R J

Trafficked

To

Hell

A deceived daughter's plight.

A mother's fight to find her

Whilst this story is fictional; real life can and is much stranger. At the end of each chapter is an abridged but true account from an actual court case where traffickers have been prosecuted. It is these stories you may find hard to believe!

Human Trafficking is said to be the second biggest International crime after the drugs trade and has an annual value of 31.6 billion US Dollars. An International Labour Organization report states that 2.5 million people are victims of human trafficking each year with 1.4 million of these being for sexual purposes. These victims are mostly women. To put this into perspective, it is equivalent to the entire female population of Albania or Jamaica being forced or coerced to leave and made to work overseas as prostitutes - each and every year.

For Victoria

*and the thousands of others who have
suffered at the hands of traffickers in the
past, the present and …….*

Chapter 1

'I don't want to go!' cried Kristina, flinging her arms around her mother and hugging her tight. Airport farewells are never easy, but unbearable when an only daughter goes far into the unknown for who knows how long? Airport wrenches need to be short and crisp and this change of heart was not helping either of them. 'Let's return the money and I'll stay here?'

The two hugged each other as they stood at the entrance to passport control - the one-way passage leading to other worlds; unknown adventures. The two women were of similar height, tall and slim. The mother, Elena, was dressed in a beige knee-length coat to protect her from the weather on her journey home, the daughter in jeans and T-shirt in readiness for the heat of her destination. At their feet, a light blue coat lay across a single small suitcase which held the meagre essentials for a life away from home – a lifetime packed into one small space. Around them milled other passengers going about their business of travel; oblivious to the domestic scene unfolding before them. Kristina held her head on her mother's shoulder so their natural blonde hair intertwined and looked as one. She whispered once more into her mother's ear. "I don't want to go.'

'No,' said her mother, 'Once you are on the plane, you'll be fine. It's what you have always dreamt of. A professional dancer, earning really good money; and it's not forever; you can always come back from Almina.'

Elena knew full well there could be no change of heart now. Banks would never entertain lending money to people like her and Kristina. She had borrowed enough money to pay the agent's fees and send Kristina off, plus a little extra to help her get on her feet before she could start sending money home. Some was spent, some saved but the interest was ticking away and rising at an alarming rate and the people who had lent her the money had a way of dealing with late payers.

Her mother held up Kristina's chin and looked into her eyes. Kristina had the same blue eyes and pert nose. She kissed her daughter lightly on the forehead, looked up and saw behind Kristina the large departures board flashing, 'Almina – proceed to gate.' Time to go love, you'll miss your flight.' The mother gently but reluctantly pushed her daughter away and smiled. Kristina picked up the coat and suitcase and proceeded down the zigzag line of people queuing at 'departures.' She looked back at her mother every now and then and attempted a nervous smile and wave. Kristina showed her ticket to the waiting official, took one last look at her mother and waved her hand with passport and ticket held high before rushing around the corner and out of sight so as not to let Elena see the torrents of tears flooding from her eyes.

She was gone.

Elena stood for some time staring at the gate through which her daughter had so recently disappeared. When all hope of Kristina returning had dissolved to nought, she wiped a tear from her eye, turned and with shoulders drooping, made her sad and lonely exit.

On the plane, Kristina cried almost all the way to Almina. As they made their final approach, she saw for the first time the yellow incandescent 'criss-cross' street light patterns set against a darkening sapphire blue sky, holding the promise of a new future. It was then that excitement overcame her tears. The plane touched down and Kristina joined in with the round of applause from the other passengers. As she emerged from the aircraft doors hot air rushed at her and hit her full in the face. It made her breathless. Kristina was reminded of the times when, as a child she would open the oven door to remove the bread her mother had baked. This place was like a furnace. She worked her way down the steps and onto the bus, hanging on as it made its tortuous journey to the terminal to deliver its exhausted travellers. Kristina couldn't help noticing the bus carried many single young women like herself but very few older people and families.

At passport control, the immigration officer, dressed in his military uniform was joking and laughing with the family in front of her, welcoming them to Almina. Kristina thought how different this was compared to her own country and the old communist ways but when her turn came he became sullen; official.

'Passport! Visa!' he demanded. The official spent a long time examining both; trying but failing to find some error in the documentation before finally and ferociously stamping the documents. 'Next!' He snapped and turned to the couple behind her, instantly replacing his stern looks with the broad welcoming face of before.

Kristina and the other passengers raced through the rest of the procedures as soon as possible and once outside she stood for a moment to take in the atmosphere. It was total chaos. Taxis were everywhere with people shouting and pushing. The heat and the humidity were unbearable but she saw a friendly face, a woman holding a hand-written sign saying, 'Kristina. Dance troupe.' The woman was older and heavily made up with greying hair almost reaching her shoulders. Her skin was dark and cracked from spending too much time out in the sun. She wore black trousers that were two sizes too small for her short plump body and a white blouse with the buttons pulling at the cotton - straining to burst open as her large bosom tried to break out.

Kristina smiled at her, 'Hi, that's me, good to meet you.'

'My name is Eva,' the woman replied pleasantly. 'Did you have a good flight?'

'Very good,' lied Kristina.

'We have a car waiting for you and I'll take you to your lodgings. You must be very tired?'

'A little bit,' Kristina replied looking around, seeing lights everywhere and not believing how much electricity was being wasted.

A large black BMW drew up; the windows tinted to keep out the heat of the midday sun and prevent any outsider seeing what lay inside. The street lights and bright neon signs reflected in its gleaming paintwork. Kristina and Eva piled into the back.

Eva introduced the driver. 'This is Na'im; he's been in Almina for five years – a long time.'

'Welcome to Almina, Ms Kristina,' said Na'im, 'I wish you a pleasant stay.' Na'im was a Pakistani in his mid-thirties, dressed in an open-necked blue short-sleeved shirt and dark slacks. His head was totally bald, clean-shaven to keep him cool in the summer.

3

'Thank you Na'im,' replied Kristina, feeling a little more at ease. Both these people were very friendly.

As the car pulled out of the airport and drove through the city, Eva pointed out the main attractions. Huge steel and glass structures brilliantly lit until they disappeared into the dark night sky. She passed over a thick wad of low denomination notes. 'Here's one hundred dollars in local currency. It's a float; we'll take it back at the end of the month when you get paid.'

Kristina had never held this much money in her hands ever before. She stared at it in wonderment. She had only been in Almina for a matter of hours and already she was driving through the big city in a luxury car and holding more money than she could earn in months back home. She fondled the bundle of notes carefully and thought of what she would buy for her mother.

'We need to start on your application for a residence visa first thing in the morning. I'll need your passport for the authorities so I can arrange your residence visa. You can have it back tomorrow evening.' Kristina hung on to the money in one hand whilst rummaging in her bag with the other. She found the passport and handed it over. What we've also done for you is to arrange a local SIM card for your phone. It's a different system here so yours won't work. If you let me have your mobile I'll change it for you then you can ring your mother later.'

'Oh, thanks', she said gazing out of the car's side window, enthralled at this new spectacular modern city and looking forward to telling her mother all about her new home. Eva changed the SIM card, collected the passport and delivered Kristina to the apartment block where she would be staying; a characterless concrete building with small windows set back so as to lie in the shadows. The building was tall, standing perhaps twelve or more floors high. Each floor had balconies staring out at nothingness whilst hiding clothes drying on racks hidden behind the balustrades. Nearly all the balconies held a satellite dish, pointing inexorably at some distant unseen alien lurking in outer space.

Kristina looked around the room as she entered. Apart from the 'en suite' bathroom the room had one set of french windows leading to a small outside balcony. She could see the tops of houses and remembered Eva had pressed the lift button for the sixth floor. She saw each girl had her own bed space with just a mattress lying on the floor. Each space was personalised in one way or another with photographs of the family back home, stuffed toys and racks of clothes accompanied by rows of bags and shoes all neatly laid out. 'How do people live like this?' she thought 'and more to the point, how long have they lived like this?' She remembered her small cosy bedroom back home and felt tears come to her eyes. The room was silent save for the hum of the air-conditioning unit blowing welcome cool air into the apartment.

There were three Eastern European girls already inside, all still in their pyjamas, with two sat on mattresses reading magazines whilst the other stood in the bathroom doorway cleaning her teeth. The girls briefly stopped reading, looked up and said 'hello' in Kristina's own language before returning to their studies. The girl brushing her teeth waved and then walked out of sight into the bathroom.

'Little bit cramped isn't it,' said Kristina looking at the four mattresses lying on the floor.

'Think yourself lucky you are not Chinese or African,' muttered one of the girls covering her mouth with her hand so neither Kristina nor Eva could hear. 'They share thirty to a room.'

'Settle yourself here for the night; we'll sort everything out in the morning. Your bed is the one on the left,' said Eva as she left the room.

It was only a few seconds later that Kristina heard the click of the key in the lock.

"Trafficking stories all follow the same pattern. A girl in a faraway village is offered a job paying five times her salary in Almina. She is met at the airport where they take her passport, lock her in a room in a high building where there is no chance of escape and then force her to work as a prostitute. The most harrowing tales involve children. You can't imagine that people can do these things to a child."

Director of rescue
shelter for trafficked women

Chapter 2

Some people have bastardism thrust upon them. Some people develop bastardism as a result of life's challenges but Pony Tail Ari was born a bastard. There is no other way to describe it.

At birth he was an ugly little shit - but was he big. Heavy I mean. The nurses doted on him, not for being pretty but because he held the record as the heaviest baby born in that hospital. Not that his mother minded. She never wanted him. If abortion had been readily available he would have been terminated from day one. He was the result of a loveless, one night stand. A business deal going hopelessly wrong! What should have been a quick fuck in return for the electricity money turned into Pony Tail Ari. As the nursing staff took the young Ari away to be seen by the doctor, his mother gathered up her meagre possessions and tip-toed out of the back door - never to be seen again. They tried to find her but since she had given a false name and address it was a fool's errand quickly forgotten.

So the young Ari was destined for children's homes and foster parents. Not that the foster parents ever lasted long. Once placed with a doting couple he would soon be returned as he had no way of returning their love; he never wanted to be loved. It just wasn't in his nature.

At school the other kids avoided him. It was his eyes really; cold, piggy eyes. Too close together for comfort and eyes that would never look you in the face – unless he wanted something. Then the hard direct stare connected with his pure white 'putty' complexion and expressionless face told you without uncertainty that you had to obey.

It was in his teens when he truly found his vocation and discovered real money; Violence for rent! That was Ari. There were two groups who controlled the town - the local Mafia and the Sportsmen and you either paid protection money to one or the other. There was no other choice.

If you didn't like someone or if someone beat up your child, you 'paid' and revenge would be 'arranged.' The Sportsmen and the Mafia had a mutual respect for each other and each had their own districts. 'Never the twain shall meet.' It was an unwritten agreement and it worked – until Ari came along. With no friends and no family, he was alien to this world. People got 'in' to the Mafia or Sportsmen through family contacts, or friends. But how could Ari? He had no-one. Never had had!

So he set up his own business - pay me or I will break your arm or leg. The Sportsmen had the area of his school and thought they ruled it, which they had done until Ari came along. Naturally this upset the 'Sportsmen' who were now losing out on a lucrative income, and so it was the Head of the Sportsmen at the school who was sent to sort Ari out; to explain this just wasn't on.

Ivan was the weightlifter; body builder extraordinaire. His physique was exceptional and combined with his deep blue eyes and blonde curly hair he was a great attraction to the girls. His job was to explain to Ari that he was 'out of order.' After all, the school was 'Sportsmen's' territory. As agreed with the Mafia. Who was Ari to upset the apple cart?

One evening, just after sunset, as Ari was walking down a narrow dimly lit passage between the backs of some houses, Ivan suddenly stepped out of a doorway immediately in front of him. At the same time, three other brutes stepped out from other doorways and surrounded him. Ari did not feel fear; this was an emotion missing from his DNA.

Now Ari,' said Ivan with a smirk. 'You're upsetting some of our friends who feel you are stealing what is rightfully theirs. These friends have asked me to explain to you that this is not a nice thing to do. In fact they are very, very upset about it.'

Ari said nothing but just stared blankly into Ivan's eyes. This had a slightly disturbing effect on Ivan as he was used to people begging for forgiveness at this point. Two thugs grabbed Ari from behind and held his arms. Ari knew he had the strength to put up a good fight but even he knew four against one was a fight he could not win. He decided to take whatever punishment they gave out in silence, without saying even a word, a grunt or fighting back.

Ivan and the man in front punched Ari in the face and the body but Ari still didn't let out even a whimper. The two holding Ari from behind forced him down and held his head to the ground as if training a dog to show him just who was the alpha male in town. All four kicked him in the head, the kidneys and groin but still Ari remained silent. When they felt they had done enough, plus a little more, Ivan motioned the others to stop.

'Let that be a lesson for you, sneered Ivan. 'This is our territory so keep out of it.' At this all four spat in Ari's face and walked off. Ivan had an uneasy feeling the boy had not learned any lesson at all.

Ari kept still until they had left and then gradually lifted himself to his feet. He was sore but unbroken. 'In a couple of days' time I will be back to normal,' he thought. 'In four days I'll have you bastards!'

"I escaped many times but was always brought back by 'pony tail Ali.' He was an enforcer used by the brothel to teach errant girls a lesson. He looked after between 200 and 300 girls at any one time and we all lived in constant fear of this man.

When a new girl was brought out they'd call Ali to visit to make sure she knew his face. If a girl did cause trouble, he would take her out to the desert, rape her and then beat her with an iron bar before bringing her back to the brothel."

Report from Court proceedings.

Chapter 3

'Why did God give me this fabulous body if I am not meant to use it?' And fabulous it truly was. Nikki was perfectly proportioned, small to medium height with long black hair hanging down to her shoulders. Her hazelnut eyes sparkled perpetually and were full of life; always holding a person's attention and hinting that maybe there was a promise of something extra. This was Nikki's philosophy in life. Some people have a brain and use it in law or medicine. Some people are good with their hands and use them to create art. Nikki used her God given bodily gifts to create enjoyment. At least this was the way she saw it. In her mind she was on a par with a doctor or a lawyer who sell the use of their brain by the hour. Nikki did the same only with a different part of her body. The difference was Nikki actually enjoyed selling this particular bit of her body. No complaints. She enjoyed the work and could do it lying down.

At the age of eleven or twelve she would give any male a quick look of her breasts (or even let them fondle them) for nothing. She would lean against the back of the school wall staring at the sky whilst amorous adventurers would attempt a quick snog, or even a bit of finger. She was always happy to be helpful; charity really. But then, as her breasts blossomed and became quite tactile, she thought 'why should I provide this service for free?'

Boys were quite happy to hand over money to fondle her blossoming breasts and, as they grew to full size, would pay even more. A quick grope with Nikki was the joke of the town. The trouble was she ran out of clients. A business of this nature needs a constant flow of 'fresh meat,' i.e. 'new customers.'

After two or three times, every male knew every trick Nikki had. She either had to change her act or find a new audience. This was when she met Philippe. Philippe was over fifty and she was just eighteen. He was handsome, awesome and cast an aura of gentility He was the first, the only man to treat her as a real person and not just as an object.

Philippe was tall and slender with short black hair greying at the temples giving him a distinguished air. When he spoke he spoke without accent and pronounced every word with a deliberation implying he had carefully selected each one especially for you.

Late one night, Nikki had been stood outside an old grey concrete block of flats. Once communist times had ended, flats had been handed over to the tenants living in them for free and those lucky enough to have a ground floor flat had quickly sold them off to have doors knocked into the outside walls. This gave an outside entrance enabling the premises to be used as shops or, in the case of the property behind her, a bar. Light, tinged blue-grey by the nicotine smoke filling the air inside, passed through the curtains and escaped from the two windows at either side of the door. It gave Nikki a surreal form of illumination and made the wares on offer even more attractive. Nikki wore a short jacket and even shorter skirt. She shivered from time to time as the evening chill bit at her thighs. She walked two or three paces up and down, taking long drags from endless cigarettes; stamping her feet every now and then to maintain circulation. Nikki had been there nearly one hour waiting for a customer, any customer, who had either had a row with the wife and was looking for comfort or was too inebriated to remember that, in Nikki, he had drunk from this cup before. It was then that Philippe came by.

'Excuse me' he said, 'but do you happen to know the way to the 'Intouristic' Hotel?' The 'Intouristic' Hotels were the only ones where foreigners could stay. Nikki smelt money.

Philippe wore a long black overcoat to protect him from the cold and had his hands in the coat pockets - providing an inviting space through which Nikki slipped her arm. He brought his own arm close to his body to squeeze and reassure her.

'It's hard to explain Sir, but I can show you if you like.' So they walked and talked about where they both came from and other small talk meaning nothing to either of them.

On the way to the hotel, Nikki's mind was churning, 'How much to charge him? 'Intouristic' hotel, old guy, how much can I screw him for screwing me? That is, if he's up to it. Maybe if he goes to sleep I

12

can take his wallet.'

Pricing is always a problem when selling a commodity – and a commodity was surely what Nikki was selling. Ask too much and you frightened the customer away. Ask too little and you regretted it later.

'My wife died three years ago,' Philippe explained as they walked along. 'We were very happy together and had few friends as we enjoyed our own company so much we didn't need anyone else. I find myself very lonely these days and wished I had more human company.'

The price went up in Nikki's mind.

'I hope you don't mind my telling you this but I find you a good listener. Since she passed away, I have problems in the err.... shall we say, bedroom department? In fact, on some of my darkest occasions of despair, I have even paid a prostitute to see if that would help. But it made no difference; I still couldn't achieve an erection.'

The price went up even more.

Eventually they arrived at the 'Intouristic' Hotel. The 'Intouristic Hotels,' again a relic from the past, had been thrown up to accommodate foreign tourists and gain what little foreign currency could be squeezed from this source. They were all the same; concrete and featureless. Square buildings covered with square windows – each hiding a small square room within.

'Well, here we are! It's been very good of you to show me the way and, more importantly, listening to me drivelling on about my problems. I hope you didn't mind. I guess I'm just a lonely old man in a strange and friendless town.'

Racing through Nikki's mind was the age old problem of how to change a friendship into a relationship – or in her mind, into a business relationship.

'I'm not a doctor.' Nikki spoke softly, 'but maybe I can help you with your err.., 'medical' problem.'

'Very kind of you to offer but I'm not sure I want to put myself in the hands of an amateur', replied Philippe.

'There's nothing amateurish about my hands. Shall we say two hundred for the night?'

'OK. And if you're good, I'll pay you the two hundred plus another one hundred in the morning.'

13

'Shit,' thought Nikki, 'I didn't ask for enough.'

The 'Intouristic' was a small hotel and since it was late at night, the 'foyer' was empty. Strewn around this open space were some leather couches, old and well worn. On each dark wooden table, sat a dimly lit lamp; an old glass oil lamp converted to electricity. A single male receptionist sat behind his desk reading a copy of the day's paper.

'Why not pop into the little girl's room whilst I go and collect the key?

She knew his suggestion was to avoid any embarrassment with the receptionist. Since only foreigners were allowed in Intouristic hotels, locals had to sneak in or be thrown out or even reported to the Police and Nikki was hardly dressed as a respectable tourist. Philippe had thoughtfully already booked a double room under the name of a 'Mr and Mrs Johnston' and opened a credit card for the bill so there was no paper work to be done. However, they needn't have troubled themselves as the receptionist never looked up from his reading but reached back, collected the key from its hook and handed it over. Philippe and Nikki met at the door to the old lift and entered. He looked around the fake walnut interior, found the brass control panel and pressed the button for the second floor. He looked into Nikki's eyes and smiled. Nikki gave the coy look she had practised many times in front of the mirror, but she could already feel the sexual desires rising.

'God, I love my job!' she thought.

They crept quietly along the carpet lined corridor; each giving the other a conspiratorial look and neither could resist a silent giggle as they turned the key and entered the room. As Philippe turned on a bedside light (only one to keep the room romantic he told her), Nikki moved behind him and placed her arms around his chest gradually lowering them until her two hands settled on his crotch.

Squeezing gently she whispered in his ear, 'Where's my money?'

'Ah', said Philippe, 'let's see how good you are first. I'm sure you're not one of them, but too many girls take the money, go for a quick but happy ending and then leave after half an hour. No, Nikki, we are going to have a full night of passion, a full night of love making and then we'll sleep together like husband and wife; in the morning, we will wake and start all over again.'

'Even three hundred is not enough for all that', thought Nikki and

14

besides, 'sleeping together like husband and wife?' If the married couples she knew were anything to go by, that meant shouting and screaming at each other all night!

But he turned around and kissed her on the lips, his hands slid under her blouse. He undid her bra with his right hand whilst moving his left hand under the now loose cup at the front and began to fondle her right nipple between thumb and index finger.

'Sod it,' thought Nikki, 'He'll pay,' and turned her attention to her work.

'Bang! Bang! Bang!'

'What the hell's happening?' she thought as she propped herself up on one elbow whilst fighting to open her eyes against the early morning light.

'Shit! I must have gone to sleep.' She looked around the room but in the semi darkness could not see Philippe.

'Bang, bang, bang!' The thumping on the door sounded once more.

'This is the manager,' said a voice from outside. 'Would you please open the door?'

'Philippe, where are you?' she cried as she dragged herself out of the bed. The long night of sex had taken its toll and she was finding difficulty getting her legs moving and placing one foot in front of the other. 'Too stiff,' she thought. 'But not as stiff as that bastard last night.'

'Would you please open this door?' The sound from outside was louder this time.

'I'm coming,' she shouted as she made her way to the bathroom.

'Philippe, where are you?' She asked as she forlornly examined the empty room. The bathroom was empty and a quick glance around the room showed her all his clothes had gone and, worse still, he hadn't left her money. Wrapping her naked body in a bath towel she made her way to the door and opened it.

'Thank you, madam. Could I please speak to your 'husband?' The short, fat, dark suited manager added a little stress to the word, 'husband' as he pushed his little chest out in an attempt to make himself look important.

'Unless he's hiding under the bed then it doesn't look like it. What's the problem, he paid for the room last night?'

'Unfortunately, when registering with the hotel, your 'husband' opened a credit card to cover the charges. We've just been informed the card had been stolen earlier in the day but it has only just been reported. I'm afraid you will need to accompany me to my office and await the police.'

This turned out to be the defining moment in Nikki's life. From this moment on she never trusted any man ever again. From this point on, it was 'screw them all!'

A woman died as she hit the floor after falling from a third floor window. She had jumped out in order to escape her traffickers who had held her captive and forced her to work as a prostitute

Three men are on trial charged with false imprisonment and running a brothel.

Despite extensive police efforts over a period of five months, her name, age or nationality remain unknown.

Report from Court proceedings.

Chapter 4

The sound of the key turning in the lock sent a wave of panic through Kristina. The realisation she was incarcerated in this room slowly dawned upon her. She looked around at her roommates but they just gave her a blank but knowing stare. She tried to ring her Mum but the new SIM card didn't work and reality started to sink in. Kristina had fallen for the oldest trick in the book. Eva had given her a large wad of notes amounting to a small sum of money to gain her confidence - and she, in return, had handed over her passport. Frantically she searched through her handbag for her old SIM card but it wasn't there! She had been so busy sorting the money thinking how she would spend it that she hadn't realised Eva had not returned it to her.

'How stupid!' Kristina thought to herself. 'I would never have fallen for this at home.' But the truth was she hadn't been in this strange country five minutes before she had been robbed blind.

Kristina realised she was now isolated. Cut off from the outside world with no passport or means of escape. Gradually a feeling of hopelessness overcame her and she sobbed herself to sleep.

The next morning, Kristina was woken by the noise of the other girls chattering to each other as they showered and dressed. She lay still, pretending to be asleep, trying to listen in to what they were saying and glean any information she could - but everyone was talking at once; it wasn't possible to hear anything clearly. She heard a key turn in the lock

'Breakfast is ready.' Eva spoke from the doorway. The girls left the room whilst she moved over to Kristina and took a long look at her; still Kristina feigned asleep. 'Sleep a bit longer love, you've a hard day ahead of you,' whispered Eva quietly as she crept out of the room.

The girls came back and chatted as they dressed and put on their make-up. Apart from a cursory nod to Kristina, they mostly ignored her – this way they did not have to avoid answering any awkward questions.

'Ah, good,' said Eva returning, 'you're awake. Now get yourself ready; you've a visitor coming later.' She left the room before Kristina had a chance to ask who her 'visitor' was.

'Any ideas who it is,' asked Kristina to no-one in particular as she raised herself to sit up.

'Probably quality control,' replied one of the girls and they all burst out laughing.

'Don't worry,' said one girl coming towards Kristina, 'You'll be alright. It's just a bit strange at first. My name's Melda by the way.' Melda hitched up her blue jeans at the knees and sat next to Kristina on the mattress; her red top striking in its vividness. She brushed her short auburn hair away from her face to reveal her Chinese eyes. 'Kazakhstan,' Nikki thought. Strange how some people expect physical characteristics to change abruptly at a country's border. 'I'm Kristina,' she took the hand proffered by Melda and shook it.

'Is the bedroom door always locked?' asked Kristina.

'Either that or the front door of the apartment,' replied Melda. 'It's to stop weirdo's breaking in – or so Eva says. Can I give you some advice?' Kristina wondered what was coming. 'Don't fight them,' advised Melda, 'do as they ask, do what they want and you'll end up enjoying it. If you fight them, you will never win and your life will be hell.'

A well-built middle aged woman came into the room. She had cropped blonde hair, was smartly dressed in a trouser suit and carried a large handbag in her left hand. Not one to be messed with.

'Morning Mamasan,' the girls chirped in unison.

'Morning girls. If everyone's ready we'll get off.'

'Get off?' laughed one girl, 'only if we're lucky.

'Bye Kristina, have fun,' one of the young pretty girls said.

They giggled as they walked out of the room.

Melda deliberately held back. She took Kristina's hands in hers and looked her straight in the eyes. 'Remember what I told you. Do what they ask you.'

Kristina heard the front door close. The flat was very quiet and she felt very much alone. Unzipping her case, she took out her toiletry bag and towel and went to the bathroom. After a shower, she threw on a pair of black jeans and a white top, and she felt a little brighter; she set off to investigate the apartment. She tried the front door but it was locked. She wasn't surprised. Kristina found the small kitchen and after a thorough search of all the cupboards and drawers, eventually found the essentials for a cup of coffee and a piece of toast. As she sat down at the small table in the middle of the room to have this makeshift breakfast, she heard the front door unlock, open and then lock again as Eva returned.

'Good,' she said, 'you've made yourself at home.'

Kristina nodded, 'when will I meet the rest of the dance troupe?'

'All things in good time,' smiled Eva, 'Dmtry is coming soon and he'll explain everything. I'll come and collect you when he arrives.' She left the kitchen and busied herself around the house, whilst Kristina sipped her coffee. The doorbell rang and Kristina heard a muffled man's voice.

'Hello, Dmtry,' said Eva, 'She's in the kitchen.'

'Good,' replied Dmtry, 'How's business?'

'I can't complain.' He followed her into the apartment. Dmtry was in his early forties and wore dark slacks and a white polo shirt; his short muscular figure and thick black hair conspicuous in this feminine domain. 'Wait in there and I'll bring her.'

Eva put her head around the kitchen door, 'Dmtry will see you now,' she said in a voice sounding as though she was announcing visiting royalty. 'Come on through.' Kristina followed her into another room obviously serving as a lounge. There was a large sofa set and television and the room was pleasantly decorated with several pictures of forest and mountain scenes on the walls. Dmtry stood as they entered the room and welcomed her, speaking in Kristina's own language. 'How was your trip?' he asked whilst giving her the broadest of welcoming smiles.

'A little long but it was OK,' answered Kristina. 'When will I meet the dance troupe?'

'The dance troupe?' asked Dmtry looking perplexed.

'Yes the dance troupe,' she continued. 'It's why I came out here. Apparently someone had an accident and broke her leg and I'm to replace her.'

'Oh, the dance troupe,' said Dmtry, realising what she was referring to. 'I'm afraid the position has been filled.'

20

'So what happens to me,' asked Kristina, 'do I just go back home?'

'No,' said Dmtry, 'it isn't that simple. You'll work in the nightclubs, but not as a dancer.'

'Then what will I do?' Kristina looked at him carefully as a feeling of apprehension took over.

'Well,' said Dmtry. 'Did the other girls not tell you?'

'No, they certainly did not,' she replied. 'In fact they seemed to want to keep out of the way.'

'Well, when I say work in the nightclubs, I mean as a working lady.' Dmtry sat back to see how she would take this.

'A working lady,' Kristina was incredulous. 'You mean a prostitute don't you?'

'Don't look at it that way,' pleaded Dmtry, 'most girls enjoy it once they get used to it.'

'Never!' said Kristina firmly, 'I'll never do it. Give me my passport back and let me go home.'

'Not possible,' replied Dmtry, 'it costs money to bring you people out here and Eva will not give you your passport back until you've repaid her in full.'

'Just tell me how much and I'll get my mother to send it,' Kristina spoke haughtily. 'I will not stay here.'

'Fifteen thousand US Dollars,' Dmtry spoke slowly and quietly so there could be no doubt in what he said.

'How much?' asked a shocked Kristina.

'Fifteen thousand US dollars,' repeated Dmtry.

"A friend promised me a good job in Almina but she lied. They were waiting for me at the airport and took me to a flat were I saw four girls and a woman who told me I would be working as a prostitute. She even told me that I needed to pay her 15,000 US Dollars to cover the cost of bringing me to Almina. I was forced to work against my will as I was alone in a strange country and I couldn't do anything. They threatened me." Eventually the 20 year old Russian woman contacted a friend who helped her escape.

Proceedings of Court case.

Chapter 5

Ari shifted his position carefully so as not to make a noise. He had been crouched behind this snow covered bush for nearly half an hour waiting for Ivan to come by. This overgrown park area between the tall grey faceless blocks of flats was lit by a single street lamp, its naked bulb casting an eerie glow as the yellow light reflected from the white covering of snow; the shadows of the leafless branches reaching out towards him like the fingers of the dead. He moved his feet delicately between the used hypodermic needles strewn on the ground; thankful no-one thought to use condoms in this district as these would be littering the place as well. He looked at the large tree which acted as the centre piece of the park where all paths met before branching out to take people on their way to the other side. Not that anyone came here after dark. These areas had been put in place for the children from the overcrowded flats to come and play but after the fall of communism there was no money to maintain them and, more importantly, to police them.

Ari looked closely at the tree and could see the glint from the steel ice pick he had stuck in the trunk earlier and knew the elastic luggage cord was resting at its base. In his hand was the sister to the ice pick; both had been especially honed to a fine point for this mission.

The silence was broken by Ivan's feet crunching in the crisp snow. He walked past Ari deep in thought as he visualised the next weight lifting competition which, if he won, would make him county champion. Ari gently raised himself and as Ivan neared the tree he sprang forward, raced towards Ivan and used his momentum to bulldoze him into the tree. With Ivan winded and confused Ari grabbed his right hand, flattened it against the tree trunk and brought the ice pick down hard, very hard. With Ivan screaming in agony, the needle sharp pick went straight through Ivan's hand and deep into the wood beneath where it stayed secure. Ari grabbed

Ivan's other arm and stretched it out before removing the second pick from its resting place in the tree trunk and drove this home. Ivan was now impaled against the tree. He started to recover and was kicking out, trying to find a target, any target on Ari's body but the pain from his hands was too great to allow him to move far. Ari bent down and picked up the iron bar which had originally been part of the suspension of an old car. Taking aim he drove each ice pick well into the tree.

"Remember me?" asked Ari as he whispered into Ivan's ear. He was so close Ivan could feel the warmth of his breath.

Ivan kicked out with his foot but missed; letting out a gasp as he pulled on the wounds in his hands.

"We'll have to stop that," said Ari as he picked up the elastic luggage cord. He wrapped one end against Ivan's ankle, walked around the tree before wrapping the other end around Ivan's other leg. Ivan was now prostrate against the tree and helpless.

"Enough," whimpered Ivan. "We didn't permanently harm you. Let me go and I'll do anything for you. Anything you want."

"Oh I want," said Ari. "I want too much. You took my respect away and you're going to give it back. I understand you lift weights." Ari stood back and brought the iron bar down on Ivan's left forearm. There was a sickly crack as both bones broke. "I think that's put an end to that." Ari moved around to the other side of Ivan and whispered into his ear, "I think you are a wanker too." Ari brought the iron bar down on Ivan's right forearm and the sound of both bones cracking echoed around the park. "Not any more. Now you just wait here until I send someone to see you. Don't go away now." Ari walked away leaving Ivan sobbing against the tree. Wasting no time, he went to a deserted shop just off the precinct. It was a large shop but completely empty and in darkness. On the side of the door was an intercom. Ari pressed the button and waited for the reply.

'Who's there,' said a metallic voice.

'I want to see the Boss,' Ari spoke confidently. 'I have some important news for him.'

'Stand back and let me see you,' said the voice in the box as if there were some sort of alien trapped inside. Ari stood back so the camera could see him.

'Open your jacket and show me you're clean,' the voice

commanded. Ari complied and a buzzer sounded as the door unlocked. Ari pushed it open and went inside. There was total darkness but as his eyes grew accustomed to the dark he could see disused shop display stands everywhere. He felt his way around them and followed a chink of light from under a distant door. The sounds of people talking and of music playing grew louder as he approached.

As he reached the door he carefully pushed it open and was immediately blinded by the glare. There were bright lights everywhere and music blaring out. The room was filled with one armed bandits, roulette wheels and card tables. Everywhere people were shoving coins into the slots or playing the tables with stacks of chips in their hands. At one end was a huge bar which held every type of alcoholic drink available on the market. Gambling was illegal in the communist world but with a few dollars handed to the police by way of 'winnings', anything was possible.

'So, what's this 'important news' requiring you to see the Boss?' asked the massive henchman eying Ari suspiciously. Ari looked him over. Grey suit with jacket open to reveal a black open necked shirt with muscles bulging through. Ari knew he could take him if needed but that was not why he was here.

'I can only tell the Boss,' Ari retorted, trying to stay calm.

'You do realise the punishment for wasting the Boss's time?'

'Trust me,' said Ari. 'This is no waste of time.'

'Sit down and have a drink,' said the henchman, 'whilst I find out if he'll see you.' Ari sat down and ordered a glass of water from the waitress. He had never touched alcohol in his life as, in this business, he always needed to be in full control of his senses. As he sipped his drink, he watched the punters playing and losing all their money; happily believing the machines were fair - but losing all their money anyway.

It wasn't long before the henchman returned. 'You've five minutes and it had better be good.' Ari was escorted upstairs into a large office; it could have been any office in any multinational company. The only difference was there were television screens everywhere, showing the gaming floor and the outside entrance. The Boss sat in a swivel chair in front of the monitors keeping a close eye on his empire. He was fat and wore a white shirt and black suit that could hold two average sized men. He was clean shaven but had a thick crop of black hair. He turned in his chair to look at Ari.

'So,' said the Boss. 'What's so important I should meet with you?'

'I want to join your team,' said Ari.

'And in this negotiation, I know what I can provide. What are you bringing to the table?'

'Just violence,' said Ari, 'violence on demand. I can do anything you want.'

The Boss smirked. 'And how do I know?'

'Send one of your men to the park in Lenin square,' Ari replied, 'You'll find my calling card pinned to the big tree in the centre.' The Boss nodded to the henchman who quietly left the room.

He turned to Ari, 'here's a thousand. Play it on the tables downstairs whilst we check your story. Don't feel grateful as we'll take it all back. Everything is 'destined' here.' So Ari returned to the gaming floor and waited nervously. He played poker against the young female dealer and even he was surprised at how quickly the money was taken from him. He sat watching a group of old women as they gambled away their meagre pensions in the hope of raising some money for next week's food. The flashing coloured lights from the machines illuminating their faces and emphasising the look of desperation printed upon it.

Finally the henchman returned, tapped him on the shoulder, and took him back upstairs.

'You'll never be a professional gambler,' said the Boss without emotion, 'but we were impressed by your credentials in the park. This means respect on the highest level. What exactly do you want from us Ari?'

'I'm tired of working alone. I want to join your team."

"Ok, but don't ever let me down. If you do I promise what you did to Ivan is nothing to what we will do to you. Let's get down to business, what do you want from me?' asked the Boss.

'An untraceable gun,' said Ari, 'one having no past. I still have some old history to sort out before I join your family.'

'Finish your business and then come back, He'll see to your needs.' Ari followed the henchman out. The next day the police investigated the shooting of three men from a well-known local gang; all fatally injured. The newspapers reported the story on a page no-one would read and since they were known criminals, no time was wasted trying to find out who had killed them. Besides the 'Boss' had paid the police not to look too far.

Overall, the Boss was pleased with his new boy.

"I arrived at the airport. They met me, took my passport and told me I would work in prostitution. When we reached the flat she immediately told me to shower as there was a client waiting for me. Then she took photos of me wearing revealing clothes to send to other clients. She kept me locked inside one room and demanded 5,200 US Dollars if I wanted to quit prostitution and return home." A Filipina housewife received a text from the trafficked girl threatening suicide if she could not get help from her embassy. Police arrested the traffickers in a sting operation.

Report from Court proceedings

Chapter 6

Nikki stood in a dark back street running between a line of empty warehouses. It was typical of the rest of Kazmenia. An ex USSR satellite state left to rot after the Russians had left. It was late evening and the only light came from two dimly lit street lamps a few hundred metres apart. She stood in the darkest spot; exactly halfway between them. It had been raining earlier and the streets were still wet allowing her to watch the full Moon reflecting in the puddles. Nikki ran her fingers through her long dark hair to pass the time. She could see her shadow cast on the floor by the distant lights. She liked what she saw. Good figure with 'goldilocks' tits and bum; not too big, not too small. Just right! She could see a figure approaching her in the distance and could hear the footsteps echoing from the warehouses lining the street.

'Good,' she thought. 'He's middle aged, drunk and all by himself – a possibility.' Nikki had moved to the anonymity of the big city to give her a larger client base and if things went wrong, as they often did, in the city she could quickly lose herself for a few days until the coast was clear.

'Are you taking a lady home tonight sir?' she asked as the man walked past; his hands in his pockets and head turned down so his eyes would not meet hers.

'Not tonight thanks,' he replied unsteadily.

This street was a good location as it was off the main thoroughfares where the police patrolled and decent people frequented - but it was still busy enough. It formed a shortcut between the popular bar area and the residential areas further afield.

Nikki positioned herself in the middle of the pavement as another 'mark' approached. This time he would have to walk around her if he wanted to ignore her. But no, he made eye contact from the start 'Would you like a lady tonight?' enquired Nikki.

29

'Depends on how much,' he answered.

'One hundred for a shot, three hundred for an hour.'

'Too much. How about two hundred for the hour?' he negotiated.

'Ok,' said Nikki. 'Give me the money and let the fun begin.' He handed over the two hundred and she quickly squirreled it away in her handbag.

Nikki thanked him. 'Now if you walk down this street to the lights and turn right, you'll see the Eros hotel on your left. I'll phone the girl to expect you.'

'But I thought I was going with you,' said the confused punter.

'No, the girls are waiting outside the hotel as I told you. You can't hand money over in the hotel, as the management won't allow it. You pay me here and then go to the hotel were the girl is expecting you. She's a really beautiful girl called Olga. Just go there. There's no problem.'

'Well there'd better not be,' said the punter realising there was no chance of getting his money back. He set off unhappily down the street in pursuit of his hour of extra-marital ecstasy. On his way he passed another man coming in the opposite direction.

'Shit,' thought Nikki as she saw the man coming back up the street. 'This one's so dim he doesn't know when he's been conned.'

'I thought you said the girl would be waiting outside the hotel,' he complained as he approached her.

'She is,' Nikki said convincingly.

'Well there was no-one waiting when I got there.' He replied. 'It was the Eros hotel you said?'

'That's right, the Eros. Straight down the road to the lights and turn right.'

'Well there were only two blokes standing outside when I arrived. Not a female in sight.'

'Ah!' said Nikki. 'She must have got a private customer. She'll be free within the hour. Look, go back to the hotel and if she's still busy then come and let me know and I'll do it for you myself. Fair enough?'

The man trudged off down the street and back to the Eros Hotel, still ignorant of the fact there was no girl either outside or inside the hotel; and the two men he saw outside the hotel were also victims of the same scam. Not to mention the other man he had passed as he was on his way back to complain to Nikki.

30

This was the beauty of the scam. If a girl actually did the business then she could only manage two or three customers a night whereas if she conned the men into thinking they were about to get sex and sent them out of the way on a wild goose chase, she can do four or five an hour. What could they do? Call the police and get their names in the papers? No, just they had to put it down to experience. The trouble was though, with this scam a girl could not stay in the same place for more than a couple of hours at most, as the 'clients' eventually started talking to each other outside the hotel or, as in the case of the last man, come back to complain.

Nikki reckoned she could manage one more hit before moving on to a different part of town and luckily she saw him coming down the street. He looked lonely and a little inebriated so she moved into the centre of the pavement once more.

'Looking for a lady for the night sir?' she asked.

'Why, Nikki?' he replied, 'I would've thought that after last time you'd be more careful of older men.'

'You fucking bastard,' she hissed; not wanting to draw attention to herself. 'Do you know what it took to get out of the manager's office without him calling the police? I had to work it off 'room servicing' his randy hotel clients for the next month, with him taking all the money and I had to give him a blow job there and then – as he put it, 'the interest' on the money!'

'If I were you Nikki,' replied Philippe, 'I wouldn't stand around here arguing in case some of your 'upset' clients of the night return for a refund. Come and have a coffee with me and maybe we can do some future business together.' They walked off in distrustful silence to find a café in the opposite direction to the Eros Hotel.

"She lured us to Almina under the pretext of finding us good jobs as saleswomen or waitresses but as soon as we arrived she took our passports and forced us to have sex with strangers for money. There were five of us locked up in a flat and so we made a pact that if one of us were to get out then that person must call the police.

One girl escaped that night and called the police who came and arrested four women and the pimp."

Report from Court
proceedings

Chapter 7

The Boss sat in his high backed chair behind a large old fashioned carved desk. Not that anyone noticed, but the chair was slightly raised so anyone visiting had to look up to him; like paying respects to Buddha. Ari stood a little behind him whilst on his right, sitting a little out of the way at the end of the table, was Ligo; a small set, thin man who wore thick rimmed spectacles. A large black ledger lay on the table in front of him. The room was furnished like a relic from the Victorian era and was very dark as the curtains behind the Boss were almost fully closed. The sound of the front door ringing and muffled voices could be heard from the passage outside. A few minutes later a small bald bearded man was shown in. He was dressed in a dark blue suit but with the jacket open to allow his stomach to protrude through the front. Ari motioned the man to sit down. He smiled and displayed a row of blackened, decayed teeth.

'How can I help you?' asked the Boss.

'I own a small tailor's shop on the high street, making men's shirts and suits,' said the visitor. 'I've always paid my donations to your charity both in full and on time.'

The Boss turned to Ligo who opened his ledger and turned over a few pages. He studied an open page for a moment and then nodded back to the Boss. 'Continue,' said the Boss.

'Well, a few weeks ago another tailor opened across the street and he's selling cheaper suits than me and taking my customers.'

'Nothing wrong with competition,' said the Boss who didn't know the meaning of the word. Anyone daring to compete with him was quickly and violently dealt with

'I don't object to fair competition' said the visitor, 'but he doesn't donate to your charity like I do. I can't compete on those terms.'

The Boss turned to Ligo and raised an eyebrow.

33

'That's true,' said Ligo. 'Our fund raiser visited him two weeks ago and he's still to make a donation.'

'I thank you for bringing this to my attention,' said the Boss. 'You can go now and I will look into it. Ligo, make sure our collector forgets to go to our friends shop here for one week as a 'thank you' for his honesty.'

The tailor smiled gratefully and began to back towards the door. 'Thank you, Sir. Thank you.'

'Ligo, arrange a visit to this new shop. Make sure he starts donating to our cause and increases his prices. Ari, don't get involved yet. I want to keep you in reserve in case we need things to turn nasty.'

Ari smiled and hoped things would turn very nasty indeed.

The doorbell rang once more and again muttered voices were heard from outside. The Boss hadn't always run these 'clinics' as he now called them in this way. Previously it had been on an ad hoc basis with people asking for help whenever they saw him in the street or in a bar. He knew it wasn't very professional doing business like this but wasn't sure how to change it but then he watched the film 'The Godfather' and saw how Marlon Brando had handled his business arrangements and was hooked straight away. As a result, the boss arranged two clinics per week between ten and twelve, where his 'family' could come and request help. In emergencies or if the money involved was large, then a private meet could be arranged but if anyone wasted the Boss's time, the consequences didn't bear thinking about.

Initially, he copied the arrangements from the film verbatim with the family members whispering in his ear but half the time he couldn't hear what they said and had to ask them to repeat a little louder - which defeated the whole object of playing the 'cool' Mafia man. Then there were those who sprayed when they talked and he was soon fed-up with an ear full of spittle so he quickly dropped the idea. He soon realised what happened in films didn't always work in real life and so adapted his hero 'Marlon's' style to a much more practical one.

The door opened and in walked a middle aged lady. She was well dressed, wearing a dark grey business suit; her hair was tied back. 'I don't think we know each other.' The Boss looked her up and down, swiftly liking what he saw in front of him. 'What can we do for you?'

'My company has bought some land near here and we want to develop it into a shopping complex and a high end residential area,' she said.

'So what do you need me for?' asked the Boss, 'you seem to know what you're doing.'

'Well,' she continued, 'it's all down to access. To put a road on this plot of land to give people access, we need to buy out another piece of land which is in the way.'

'So why don't you make the owner an attractive financial offer.' The Boss continued to run his eyes over her body, stopping at her tits and thinking he wouldn't mind juggling with them one night.

'We've tried,' she replied, noticing his fascination with her breasts and so pushed them out further, 'but he won't listen.'

'Then offer him more.'

'We've tried,' she repeated. 'In fact we've offered him a life of luxury in one of our new homes or even to relocate him to a mansion on the Black Sea, but he won't listen.' At this she manoeuvred her arms so her jacket opened to reveal a tight silk blouse leaving nothing to the imagination. Her nipples were now clearly in view as they pushed the fabric forward. 'Thank God I had those injections last year to make them permanently hard,' she thought. 'It's going to pay off sooner than I expected. The guy's getting excited.'

'So why won't he accept?' The Boss asked.

'I don't know. He just keeps saying no.'

'This is not an easy problem. If the guy doesn't want to sell then he doesn't want to sell. Do you have the contract of sale with you?'

'Yes,' she replied, placing it on the table.

'This is straight,' said the Boss, 'I'll not cheat him – and you understand the difficulties arising if this contract is not abided by?'

'It's straight,' she said, 'and if we need to, we'll pay him more. We're desperate for the access, otherwise the whole deal is off.'

'Come and see me tomorrow at eight pm and we'll see what we can do. I think we can solve the matter but it will require money and 'hard work' on your part.'

The lady rose, thanked the Boss for his time, turned and left - smiling on the way as she thought of the great business victory that was to be hers.

This concluded the business for the day.

'Send the two new boys to see the tailor,' said the Boss turning to Ligo.

'Ari I want you to go and talk to the old guy.'

The Boss had no children and no real second in command and he was wondering if he could groom Ari as his successor but Ari lacked diplomacy. He knew eventually Ari would be needed to deal with the tailor but like all managers, he needed to provide professional development for his team. The two new boys needed experience and he wanted Ari to develop the skills of negotiation rather than just beat people into submission in order to get his own way.

'Ari,' he continued, 'don't harm the old guy. We must respect our elders. He's done nothing wrong; he just wants to stay in his home. However, no-one can stand in the way of progress. This new development will bring jobs and money to our town and bring hope to young people. He's been offered ten times the market price which is a very good offer. Make him see he should take it but nicely huh? No heavy stuff.'

The Boss had hoped he had given all the reasoned arguments Ari needed to make the old guy understand and sell. 'Do you understand,' said the Boss, 'try to do it by reason.'

Ari picked up the contract of sale from the table and left.

The next morning Ari was driven out to the old man's house by his driver, Boris.

'What's on the agenda today,' said Boris.

'We've to talk a guy into giving up his home when he doesn't want to do it,' replied Ari.

'Why don't we just force him into it as usual?'

'The Boss says, no.' Ari was disappointed. 'We just have to talk this guy to death. That's a new one isn't it?'

'Sure is,' Boris knew better than to say the Boss had 'gone soft.'

The black Moskvitch car pulled up in the front of an old wooden dacha set amongst the trees. The dacha had a raised wooden porch with veranda; an empty chair stood to one side waiting for better weather. It didn't look like it would take much huffing and puffing to blow this house over. The curtains on one window twitched ever so lightly. Ari and Boris carefully climbed the creaky steps and knocked on the front door.

'Who's there,' cried a voice from inside.

'You know dam well who's 'there',' retorted Ari. 'You saw us drive up. Now open the fucking door and let us in.'

The door opened to reveal a man in his eighties. Grey hair and wrinkled head. He wore an old blue boiler suit covering a dirty red checked shirt. In his hand he held a shotgun.

'Put the gun away old man,' said Ari. 'Do you want to get us all killed?'

'I know why you're here,' the old guy looked him straight in the eye, 'and I'm not selling.'

'OK, my Boss said I had to respect the old and not harm you. I'm here to reason with you. Now can we come in; it's fucking cold out here.'

The old guy opened the door fully, stood to one side and let them in. 'Sit down then. You want some vodka?' The room was devoid of photographs or any item of a personal nature. Two tatty arm chairs, covered in old blankets were positioned either side of a cast iron wood burning stove. By the window was a table with the remains of lunch; bread, cheese and a half drunk litre bottle of beer. Everything being of wood gave the place a peaceful atmosphere – like communing with nature.

'Sounds very civilised. Yes, why not?' The old guy poured two tumblers full of vodka. Ari, who did not drink placed his on the table and thanked the man.

Boris took several gulps of his to Ari's disgust.

'Now look old man,' said Ari putting on his most placating voice, 'We've got kids out of work in this town. There's no money. The people need this new development. It'll take hundreds of folk off the breadline and give them a decent life.'

Ari hoped he had remembered the Boss's words correctly.

'It's a good offer; ten times what the place is worth and I think I can up the price a bit more.'

'I'm not selling,' repeated the old man.

'Do you have any children to leave it to?'

'No,' replied the old man. 'I never had any children.'

'Seems like we have a lot in common,' said Ari. 'You never had any kids and I never had a father. Not one I ever knew anyway, so if you

37

don't have any kids why are you holding onto this place? If I were you, I'd take the money and enjoy the rest of what's left of my life.'

'I have a dog,' the old man spoke as he sipped his vodka. 'He's lived here twelve years. He's too old to move.'

'I always wanted a dog,' said Ari opening up to this old guy more than he had ever opened up to anyone else before. 'But I was always in homes or being fostered so I never had the chance. One day I'll have my own dog. That's the only thing I wish for.'

'Rusty,' called the old man and a small pale brown Pekinese dog who was anything but a rusty red colour, slowly padded in from the kitchen.

'Why do you call him 'Rusty' said Ari, he isn't red.'

'I forget,' said the old guy smiling, 'It's a joke. Get it? Why is he called Rusty? I forget?'

'Oh,' said Ari, 'Yeh, I get it now,' He quite liked the old man in spite of his stubbornness. 'You know, I would've loved to have had a father like you.'

'Well thanks,' said the old man not sure he wanted a son like Ari.

'Here boy,' called Ari snapping his fingers close to the floor. Rusty sidled over to Ari and cautiously sniffed his hand. 'There's a good boy,' cooed Ari, and Rusty started to lick his fingers. 'You know, a dog is a friend for life. Dogs don't know the meaning of the word 'divorce.' A dog is for keeps.' Ari picked Rusty up and tickled him between the shoulder blades with his right hand. The dog sniffed and sneezed as, like all Pekinese dogs, too much designer breeding meant he struggled with his breathing. 'Did you never think of getting something a little bit bigger?' he asked as Rusty started to play up to his attentions.

'No,' said the old guy, 'Rusty is a big enough character. He is perfect for me.'

Ari moved his hand and started to tickle Rusty behind the ears.

'The old man chortled, 'You can do that all night. He loves it.'

'Yes,' said Ari, He sure does,' and then in one rapid movement he twisted Rusti's shoulders clockwise whilst turning the dog's head one hundred and eighty degrees anticlockwise. The crack of the dog's spine breaking echoed around the room.

'Sorry old man, I mustn't know my own strength.'

He placed Rusty on the floor and watched as his legs twitched for several minutes before the life ran out of him and he was gone.

Tears welled in the old man's eyes as he looked at his lifelong friend, now gone.

'Anyway,' said Ari, 'look on the bright side. There's no reason for you to hang on here anymore. You might as well sign this.'

Ari took the contract from his pocket. The old man signed with Boris a witness and at that they left the old man to cry alone.

'Pity,' said Ari to Boris as they drove back home, 'I liked the dog.'

'You didn't hurt the old guy did you Ari?' asked the Boss on their return.

'No,' replied Ari handing over the contract, 'I just reasoned with him like you said.'

'Good,' said the Boss breathing a sigh of relief, 'I'm glad you're starting to show some maturity.'

'Now,' I don't want disturbing tonight. Our young lady is coming to collect this contract and we need to conclude our business.'

Early next morning, two young men entered the new tailors down the high street. They were dressed in suits and each wore a black trilby as if they had walked in from a thirties gangster film. A third stood outside deterring new customers from entering.

As they entered the tailor greeted them.

'How can I help you gentlemen?'

One hood reversed the sign hanging on the shop door so it read 'closed.' 'We understand you were given the chance to donate to some local charities a few weeks ago. Have you decided how much you wish to donate?' asked one of the hoods. The tailor eyed the baseball bat he kept under the counter as protection.

'I donate to charities by direct debit,' he said as he moved towards the bat, 'I've no desire to give more at this time.'

'That's a pity,' said one of the hoods, 'as people get upset when businesses don't subscribe.'

The tailor reached under the counter, produced the baseball bat and banged it down hard on the work surface. 'Look!' he said, 'you people don't frighten me. Come into my shop once more and I'll talk to the authorities and report you.' The tailor came around the counter wielding his bat. 'Now clear out of my shop and go back to the gutter you came from.'

'OK, OK,' one hood replied 'we're going,' and thought 'what a stupid prick.'

The Boss wasn't at all happy when he heard the news. His night of lust had turned out to be a disaster. The woman had tried to please but she was an insult to his dick. She just didn't have it. Besides, he liked to feel ladies nipples stand up as he teased them with his tongue. These seemed to be permanently hard - like a pair of metal rivets welded on. No, when it came to sex, 'forget the intellectual,' he thought, 'always go for waitresses. They try harder; serving up sex is what they do best.'

Of course there was this stupid prick of a tailor. Who the fuck did he think he was? Sending my guys away like that. The story was all around town and something had to be done. 'What would Marlon Brando have done in this situation,' he thought. Marlon Brando was always his source of inspiration.

'Leave it to me,' said Ari when he heard the news, 'I'll be glad to sort it.'

That night the tailor was working late in the untidy work room at the back of the shop. Shelves stacked with rolls of black, blue and grey suiting material lined the walls. The room was lit by a single bare electric lamp hanging from the ceiling. He was working on a jacket hanging on a tailor's dummy and he was putting in the finishing touches by stitching in a bright red silk lining. He was making small hand stitches which he knew no-one else could match and he stood back to admire his work; feeling a sense of pride in his achievement. Having finished stitching, he cut off the thread with his teeth and placed the needle amid many others in a soft velvet pad lying on the table.

'Clap, clap, clap,' came the noise from behind him. The tailor had been so intent on his work he had not noticed Ari and his accomplice enter the shop and who were now applauding his work.

'Nice piece of work,' said Ari walking round the jacket and feeling the fabric with his fingers. 'A perfectionist; just like me!'

'What do you want?' asked the tailor moving towards the baseball bat he now constantly kept at his side after the incident, a few days ago.

'Me?' said Ari, 'what do I want? I want to teach you a lesson.' The tailor picked up the baseball bat and wielded it once again in the air.

'Come near me and I swear I'll hit you with it.' Without a second thought, Ari moved towards the tailor, who swung the bat at him but Ari moved his arm across his face and caught the end of it with his right hand. He ducked as the bat moved over his head, placed his left hand over the handle and moved forward pushing the bat against the tailor's throat - pinning him against the wall.

Ari brought up his knee and hit him in the groin. 'Now, we've asked you nicely and you've said no. So now we're here to tell you not so nicely. You pay. Understand? You pay.' Ari and his accomplice dragged the tailor to a chair and sat him down. They handcuffed his arms behind him and tied him to the chair.

Thence came the moment when the victor knows he has won and the vanquished knowing he has lost the game.

Ari said nothing. He knew silence in these sorts of situations was far more frightening than any threat. Let the victim imagine his worst fears. This would scare him most. Ari moved around to the front of the tailor, stooped and looked him straight in the eye. 'So,' said Ari quietly, 'Do you still not want to contribute to local charities?'

'I didn't understand what the local charities were,' said the tailor meekly. 'Now I know of course I will donate; just let me go.'

'Difficult, because people know you have refused.' Ari looked straight into the eyes of the tailor but gave no clue as to what was to come next. He picked up a long strip of cloth and moved behind the tailor, placing the cloth under the tailor's jaw and bringing it up above his head, where he tied it tightly. The tailor looked like an old cartoon character with tooth ache but try as he could the tailor was unable to separate his lower and upper jaws. His teeth were held clenched together. Ari moved to the front so the tailor could see what he was doing. He slowly picked out the largest needle from the pad on the table and held it high so both he and the tailor could see it clearly. Picking up some thread from the tailor's supply, he carefully licked the end and threaded it through the eye of the needle. Gently, he pulled the thread through the needle, cut it from the reel and knotted the end. 'Now,' said Ari. 'I hear you were going to talk to the authorities. Is that right?'

'No,' the tailor tried to scream but could only let out a whimper through his clamped teeth.

'Too late,' said Ari as he moved towards the tailor. His associate moved behind the tailor and held his head firmly from behind. Ari moved closer and grabbed the tailor's lips, forcing them together. He took the needle and thrust it through the bottom lip. The tailor tried to scream, as Ari brought the needle through the tailor's top lip and pulled the thread tight before tying it to fix the end. He then stuck the needle through the bottom lip again followed through the top and pulled the thread tight once more. The tailor was in agony. He had never imagined such pain. Ari continued until he had completely stitched the tailor's lips together. At the end he finished with a beautifully neat knot his mother would have been proud of – not that he knew his mother but that was immaterial.

'Now,' Ari whispered into the tailor's ear, 'do we have a problem here?' The tailor shook his head. 'Because, if I have to come back I will sew up your arse hole and feed you until you burst. Is that clear?

"The manager of the night club forced us to work as prostitutes. He told us that if we refused he would hurt our parents back home. We pleaded with him to let us go back to our home country but he demanded money to hand over our passports and let us go. The manager was arrested after a tip off. When police raided the flat where the women were kept they found a large amount of drugs 'used for sexual purposes."

Report from Court proceedings

Chapter 8

'You mean I can't go home until I pay Eva fifteen thousand dollars? You are joking. Please tell me you're joking.'

'No. I'm not joking.' Dmtry spoke curtly. 'Most girls repay it in less than a year. It depends on how much work they get and that depends on how hard they try.

'But I'll never have so much money,' said Kristina, 'I'll be stuck here forever.'

'If the other girls can do it, then surely you can,' said Dmtry. 'It's only natural.'

'It is not natural at all!' said Kristina. 'I came here to dance and dance is what I'm going to do. I am not a prostitute and never will be.' She was furious. She realised that she had been duped.

'You'll have to do a lot of dancing to repay that sort of money,' reasoned Dmtry. 'Why don't you just play the game and end up rich?'

'And just what is the game?' asked Kristina.

'Well, you let me screw you here and now, and then we decide whether you go on to work the nightclubs or work inside. It's your choice.'

Kristina remembered the blonde girl's words from earlier. 'Quality control.'

'And working 'inside' being?' asked Kristina.

'Working inside means in a safe house where the men come to visit,' said Dmtry. 'Some girls prefer someone else to tout for business rather than having to find it for themselves. They feel embarrassed asking.'

'You mean working in a brothel?' said Kristina.

'Sort of, but more pleasant. More upmarket,' said Dmtry 'Well I'm doing neither,' retorted Kristina 'so you can go and tell 'Madam' Eva just that.' She stood up and stomped out of the room. Falling on her mattress, she burst into tears.

Dmtry returned to the kitchen where Eva was sipping a cup of coffee as she waited for the outcome of the discussion. 'Nothing doing,' said Dmtry. 'She says she won't do it.'

'They all do 'it' in the end,' replied Eva. 'We'll let her starve for today and I'll talk to her tomorrow.'

'I hope she does see sense,' said Dmtry. 'She seems a nice kid.'

'Thanks for trying.' Eva smiled gratefully. 'Anytime you're feeling lonely just say the word and I'll send someone over.'

'I've a Chinese 'live in' at present but I'll bear the offer in mind.' Dmtry shrugged his shoulders. 'You never know.'

Eva took a bottle of water from the fridge and went to see Kristina. She unlocked the door and saw her lying on her mattress, facing the wall and sobbing quietly to herself. 'Don't make life difficult for you or for us,' said Eva firmly. 'We're giving you the opportunity to make a lot of money for your mum and family back home. Most girls would jump at the chance.'

'No,' sobbed Kristina. She refused to look at Eva but continued to sob quietly. Eva placed the water by her side and left – locking the door from the outside.

"I was brought to Almina from Bangladesh on the offer of a job along with several other women. When we arrived we were kidnapped and taken to several apartments around the city. The trafficking gang consisted of one woman and five men and the men assaulted and raped us before forcing us into prostitution."

Report from Court proceedings

Chapter 9

Nikki arrived at a restaurant in one of the better class hotels in the business district of the city. A relic from bygone times but with the crystal chandelier hanging from the ceiling and the luxuriously decorated tables scattered across the carpeted room, it still oozed class. The round tables, each with their starched white tablecloths providing a splendid setting for the silver cutlery whilst the single red rose held in a cut glass vase in the centre finished the magnificent curio off. Nikki, hair in a classic up do, was wearing a long red, off shoulder evening dress with a small silver bag that matched her shoes held in one hand. The maître d' watched as she glided down the few steps on entering and quickly summed up the purpose of her visit. He showed Nikki to a table in a secluded corner of the restaurant – far away from the respectable 'family' hotel guests.

'Oh no!' Nikki appeared to be shocked and spoke more loudly than normal, keen to point out she was a respectable lady. 'I couldn't possibly sit there. What would people think? I'm here to meet my grandfather who's treating me to dinner on my birthday.' Looking around the restaurant she chose a table near the centre of the room.

'May I sit here?' she pulled out the chair and sat down before the maître d' had a chance to say no. However, since the young lady turned out to be respectable and after all, merely waiting to dine with her grandfather on her birthday, he breathed a sigh of relief as he didn't like serving 'that sort' who usually came here 'on business.'

'I'll arrange a cake with candles,' he thought and went off to see the Chef.

Nikki had deliberately chosen this table and this seat as there was a middle aged business man sitting by himself at the next table, who would now be in her direct line of sight. She smiled at him and he nodded back and returned to his dining. Meanwhile, the maître d' was guiding Philippe to the table and seated him opposite Nikki;

47

his back to the man behind. Philippe was dressed for the occasion. Distinguished looking with a light grey suit and red carnation in one lapel. As Nikki talked to Philippe, her eyes drifted over his shoulder and caught the attention of the man sitting by himself, who looked somewhat lonely on his own.

Throughout the meal, Nikki kept looking at the man opposite and smiling at him. At one point, the man was almost certain she had actually blown him a kiss. The cake arrived; Philippe toasted Nikki and congratulated her on her birthday and passed over a present – a small box beautifully wrapped with a pink satin bow on the top. Nikki slipped it into her purse and said she would open it later.

'If you don't mind,' said Philippe as he rose and kissed Nikki affectionately on the forehead, 'I'm getting old and it's time for my bed. I'll ring you tomorrow and we'll meet up before you go back home. Enjoy the city whilst you're here.' He paid the bill and left and again Nikki smiled at the man who was still alone and sitting directly in front of her. He had clearly been waiting for Philippe to leave as he had finished his dinner long ago.

'I don't like to think of a beautiful young lady on her own on her birthday. Do you mind if I join you?' The man rose from his table and sat down next to her without waiting for an invitation.

'Not at all.' Nikki smiled sweetly. 'To be honest I would be glad of the company. Granddad is very nice and I love him terribly but I don't come to the city much and I was hoping to see some night life. Granddad had arranged a young friend who was to show me the city's 'life,' but he had to cancel at the last minute.'

'Well maybe I can be of assistance. I'm in the city on business and at a loose end myself. I finished a lucrative deal today so I want to celebrate. Why don't we go out together and party? My name's John,' said Cyril - careful not to use his real name.

'My name's Ingrid.' Nikki did not want to give her real name either. 'Just let me go to the loo to freshen up and we'll be off.' In the toilets, she entered one of the cubicles and sat fully dressed on the closed toilet seat. She took out Philippe's present and opened it, throwing the wrapping into the bin and placing the set of house keys it contained into her bag before returning to the table.

'Right, John, I'm in your hands.' She linked her arm through his and together they walked to the taxi rank, leaving their choice of venue in the hands of the taxi driver.

'Take us to the best nightclub in town,' said Cyril; neither of them wanting to admit that in reality, they both knew the city inside out. After two or three night clubs they decided to call it a night. They had drunk enough, though even in Cyril's inebriated state, he was surprised as to how sober Ingrid was after so much alcohol. For his part, he was decidedly tipsy but they had both enjoyed themselves.

'Where are you staying?' asked Cyril as they left the club.

'All by myself,' Nikki replied. 'I'm staying in a friend's house nearby. They're away on holiday so it seemed pointless wasting money on a hotel. Why not drop me off and come in for a night cap? It would be the perfect way for me to say 'thank you' for a wonderful evening.'

Nikki opened the front door with the set of keys Philippe had presented to her and let them both in. She placed her finger vertically across her mouth and mouthed a surreptitious 'Shhhhhh!' before leading Cyril upstairs. Cyril despite the intoxication and excitement noticed how few personal effects there were in the house but thought it was possibly because the owners travelled so much.

As they entered the master bedroom, Nikki closed the door and pressed Cyril back against it. She stood back and slowly removed her dress, revealing her naked body since she had worn no underwear all evening. She knelt down, slowly unzipped his trousers and massaged his penis until he had a firm erection. Carefully manoeuvring her hands and tongue she brought him to a climax in less than a minute.

'Let's do something else until 'big boy' here recovers,' she said and moved across to the wardrobe, removing some silk ties and a hood. 'This is what I like,' she said as she moved over to lie on the bed. 'Tie me up to the bed with my hands and legs outstretched and put the hood over me,' she asked. 'Then I want you to kiss me and do things to me in such a way I don't know what or where the next delight is coming from.' Cyril, who had already taken off his clothes, readily agreed and started to tie Nikki down.

'Not too tight,' said Nikki, 'I don't want any marks when I get home to Mum.' With a firmly bound and blindfolded Nikki, Cyril started on his limited repertoire. He started licking her nipples before moving down to try to bring her to a climax. Meanwhile, she was trying not to go to sleep in the darkness of the hood and the only thing keeping her awake was her professionalism and the cold wet tongue failing miserably to raise even the slightest interest from her private parts. 'That was unbelievable!' lied Nikki as Cyril untied her and removed the hood.

'Have you ever tried it?' she asked.

'No. Never, my Wi..' Cyril corrected his mistake at once. 'My girlfriend is much more conservative.'

'Try it.' Nikki pushed him down on the bed and started to tie him up. 'You are just going to love this next bit,' she said, placing the hood over his head. 'Now I'm going to wait a few minutes to build tension and then, I promise, you'll have the experience of a lifetime.' Quietly, she picked up his wallet, watch, hotel room key card and crept out of the room.

As Nikki left the house, a car coasted up silently; she climbed in and gently closed the car door.

'Ingrid? Ingrid?' came the muffled noises from inside the hood in the bedroom. 'Where are you? Come on Ingrid, stop messing about.'

'What took so long?' asked Philippe as they drove to Cyril's hotel.

'Don't ask. He wouldn't give up until he gave me an orgasm and so I had to fake three in the end.'

At the hotel, they presented the key card to the night porter, who handed the room key over to the respectable couple in front of him without a second thought. Indistinguishable from any other hotel guests, they went up in the lift quickly and made their way to the room. Within seconds, with expert hands, they cleared the room of anything valuable and left as unobtrusively as they came. The credit cards were sold off to a 'fence' who would spend the rest of the night turning Cyril's credit balance into cash.

Meanwhile, Cyril had spent a restless night; every now and then calling out for Ingrid until the alcohol overcame him and he fell asleep.

'This is the kitchen, a little small but well organised' said the Estate agent to the young couple with her. Moving on she carefully opened the door to the lounge, stood back and let them enter.

'Always remember to let the buyers into a room before you enter it,' she remembered from her training; that way the rooms always look bigger.' The young couple walked in first and looked around in silence. 'If you come upstairs we'll view the bedrooms and bathroom' she said leading them up the stairs. 'The house is to be let fully furnished and if you want it, you'll have to move very quickly, as there was an elderly gentleman who viewed the house yesterday and he seemed very interested.'

She led the couple upstairs whilst explaining the terms of the lease and wondered if she had really heard a muffled man's voice asking for Ingrid. 'Maybe the house was haunted,' she thought. 'Better not let the clients think this or they would never rent it.'

'This is the master bedroom,' she spoke knowingly as she flung back the door, standing aside to let the couple walk into the room. The young girl let out a shriek as they all stared and saw Cyril, lying naked, hooded and tied to the bed.

"I met a woman calling herself 'Mistress Pain' on an adult dating website and she promised me an afternoon of 'tying and teasing'. She promised to whip me if I was bad. I received an SMS saying 'I am here slave, open the door and go upstairs'. She followed me up and told me to kneel naked on the bed where she used Velcro to tie me down. At that moment, her boyfriend burst in and tied me down fully using plastic cable ties. He gagged me and then ransacked my house taking away all my electronic goods and jewellery."

Proceedings of Court case.

Chapter 10

Ari hung his head a little and shuffled his feet like a naughty boy in front of his headmaster.

'I thought I said no violence?'

'No Boss,' said Ari, 'You said 'don't hurt the old guy'. You never mentioned anything about the dog.'

'But I asked you to reason with him.'

'I did,' pleaded Ari. 'His only reason for staying in the house was the dog, so I explained to him with the dog gone there was now no reason for him to stay. He signed, took the money and left. They've already started on the construction at the site.'

'But you have really upset the woman,' continued the Boss, knowing already this line of thought was a lost cause with Ari. 'We may have been able to use her again but now she's more upset about the dog than she would've been if you'd killed the guy.' The Boss sighed as he realised what he had known all along. Ari could never take over the reins from him. To be in charge meant being responsible for those who could not help themselves. The Boss needed a son, a successor. He'd hoped it would be Ari but no. As much as the Boss loved him, there was no way Ari could take over once he had gone. He was destined to be the faithful disciple but never the master. Ari brought the conversation back to the business at hand.

'You mean, 'you' might have been able to use her again,' joked Ari; being careful not to go too far.

'Not likely!' The Boss frowned. 'Frigid cow! I liked the work you did with the tailor though. He pays his dues regular and townsfolk respect us even more. They say when he smiles he has them in stitches! No, that was a nice touch.'

'Thanks,' smirked Ari, 'I enjoyed it too.'   'Tonight, I have a special visitor coming,' said the Boss, 'So I want the place empty. Tell the cook to prepare dinner and put it on the side - goulash or something similar. It'll stay warm and we can serve ourselves. Tell the staff everyone must go out for the night and not return before eleven.'

'Who'll open the door?' enquired Ari.

'I will. No-one must see this visitor.' The Boss looked serious.

'He must be pretty important,' said Ari. 'Are you sure this is safe?'

'I'll be fine,' replied the boss, 'but I want you to stay in the kitchen and have a wander around outside every now and again. You know, make sure no-one is listening from the outside.'

'Ok,' Boss, 'if it's what you want.'

'No Ari, it's what my visitor wants.'

That night the cook prepared soup, goulash with dumplings and a rich chocolate cake for the 'important guest' and set it out on the table at the side of the Boss's office. Whilst this room was not the most comfortable for dining, it was soundproofed and had closed circuit television installed so he could watch for anyone listening outside the door.

Just after nine, a black Mercedes pulled up at the outside gates. A buzzer sounded under the Boss's table. He checked the gate camera on the closed circuit television and flicked the controls to give him a close up view of the car but he was still unable to make out who was inside. The Boss checked his watch and nodded.

'This must be him,' he thought and pressed the buzzer on the intercom. 'You ready Ari?'

'Ready and waiting.' Ari was intrigued.

'OK. Keep out of sight unless I need you. I'm letting him in.' The car drove through the gates which closed silently behind. It drove slowly up the drive until it reached the front of the house and came to rest under some trees where it could not be seen from the road. A man climbed out of the car and walked to the front door; his feet crunching on the gravel under his shoes. As he tapped on the front door, the Boss looked into the closed circuit television so he could see him. The man looked up and smiled into the camera to give the Boss a good look at his face. Security had to be tight. The Boss walked over to the front door and opened it slightly so only a little light was visible. The visitor wanted to remain in the dark.

54

'Welcome Mr Mayor,' he whispered. 'Come in.' He led his clandestine visitor to his office and the door closed with a reassuring thud as the sound proofing kicked in. The Mayor was casually dressed in jeans, open shirt and blue cardigan to complement his fair hair. He may well have been the same age as the Boss but as someone who had to present a public image, what bulk there was on his body was pure muscle. The Boss poured his visitor his favourite drink, a tumbler full of whisky, and they sat and talked of old times. Of school together, the teachers they hated and the girls they had sometimes fought over and of course, the girls they had sometimes shared. They picked at the food but neither was really interested; only eating enough to be socially correct but no more. Drink and reminiscing were more important.

'So what problem has brought you here this evening? The Boss finally asked.

'You and me,' replied the Mayor, 'are dinosaurs. There's a new breed of politician who wants us out. Well, actually 'me' if I'm honest. They want an end to corruption and a new beginning.'

'I thought you'd been making a drive against corruption yourself. I certainly sent you two scapegoats this year to be prosecuted and you to take the glory for removing this scum from our streets.'

'Yes, and I thank you again,' replied the mayor. 'I know when one of your men cheated, you could have simply killed him but in view of our business relationship you gave me all the evidence I needed to prosecute him and put him in prison. Helped you, as it got rid of these people for a good few years and it also helped me, since I, as Mayor, was seen to be taking action against organised crime. They served their time in prison and said nothing as they feared what would happen to them or their families if they did.'

'So what's the problem?' The Boss wanted him to get to the main point.

'I'm up for re-election this year and I don't think I'll win.' The mayor was clearly worried.

'Why not? You've won it for the last twenty years - so why not once more?'

'There's a new opponent,' continued the Mayor, 'and he's fighting the election on a clean-up campaign.'

'Nothing new in that,' the Boss responded. 'Didn't you do the same?

Why not just publish the dirt about him?'

'The problem is,' said the Mayor, 'this guy is clean.'

'Well, why not invent some dirt, or at least plant some on him?'

'Not that easy, I'm afraid,' said the Mayor. 'He really is clean. He goes jogging every morning, attends church every Sunday and visits the old and sick - and even mixes with the young at Youth Clubs. The idiots who got rid of the 'Party' system where your friends voted you 'in' rather than the public, need their heads seeing to. No, if we try to plant something on him, believe me, it will come right back to me.'

'Let me give it some thought.' The Boss already knew what the answer would be. 'Now enough business talk! Do you remember the redhead we fought over in our last year at school? What was her name?'

'He needs to vanish into thin air,' said the Boss later that evening. 'No witnesses, no noise, just disappear forever.'

'That's not easy! There's always someone who'll talk a little and then a little more until everyone knows everything,' replied Ari.

'Not if we don't tell anyone. What we need is one person who will do everything.'

'There are always questions to be answered.' For once Ari was trying to be sensible. 'People, politicians, the police and even though nothing is ever said they still get the hint and put two and two together.'

'But what if our assassin disappeared too?'

'You mean someone kills the assassin straight after.' Ari did not like where this conversation was going.

'Of course not you bloody idiot,' I mean he goes away for a while until things cool down and the Mayor is re-elected.'

'Maybe.' Ari thought about it for a minute. 'Any ideas where our assassin would go until things calmed down?' He realised where things were going. If it were to be a 'one man band' then the fact the Boss was talking to him already, meant he'd been chosen to carry out the plan.

'I do have an idea. In fact it is more of a 'working holiday' than a place of work. You must admit Ari, there's not been much in your line of work recently. The tailor was the only real job in the last two years.' The Boss knew Ari could not refute that fact.

'True,' said Ari, 'it's been a bit boring of late.'

'And this job is important not just to the Mayor but to us. If a clean guy gets into the mayoral office we'll have problems. Get rid of this guy and we maintain the status quo.'

'Whatever you say Boss.' Ari had no choice but to agree with him.

'This is the guy. His name is Vladimir and this is all the information we have on him.' He passed over the dossier the Mayor had given him. I don't want to know anything about it other than when you want your ticket out of here. Make it soon! The sooner the better - before he gets onto a roll with the election campaign.'

Ari took the folder and stood up to leave.

'In fact,' added the Boss, 'I don't think we should meet again until the job is done.'

Ari went home and spent all night pouring over the dossier until he knew it all by heart. He considered a suicide due to a contrived scandal or even a road accident - but this would cause investigations afterwards, which no-one wanted. 'No,' he thought, 'the Boss is right. 'Vladimir' just needs to disappear from the face of the Earth and do it fast.' That gave him two problems:

Problem one: how to kill him with no-one seeing it happen.

Problem two: How to get rid of the body where no-one would ever find it.

The politician shared a house with two male friends, so killing him at home was out of the question. A silenced gun could be used for the act but carrying a dead body out of a strange house was bound to raise an alarm, even when carried by a man with Ari's strength. Every morning, Vladimir went jogging and this seemed to be the best opportunity. He was as regular as clockwork, set off at six, jogged round a path in some nearby woodland and returned at seven. The only problem was how was Ari to catch him? He was strong but no athlete. To lie in wait and shoot him as he passed was possible but not a certain death and this plan had to be one hundred percent certain of success. As for getting rid of the body, this had to be done straight after he had killed him.

'If I kill him between six and seven,' pondered Ari, 'then I need to dispose of the body by eight at the latest.' He was at a loss as to how he was going to do it.

There were always the 'cement shoes' followed by dumping him in the lake, as they did during the gangster wars in the States; but where would he get enough cement so quickly? He also needed a boat. It was difficult doing all this by himself. He could just sink the boat but then he couldn't swim. This posed yet another problem.

'One thing at a time,' thought Ari and picked up the phone.

'Hi,' said Ari, 'I need some cement, two bags should be enough. When can you deliver?'

'Any day but Wednesday; we're tied up at the new development all day.'

'I'll leave it for now,' said Ari and hung up, as an idea formed in his mind.

The next morning Ari arrived early in the woods to check the layout and sat behind some bushes near the place where the path crossed a stream. He had walked the path the previous afternoon and selected this particular spot as the best place of ambush. Amid the sounds of the stream trickling by and the birds singing as they awakened, Ari felt quite calm. He moved further into the greenery as he heard the thudding of jogging feet and saw Vladimir approaching. He checked his watch; six twenty am. Once Vladimir had passed, he finalised his plans. He would need a canvas sheet to wrap the body in so there would be no trace of blood and he calculated ten minutes would be enough to finish off the job. He made his way to the parked truck, which he had stolen especially for the occasion the night before and which was now parked across the stream, hidden down a narrow tree lined track. Ari mimed throwing the body into the back of the truck and drove to the new development. This was being built on the land Ari had secured from the old man. His house had completely gone and he could see the mud and dirt caused by a constant stream of construction vehicles accessing the site. He parked and walked over to what looked like a war zone, with deep trenches everywhere. At the bottom of the trenches was a layer of gravel. Ari wandered around the site for some time and realised it appeared to be devoid of people.

'Can I help you?' said a voice from behind. Ari swirled around fast. The voice took him by surprise. In front of him was a worker dressed in dark blue overalls and muddy boots. Despite the peaked cap worn on his head his face had a dry, cracked, weathered appearance.

He looked at his watch; five minutes past eight. 'No,' he replied. 'I'm just looking. I've put my name down for one of the flats and just wanted to see how they are coming along. Hope they're building them right.'

'Nothing wrong with these mate,' the workman said as he sidled up to Ari's side. 'Look at those foundations and see how deep they are. Nothing will move this building.'

'According to my schedule,' continued Ari, 'the foundations should be in by the end of the week.'

'I don't know about schedules but they'll be in by the end of tomorrow morning. That's for sure.' The workman seemed pleased at being able to give the man news on the latest progress.

'Thanks,' said Ari, turning and walking away whilst looking out for the last piece of his puzzle. As he glanced around, he saw it at one side near some trees; a pile of loose gravel at the edge of the site. As he drove back into town, he rang the Boss and said. 'I'll collect the needful at ten tomorrow morning.'

'No problem.' The Boss put the phone down, pleased things were moving.

The next morning Ari arrived early and stretched a thin piece of fishing line between two trees so it ran parallel to the bank of the stream and about twelve inches above the ground. Having done this, he lay in wait; it was drizzling with rain which bothered him, as he had to keep the silenced gun under his jacket to keep it dry.

'At least the rain is keeping the bloody birds quiet,' he thought, 'so I can hear him coming.' At last he heard the thudding of feet and looked at his watch. It read ten past six. He was early but then he realised it wasn't Vladimir at all. It was a woman in her thirties, dressed in a blue track suit with a white stripe down the side of each leg and arm and her long dark hair swaying from side to side as she ran. She ran up and stopped just before the fishing line, jogging on the spot, stopping only to look at her watch

'Stupid bitch,' groaned Ari. 'She's is in the wrong place at the wrong time and she's really going to regret it.' Suddenly he realised what was happening. 'Shit! She's waiting for him.' He took the gun from under his coat. This complicates things. The Boss had said no witnesses, which meant the 'kiss of death' for this woman. She was only a matter of feet away from him, when she turned, appearing to look straight at him. Ari shot twice and the bullets struck home both times. The woman fell to the ground. He walked over and put a third bullet straight through her head to make sure she was dead before dragging her behind the same bushes he had been lurking in. He had to work quickly, kicking leaves and dirt over the drag marks left behind on the ground by her feet.

Blood stains! They were definitely not what Ari wanted. His victim was supposed to disappear into thin air. Blood stains on the ground were not conducive to this idea. He put more leaves over the blood stains and returned to his hiding place. 'Sorry love,' he whispered, as he pushed her to one side to make room.

More thudding noises could be heard as more feet trod the ground. Vladimir slowed but kept jogging as he reached the river bank, looking round as if he was expecting to see someone. He was not concentrating on where he was going so he tripped over the fishing line and fell forwards into the stream. As he fell, two bullets flew from Ari's gun; one hit him in the back of the head and the other landed in the middle of his back. He never even knew what had hit him. There was a splash as his body hit the water.

Ari raced out of his hiding place and checked his victim, who was now face down in the water, the blood being carried away by the water, leaving no trace. 'Now this is how it should have been,' muttered Ari, 'sweet and clean.' He had to think quickly what he was going to do with the woman? There was bound to be a search for Vladimir. Everyone knew he had left to go jogging and so the path would be searched and the blood stains found. It would complicate things when they found it wasn't Vladimir's blood. A forensic examination would soon determine this and so Ari had to think of a plan B – and fast.

Ari removed the fishing line and was pleased there was no scarring on the tree trunks. He brought the sheet of canvas and wrapped it around the corpse but it was a real dead weight as he lifted it from the stream. The wet canvas and body left a trail of water on the ground as he carried it back to the truck. 'At least the rain will hide that,' thought Ari, thankful it had not been a dry night. Dumping the body in the back of the truck, he removed Vladimir's trainers and returned to murder scene. He carefully went over the area, placing Vladimir's trainers down and stamping on them to leave footprints at certain points. Going back to the truck, he threw the trainers in the back and drove to the building site, parking a little out of the way by the side of the gravel, where he waited and watched. As he parked, he knocked over a small wooden stake in the shape of a cross stuck in the ground by the edge of the trees.

'No-one here yet,' thought Ari giving it a few more minutes to make sure. He drove over to the trenches which were to be the foundations of the new shopping centre and parked nearby. Clambering out, he went round to the back and lifted up the corpse wrapped in the canvas shroud. Thankfully Vladimir was a light weight for someone with Ari's strength, so he easily tossed the corpse to the bottom of the trench. A loud crunch could be heard as his body hit the gravel. With a grunt of satisfaction, Ari went back to the truck, took out the trainers and tossed them after their unfortunate owner.

He drove the truck back to the pile of gravel, parked and loaded the stones onto it. The front tyre rested on the wooden stake and pushed it into the mud. As it sank, to be lost forever; there was one word written on it, 'Rusty.' The poor little dog who had not wanted to leave this land. Driving back to the trenches he stopped and shovelled gravel over the corpse until it disappeared from sight.

Once he was sure the corpse was totally hidden, he drove the truck away and he parked out of sight - amongst the trees but near enough for him to walk back and watch the 'burial ceremony' as the concrete filled the trenches. He took the gun with him, in case things went wrong. The workers arrived first, followed soon after by a convoy of cement trucks, which poured line after line of concrete over Vladimir's body and into the trenches, until they were full and level with the ground.

Ari drove back to the outskirts of town, where a black limousine with darkened windows was waiting for him. As he neared the waiting car, the front passenger door opened and Boris climbed out to meet him. Ari passed him the truck keys and the gun. 'Get rid of these. Did you pick up my stuff?'

'Yes, replied Boris, 'it's in the car.'

Ari got into the back of the car.

'Everything go to plan?' asked the Boss.

'A slight complication,' replied Ari, 'but I fixed it. Now, where am I going for my holidays?' As the car set off in the direction of the airport, the Boss handed Ari an envelope full of crisp, new one-hundred dollar bills.

'That's for now. I'll send you regular money once you're there. It's a new business in a new patch and so it's going to be something like the Wild West used to be. You'll have fun.'

'Sounds too good to be true,' grinned Ari. 'Where exactly is this place?'

'It's called Almina.' The Boss handed over Ari's air ticket and passport. 'When you reach the airport, you'll be met by a woman named Eva who'll explain everything. She's setting up a new racket; mainly prostitution. There are no drugs as yet but she needs an enforcer. You'll work for her over the next two years; helps the Mayor, helps me, helps her and helps you. Everyone's a winner. I'll miss you Ari.' The Boss smiled. 'We've had some good times together you and me. I only ask one thing of you.'

'And what's that?'

'Come back,' replied the Boss. 'Just come back.' The car pulled up at the airport and Ari got out. The driver opened the boot and took out Ari's suitcase and went to find a trolley. A police man was on his way over to tell them to move the car but fortunately for him, he realised whose car it was and turned around just in time to avoid an embarrassing incident.

And then Ari was gone.

Vladimir's disappearance was news the next day along with the discovery of the woman's body. The press quickly linked the two stories together, particularly when it was found she was the wife of a close friend of Vladimir. The following day the press announced the two had been having an affair and surmised a lover's tiff which had led to the shooting of the woman and consequent absence of Vladimir. Why else would he disappear into thin air? The burned out truck was found several miles away and didn't even make it into the newspapers.

'Well done Ari,' thought the Boss. 'Perhaps there is hope for the boy yet as my successor.'

"The three Asian men lured us to Almina with the promise of jobs as housemaids but when we arrived they took our passports, locked us up in two apartments and forced us to work as prostitutes. We were locked in our rooms and they threatened to torture us if we did not co-operate." The three were sentenced to 15 years in gaol, fined 130,000 US Dollars and made to pay each woman 2,800 US Dollars in compensation.

Proceedings of Court case.

Chapter 11

My Dear Jonathan,

It was such a pleasure and relief to receive your last email. I thought you had forgotten me. You cannot understand how much your words mean to me. They give me hope and a wonderful vision of the two of us together in the future. It truly warms my heart. I thought that as a woman at the age of thirty two, my life was over. I thought I was too old to attract another man but now you give me the hope I am still young enough to find a loving relationship with such a truly amazing man.

Please send me more photographs of you, your life and your friends.
Your loving Gina
P.S. I will not sleep until I receive your reply.

'All this makes you want to puke,' said Nikki. 'What's up with these sad guys?'

'Everyone wants to be loved. That's the whole point of the scam.' Philippe said philosophically.

'Why do we go to all the trouble of setting people up and then stealing their money?' she pondered. 'I mean, like with the scam of tying the naked punter to the bed and leaving him in a public place before stealing his money and all his worldly possessions. Why didn't we just steal his money at the start and be done with it?' Nikki and Philippe had been working together for nearly a year and between them had swindled a growing number of victims. They had used some of the money to set themselves up in a small rented flat and were living together in the city. Nikki was busy at a computer set against one wall whilst Philippe sat in his favourite arm chair by the window. The small room was cluttered but snug. The wallpaper had seen better days, faded but still hanging on to the walls; just. Framed old prints of country scenes hung on the walls to brighten the room

'And tell me, my dear,' Philippe replied, 'have any of these 'ripped off' gentlemen ever complained to the police?'

'Wait a minute, here's one from Eric.' Nikki turned to the computer and tapped away at the keyboard.

My Darling Eric,

I can't tell you how much your last words of comfort meant to me. I also thank you for the cable transfer which arrived just in time to allow me to pay the electricity bill and keep myself and my young son not only warm but alive this dreadful winter. I am absolutely desperate without a man to look after me. Hopefully this situation will be sorted out soon and we can be together and keep each other warm,

Your loving Olga

'Well no,' she finally answered Philippe's question, 'at least not that we know of.'

'And they won't,' he responded. 'If we just take their money they'll make a complaint to the police and they'll eventually catch us. By taking their money and humiliating them they'll never report it. Take that John guy last year.'

'Oh him! The first time was fun but after a birthday party every week, each at a different restaurant, it gets a bit hard to keep up the appearances.'

'Well yes. But how could he possibly say anything?' Philippe took a long breath and continued, 'well officer, it was like this, I met this girl in a restaurant and we went back to her place only it wasn't her place, it was a house up for rent and I tied her to the bed and made love to her and then I let her tie me naked to the bed and blindfold me and then she took off with all my money and hotel key. Oh, then an estate agent and a young couple found me bound naked on the bed in the morning and untied me and let me go. Please officer, don't tell my wife about this. Oh! Don't let it get into the papers or I will be the laughing stock of the business world.' No dear, that is why we set them up and embarrass them and that is why we will continue to do so.'

'Ah George,' Nikki returned her attention to the computer keyboard. 'Let me reply to him as he's about to send us the big one.'

Dear George,

The prospect of our impending marriage thrills me so much I can no longer work – so I have given up my job. This leaves me very short of money as you know. But you were right; if you don't like your job quit it, so I have. If you could transfer me some money to pay for the rent whilst we wait for the visa to come through I would be ever so grateful. I will repay everything when we meet.

All my Love,

Helena

Whilst Nikki worked at the computer, Philippe sat quietly completing the crossword in the newspaper. He and Nikki liked this. They had become a couple even though he was so much older than her. The nature of her job meant she could have sex anytime she wanted and the punters paid for it, so she didn't need a man at home to keep her happy. Philippe provided the security and they were 'comfortable.' An old word, but a good one; one that described their relationship perfectly.

'Shit, this one wants to fly out and meet me before he marries me.'

'Just say to him err, what's his name?' said Philippe.

'Andrew, Andrew from the States.'

'Well just tell Andrew it's unsafe for an American to travel in the rural areas of Kazmenia and also, sorry, what name are you using with Andrew?'

'Ena.'

'Well let Ena tell Andrew he can't come over here until they're married as there would be shame on her if the neighbours thought she'd met a westerner over the internet. When they're married there'll be no problem,' advised Philippe. He reached over to a small table by his side and picked up the thesaurus to help him solve a particularly difficult clue. Mostly Philippe and Nikki enjoyed the 'domestic' aspects of their life together. Sometimes he and Nikki did make love together but not often. Theirs was a professional relationship in every sense of the word - but 'comfortable,' as we said.

If he did ever want sex, he could always buy it but in reality Philippe never bought anything. He was addicted to the excitement of cheating people – and the thought he was conning a girl into having sex with him for free, was far more exciting than the sex act itself. Philippe had set up a female escort agency and he advertised on the net that the agency was looking for new girls to work for them. A girl would ring up and Philippe would ask her some questions about her age, hair colour, reasons for wanting the job – anything really because the answers didn't matter as he would invite her to meet him anyway. At the end he would thank her for her time, tell her he was very interested and asked for a photograph. 'Just a shot of the head and shoulders for now,' he would tell her. As soon as the photo arrived and, if she looked half decent, she would be invited for an interview. Philippe wasn't really concerned about looks; that was not what he was after. It was usually Nikki who rang and explained theirs was a respectable agency with a loyal client base so they had to make sure new girls knew how to give customer satisfaction before sending them out on jobs. Some girls backed out at this point but not many as Nikki was good at what she did and exuded confidence. Besides, most of these girls were so desperate for money they would believe anything.

The girl would arrive at the appointed hour; Nikki would let her in and lead her to the bedroom where Philippe was waiting. She would do a quick introduction and leave them to. The girl would not hear from the agency again and if she rang, she was simply told she had been unsuccessful in the interview. Some girls even asked what they did wrong and how could they improve their performance. Nikki once thought of offering them private tuition, at an inflated price of course but thought better of it. As Philippe always said, 'never get greedy.' No matter how good the last scam was, do not go back for a second helping.

However, not all scams could be for pleasure as they needed money and so they carried on with the old ones and also introduced a few internet scams to keep up with the times.

Their latest scam, 'the www.RussianWives.org/asm' website had been going for three months now - not that Philippe or Nikki were Russian or had ever lived there but Russian wives were fashionable and 'www.RussianWives.org/asm' had a ring to it which would attract men from all over the World. Initially Nikki had asked a few of her attractive girlfriends to provide mug shots and Philippe set up a website advertising Russian girls who were looking for husbands from the West. Naturally, Philippe and Nikki wrote all the emails and took the money.

Dear Greg,

Thank you for your message. I was in real need of cheering up. These past few months have been some of the best in my life. I feel I have someone whom I can talk to. My son has been terribly ill and the Doctors say he needs an operation. But that will cost me two thousand dollars and I just don't have it. The Doctors say he could be permanently crippled if he does not have the operation soon.

All my love
Gina.

'We need to try something else,' said Nikki, 'something big.'

'Like selling the Kremlin to a Texan?' replied Philippe? 'What would they do with it? Put it next to London Bridge?'

'No, not like that,' she mused, 'how about online dating sites?'

'Go on, I'm listening.'

'I read somewhere where one con artist went to online dating agencies looking for widows of soldiers. He spun the tale saying he was a soldier serving in Afghanistan. After he'd reeled her in with his stories of how lonely he was and when she was finally hooked and 'in love,' he asked her if she would mind if he sent her his war medals to look after.'

'Now that's real class,' said Philippe. 'Medals to a war widow is like manna from heaven. So what happened next?'

'Well,' she continued, 'she received a phone call from a courier company saying the medals had arrived but were stuck in customs. He told her over the phone the customs duty was two thousand dollars since the medals were so valuable.

'I take it the representative from the courier company was our old friend 'the soldier' in disguise?' asked Philippe.

'Of course it was. Anyway, she passed the information on by email to the soldier boy whom she thought was back in Afghanistan and he replied asking her to pay it. He would give it back as soon as he met her after his tour of duty.

'So she paid up?'

'Of course; but as soon as she'd transferred the money into the 'courier's' bank account, she got another call from the 'courier' company saying it would cost another twenty thousand to change the parcel into her name so she could collect it!

'I was liking it until now,' said Philippe.

'So she mortgaged her house and transferred that too,' continued Nikki ignoring his comment. 'Afterwards she heard no more from the 'courier' or the soldier boyfriend and never even got the medals. Now that was cool.'

'Didn't she check the soldier out when she first heard from him?' enquired Philippe.

'Of course, No-one's that stupid. He was using a real person's name who actually was serving in Afghanistan and so it all appeared to be real.'

'And is there an end to this story?'

'Well yes,' continued Nikki, 'she complained to the police and they were all arrested. They found the courier and the soldier were the same person and he'd never even been in the army, never mind Afghanistan.'

'Precisely my point,' said Philippe, 'they got greedy. They should have stuck at the two thousand. Oh, and stick to blokes. Women get sympathy, men get laughed at.'

'Have you not finished your crossword puzzle yet?' asked Nikki as she returned to the computer and studied the next email. Philippe, are you listening to me? Philippe, Philippe! She screamed as she ran towards him.

'Heart attack,' said the Doctor. 'He's known about it for several years. I told him many times to take things easier but he wouldn't listen.'

'But he never mentioned it to me,' she sobbed desperately trying to come to terms with the loss of her best friend.

'Sorry,' said the Doctor. He shrugged his shoulders and left, not knowing what else to say.

Nikki had never felt so lonely. She picked up his picture standing proudly in its frame in the centre of the table and held it close to her. Stumbling across the room, she fell into a chair and the floodgates opened. The sense of loss overwhelmed her and for the first time in her life, she gave in to her emotions and allowed herself to cry real tears. She had not realised it whilst he was alive, but now he had died, she knew she had loved Philippe with all her heart.

But it was too late for all that now.

"I lived in South America and met him on the internet; he said he was in love with me. He brought me to Almina for a visit but when I arrived he had sex with me and then forced me to work in night clubs and find clients. If I came back without money he would assault me." Police raided the flat after a tip off. When the door was opened, three women ran out in an attempt to escape the man.

Proceedings of Court case.

Chapter 12

The rest of the morning and afternoon passed quietly. Eva had unlocked the door once to check on Kristina but she was just lying on her mattress staring at the wall. The girl was obviously very unhappy but Eva had seen this many times before.

Around five o'clock, two of the girls returned and were let in. Eva opened the door to let them pass and smiled as she saw Kristina lying on her back now staring at the ceiling. 'She must be feeling hungry by now,' thought Eva. 'Let's see how she feels in the morning.'

Kristina waited until Eva had left before looking at the two girls. 'Where's Melda?' she asked.

'Melda got lucky,' the blonde girl whose black roots had started to show answered her question. 'Two 'quickies' in a car and then back to someone's home for a siesta. She asked me to tell you not to fight them and she also asked me to give you this.'

She threw her a chocolate bar. 'Thanks,' said Kristina picking it up and tearing off the wrapper. The hunger pangs had started and she appreciated the chocolate.

The two girls stripped naked and spooned up to each other on one mattress. 'Care to join us Kristina?' giggled the blonde girl.

'Piss off,' Kristina was repulsed by their antics.

She attempted to ignore the rustlings and noises from across the room and tried to sleep. She needed to think about what she was going to do but try as she may, she couldn't think of a way out of this intolerable situation.

At about seven o'clock Eva unlocked and opened the door. The two girls had showered, dressed and were ready for the evening's work.

'OK girls. Let's go!' Eva followed them out, locking the door behind her. Kristina was alone once more. She spent the rest of the evening thinking of life back home, of escaping or worrying she would be harmed by her captors. The thought kept coming back to her. Fifteen thousand dollars to get her passport back. It took most people back home a lifetime to earn that sort of money. She thought of stealing her passport but she didn't even know where it was kept. She was restless but finally she fell asleep.

She remembered hearing the door open and the voices of some girls returning home. She thought she heard Eva asking the girls to be quiet saying 'that girl has a hard day tomorrow' and one of the girls (the blonde one she thought) saying 'you can say that again' but Kristina was only semi awake and then the door locked and she fell asleep again.

The other girls gathered in the far corner of the room and spoke in hushed voices.

'That bastard Ari,' the blonde girl spat. 'Did you see her face?'

'I know she'd been withholding money but there was no need to go that far' said Melda. 'She won't be able to work for months.'

'Why what happened?' asked the third girl.

'One of the girls in the flat opposite kept some money back. Madam Eva found out and sent Ari. He came into the bar, dragged her out by the hair. She was screaming in front of everyone but he took her out into the desert, beat her with his fists, had his way with her and if that wasn't enough, he took out an iron bar and beat her time and time again with it. She's cut, bruised and bleeding. The bastard!'

The meeting broke up with each girl going back to her own bed space in silent thought - vowing never to hold back any money in future.

'Kristina, it's me,' whispered Melda's voice in her ear. She felt a hand on her shoulder.

'Don't fight them,' Melda said. 'Promise me you won't fight them.'

She remembered nothing else until the next morning.

The other girls were still sleeping when Eva unlocked the door and entered. She crept over to Kristina, tapped her on the shoulder and motioned for her to follow. 'Get yourself showered and dressed and come to the kitchen,' said Eva. 'We need to talk.'

Kristina did as she was asked and joined Eva in the kitchen. Sitting in the corner was a big guy with a pale complexion and cold piggy eyes who just sat and stared at her. 'Morning,' said Kristina looking him straight in the eye, but he gave no response or acknowledgement. He just continued to stare at her whilst his eyes followed her across the room until she sat down.

'Coffee?' asked Eva.

'Please,' replied Kristina.

'Now, I want to ask you if you've come to your senses about working with us,' said Eva. 'You're a very silly girl if you continue to hold out in this way.'

'If you mean work for you as a prostitute,' answered Kristina, 'then the answer is still no. I'm not going to cheat you but I was promised a clean job dancing and this is what I intend doing – and nothing else.'

'The people we work for won't like it, Kristina.' Eva continued. 'They won't like it at all.'

The man in the corner still sat staring at Kristina as if he was bored by it all.

'Then they'll have to get used to not liking it,' retorted Kristina as the boldness of youth outvoted common sense.

'I asked you down here to Meet Mr Ari,' said Eva as she motioned towards the man; who responded by nodding his head slightly. 'Take a good look at him because if you ever see him again you'll wish you'd never been born. Mr Ari is in charge of punishing naughty girls.'

A feeling of unease crept over Kristina as she began to realise this was a horrendous situation and it was very serious.

'Now go back to your room,' continued Eva. This afternoon, whilst the girls are on their break, I'll take you to the owners who'll explain things to you in detail. You can ask then about being a dancer. But, if you see sense and change your mind knock on the door and tell me. It's never too late to join our business and to be honest, you don't have much choice.'

Kristina returned to her mattress and threw herself down on it. She heard the key turn as Eva locked the door. Had she listened in to the girl's conversation of last night, she might not have been so stubborn.

"We were lured to Almina with the promise of good jobs. On arrival one of the Bangladeshi men raped me and they forced us to have sex with strangers in return for money. He took me outside to find a taxi to visit a client but I rushed to a passing pedestrian and asked for help. He restrained my captor until the police arrived. I was crying in fear but told the police of my friend who was locked in a garbage room." Police broke down the door of the room, and freed her friend. They found condoms and lubricants in the garbage room which contained a curtain separating two beds. The men pleaded not guilty saying the girls did so willingly. The second man gave evidence from a wheelchair as he had injured himself during the raid having jumped out of a second floor window to escape.

Proceedings of Court case.

Chapter 13

It had been six months since Philippe had died and Nikki had spent those months lonely, upset and, as the saying goes, like a ship without a rudder. Or as Nikki preferred, 'like a man without a prick.' She had not only lost direction but her heart just wasn't in the business any more. At one point she even thought of getting a real job (though this was only for an hour or two on a night when she had drunk too much wine).

Philippe's picture was still on the table and she would still have a little weep from time to time. She picked the picture up, held it to her breast and remembered the happier times when they had had the photograph taken. She also remembered how they would find a lonely middle aged widow and do some background research on her. Details such as where she came from, the names of a few family members and so on. Nikki would then visit the lady and ask if she was 'Mrs so and so' from wherever and the victim would readily, if a little warily, agree. Nikki would produce fake ID stating she worked for a law company, who specialised in tracing the long lost relatives of people who had died without making a will.

She smiled as she remembered one customer in particular, Mrs Dolgov. She had once lived in Chechnya but had been forced to move with her family because of the war. Mrs Dolgov had shuffled to open the door in response to Nikki's call. She had worn an ankle length, shapeless black dress which reached down to her pink fur lined slippers. A red babushka scarf covered her greying hair. 'We believe you could be the next in line of one Gregor Paluski who died intestate three years ago, leaving a house and a considerable sum of money,' Nikki had told her. Mrs Dolgov had no reason not to believe her; Nikki was confident and assured; her Christian Dior business suit and the high Louboutin shoes only added to her authenticity. 'I wonder if I could come in and ask you a few questions?'

'Yes,' the lady was trusting and interested. 'Would you like some tea, or something a little stronger?' She raised her bushy eyebrows as she asked the question. Excitement now showing in her twinkling brown eyes.

'Tea will be fine as matching distant relatives with lost money is a tricky business,' Nikki remembered saying. 'Did your family once live in Chechnya?' she had asked – knowing full well they had.

'Oh, yes, we lived there up until fifty eight.'

'That's good,' Nikki had replied 'because Gregor lived there then. Could you tell me the names of any other family members?'

Mrs Dolgov had thought for a minute or so before replying, 'Let me think. 'There was Auntie Maria and, and, oh what was the other one's name? Oh! I know, Uncle Giorgio. That's right, it was Uncle Giorgio. I am sure now.'

'Well this is very important because Gregor had a half-brother of the very same name,' Nikki wanted to reassure her. 'I think we're on to something important here.' She gave Mrs Dolgov a knowing look. 'I've a photograph of Gregor here if you would like to see it.' She pulled the picture of Philippe from her bag. They'd had this photograph taken specially, with Philippe looking very grand in his borrowed suit. 'Look, there's a likeness between you and Gregor. You have the same nose and chin.'

'You know, I can see it too.' Mrs Dolgov was playing into Nikki's hands; the excitement of the future inheritance and the thought of how it would bolster her meagre savings masking the fact there was not one iota of likeness between her and man in the picture.

'Strange,' thought Nikki to herself, as she broke off from her thoughts. 'Philippe had always refused to have his photograph taken and yet on this scam he was insistent it was his photograph that had to be used. He always said photographs were for police and not fraudsters.' She returned to thinking about Mrs Dolgov. Before leaving, she had told her, 'I need to get back to the office and check out this new information but I'm becoming more and more certain you are indeed the heir to Gregor's estate. 'I will come back to you in a few days when I've more information.'

She had spent the next few days working on other cons without giving a single thought to Mrs Dolgov and her inheritance before calling her back. 'Ah Mrs Dolgov, I have some good news for you. All the information checked out and I am fairly sure you have a claim on Gregor's estate.'

'Do you really think so?' The woman was ecstatic. 'I could certainly use the money.'

'Ninety five percent certain,' Nikki had lied. 'We now need to lodge our claim with the courts but I'm afraid this will cost a little money. We need four hundred in Court fees and another two hundred to draw up the papers. I'm happy to proceed with the matter but I'm afraid we'll need the money first. For our part, we'll wait until you have your inheritance before we collect our fees. We charge ten percent.'

Mrs Dolgov had been taken aback a little. She had only been thinking of receiving money and not about paying any out. There was a pause in the conversation whilst she was thinking.

'It's really up to you Mrs Dolgov,' Nikki broke the silence, 'but we really have to do this to secure your claim. I can come around tomorrow to collect the money. The Courts only accept cash I'm afraid.'

'I'll have the money ready for you,' Mrs Dolgov replied, having decided this nice young lady would not cheat her and after all, she really wanted this money; needed it if truth be told.

Nikki kept returning for more money to cover legal fees, Court costs and so on until Philippe had said 'enough.' His policy was not to get too greedy and not to keep going back for more, as this greatly increased the risk of being caught.

Of course, Mrs Dolgov had heard no more of Nikki and the long lost Gregor's money. Every now and then she thought 'I wondered whatever happened to that nice young lady and Gregor's money' – when she should have been thinking 'I wonder what happened to all the savings I had in the World!'

She was a nice old lady, Mrs Dolgov,' thought Nikki as she replaced Philippe's photograph on the table and thought; 'I wonder what she's doing now. Probably homeless, broke and on the streets,' she said to herself and quickly forgot about the now penniless old lady as a conscience was not something one should have in her line of work.

She still did the odd trick but mainly with regular customers. Nikki only plied her trade on the streets when she was short of money. She smiled as she thought that in real life 'making ends meet' meant saving money, yet for Nikki, it meant making money. Nikki still had the 'RussianWives' website where she was ripping off Western men of seventy and above, who actually thought desperate young Russian women actually wanted them for love. Oh well, she thought, 'there's no fool like an old fool,' and so this scam continued to provide a valuable source of income for her but she needed new faces. The site had grown so much she employed two fake 'Russian Wives', in the back office to speak to the sad old men and write to them , making them think they could buy love, in return for a passport. The two girls sounded attractive over the phone and wrote passionately - but were not what you would call sexy or even good looking.

Nikki needed a constant source of 'new girls' and different pictures on the internet to bring the rich western flies to the waiting black widow spiders who would strip them of their money and then spit them out. Why else was it called the web?

She also had a small clientele who bought pornographic pictures from her - again over the web. "Adults only," as Nikki had standards and those standards meant there would be no child pictures. She had had more than her fair share of attention from paedophiles herself when she was young so she refused to even consider it but the trouble was, she only had a limited number of pornographic pictures and her clients wanted more.

It was at this point she remembered Philippe's scam where he obtained sex by deception and so she started to make arrangements.

Angelina lay in her dingy home reading the newspaper. She wore a pair of dark green trousers and an old red pullover with sleeves rolled up to cover the holes in the elbows. Her long black unruly hair hung over her shoulders. Angelina's almond eyes were widely spaced about her straight nose. Resting on an old and soiled sofa, she held a glass of vodka in one hand, a cigarette in the other and the soon to be empty bottle by her side. Times had treated Angelina badly. Her husband had left her long ago and her day job was not only boring but didn't pay her enough to live on. Yet, she still had her looks and her figure. An advertisement leapt out at her from the classified section.

Seventh Heaven Escort Agency

We are a respectable escort agency providing companionship to business men visiting the city.
Special offer! No registration fees, nothing to pay for the first month

'What have I got to lose? No registration fees, nothing to pay for the first month' – it was too good to be true. Angelina pondered the thought for a while. 'No,' she thought, 'nothing's that good. Getting paid to go out with a man? No-one's that foolish. It must be sex; but then again, I could do with a bit of that myself. I can't remember when I last had it. I'll give them a call in the morning.' She finished the bottle of vodka as a kind of celebration. Something she did every night to be honest but up till now it had always been to cure depression.

The first thing next morning, the telephone rang in Nikki's apartment. Nellie, one of the two 'girls' employed by Nikki answered. Nellie was well past fifty, her short skirt hitched up as she sat by the phone revealing thighs the size of tree trunks.

'Hello, how can I help you?'

'Well you can get your lovely little backside over here to the States and marry me,' said the voice on the phone.

Nellie frantically went through the names of all the men she was presently 'cyber shafting' and suddenly remembered the voice. 'What a lovely surprise,' she cooed, sounding young and virile, 'but Arthur, you shouldn't ring me at work. You'll get me sacked.'

'It doesn't matter,' said the voice on the phone, 'you'll be quitting soon so you and your boy can join me over here. How is he by the way?'

'He's doing well after the operation. I can't thank you enough for sending the money. It was a real life saver. There'll be a few more expenses but we'll talk about it later.'

'No problem,' the voice on the phone was gentle now, 'Just let me know and we'll sort it. I love you. Bye.' Nellie put the telephone down, sighed with relief at another one placated when the phone rang again. 'Christ,' she muttered 'they never stop.' However, this time it was a female voice.

'Is this the Seventh Heaven's escort Agency?' It was Angelina.

'Why yes.' Nellie was surprised as it was usually men on the other end of the line. 'How can we help you?'

'I'm ringing about your advertisement in the paper, Escorts wanted.'

'That's right,' said Nellie. 'Are you interested in joining us?'

'I was wondering how much call there is for this sort of thing here.'

'It takes a little time to get clients,' said Nellie, 'but most of our clients prefer to use the same escort each time and so you can build up your own clientele. You only pay the registration fee at the end of the first month and by then you should have earned more than enough to cover all your agency fees. Of course if at the end of the first month you feel you don't want to work with us, then you're free to walk away with no charge or commitment.'

'Does the work involve.....' stuttered Angelina. 'Well, I mean do I have to ..'

'If you are asking whether our Escorts are expected to provide sexual services then the answer is no. We arrange companionship duties only. Of course, if the client and Escort decide to make a private arrangement, then it is up to them but as a respectable agency, we don't want to know anything about such delicate matters.'

'Sounds too good to be true,' Angelina correctly but unknowingly stated. 'What happens now?'

'Come and see us tomorrow at eleven and bring some photographs with you. Don't have any taken specially; if we feel we need more we'll arrange it. We'll see you tomorrow. Please don't be late.'

Angelina hung up. A tinge of excitement ran through her body and she thought. 'At last, there's a chance coming my way.'

'Who was that?' asked Nikki.

'Another sad woman looking for an easy way out of debt and alcohol,' replied Nellie as she replaced the receiver. 'This time next week she'll be further down the bottomless pit of despair.'

The next morning at ten forty five the doorbell rang. 'Shit, she's early.' Nikki looked at her watch. 'Why can't these people arrive when they are told to? This one must be desperate for money.' She looked at Nellie who was busy on the phone to one of her would be Western husbands and so she went to open the door.

The woman was wearing plain cheap clothing. She was probably in her mid-forties and dressed in a drab grey coat which reached down to the hem of her full length black dress. Perched on her head was a plain grey felt hat. There was nothing wrong with that but the accessories she had brought with her stunned Nikki. At one side of the woman stood a girl of about five years old and at the other, a boy of about eight; both dressed in their school uniforms. There was something about the boy. Nikki had a strange feeling she had seen him somewhere before.

'What does this woman think she's playing at?' she thought to herself. 'It's one thing not to realise you're past it for escort work, but bringing children along? She must be crazy.'

'Hello.' She tried to smile. 'Angelina?'

'No,' said the woman, 'I am looking for Philippe Voltaria.'

'Who?' asked Nikki, as her heart missed a beat.

'Philippe Voltaria,' said the woman, 'I understand he used to live here.'

'You'd better come in.' Nikki was feeling sick. What was all this about?

The woman sat down but the two children stood silently by her side. 'We haven't heard from him in months and he used to write or telephone us every week - sometimes twice a week,' she added proudly.

'How do you know this err.... Philippe Voltaria?' Nikki already knew the answer.

'He's my husband. Been married twelve years next June,' she said and raised her head a little to emphasise this achievement. These are our children Anna – she's five and Bennie who's eight. Say hello to the lady children.'

The children stared at Nikki, saying nothing.

'Bennie is the spitting image of his father,' said the woman. 'Such a handsome boy.'

'He certainly is,' thought Nikki now realising where she had seen the boy before.

'There's no work in our village for someone of Philippe's talents so he moved to the city,' she continued. 'He worked in a bank but he always saw us right. He sent us money regularly and last year, he even bought us a small house to make us 'financially secure' as he put it.'

'So that's where the money I worked for went,' thought Nikki, 'and I thought I was the one being provided for.'

'But these past few months we've heard nothing,' the woman continued. 'There's been no money but it doesn't matter as I have a small job that keeps us. No, worst of all is he never rings or writes to us anymore. We miss him terribly; especially the children, so we came to look for him. He gave me this address and said if I ever needed him, I would find him here. He told me if he wasn't in then his cleaner would help me. Someone called Nikki?'

'Yes,' Nikki felt dejected. 'That's me. I clean here two or three times a week.' 'Bastard,' she thought. To think I actually loved the guy. The only thing I vacuumed and cleaned for him was his dick.'

'We don't even have a photograph of him at home,' said the woman clearly upset.

Nikki took a deep breath, 'I've some bad news for you.' She turned to the children. 'Why don't you two children go next door and ask Nellie for a biscuit. She'd love to see you.' Without waiting for an answer, she bundled the two children into the next room and closed the door. Turning to Philippe's wife she spoke softly, 'I'm very, very sorry to have to tell you this but Philippe died of a heart attack some months ago. I tried to contact you but I couldn't find your address. His last words were of you and the children.'

The woman looked shocked and tears sprang to her eyes. 'Oh my God,' she whimpered. I had a feeling something had happened. He'd never desert us. He was the kindest, most honest man you could ever wish to meet. I loved him so much.'

'I know,' lied Nikki. 'You were lucky to have found him.' It was not what she was thinking.

'And after all these years we don't even have a photograph of him for the children to remember him by. He always refused to have one taken.'

'The bastard,' thought Nikki. 'The doctor said Philippe knew he was dying and this was his last joke to make me give his wife and kids a photograph so they'd have something to remember him by. He never used his own photo in a scam; he always used someone else's but on that one occasion, he had insisted it had to be his photo; in a suit, looking respectable. Why couldn't he have trusted me just this once? Better still, he could have just sent the bloody thing by post.' But that was not Philippe's style. Pulling cons was in his nature. That was what he was. Love it or hate it. There you go.

'Look,' said Nikki composing herself, 'there are some of Philippe's personal belongings here and I am sure there will be a photograph. Let me find them for you.'

She stood up, walked over to the table and picked up Philippe's framed photograph and took it into the bedroom. She pulled down the box where she had stored his belongings and placed the photograph in amongst them. Opening her purse she emptied it of cash and put it all into the box too. Nikki had never shared anything in her life before and she was not going to start now. She would not share her grief or her memories with this woman and her kids. It was time to move on. She picked up the box, carried it through and handed it over.

The woman lifted the lid and took a peek inside. Her spirits rose when she saw the money. She lifted a gold Rolex watch and displayed it to Nikki. 'Is this real,' she asked. 'I never saw him wearing this before.'

'Oh yes its real,' said Nikki. 'I can vouch for that myself. It was his pride and joy.' She could not take any more of this. It was time for Philippe's wife and kids to leave.

'If you don't mind I've some more 'cleaning jobs' to do,' Nikki added as she moved to the door.

'Well thank you very much,' said the woman and rose from the sofa.

Nikki retrieved the children from Nellie and escorted them to the door.

'Well thank you again,' said the lady, 'you've been most kind.'

As the three of them left Angelina walked in through the open door. She looked at the lady with the two children incredulously. Once they had gone and the door closed Angelina asked, 'Is SHE an escort too?'

'Oh yes,' said Nikki, 'she's our biggest earner. Most men like the homely sort when they're away on business. Mind you, she fucks like a rabbit – that always helps.'

"I married a man in Pakistan against my family's wishes and my husband sent me to Almina with his brother for a holiday until things cooled down. As soon as I arrived I was locked in a brothel and forced into prostitution with my husbands consent. I refused but the brother beat me up and then started sending different men to have sex with me." Police raided the apartment and freed her. Records show that she was sent to parties, danced with customers and then had sex with them.

Proceedings of Court case.

Chapter 14

'No, don't let Ari near her yet. He's only used as a last resort.' Eva replied quickly. This young lady is a valuable commodity and so we must treat her with care. Nobody goes to the supermarket and buys bruised fruit and it's the same in our line of work. No, firstly we will hurt her where it doesn't show, inside her head.'

'So what do you plan to do?' said Dmtry leaning forward in his chair with interest as he had a good idea what was coming next.

'I have two clients who are willing to pay a considerable sum of money to break in one of our unwilling girls. '

'You mean they will pay you money for this?'

'Yes,' replied Eva. 'But they want a girl who'll fight back. They want someone who will kick and scratch and put some resistance up. I think our Kristina fits the customer's requirements.'

'Sounds like your Kristina will be one of your best earners this week,' said Dmtry rising from his chair and walking to the door. 'Do you want to do it here so the other girls can hear what's happening and learn to be good.'

'No. I'll arrange for the interested parties to be at the office this afternoon. It's quiet there.'

'I can't wait. Bye.'

Oh Kristina, she thought to herself. Please see sense and work with us.

Sometime, in the mid-afternoon, Kristina heard the key turning in the lock again. She closed her eyes, wondering what was going to happen next.

'Time to get ready,' said Eva. 'We'll be going soon. Shower and wear something attractive if you want to make an impression. I'll wait for you in the kitchen.' Kristina showered and then sorted through her suitcase for something to wear. She chose a black skirt and the lacy top her mother had presented to her as a leaving present. 'This is for the special occasions,' her mother had said. Kristina almost burst into tears as memories of her mother and home swam through her head. She hung her clothes over Melda's clothes rail and busied herself with her makeup. It took some time to cover the black rings under her eyes caused by too much weeping but in the end she looked into the mirror and thought she had just about managed it. That done, she slipped into her clothes and joined Eva in the kitchen.

'You look very pretty,' Eva smiled. 'Now, no more tears. Have you changed you mind about joining us? I wish you would. You're making life very difficult for everyone.'

'No,' said Kristina, 'I came here to dance and dance is all I want to do.'

Voices could be heard as the girls returned from their afternoon shift. They could hear the blonde girl complaining. 'Not much doing today,' she grumbled. 'Too close to payday.'

The voices disappeared as the girls were locked into their room.

'The stupid cow,' said Melda, as she saw Kristina's bed was empty. 'She's determined to fight them.'

'I don't know what's special about her cunt,' said the blonde girl. 'Maybe its gold plated.'

'Don't be cruel.' said Melda, 'She's just not 'that' sort of girl.'

'She soon will be,' replied the blonde girl.

Melda picked up a large teddy bear from her bed. It had belonged to her three year old daughter who had presented it to her when she left to come to Almina.

'This is to give you hugs from me,' her daughter had said. It broke Melda's heart to leave her. Neither had wanted to part but her husband had left her for someone else and there was no money. What else could she have done, except leave the child with Babushka and come and work here. Of course, her grandmother knew what Melda was doing and was grateful for the money. Her only stipulation was when she went home, Melda had to leave her 'business' in Almina and become respectable in the eyes of the neighbours. On one of her home visits, Melda had taken her mother out for dinner in an expensive restaurant in the city centre. Her mother was preening herself, wanting everyone to see how her daughter had 'made good' and was treating her Mum to a feast, when in walked one of Melda's customers from Almina. Their eyes had met and a knowing smile had passed between them but neither acknowledged they had even met let alone spent several hours writhing in naked bliss.

Melda quickly shook the thoughts of home from her head and tucked the teddy bear into Kristina's bed, thinking she would need it when she returned. The girls retired to their own bed spaces to rest before the next shift. In the Kitchen, Eva and Kristina were joined by the Mamasan.

'This is Rula,' said Eva. 'You've seen her before but Rula looks after our girls when they're out at work. She's their manager.'

'I hear you don't want to join us.' Rula stared at her coldly. 'Pity, a lovely girl like you would make a lot of money.'

'Let's go said Eva,' not waiting for the girl to reply.

Eva and Rula stood at each side of Kristina and walked her outside into the corridor. No-one spoke as they waited for the lift to come.

It descended in silence; still no-one spoke until they left the building. 'Now I know what it's like being taken to the death chamber,' thought Kristina, and then reminded herself the situation she was in was no joking matter. The heat hit her as they left the air conditioned building. There was a taxi waiting opposite the entrance to the building. Rula must have told the driver to wait when she and the girls came back to the apartment. She opened the rear door of the taxi and clambered in. Kristina found herself being pushed inside; she had no choice but to do what they wanted.

'OK, said Eva, 'you know where to go.'

As the taxi pulled away, Kristina realised there was no chance of escape, sandwiched as she was between Eva and Rula and besides, if the taxi driver knew where to go, then he was part of the business – so it was no use asking him for help. She also realised no passer bye spoke her language and so she could not ask anyone for help. The taxi drove through busy streets and traffic until the tall high rise buildings ended and they entered a residential area comprising of tree lined avenues and villas. After several twists and turns, the taxi pulled up at a large two storey villa built like a Spanish hacienda.

Eva opened the door and climbed out first, motioning for Kristina to follow her.

'I'll wait here until you are inside,' said Rula, 'and then I'll return to the other girls back at the apartment.'

87

Eva and Kristina walked to the front entrance which had a large metal gate, decorated with imitation wrought ironwork. This villa, like the others in the street, had tall surrounding walls, adorned with lamps decorating the top.

Eva rang the buzzer and a crackly voice came over the intercom.

'Yes?' enquired the voice.

'It's Eva; we're here.'

A buzzing sound came from behind the gate as the automatic electronics worked their wizardry and it opened a little. Eva pushed it wide open; they walked in. She turned and waved to Rula in the taxi who returned with a 'thumbs up' and the taxi drove away. Kristina noticed the villa was surrounded by lush green grass and she wondered how it managed to survive in the heat. They reached the door of the villa and entered. Inside was a reception area with several comfy leather armchairs and a reception desk at the far end. Behind the desk sat a young Philippina girl who was smartly dressed in an expensive trouser suit.

'We're expected,' Eva told her. She turned to Kristina, 'sit down a moment; I'll go and tell him we're here.' Kristina sat down whilst Eva went to a door at the back of the reception area; tapping lightly, she walked straight in and approached Dmtry who sat behind the desk. 'She's here,' Eva announced as she closed the door.

'Ah, our reluctant call girl.'

'She'll be Okay. It's like a car with a flat battery. Once you get it going it goes on forever.'

'And you want these two gentlemen here,' said Dmtry, waving his arm around the room to point out two other men sat by the far wall, 'to give her a 'jump' start?' Sat at the back of the room were two Eastern European men in their early forties. Casually dressed in trousers and shirts they gave a broad smirk as Eva looked their way.

Eva returned her gaze to Dmtry, 'you're so good at it.' Eva gave him a knowing smile, 'and you enjoy it really.'

Dmtry looked across at the two men, 'this one actually thinks we brought her here as a dancer!'

'A dancer!' snorted one of the other two men in the room. 'She actually believed that?'

'When you're broke with no future, you believe anything,' replied Eva. 'I'll leave you to it and go back home. Send her by 'special courier' when you've finished but no bruises; Now remember you two, If you damage the goods you will have to pay extra. No bruises on the face.'

Eva took out her mobile and ordered a taxi. As soon as it arrived she left through the back door so that Kristina would not know she had gone.

Simon, the larger of the two men approached Dmtry's desk.

'So what's the plan?' he asked.

'Ari said to have fun, get your money's worth but break her in good and proper,' replied Dmtry.

'I wish I hadn't had that wank before I came here,' joked John, the third man in the room, and all three fell about laughing.

Simon and John pulled their chairs up to Dmtry's desk. He placed a bottle of whisky on the table along with three glasses and poured them all a drink. Passing round the pack, they each took a small blue diamond shaped tablet and washed it down with the whisky.

'It takes thirty minutes for the tablets to start working,' said Dmtry. 'Fancy playing cards?'

'Dollar a point?' added Simon.

Dmtry pressed the switch on the intercom and spoke to the receptionist.

'Mr Dmtry has someone with him at present,' she said to Kristina. 'He asks if you wouldn't mind waiting.'

'No, that's alright,' replied Kristina.

She sat there and composed herself, deciding upon a reasoned approach. No hysterics; just reason with him that she had come here for a dancing job and that was all she was asking for. 'I'll tell him that I'll make more money for you as a dancer than I will selling sex,' she thought. 'I'll just not be any good at approaching men to pay me money for sex. Come on...,' she said to herself wanting to get the ordeal over, your meeting must be over by now.' Across from her hung a poster of a rocky coast line in some far off exotic place. Kristina glanced at it and wished she were there, as far away from Almina as possible.

'I'll raise you two and see you,' Simon told John.

'I have two pair,' replied John. 'That's not including the pair sitting outside!'

'Not enough said Simon, 'Full house.' He scooped up the money and placed it with the rest of his winnings in front of him.

'I don't believe this.' John was not amused. 'Look at all those winnings. You've just about cleaned me out.'

'How are we doing for time,' Simon wanted to know.

'Twenty five minutes gone.' Dmtry checked his watch. 'I don't know about anyone else but I am starting to feel something waking up between my legs.'

'Well we're not packing up yet.' John was petulant. 'I want a chance to get some money back.'

'I'll happily take more money from you,' Simon laughed. 'Let's give the tablets the full hour to ensure maximum effect. Whose deal is it?'

Dmtry spoke into the intercom. 'We don't need you any longer, Maria. You can go home now. Please tell Miss Kristina that I'll collect her as soon as we have finished our meeting – there are just a few loose ends to sort out.'

'Thank you, Mr Dmtry,' Maria answered, 'I'll see you tomorrow.'

'Mr Dmtry sends his apologies and says he's almost done,' the receptionist told Kristina. 'If you don't mind, I'll leave you here as it is past my finishing time.' She busied herself, checking for her keys and phone and checking the contents of her bag as she left Kristina alone in the reception.

Kristina took out a small mirror and checked her makeup. Happy that she was looking good she tossed her hair a little and put the mirror away. 'Come on Dmtry, come on,' she said to herself, 'I want to sort this matter out. They must've me mixed up with someone else. Maybe I could offer to audition for him - that would convince him that I'm here to dance.' She looked again at the poster and the waves crashing against the rocky shoreline. By now she knew every detail since she had studied it for so long.

'He's done it again,' John moaned as Simon won yet another hand of cards.

'You either have it or you don't' bragged Simon, scooping up yet another pile of money.

'We're at fifty minutes now.' said Dmtry. 'By the time we've put the cards away and brought her in, we'll be at the magic hour mark. I don't know about you two but I think I'm ready.'

'Fine by me,' John was relieved. 'I'm just about cleaned out anyway.'

'Sure,' Simon agreed. 'Let's collect her and put her into her misery!'

Dmtry rubbed his hands as he walked towards the door and opened it.

'Ah Kristina. Good to see you again.' Dmtry smiled. 'Sorry to have kept you waiting. Won't you please come in?'

She stood up and shook hands with Dmtry. He stood back and motioned her to go in first before closing the door and followed her, watching her pert little bottom move from side to side as she walked.

Kristina stood near the desk, not sure whether to sit or stand. He walked behind it and sat down.

'Please take a seat Kristina,' Dmtry pointed to a chair in front of the desk. This is Mr John and Mr Simon who are my business associates.' Kristina nodded to them as she sat down.

'Now what's the problem?' he asked. 'Eva tells me that you're still unhappy.'

'I think there's been some misunderstanding,' said Kristina in the confident voice that she had been practising in her head, whilst waiting outside. 'I applied for a job as a dancer to replace someone already out here, who met with an accident.' Kristina stopped and went quiet.

'So?' asked Dmtry, 'what's the problem?'

'Well,' continued Kristina, Miss Eva seems to think that I came here to be a...' Kristina went bright red with embarrassment.

'To be a what?' Dmtry prompted her, knowing full well what the answer was.

'A prostitute,' said Kristina at last. 'I just can't do that. I only came here to dance.'

'A dancer,' Dmtry turned to look at Simon. 'The girl says she's a dancer.'

'Would you mind standing up?' asked Simon, 'and push that chair away so we can see you better. It's in the way.'

Kristina stood up and pushed the chair with her foot and it slid to one side on its rollers.

'Nice footwork,' John commented. 'Now just turn around so we can see you properly.'

She pirouetted slowly on the spot, smiling at the men in turn as they came in to view, not realising what was happening.

'Thank God mum bought me this top,' thought Kristina, 'she must have known I'd need it for interviews.' In her innocence, she felt confident that she would convince them to let her dance.

'What do you think Mr Simon?' John was dying to put his hands on her.

'A dancer? I can't see it myself,' Simon replied, 'The poise, it's all wrong. No dancer stands like that.'

Kristina turned quickly to look at him. She knew her poise was perfect; she was so well practiced. 'That's perfect,' her old dance instructor had always told her when the dance class had been asked to stand. 'So what did I do wrong here?' Kristina was puzzled as she did a quick mental check of how she had stood and turned. 'There was nothing wrong with that,' she retorted, 'my poise has always been perfect.'

'It may be perfect for a village but in a city it's all wrong.'

'Look at her nose too,' observed John, 'it's too big. Dancers have to be pretty and this one's not.' Kristina was hurt, wondering why he was so rude.

'I have a nice nose.' She turned to look at John. 'I've never had any complaints about my looks. In fact I always receive many compliments.'

'Well you're getting complaints now,' John replied rudely. 'Maybe your nose has grown whilst you've been here.'

Simon stood up and walked towards Kristina. Slowly he walked around her, studying her body very closely, looking her up and down.

'Piss awful tits too,' He stopped in front of her and stared at her chest. 'Too small; far too small for a dancer.'

Kristina found herself defending the size of her breasts. 'They're big enough,' she snapped. 'Dancers don't have huge breasts. They just don't. It's all to do with balance.'

'Well you certainly couldn't balance these in each hand,' Simon guffawed.

She could smell the whisky on his breath. The other two men were laughing and Kristina remembered that the receptionist had been sent home. She trembled with fear as she started to realise what was happening. They were never going to listen to her. They never had any intention of listening to her in the first place.

'Let me have a proper look,' Simon reached out and, grabbed each side of her blouse, ripping it open. She felt a wave of terror pass through her, as she saw her mother's going away present, now torn and ruined, fall to the floor. Dmtry and John came up beside her and stood behind, one at each side, so that she was now surrounded.

'She's got a flat arse,' said John. 'No shape to it at all.'

Kristina swung around to face him, holding her hands over her cleavage in a futile attempt to retain some modesty and stared him in the face.

'Go to hell! There's nothing wrong with my figure or looks,' she shouted as tears welled in her eyes.

'Let's see then,' said Simon, as he started to undo the top button of her skirt.

'Take your hands off me,' her voice was rising as she spun around and smacked Simon across the face. As she did so John undid the clasp of her bra so she spun around to strike him too, but with her bra undone and her hands being used as weapons, it left her wide open for two of the men to touch and play with her breasts anytime they liked – and did they like.

Before she knew what was happening, Kristina found herself stark naked and being passed from one to the other. They touched, squeezed and fondled her body and she was powerless to stop them. She tried to kick and scratch but this just made the situation even more frenzied.

Just as a cat plays with its victim before going in for the kill, her screams and protestations not only went unheard, they just raised the level of excitement of the animals playing with her. Eventually, the combination of whisky, pills and primeval forces took over and Kristina was forced to the floor.

'There are plenty of condoms in the desk drawer,' said Dmtry as he made for the door and left John and Simon to enjoy their purchase. 'Don't let the little bitch give you anything nasty.' As the afternoon turned to evening, they each took turn and turn again until the screaming eventually stopped as Kristina gave up fighting.

Finally, after what seemed like a lifetime, Dmtry returned and took her himself. By now the fight had gone and Kristina just lay there; sobbing quietly and desperate to leave.

'Get dressed,' said Dmtry as he climbed off her. 'We'll take you back now. Don't worry, I'll keep in touch.' Kristina dressed as best she could. She could only hold the top of her blouse together, as some of

93

the buttons had been ripped off and it was badly torn. Simon pushed her towards the door and dragged her out. He and John were to deliver her back to Eva on their way home. Dmtry pulled up two chairs to the desk and poured some more whisky. Ari, who had been enjoying every moment listening from an adjoining room walked in.

'Hi Boss,' Dmtry stood up as Ari entered.

'Everything go alright?' asked Ari. He still felt a buzz of pride when one of his men called him 'Boss.'

'Yes,' Dmtry smirked, 'I could have sworn she was pushing back at the end.'

'Just like horses,' Ari laughed. 'I told you, once you break them in anyone can ride them.'

"I came to Almina just after my seventeenth birthday because of a job offer. On arrival I was taken to an apartment and told I was to work as a prostitute. When I refused I was stripped naked. They took pictures of me and threatened to post them on the internet. They raped me and then chained my hands together so that a customer who had paid 14 US Dollars could have sex with me." Four other Bangladeshi women testified that they had been treated in the same way.

Proceedings of Court case.

Chapter 15

'Where is she?'

'Please tell me; where is she?' Elena demanded of no-one in particular. 'You bring them up, love them and then they do this to you. Just how much money did I spend on her education – money I could not afford I might say and then she does this. I scraped, did without to give her the best I could offer and then, without a bye your leave, nothing. Just where is she?' Elena looked across at her sister and with her eyes, silently demanded an answer; one that never materialised.

'We never had any problems when she was at school.' She continued, 'she was always the teacher's pet, the blue eyed kid who could do no wrong, top of the class; we were all so proud of her. She was beautiful. The best daughter anyone could wish for. But where on Earth is she?'

'I don't know love.' Tasha shrugged her shoulders as she struggled to find any word of solace to console Elena; but found none. When it came to comforting her sister about her missing daughter, the words were close but always tantalisingly out of reach. The two women were the wrong side of their mid-thirties but were attractive and had a strong likeness of appearance. Tasha had auburn hair that fell onto her shoulders and she kept brushing it to one side to keep it away from her face. They sat dressed in jeans and T-shirts in the small sitting room with the curtains drawn as if someone had died. They occupied arm chairs placed at opposite sides of the coffee table. An empty two seater sofa at one side advertising the fact that someone in the family was missing. Against the wall was the fireplace with a gas fire hissing away. Above, on the mantelpiece and taking pride of place amongst life's nick knacks was a framed photo of a young girl beaming as she held up a trophy she had clearly won. Tasha leaned forwards, picked up the bottle of vodka and filled the two empty glasses; passing one to Elena and keeping the other for herself.

Elena looked longingly at the photograph and sipped her drink. 'I mean, she was always smiling and extrovert and could she dance!' Elena pictured her daughter Kristina in the dance competition where she had won the trophy proudly displayed in the photograph. 'It was like she was part of the music; as if she and the rhythm were as one. I remember how she would stride onto the dance floor as if nothing else around her mattered. She was in a world of her own where all that existed was the music.'

Tasha nodded in agreement and drained her glass in one go. She reached over for a refill, looking over at Elena to see if she too was in need of a top up.

Elena shook her head to reply in the negative. 'Talented! That's what she was and why we sent her to those dance classes. We wanted to do the best we could for her.'

Tasha raised an eyebrow at the mention of 'we.'

'Oh all right then, why 'I' sent her.' Elena thought silently of Peter, her long gone husband. She remembered how she had loved him when she first met him. His long dark hair, the strong bony features of his face, his idealism and visions of the future and then how it had all disappeared. Too much depression; too much vodka; too much of a problem! He did have a job when they first met but with the end of communism that was it. Goodbye job, hello uncertainty. He never worked again. He was never sober again.

'It was perestroika that finished him,' Elena continued. 'We suddenly had all the designer products in the shops we'd never had before. The trouble was, when the communists were in power, we had plenty of money but there was nothing in the shops to buy. But now, after communism, we have everything in the shops to buy but no money to buy it.'

'I don't think you can blame what Peter did on perestroika.' Tasha spoke softly not knowing how her sister would react.

'Floosy! There he was spending what little money we had on her when his only daughter needed medical attention we couldn't afford.'

'Kristina did pull through though,' soothed Tasha.

'Yes but no thanks to him. I kept asking him why he kept going out and he said it was to look for a job. I used to make him sandwiches to take with him. They probably shared them in her bed!'

'Don't keep going over it Elena, you will only make things worse. What's done is done. Kristina is all that matters now.'

'He didn't even have the courage to tell me when she was pregnant. The whole village knew before I did. What a fool I was. They were all laughing at me in the street and worse still, Kristina was taunted by the other children at school for the rest of the year. I threw him out as soon as I realised what had happened and neither Kristina nor I have spoken to him since.'

'Here, have this.' Tasha passed over a tissue for Elena to wipe away the tears.

'It's been three months now since my Kristina went. Where is she?'

'Where is Mikhail tonight?' asked Tasha trying to change the subject from the missing Kristina. These evenings filled with vodka, remorse and worry were becoming more and more frequent. But what could she do? Elena would ring her and sob into the phone, begging her to come over to talk.

'Mikhail is staying with school friends tonight. It's good for him to get away from all this. I'm so sick with worry, I can't think of anything but Kristina. Mind you, he's worried too. After all, it's his sister that has gone missing.'

'We all worry about Kristina but don't neglect Mikhail. He's a good boy and needs your support.'

'The dancing lessons went really well.' Elena returned to the theme of her missing daughter. 'As she grew older, she matured and developed into a beautiful young woman.' Elena smiled, 'She inherited my bright blue eyes and long blonde hair. Kristina always had a brain but all she wanted to do was dance. She took the examinations and passed them all with flying colours and then she was spotted by a local business man who offered her a job as a dancer at his night club. I can see her now. As the customers drank and flirted on the floor Kristina was gyrating in a cage suspended from the ceiling. To be honest, I was unhappy with her job but I never said anything. Everyone could see she was gifted. It was an art form rather than an erotic performance. If only she hadn't seen that stupid advertisement in the paper.'

'Do you mean the one for a dancer needed for a troupe in Almina?' Tasha knew the answer full well as they went through this story three or four times a week.

'I didn't want her to apply as I needed her company, I needed her around me; I was lonely. But what could I do? I have to find the money to send Mikhail to university from somewhere and this money was good. Kristina promised to send some home every month. Not only do we need the money but this was something she lived for – dancing. To be paid huge sums of money for doing something you love has to be the equivalent of the American dream; hasn't it?' Elena looked at Tasha for reassurance. 'Oh Tasha, where is she?'

'I don't know love, I just don't know.'

'She went to the auditions along with over a dozen other girls but my Kristina beat the lot.' Elena held her head up in pride. 'She was the lucky one – or so everyone thought. Do you remember how the local paper did an article about her? Elena leant back in her chair and looked towards the ceiling. She held up her arm and moved her outstretched hand through the air as if to mime the newspaper headline banner written across the sky, 'Kristina wins a future away from it all.' How wrong could they be? Off she went. Waved goodbye. See you soon Mum. Love you; and then she was gone. I lost her.'

Elena broke into a sob. Eventually the tears subsided. She looked up at Tasha.

'Just where the Hell is she?'

'I'll kill her when I find her!'

"I came from Bangladesh on the offer of a job but when I arrived at the airport they moved me to a flat were two other women worked as prostitutes. I was locked in and when I refused to work in the sex industry they beat me and used force to make me have sex with strangers. Three of my captors raped me repeatedly. After 17 days locked up I tried to escape using a cloth ladder to climb down from the first floor balcony but it broke suddenly when I was half way down. I fell down and broke my orbit bone. The building's watchman saw me fall and called the police."

Proceedings of Court case.

Chapter 16

Angelina sat down feeling more confident. 'If that plain Jane can pull the punters in then I'm sure I can,' and as this thought passed through her mind, she leant forward and squeezed her arms to her body a little to emphasise her cleavage.

'So,' said Nikki, 'you're interested in joining the 'Seventh Heaven Escort agency.' I believe Nellie has filled you in with most of the details?'

'Yes,' Angelina replied, 'Nothing to pay for the first month, the agency takes thirty percent of fees. There is a registration fee to be paid at the end of the first month but you should have earned enough by then to cover it. If not, you can walk away and not pay anything.'

'Got it in one.' Nikki smiled, 'The idea is, any money you do have to pay out should come from your earnings.'

'Great,' said Angelina, 'where do we go from here?'

She heard Nellie's voice in the next room. 'Hi Eric, what's the weather like in California?'

'Glorious,' came Eric's voice over the hands free Nellie was using. 'Say, did you get the two thousand for your air ticket?'

'Is that, I mean, has 'she', I mean has that lady met a husband in the States?' asked Angelina incredulously, looking at the figure and face of Nellie.

Nikki rose to shut the door.

'Oh yes,' said Nikki, 'Seventh Heaven is an international agency. Nellie met him as an Escort when he was over here on business and they've kept in touch ever since. Now he wants her to go the States and marry him.'

'God!' thought Angelina, If Nellie and the woman with the kids can do it then I'll wipe the floor with the men.'

'Did you bring some photos with you?' asked Nikki. The photos Angelina handed over were a mixture of sizes and many of them were from long ago, in better times.

'Mmmmm,' Nikki murmured, 'the trouble is on our website, we have a standard format to give an overall 'look' to the agency. I don't think these will match.'

'Is that a problem?' asked Angelina, seeing her prospects of future earnings taking a sudden dive.

'Tell you what,' said Nikki, 'we'll run with these for now and see how it goes. When the money starts coming in we'll arrange a professional photo shoot for you. You don't have any topless ones do you?'

'No,' Angelina was surprised, 'I thought it was pure escort work, no sex!'

'It is,' replied Nikki, 'but our customers sometimes like to imagine you undressed as they wine and dine you and so a quick peep on the web as to what you really look like helps the evening along. Anyway we can do those later as well, when the money is coming in.' Nikki liked to repeat this phrase 'when the money is coming in' as much as possible to excite the girls.

'Fill in this registration form with your name, address and contact details and we'll put your face out there for the World to get a good look and then we'll be in touch. I don't think it will be long before I have a client for you – I've a feeling for these things.'

When Angelina had left, Nikki placed one of the better photos of Angelina into the scanner, scanned it and uploaded it onto their website adding a few exaggerated details. She looked shabby and out of place amongst the glamorous girls already on the web page, but no matter. At least Angelina existed in real life which is more than most of the others did. Every now and then, a real client would contact them for an escort and in these cases Nikki would do the job herself; telling the client the cyber dream of his choice was sick so she had come instead.

Angelina was late home as she had stopped off on the way for a bottle of vodka to celebrate. She had drunk most of it with some 'friends' who, had disappeared as fast as they had come as soon as the bottle was empty.

She didn't have a computer to check the site and if she had owned one once it would have been traded long ago for the alcohol she needed to survive.

'I must pay the phone bill and get it reconnected,' she thought, as she fell asleep on the sofa, dreaming of a night out with Eric from California.

Nothing happened for several days but then on the tenth day (she was counting) her phone rang. She was confused as to what it was at first; partly because it never rang and so she had forgotten the ring tone but the vodka in her bloodstream didn't help either.

'Hello.' It was Nikki. 'This is the Seventh Heaven Escort agency. Is Angelina there?' She knew a real escort agency would be more discreet and make sure they were talking to the right person before announcing who they were – but Nikki knew it would be Angelina and so wanted to sound important.

'Yes,' replied Angelina, 'speaking.'

'Congratulations, we've a client for you,' said Nikki. 'He's in town for three nights and wants an escort for the first night. If all goes well, he'll retain the escort for the next two nights. The dates are the fourteenth, fifteenth and sixteenth of this month and he's asked for you. Are you free on those days?'

'Let me check,' said Angelina and rustled some cigarette packets and newspapers on the floor to make it sound like she was checking her diary.

'Yes I'm free those nights.'

'Good.' Nikki sounded pleased. Can I make a booking? He's in the oil industry and is interested in golf so you might like to research those topics in the meantime – just in case he wants to talk about them.'

'Yes, no problem,' Angelina responded happily.

When the conversation was over, Angelina felt a rush of excitement and vowed to swot up on oil and golf, deciding on some vodka to celebrate.

Angelina got as far as the vodka but never quite got round to the research, which was just as well because on the afternoon of the thirteenth, her phone rang for the second time. It was Nikki.

'I've some bad news for you I'm afraid. Your client's wife has been taken ill and he's been forced to cancel his trip – so I'm afraid your booking has been cancelled. Since he's given more than twenty four hours' notice, I'm sure you understand there's no cancellation fee. Better luck next time. These things do happen and you just have to put up with them.'

'Oh, all right. I understand.' replied a dejected Angelina who didn't understand at all. She had been relying on this client.

'Look,' said Nikki, 'I've been looking at the 'hits' on our website and your photograph is only getting one tenth of the 'hits' the other girls are getting. I'm sure we could increase your client base if we had some professional photographs taken.'

'But how much will it cost?' Angelina was worried about the money as she didn't have any.

'Not as much as you're thinking,' Nikki reassured her. 'We've our own photographer who does all our work and as such, he does it at a bulk rate. Eight hundred will cover it all. I don't need to tell you how reasonable it is.'

'Eight hundred,' repeated Angelina knowing she was right. If only she had the money but there was no chance, unless.....

At eleven the next morning, Angelina turned up at Nikki's and handed over eight hundred. She had spent all night hunting down old friends and relations in an attempt to beg, borrow or in one case, steal the money. She had gone to visit her mother and dibbed into the nest egg which she knew her mother kept in the sugar caddy in the kitchen. Her mother's visits to the caddy were few and far between, Angelina had a good chance of returning it before her mother found out.

Nikki picked up the phone. 'Hi, Sami? I've a pretty young lady here I want you to make love to with your camera. Are you free tomorrow? No? Ok then it will have to be next week. Ten o'clock Monday morning. Yes we'll meet up soon. Bye.'

'Right,' said Nikki, 'You heard? He can't fit you in for a shoot until Monday. Is that OK with you Angelina?'

'Well it will have to be.' Angelina wanted things to go a little faster so she could repay her debts. 'Is there any news of any more clients?'

'Not as yet. Your photo on the web is getting a little interest but I'm sure they'll come flooding in once we have some pro shots of you out there.' Angelina hoped she was right.

Nikki was feeling depressed. The look of desperation on Angelina's face had started to get to her. In fact the whole business of lying and cheating had started to affect her of late. She was losing interest and needed something new.

She rang Sami again. 'I need cheering up. Are you free tonight?'

'I'm always free for you dear,' replied Sami. 'Why don't you come over…' a pause then, 'come over me later that is! Shall we say eight?' She giggled and put the phone down.

As Nikki rang the doorbell, Sami opened it. Sami was young, in his early twenties, and had wide lively eyes that sparkled and welcomed Nikki. He wore a light polo necked jumper which hung low over his jeans.

She handed him two bottles of wine, 'I'm not drinking the shit you usually keep.'

'Let me take your clothes.' Sami was always fond of a 'double meaning.'

'Later.' Nikki took off her coat. 'We need to talk business first.' They moved into the front room and it seemed every available space from walls to tables was covered in photographs of ladies in various stages from naked to evening dress.

'Ok, I charge three hundred per hour for the sex; put your money on the side before I start,' Sami joked.

'Stop pissing about,' said Nikki, 'I'm not in the mood. Firstly here is one fifty for the photo shoot with Angelina on Monday and some digital editing I want doing.'

'One fifty,' Sami grumbled. 'That's not much.'

'Well, I'm going to pay the rest in kind tonight,' Nikki replied with a smile.

'Me and the whole street to make up that sort of money,' moaned Sami.

'Secondly,' Nikki went on, ignoring him, 'I have some old customers who want some more Lesbian photos.'

'So what's the problem?' asked Sami.

'The problem is I've already sold them all the ones I have. I need some new ones.'

'Ok,' said Sami, 'that can easily be solved. Angelina is coming over on Monday. Is she any good?'

'If you are thinking about my selling photos of a one girl lesbian act then forget it, but I think we can use her. If she would drop the vodka for a while she could look good.'

'Is there any more business on hand?' asked Sami sliding his hand down the front of Nikki's dress and cupping her breast. 'I'm completely free till Monday morning,' said Sami.

'Yes,' said Nikki 'you can remove your hand, stop playing with my nipple with your thumb and pour me some wine.'

On Monday morning Angelina arrived in good time. She was sober and quite nervous as she knew she had to look good.

'Hi Angelina, come in,' said Sami opening the door wider.

'Thanks,' said an almost sober Angelina. 'I'm a little bit early as I wasn't sure of the directions.'

'No problem,' replied Sami knowing full well she was just keen to get on with the job.

Sami led the way to a back room which had a white backdrop at the far end. Two large studio flashes with umbrellas stood at either side pointing ominously at a stool placed centre stage. A camera was on a tripod and connected to a computer placed nearby. The screen was turned away from the stool so the model could not see her photographs as they were being taken. It wasn't the best equipped studio in the world but there again Sami wasn't the best photographer. If the truth were known, these little 'jobs' for Nikki were the only work he had. He was a bar tender in 'real life' but he had dreams of becoming a fashion photographer and these jobs from Nikki gave him the chance to practise without having to pay model fees.

'Pull the front of your neckline down a little to show the camera your beautiful cleavage,' ordered Sami as Angelina posed on the stool.

'That's great,' he tried to reassure her. 'Now turn sideways and look at the camera. Great, it's in the bag.'

The lights seemed to flash a thousand times but finally the moment Angelina had been dreading arrived.

'Ok,' grinned Sami. Nikki wants some topless shots, so if you would like to go into the bathroom and take your top off we can get started. If you're embarrassed, I don't mind taking my shirt off too,' joked Sami.

'No, I'll do it here,' said Angelina taking a deep breath and removing her top and bra in one swift practised movement.

'Things are looking up,' thought Sami. 'Well, at least her tits are so there's a start.'

After a few formal poses, he pressed a few keys on the computer keyboard.

'Now I want to try a few different poses,' said Sami, 'some 'artistic shots.' Just hold your head a little to one side.'

He looked at the computer screen and studied it for a moment.

'A little bit more, great. Nearly finished.' He spoke whilst looking at the computer screen again.

Now turn your head to the left, slowly, slowly. Stop! This is definitely your best side. Now hold it just there.'

The flashes went off, the strobes beeped and Sami turned to the computer screen again. On it was a photograph of two naked girls; they were holding each other closely with one arm around each other's back and the other hand caressing each other's breasts. The girl on the left was holding her head in exactly the same way as Sami had posed Angelina.

Sami moved the mouse and another picture appeared. This time it was of a woman's face straight on, framed between the legs of a naked second woman. Sami turned to Angelina.

'OK. This time I want you to look straight at the camera and put your head down a little.'

He turned to the computer screen once more.

'Now, pretend you are licking an ice cream. That's a real turn on for some guys. Good. Now keep your head where it is and bring your eyes to the camera.'

He took one last look at the computer screen, and fired the shutter. Half an hour later he had finished.

'I think the pictures are in the bag. You were great, well done.'

'Can I see the photos?' asked Angelina.

'No, sorry,' said Sami. 'Rule of the house. No looking until they're finished. There's quite a bit of digital editing to be done yet. We want you to look your best.'

Angelina dressed and Sami showed her to the door.

'The photos will be with Nikki in two or three days,' said Sami. 'You'll look good. Trust me.'

Sami went back inside and phoned Nikki.

'All done,' said Sami, 'I'll do the digital editing on the photographs tonight. It'll be easy enough to replace the faces of the girls in the photographs with Angelina's face and the girl you sent last week. I'll have them done by tomorrow so you can flog them to your internet perverts straight away. The bodies are the same but the faces are different. Poor sods will never know.'

'Thanks Sami,' Nikki was happy. 'I owe you one.'

'You owe me three or four if the truth were known,' joked Sami and hung up.

Nikki received the photos and was pleased with them. She uploaded some of Angelina's clothed pictures to the escort website. The new pornographic pictures showing Angelina in some very compromising positions with the girl sold very quickly, as she already had a waiting list of customers eager to buy.

A few days later she rang Angelina.

'I just knew it was the photos holding you back,' said Nikki excitedly. 'We have a booking from a client for the evening of the fourth of next month and then we have a two day booking for you for the eighth of next month – and they have both asked specifically for you. Congratulations!'

'Wow!' replied an excited Angelina, 'that's brill,' and went to buy some vodka to celebrate.

A few days later, on the twenty eighth of the month Angelina received another phone call from Nikki.

'I'm sorry to have to tell you this but the owner has been going through the books and your one month free trial is over. You'll need to pay your registration fee of one thousand. I'm sorry, I hadn't realised time had gone so fast.'

'But, I have two bookings coming up soon,' replied a desperate Angelina. 'Couldn't you take the money out of my earnings?'

'No, I'm afraid not. The owner is very strict on this,' said a sorrowful sounding Nikki. 'In fact, I'm afraid the two bookings cannot go ahead unless we receive the registration fee first. Think about it for now and let me know what you want to do. You've been unlucky really; your first client's wife falling ill, your needing new photos and the photographer being too busy to fit you in straight away - and then the free month was gone. Yes, unlucky.'

'Unlucky is the story of my life,' thought Angelina as she hung up.

'What have I done so wrong in life to make things always go pear shaped?' She screamed after she put the phone down and sobbed.

'I have just got to get the money,' she thought. 'It's only for a few days and then I'll have the money back from these clients and more besides. Now think, Angelina, think.'

Angelina went back to her mother's home and as her mother watched television, she went to the kitchen and raided the sugar caddy of all its contents.

'Seven hundred,' she muttered to herself, 'not enough' but she took it anyway. She bade a hasty and guilty farewell to her mother and headed for one of the less salubrious districts of town.

There was now no other route left for her. She had to have this money in order to make a new start in life. Having already borrowed from everyone she knew to pay for the photographs, she had to think of something else. Standing outside a dingy corner shop which displayed a range of dirty, second hand goods of little use to anyone she looked at the sign over the door.

'Money Lender. Salary cheques cashed.' Angelina pulled her coat tightly around her (to prevent being infected by what lay inside), took a deep breath to pluck up courage and went inside.

The Dickensian character behind the counter peered through his thick spectacle lenses and asked pleasantly, 'Hello my dear, what can I do for you?'

Angelina looked around and inspected the pawned goods as she slowly made her way to the counter. There was a broken guitar with only two strings, a pram with several spokes missing from the wheels and many other soiled items no-body would ever want.

'I need to borrow some money,' whispered Angelina.

'Sorry my Dear, I can't hear you. You will have to speak up a little,' said the loan shark - who had heard her perfectly well the first time.

'I need to borrow three hundred and fifty for two weeks,' said Angelina a little louder this time. The extra fifty was for the vodka she needed to get over the coming days.

'And what are you going to put down to guarantee the loan?' asked the loan shark.

'I don't have anything,' said Angelina, nothing at all but I'm starting a new job in two weeks' time and can pay you back then.'

'No collateral? Then the interest is ten percent per day and it must be paid back. You do understand?'

'Yes,' Angelina remained undaunted, 'I understand.'

The loan shark reached under the counter and produced a camera. 'Stand here whilst I take your photo.' The camera clicked and the flash lit her face. She felt totally embarrassed and ashamed. Now, write your details on this paper.'

She left the shop feeling dirty and used but she had the money which she took straight around to Nikki.

'Thanks,' Nikki smiled whilst writing Angelina a receipt, 'I know you're doing the right thing.'

Angelina went off to celebrate with her usual vodka but a part of her felt there was something not quite 'right.'

On the third day of the next month Angelina received another call from Nikki.

'I'm very sorry to have to tell you this but both your clients have cancelled their appointments. It does happen. I'll be in touch as soon as I have news for you.' Nikki hung up without giving Angelina chance to say anything at all.

'I hate this part of it,' she told Nellie, as she hung up. 'We can't take the scam further so it's time to end it here and now. She'll get over it'

Meanwhile, realisation started to dawn on Angelina. There never were any customers; she knew now. Nor was there a free month's trial. The photographer wasn't busy; they were just collecting money and waiting for the month to end so they could collect the fees.

She lay down on the sofa and the phone rang again.

'Maybe it's Nikki with a new client,' she thought for a moment but her illusions were soon to be dispelled.

'You shit of a daughter,' where's my money? What have you done with my pension fund?' her mother was fuming.

'I'll pay you back,' replied Angelina, 'I really will pay you back.'

'Well don't come around here till you do.' The phone slammed down at the other end and Angelina threw herself down on the sofa in despair.

As she lay there, trying to fathom how to put her life back on track, the phone rang again.

'Hi Angelina,' said the smooth voice of the loan shark at the other end. 'Remember the interest is ten percent per day. We need some money soon.'

'It's ok,' said Angelina, 'my job starts soon and I'll repay it then.'

'Let's hope so,' said the voice and the phone went dead.

Angelina returned to the sofa and was given an hours rest before the phone rang once more.

'You slut!' Her father screamed at her. 'How could you shame me and your mother by having those filthy pictures taken?'

'But Dad,' refuted Angelina, 'I didn't have any filthy pictures taken.'

'Well there is a bloke in the pub selling copies of some pornographic pictures of you and another girl and it's certainly your face. Don't lie to me. Whore!'

Again the phone went dead.

Angelina thought quietly and deeply for some time before making a decision. She put on her coat and went to the shops where she bought a large bottle of vodka. When she returned she ran a very hot bath and stripped naked. She took the bottle of vodka from the bag, opened it and placed it next to the bath. She took the razor from the shopping bag, removed the blades and placed them on the side before lowering herself into the water.

Angelina lay back, sipped the vodka and dreamed of escorting clients, being taken out to dinner; even marrying one and going to California to live happily ever after.

Once the vodka bottle was empty Angelina tipped it upside down to make sure there was none left. She took the razor blade and in two deft movements, slit both her wrists. Blood ran from her veins until, like the vodka, there was not a single drop left.

"My boyfriend opened the door to a group of men claiming to be CID officers. They said I was wanted for questioning regarding a theft but my boyfriend became suspicious when they took me away in a taxi and so he called the police. They took me to a brothel but I escaped within hours and raised the alarm." Police made 23 arrests in the case and said that a second maid had also been abducted by the same gang but she had been dumped at the side of the road when they could not find a buyer for her. The boyfriend was also arrested for having an illegal affair with the girl.

Report from Court records.

Chapter 17

Elena took her time looking through the selection of biscuits on the supermarket shelf. It wasn't that she was fussy about what she or her son, Mikhail ate, she was just looking for the cheapest. Once, before Kristina left, the price would not have mattered as much. But now, with no money as yet from her and worse still, no news, she had to be careful. Having made her final choice, she moved to the exit.

'How's Kristina doing?' asked the girl at the cash desk as she placed the pitiful pile of groceries on the counter to be priced.

'Settling in nicely,' lied Elena.

'You must be very proud,' said the fat lady standing in the queue behind her.

'Yes we are,' she replied; wishing she could tell them how worried she was.

'I wish my girl had done something to bring money in,' said the lady behind her.

Elena quickly handed over a few coins, gathered up her provisions and left the store before anyone could ask any awkward questions.

'Any news?' asked Elena of her son Mikhail, as she opened the door and rushed into their home.' No,' replied Mikhail, 'the phone rang a couple of times but whoever it was hung up when I answered it.' Mikhail was a typical fifteen year old teenager. He had inherited his father's strong cheek bones and dark hair which he kept short to give an overall clean appearance any mother would be proud of.

Elena shuddered at the thought of who it might have been. They had started their telephone vigil four weeks ago when they had agreed there would always be one of them by the telephone in case Kristina rang. On the days neither could be there owing to school or work Tasha, Elena's sister, would man the phone. Tasha was the only other person outside the close family who was aware Kristina had vanished into thin air. They could not risk the chance of her telephoning and no-one being there to speak to her. All three were extremely worried and knew something was wrong. Kristina would have contacted them by now, even just to let them know she was safe.

'You'll have to go to the police,' said Mikhail, 'something's very wrong.'

'I know,' said Elena, 'but if I go to the police, the whole village will know she's missing.' Elena remembered the police from communist times and had been brought believing the police were basically corrupt and were to be avoided like the plague. Besides, there were certain people in the village, those from whom she had borrowed the money, who she certainly didn't want to learn of Kristina's disappearance. Elena knew it was these people on the other end of the telephone who were hanging up whenever Mikhail answered it.

'Then why don't we go to the police in the city and ask them,' said Mikhail. 'We could say, since it's international, we didn't know who to go to and thought our local police wouldn't have the resources.'

'Let's give it another day,' replied Elena putting off the inevitable once more.

The next day came and went but still no news. Eventually Elena came to realise she needed to try to find her daughter. She kept picturing Kristina lying in hospital, in intensive care no less, unable to speak after a road accident or worse. Or, on bad days, she would imagine her dead in a plane crash the local television had not reported as it was so far away. Elena eventually gave in deciding Mikhail's idea of the main police station in the city was their only option.

'So how did your daughter first hear about this job in....' asked Captain Ilya, resplendent in his highly decorated uniform and sitting behind a huge desk.

'Almina,' said Elena, 'she saw an advertisement in the newspaper which said they needed a dancer to replace one who'd had an accident. There were vacancies for several other jobs – shop assistants, maids and so on.'

'And who were 'these people?' the policeman asked.

'They said they were a recruitment agency who find workers to go out there. Apparently companies tell them what they require in the way of employees and they advertise, interview and recruit. It saves every company doing the advertising and travelling separately.'

'And so your daughter, Kristina?' the Captain queried, looking up from the notes he was writing, 'your daughter Kristina, went for an interview?'

'An audition actually,' replied Elena, perking up a little.

'How many others were there for this audition?' he asked.

'Twelve I think they said. Well I don't know actually.' She was feeling a little foolish. 'They said the applicants were all coming at different times.'

'So it's possible Kristina was the only applicant.' Captain Ilya was not looking at Elena but continuing to make notes.

'I suppose so.' She was feeling even more foolish, 'but I don't see why they would have only auditioned one girl.'

'So tell me what happened after the audition.' He looked up and smiled at Elena.

'Well, Kristina completed the audition; they said she did very well and they would be in touch. Two days later she received a phone call saying she'd been successful and they'd be sending the air ticket by the end of the week as the dance troupe needed an urgent replacement because they had performances booked. The ticket arrived along with a copy of a visit visa, and everything was dated for two days later. Luckily she'd been abroad the year before with some friends so she had a passport. In fact they asked her about the passport at the audition and took a copy. We rushed around buying her things to take with her, clothes and toiletries and then she was gone.'

'Were there any fees to be paid to the agency?'

'Yes, we had to pay their fees in cash. Kristina met them in the same hotel and handed it over.' Elena had been trying to avoid the question of the fees.

'It must have taken quite a bit of money to sort it all out,' the Captain commented and looked quizzically at Elena. 'How much were the fees?'

'Two thousand Dollars,' she replied sheepishly, 'I managed to borrow a little from some good friends.'

The Captain raised an eyebrow, 'and this is why you came here instead of the local police,' he thought.

'So let me see if I've got this right,' he continued, 'your daughter Kristina went to a place called Almina to work and from the time she left on the plane you've heard absolutely nothing from her. Have a you copy of her passport?'

'Yes.' Elena rummaged in her bag and produced a creased copy. She felt her heart give an extra beat as she saw Kristina's photo once more.

'And you've nothing at all, no documents phone numbers from this recruitment agency?'

'No. Everything was done by telephone except the, the fees and when the air ticket and visa arrived, they were the only things in the envelope.'

'No receipt for the agency fee?'

'Well, yes but Kristina had to take it with her as it would be refunded by her employer in Almina when she arrived. Unfortunately, we never thought to copy it first.'

'What happens next is,' said Captain Ilya, rising to indicate the interview was over, 'I will send the details to the police in Almina and see what they can find out. They're usually very helpful in situations like this.'

He moved over to the door and opened it.

'I'll be in touch as soon as we hear anything. I have your contact details. Don't worry we'll find her.'

Elena left and despite the Captains' reassurances, she worried even more all the way home.

Elena, Mikhail and her sister spent a fretful week imagining every possible calamity that could have happened to Kristina had happened, except, that is, the real one. None of them could have imagined that for one moment.

Towards the end of the week the phone rang and Elena raced over to answer it. Mikhail looked at her expectantly as Elena lifted up the handset.

'Hello,' said Elena a little too quickly,

'How's Kristina doing?' It was a man's voice at the other end of the phone.

'Oh! Sorry yes,' answered Elena, not letting her disappointment show in her voice. 'Kristina is just fine and settling in well.'

'Good, so we can expect some repayments on the loan soon can we?'

'Yes,' she replied, 'Just give her a few more weeks to settle in and then she'll be sending money home.'

'Good. There's no problem, just checking.' The phone went silent.

Elena placed the receiver down slowly. Mikhail, concerned about his mother, looked at her with a worried frown.

'Why doesn't she just tell us where she is?' muttered Mikhail, more to himself than anyone else.

'I don't know love, I just don't know,' Elena sat on the arm of Mikhail's chair and held him to her. 'I just don't know.'

Two days later Captain Ilya phoned. 'We've had a reply from the Almina police force regarding Kristina.'

Elena almost fainted.

'Oh no,' she thought, 'she's dead.'

'Elena?' Are you still there?'

'Yes,' replied Elena, 'I'm here.'

'Well firstly,' he continued, 'they've checked the records and there is no-one of Kristina's description either fatally injured or in hospital over the period Kristina has been there so we know she has not been harmed.'

'Thank God!' Elena let out a sigh of relief, 'but where is she then.'

'Well that's the difficult part,' continued Captain Ilya, 'she went through immigration and her sponsors applied for a residence visa and work permit but since then they've reported Kristina as an absconder.'

'Absconder?' asked Elena, 'what's an absconder?'

'It means she's run away from her sponsor and they don't know where she is.'

'But Kristina would never run away,' Elena said incredulously.

'Apparently it happens a lot. Girls go over there, find a better job offer and run away from their original sponsor to take it.'

'Even so,' said Elena, 'it doesn't explain why we haven't heard from her at all; even when she first arrived in the country.'

'Well the Almina police will continue to look for her. In reporting Kristina as an absconder, her sponsor has kept within the law and now it's Kristina who's in trouble. We can't do any more I'm afraid. Sorry.'

She sat down and felt a wave of deep depression come over her.

'Kristina would have phoned. She would never let anyone down. I just know she would have phoned.'

Elena spent the next few days wondering what else she could do to find Kristina but there was little she could do. The police had tried but if Kristina had absconded, then short of searching every house in Almina there was little they could do. She would just have to wait and hope.

The phone rang and Elena raced to pick it up.

'Hello, Kristina?' pleaded Elena. Please let it be Kristina she prayed.

'No,' said the voice, 'we were just wondering about Kristina.'

'Oh, sorry,' I thought it was her when I answered. She promised to ring tonight.'

'Well when she does,' replied the voice, 'ask her when we can expect some money. The interest on the debt is rising fast.'

'I'll do just that,' said Elena, 'bye.'

Reality struck Elena. Regardless of Kristina's plight, she was going to have to do something about this loan. She still had some of the initial money left that she had prudently added to pay for the first few instalments and any early emergency but this would soon run out. Elena needed money and fast, or else she would be in real trouble.

'What I need is a part time job,' she thought, 'one I can do in the evenings.' She dreaded the thought of leaving Mikhail at home at night but there was no alternative. Picking up the paper she turned to the jobs vacant section and this is when Elena saw it........

Elena stared at it in disbelief but there was no mistaking it. It was the very same advertisement Kristina had responded to.

Almina Recruitment Agency
We have been asked to fill the following vacancies for clients in Almina:

Dancer for dance troupe (female) –	1 number
Shop assistants (female) –	4 numbers
Tailors (female) –	1 number

Applicants should ring 0775 583211 for an appointment.

Since these vacancies are to be filled with immediate effect all applicants should hold a valid passport.

'Look Mikhail look.' She rushed into Mikhail's room and thrust the advertisement under his nose.

'It's them. The people who took Kristina from us,' screamed Elena.

'It looks like it,' said Mikhail turning away from his school books to inspect the advert.

'It not only looks like it but it is. I'm going to ring Captain Ilya right now,' and she rushed off to the phone.

'Captain Ilya,' she said, 'this is Elena, I came to see you about my daughter Kristina who went to Almina and then disappeared.'

'I remember,' said Captain Ilya.

'Well they're here again. The recruiting agents; the same recruiting agents who took Kristina away. Look at page twenty three of the paper and you'll see their advertisement.' Captain Ilya had a copy of the paper on his desk and turned to look at the advertisement.

'I see it,' he said, 'but how does this help?'

'They might have some information about Kristina,' said Elena. 'Please go and talk to them.'

'I can't see it doing any good,' said the Captain, 'but if it makes you feel better I'll go and see them in the morning.' He felt sorry for Elena, knowing how frustrated and depressed she was feeling and aware of how much trouble she would be in once the money lenders started to push for repayment of the loan.

'Oh thank you, thank you,' said Elena and hung up.

Elena did not sleep at all that night and spent the next day pacing up and down in front of the phone until it finally broke the silence and rang.

It was Captain Ilya.

'I went to see them this morning,' he said in a business-like manner. 'They were very helpful; told me Kristina had gone over there and how they'd met her and applied for her residence visa but then she'd just run off. They're very disappointed as they'd spent a lot of money taking her out there and now they've to start all over again. If the police find her, the lady in charge says they'll press charges and make Kristina pay back all their expenses.'

'But they must know something,' replied Elena disappointedly.

'Nothing,' said the Captain. 'To be honest, they seemed like nice people who've been let down badly by Kristina. I'm afraid there's nothing else I can do. Goodbye.' He hung up.

'Oh Kristina,' she thought, 'how could you have done this to me, Mikhail and all these people.'

Elena sat quietly thinking and then thought some more. Then with a sudden movement, she sat bolt upright.

'No, she couldn't,' she thought to herself, 'my Kristina would never leave me and Mikhail without saying a word, nor would she abscond from 'nice people.'

A way forward started to evolve in Elena's mind and she set herself the task of carrying it through.

"They forced me into prostitution and made me sleep with several men. They told me that I would never see my country again if I did not sleep with men. I slept with 10 men on different occasions before I managed to escape." The 17 year old Bangladeshi girl freed herself whilst her captors were taking her to a client in a taxi. When the taxi stopped at a red light, she jumped out and ran into a grocery store where the shopkeeper let her use the phone to call the police.

Proceedings of Court case.

Chapter 18

'Have you seen the papers?' asked Nellie as she threw two of them down on the table.

'Of course I have seen the fucking papers,' replied Nikki. 'Every sodding one of them! This isn't supposed to happen. You don't commit suicide the moment someone has scammed you. You just don't do it.'

'Well this one did.'

'Well this one was a stupid cow.' Nikki was furious. 'When you are scammed you go away and shout, maybe scream, but you get on with your life. You don't end it. It's not in the plan.'

Nikki couldn't help thinking if Philippe had been around he would have stopped her. Philippe never took a scam so far that people had to kill themselves as a result. No, it was his fault for not being here. No, it was her fault. Nikki had killed Angelina as much as if she had taken the razor blade and cut her wrists. To make matters worse, she actually liked the kid.

The phone rang and Nikki answered it. It was Sami.

'Have you seen the papers?'

'Are you looking for a degree in stating the fucking obvious?' Replied Nikki, 'of course I've seen the sodding papers. They even printed one of your photos of her; well one of the decent ones.'

'It's OK.' Sami tried to calm Nikki down. 'The papers say no-one knows why she killed herself as she had told everyone she'd a new job and things were definitely on the up. There's no way they can pin this on us.'

"THEY', don't need to,' said Nikki, 'I know it was me who killed her.'

'Why not come around tonight for an orgasm? Or two?' asked Sami. 'Just to cheer you up.

'No,' said Nikki, 'I might cheat, I might thrill - but I don't kill them. I need to think. Bye.'

She put the phone down and started to think about what she had done - which for a con artist is not a good thing to do.

Nikki spent the next few days brooding. The problem was she had grown too close to Angelina and actually liked her. The problem was she had pushed her too far. The problem was Angelina had wanted it too much and borrowed out of her depth. The problem was it was all too much of a problem.

Nikki looked at her position, past and present, and did a quick audit of her life: businesses and social.

Fact one.

If Nikki had left Angelina alone, she would still be alive today.

There was no way of getting around it.

Fact two.

The 'Russian Wives' website was dying. The web is a great place for putting yourself out there but it is also a great place for people to report scams. More and more of their clients were warning punters not to use their services as they had been cheated.

Fact three.

Sales of pornography over the web were now non-existent. There were just too many bored housewives doing it for free. What punters searched the web for now were free videos of amateurs 'fucking away,' whilst they vacuumed the house or did the gardening.

Fact four.

Nikki needed money. There was just not enough coming in.

Fact Five.

Nobody loved her. If she disappeared tomorrow not a single soul would miss her or even show any sign of sorrow. To Nikki this was the final straw. What impact have I made on this world if I don't leave something behind? If there's no-one to cry for me. Nikki began to think.

'Sod it,' she thought, 'I'm not so far down the hill I have to find a job. What I need is a new challenge. One where people don't kill themselves.'

And then the telephone rang.

'Hi Nikki,' said the voice on the phone. 'It's Julie here. Remember me.'

'Julie,' thought Nikki, 'who the Hell is Julie? Oh that Julie.'

'Hi Julie, long time no see,' replied Nikki who now fully remembered who Julie was. They had worked together on the streets from time to time before Nikki had met Philippe. Now they just kept in touch at Christmas or when one of them was in the depths of depression.

'What are you up to now? Still with that creep Philippe?'

Nikki explained Philippe had died nearly a year ago.

'Sorry,' replied an embarrassed Julie.

Nikki explained about Angelina and how the business was dying and how life was generally not good.

'Then why not join me over here,' said Julie. 'It's fantastic, lots of work and plenty of fun.'

'And where exactly is over here,' enquired Nikki.

'In Almina. It is unfuckingbelieveable. You just stand at the side of the road in the centre of town. You write your price on the palm of your hand, usually two or three hundred dollars and hold it up like a fucking policeman. The punters drive their cars round and round, stop and whisk you away. You do the business and then they bring you back to start all over again. You can do two or three jobs a night easy, more at weekends. And the police! Well they've never met real working ladies before so they haven't a clue how to stop us.'

'Did you say two or three hundred DOLLARS, as in US?' asked Nikki with amazement.

'Correct, US dollars,' she replied.

Nikki was lucky to earn as much in one month never mind on just one job.

'How much is the air fare?' She was mentally calculating how much cash she could get together at short notice.

'Damn,' she thought, 'why didn't I keep Philippe's Rolex watch? His family would never have missed it.' But then she didn't know his family had existed until it was too late.

'No problem,' replied Julie, 'We get paid two thousand dollars for every new girl we recruit. I'll send you the air fare and you can pay me back once you get your arse wiggling.'

'It wasn't my arse I was thinking of wiggling,' thought Nikki.

'OK, you're on.' She was convinced. 'This is exactly what I need - a fresh start and a new life. Better still, I'll be venturing into a new business at the very beginning.'

A new feeling ran through Nikki's veins – a mixture of excitement and relief. She felt like the missionaries must have felt taking religion to pagan lands except she was one of a band taking organised prostitution to moral lands.

'Duty free,' shouted the cabin crew as she came down the aisle, 'duty free.'

Nikki was brought back from her dozing. It had only been seven days since Julie had made her this life changing offer. A 'life saving' offer if she was being honest. She had presented the entire scam empire to Nellie as a gift. The flat wasn't hers but rented anyway. The client base was falling and the computers she owned were obsolete.

'Duty free Madam?' enquired the trolley dolly looking at Nikki.

'No thank you.' Nikki well remembered reading in the paper about a court case where a man had bought a duty free watch on an aircraft. Six months later, when the watch stopped working he took it back to the dealers under guarantee only to be told the watch wasn't original but fake. He took the airline to court of course but his case failed as no-one could prove when the switch had been made. He could have made the switch himself in the time since he bought it but so too could any of the dozens of airline staff who had handled it.

But Nikki knew. She and Philippe had flown together between cities to find new punters. He had always worn a fake Rolex on purpose. People assessed a person's wealth by their watch. He had pushed his own fake watch up his arm so it was hidden by his coat sleeve. When the trolley came to him he asked if they had any watches. The girl showed him the most expensive Rolex they had.

'Nice,' Philippe had said but do you have same make but a little cheaper?'

Philippe had handed back the watch and the Crew member passed him another. This time it was exactly the same model of Rolex as the replica on his arm.

'Now, I like this one,' Philippe had said, 'Let me just see how it looks on my arm.' Philippe had taken it from the box, placed it on his wrist and was waving his arm about in the air looking at the watch from all angles.

'What do you think?' Philippe asked Nikki. 'A little too much or is it classic? I want to look distinguished and not flashy.'

'Excuse me ma'am,' asked a man in the seat on the other side of the aisle, 'do you have any cigarettes?'

'Just let me finish with this gentleman first.' The girl was thinking of her commission and quickly returned her attention to Philippe.

But it had been long enough. In this brief moment Philippe had removed the fake watch and pushed the real Rolex up his arm and out of sight.

'It's a lot of money so I want to think about it before I buy.' He smiled at the girl as he placed the fake watch back in the box and handed it back.

A jeweller would have spotted it straight away but this was a girl trained to save lives on the rare occasion an aeroplane crashed, and at present she was only interested in the commission the airline gave her on sales.

Nikki had spent the rest of the flight panicking in case anyone noticed but of course no-one did. That was the way with Philippe. Even when the scam was later discovered, there was no need for anyone to kill them-self.

'Stop right there,' Nikki chided herself. 'All this is in the past and you're starting afresh. No past memories are coming back to haunt you from now on.' One good thing though. Nikki had been able to honestly vouch to Philippe's wife and family the watch was real!

Nikki had to change flights on her way to Almina, and as she was on her way through transit she saw a huge queue leading up to the help desk. 'What's going on?' she enquired of a uniformed member of staff, who looked like he should know.

'Huge storms earlier have wreaked havoc with the schedules,' he replied - always ready to assist a pretty young lady. 'Lots of flights have been delayed and many cancelled. Where are you flying to?'

'Almina,' replied Nikki, 'three thirty flight.'

'Sorry love, your flight's been cancelled. You'll need to join the queue and be rescheduled. Get a ticket from the machine over there and when your number comes up, go to the counter to be served.'

She moved to the machine and took ticket number nine hundred and fifty three. Looking at the display she saw they were only serving number one hundred and twelve so she went back to the airline official and showed him her ticket.

'How long?' asked Nikki.

126

'I'm sorry,' apologised the official. 'You're looking at a four hour wait; If not longer.'

'Thank you,' said Nikki and turned and walked away. As she did so a smile came on her face.

'Better get to work then,' she thought and idled back to the machine and took two more tickets. Nikki then went off to the coffee shop and bought a coffee. Half an hour later she returned to the queue and pretended to check the progress of her ticket. Seeing there were no officials looking she took three more tickets. She continued with this process for the next three hours until she had quite a collection of tickets.

The display showed they were up to ticket nine hundred and twenty and only thirty or so places to go before her turn arrived. She decided it was now time to cash in and sidled up to a business man who was looking very concerned at the flight information display.

'Terrible isn't it? You'd think they would have more staff on at times like these. What number do you have?'

'Who, me?' replied the business man not used to pretty young ladies starting up a conversion with him, 'I have ticket four hundred and twenty. They've gone around the clock and started again. I've a meeting in the morning and I'll never get there at this rate.'

'My ticket is up soon but even if I get a new flight I can't go on it. I've excess baggage and they want me to pay thirty dollars which I just don't have. How about if we swap tickets and you give me the thirty dollars? This way you make your meeting and I get my luggage home. Helps me, helps you.' She gave him the most beguiling smile he had ever seen.

'I don't know' said the business man, 'what if your ticket doesn't work?'

'No problem,' she said confidently. 'Take my ticket now and go to the counter. Keep your own ticket. If it works I'll be over there and you can pass me your old ticket and the money. I trust you but hand me the ticket and money quietly so no-one notices, otherwise they might not let me on the flight.'

'Sounds good to me,' said the man and took Nikki's ticket to the counter.

Nikki moved over to a family of four. With the kids crying and the wife giving the husband grief, Nikki went through the same process but increasing the price a little because of his situation.

The businessman came back to Nikki and slipped her his ticket and the money plus another ten dollars.

'Thanks,' he whispered, 'I can't thank you enough.'

'Now this is the sort of scam I like,' thought Nikki, 'one where the punters are actually grateful.' And scam it was because one of the reasons the queue was now so long, was because of the wodge of tickets held in Nikki's bag.

She worked her way around the crowd and gradually exchanged her cache of tickets for dollars.

There was one scary moment when a middle aged man came up to her. He was tall and well dressed and at first Nikki thought he was going to make a move on her.

'Excuse me, but I see what's going on here. I've been watching you for a while.'

'Oh,' said Nikki, not sure what to say and choosing silence as the best policy.

'So let's cut the crap.' said the man. 'Do you have any more of those tickets left? If the number has less than twenty to go I'll give you one hundred dollars for it. I admire a smart lady when I see one and besides, I need to get out of here.'

'Sure,' replied a relieved Nikki, have this one; it only has four to go but be quick as I am right behind you.'

She finally took her turn at the counter and was booked onto the next flight to set off on the final leg of the journey. As the aircraft reached cruising altitude and the seat belt signs went off, Nikki relaxed.

'So you're going to Almina too,'

'Yes,' Nikki recognised the man standing in the aisle, who had not only bought her last ticket but had almost given her a heart attack into the bargain.' He was a young looking forty(ish) with a kind face and pleasant smile.

'My name's Victor, Is this your first time out here?'
'Yes, and you?'

'I've been here five years,' he replied. 'You'll either love it or hate it. 'Here's my card; if you need anything or just a shoulder to cry on, give me a ring.'

Victor returned to his seat and Nikki studied the card. 'Victor

Musgrove,' it read, 'supplies for the oil industry.' Nikki carefully placed the card in her bag knowing too well in this life one can never have too many friends.

"I was offered a job in Almina as a waitress on 550 US Dollars a month but when I arrived at the airport I was met by a Filipina who took my passport. She told me I was to work as a prostitute and took me to a flat. Once there she told me there was a client waiting for me. I cried but she said I would die in Almina if I refused and that my family back home would be harmed. She brought in a man who raped me even though I begged him not to and told him I had a daughter back home. I was forced to have sex with many customers but I could not get help as the door to my room was constantly locked." The girl managed to escape one night when the madam got drunk and asked her to have a threesome with a customer. She let me use her phone so I sent a text to a friend who called the police.

Proceedings of Court case.

Chapter 19

The door opened and Kristina walked into the bedroom like a zombie. There was no emotion; she just walked in, head down, dragging one foot behind the other.

'They said you were very good – all three of them commented on it,' Eva's voice drifted in from outside the door, 'I think you'll do well. We'll talk in the morning.'

The door closed and Kristina heard the key turn in the lock. She threw herself on the bed, face to the wall with her back to the room, so she could ignore its contents and the other girls when they returned. She found the teddy bear Melda had left for her and hugged it tightly. At least that couldn't hurt her. Reaching for her handbag at the top of the mattress for some tissues, she found her mascara pencil. Taking it out and using her small neat handwriting, the same handwriting everyone had complimented her on at school, she wrote on the base of the wall:

'I want to go home,' and she signed it 'Kristina,' adding the date.

She spent the rest of the night staring at these few words and wishing she were dead. After what had happened to her today, how could she go back to her village or her mother?

Hearing the girls come home in the middle of the night - at least those who had not been booked for an 'all-nighter,' Kristina pretended to be asleep; hugging the teddy bear tightly. She felt a hand on her shoulder.

'Kristina? Kristina?' said Melda. 'Are you OK?'

Kristina shrugged the arm away, hugged the teddy bear until it looked as if its head would come off and stared more intently at the words written on the wall.

'I want to go home, Kristina.

The next morning Eva entered the bedroom and quietly crept over to Kristina.

'Follow me to the kitchen,' she whispered.

Kristina looked around and stared blankly at Eva but followed her like a dutiful dog.

'Now you're one of us,' said Eva, 'I want you to go out with the other girls just to get the feel of things.' She looked at Kristina's torn blouse that she still wore from the day before.

'Don't worry,' said Eva looking kindly at the young girl. 'We'll soon replace it with something better.'

Kristina said nothing but she resented those words. 'How can you replace something my mother bought me?' she thought.

'I want you to go out with the girls today,' Eva repeated, not to work but to get you out of the flat for a while. Go and shower and change and I'll make you something to eat. You must be starving.'

Kristina left the kitchen and collected her bathroom things in silence. She showered and dressed, selecting the most revealing clothes she had brought with her. On returning to the bathroom she looked into the mirror. She started with her eyes - applying the eye shadow and mascara as thickly as she could.

'If they want a prostitute, then a prostitute is what they can have,' she thought.

There was a bright red lipstick on the mirror tray belonging to one of the other girls. She caked it on her lips too until she looked totally unlike the Kristina of old.

'This isn't me doing this,' she said to herself, 'it's someone else. I'm just an actor playing the part and this is my makeup and costume for my part in the play.'

'Oh, no, far too much,' thought Eva as Kristina returned to the kitchen playing her new role. In fact, she almost said it out loud but stopped herself just in time.

'Very nice,' Eva commented. 'Sit down and have something to eat.' She had set out a cup of coffee and some cornflakes.

Kristina left the cornflakes untouched but sipped the coffee.

Eva gave up trying to make polite conversation and busied herself around the kitchen until the noise of doors being opened and closed could be heard from outside, along with voices of the girls chattering. The kitchen door opened and the Mamasan stuck her head through the gap.

'We're going now. Are you ready Kristina?'

Kristina stood in silence. She followed the Mamasan into the hallway were the other girls waited. Melda's face fell as she saw the state of her.

'Kristina is coming with you today,' Eva announced as she emerged from the kitchen, 'not to work but just to get the feel of things.'

'Make the most of it,' said the blonde girl 'from tomorrow the 'things' will be getting the 'feel' of you!'

The blonde girl and the Mamasan laughed.

'Don't,' said Eva, 'Kristina is a little shy. She'll be fine.'

The Mamasan took out her key and unlocked the front door and they all filed out into the corridor. Everyone stopped and waited and seemed to know what to do as the Mamasan opened the front door of the flat opposite and another five girls trooped out. After a brief exchange of greetings between the two groups of girls she introduced Kristina.

'This is Kristina, a new girl, look after her.'

They crammed into the lift and went downstairs where two taxis were waiting. Kristina started to tremble as she remembered her previous ordeal.

'It's alright.' The Mamasan tried to placate her, 'no-one's going to harm you.'

They all piled into the taxis, each girl knowing exactly where to sit. The Mamasan sat in the front. Melda took hold of Kristina and the two of them and another girl sat on the back seat whist the blonde girl half sat half resting across them. With all doors closed the two taxis sped off and drove through the city streets. Kristina could hardly see out through the windows but what she did see looked striking. New tall buildings of glass, metal and concrete set in front of a brilliant blue sky.

'My local priest back home was wrong,' thought Kristina, 'Hell can be beautiful.'

The taxis pulled up outside a hotel named 'The Almina Towers Hotel'. A few girls stood outside the hotel hoping to catch a customer on the way in or out. These were the 'self-employed' girls who hadn't caught a customer for some time and couldn't afford the entrance fee to the bar. The Mamasan, Melda and the rest ignored them as if they were dirt on the pavement and walked into the hotel foyer.

There was a door off to the left with a security guard on duty but he just nodded to the Mamasan and they all walked past him. Kristina was unable to see anything at all as it was so dark but gradually, as her pupils widened and her eyes became accustomed to the change from the bright outdoors to the seedy interior, she started to make out the room. There were no windows and the room was lit by artificial lights. At one end stretching almost all the way across the smoke filled room was a bar with beer pumps, spirit optics and just about any type of alcohol one could think of. What struck Kristina immediately was the number of women; they far outnumbered the men.

'Don't worry,' said Melda to Kristina, 'it will fill up once the football starts.'

'Doesn't bother me in the slightest,' thought Kristina, 'I've no intention of doing anything anyway.'

The girls moved over and stood next to an empty pillar at the far side of the room and took over the space. It puzzled Kristina as to why, in such a busy place this space was empty but she kept her thoughts to herself. The Mamasan moved over to the bar and ordered a pint of beer. She took two straws and sat down on a chair in the corner which seemed to have been left empty for her. Placing her handbag on her knee, she sat like an eagle in its eyrie watching the room, taking the odd sip of beer through the straws as she did so.

Kristina looked around her new surroundings. The area around her was filled with Eastern European girls, whilst the far side of the room - nearest the entrance, was filled with a group of Chinese girls. The smoke and murk concealed the seedy and tackiness of both the place and the girls. The door was kept firmly closed as the merest glint of daylight would destroy the whole seductive fantasy in an instant.

Melda leaned across to Kristina and whispered. 'This is our area. Don't stray into the Chinese territory over there or all hell will break out. The single girls are 'self-employed.' They generally stand at the bar so the guys have to lean over them to get service and buy their drinks. This way the girl can start a conversation. We just find a guy looking our way, stare them straight in the eye and smile at them, in the hope of attracting them over.'

Two men walked in and looked around. All the girls looked straight towards the newcomers and smiled. As they walked to the bar, nearby girls on their route said 'hello' or put their arms out to touch and stroke them.

'It'll start to fill up now,' continued Melda, 'but everyone is just weighing each other up and window shopping. The bars have to close between four and six in the afternoon so, if we're to make money, we need a punter before four. The Mamasan pays the security for us all to come in but if none of us score then she gets very angry and it's not worth thinking about. The Mamasan hates to lose money.'

A group of three more men came in and received the same treatment as the last two, with girls pawing them or standing in the way. 'It's like the girls work as automatons in a theme park,' thought Kristina, 'springing into life whenever the tourist coaches pass but returning to sleep mode afterwards.'

Melda was feeling uncomfortable by Kristina's extended silence so she continued with her monologue for something to do. 'Not all the men are here to '*take a lady*,' some come for the cheap beer and the sport on the television. Some just like to take a walk on the 'dark side' and get a kick out of being on the side-lines. Thankfully for us, some are here to play but they mainly wait till the bar is about to close. The tight bastards know if they pick up a lady too soon, they'll have to buy her drinks and this adds to the overall cost. They also know we need customers before the bar closes at four in the afternoon otherwise we go home losing money. This means they can bargain and get a better price. The result of all this is we spend most of our life as prostitutes, bored, sipping water so we don't get drunk whilst we wait for closing and a punter.

An older guy in his fifties walked in. He was dressed in cheap knee length shorts, a polo shirt and sandals, with socks! He seemed to know all the girls by name and they swarmed around him like bees around a honey pot. He brushed passed them but looked Kristina directly in the eyes. She turned away to avoid his glare.

Kristina saw the clock on the wall had moved to three thirty and the place had started to liven up. It was now full and the men and working girls had started to chat and mingle. On Kristina's right the blonde girl was in full flow talking to a tall European guy. She laughed at all his comments and took every opportunity to place a hand on his chest or just hold his hand. To her left Kristina could overhear another of the girls negotiating.

'Your place or mine?'

'One hundred dollars for one hour, one fifty for two hours.'

'What do you get for your money? Sheer bliss is what you get.'

'I'll do an 'O Level' but I don't do 'A Levels'.'

The girl left, followed by the man a few steps behind her trying to convince the rest of the room they were not leaving together. The blonde girl and her 'man' were the next to leave and then to Kristina's surprise she saw Melda, who had snuck off whilst Kristina was concentrating on her eavesdropping and was now leaving with an Indian guy. 'When did that happen?' she thought.

Last orders were called, and the bar shutters came down. Kristina looked towards the bar and accidentally caught the eye of the old guy in the shorts. She quickly turned her gaze away to avoid him. The remaining girls went outside and stood by the front door of the hotel where a number of other girls had gathered in a last ditch attempt to catch a customer as the remaining men drank up and left. Kristina followed them and stood at the side of the group and was joined by the Mamasan. As the girls plied their trade, taxis pulled up knowing there were fares to be had. Two by two the girls and their newly found punters (whose good intentions had been forgotten in the haze of alcohol), drove away until it looked as if no-one was left in the bar. The Mamasan was about to say 'come on girls, time to go' when the elderly man staggered out of the hotel and looked around at the wares on offer. He breathed heavily through his mouth puffing out his cheeks as he did so. The other girls smiled back at him and there were calls of 'would you like a lady?'

Kristina was petrified as he took one look at her face, smiled and wobbled straight towards her. 'You! Come with me,' he ordered and took hold of Kristina's arm dragging her towards a taxi.

'Piss off!' she shouted and shook herself free. The man looked startled. This had never happened to him before. He looked at Kristina and at the Mamasan, shrugged and moved over to the other end of the group and selected two Chinese girls using the same amount of charm he had shown to Kristina. He piled into the back of a waiting taxi with one girl at each side of him and they drove off. The two Chinese girls stared back at Kristina through the rear window with a smug smile on their faces; looking like two cats who had caught the mouse.

The Mamasan looked at Kristina with hate in her eyes. 'You could at least have been polite. Next time you go with the punter, any punter.'

Two taxis pulled up and they all clambered in. Going home was a lot more comfortable than the journey out as there were fewer of them. The Mamasan returned them to their bedroom to be locked in once more until the evening came.

She went to the kitchen where Eva was waiting, along with a pot of tea and they went through the afternoon's deals, like a printer spewing out the weekly takings of a large shop. Mamasan, in her corner had memorised every move the girls had made. She reported on who had made a score and gone off with a punter, who had nipped out to give someone a quick blow job as they drove around the city, who had tried and failed and in particular those who hadn't tried at all. Eva made a note of the money they expected from each girl on their return.

'How about Kristina?' Eva asked.

'This one's going to be a problem.'

'Why,' asked Eva and she was told of the events of the afternoon. 'I know we said Kristina was only going to get the feel of the place but she told a prospective customer to 'piss off.' He knows who we are and has been with several of our girls before. He's usually too drunk to do anything and if we're not careful we may lose him.'

Take her out tonight and fix her up with someone,' suggested Eva. 'Life's too short to lose money.'

That night the process repeated itself and Kristina found herself in the same bar, standing in the same place as she had done earlier. The Mamasan had taken up her position at the corner of the bar with her bag on her lap, sipping her pint of beer through two straws.

'Same as before,' said Melda turning to Kristina, 'only this time we try to get an early shift and then a late one so we can have at least two hits per night.'

The girls did a lot of smiling and staring but there was not much action. Kristina saw the Mamasan put her drink down on a shelf and placed a beer mat on her stool to reserve it before walking over to her.

'Come with me,' the Mamasan said to Kristina, 'I'll introduce you to some people and help you find a customer.' She took her by the arm and walked her over to a group of men enjoying their beer whilst they watched football on the television.

'You taking a lady tonight?' The Mamasan asked. The man nearest her turned his attention from the football and looked her up and down. He smiled as he thought 'You must be joking, not an old bag like you.'

'This is Kristina. She's new. She's tight.'

He gave the younger girl the once over and was clearly impressed.

'Maybe later; after the match has finished.'

'Ok, see you later.' The Mamasan took her over to a young guy sitting by himself and staring into his beer.

'You like to take lady?' she asked. 'This is Kristina. She's new. She's tight.' The young man looked up from his beer, looked first at the Mamasan and then at Kristina. 'How much?' he asked.

Kristina stood still, her shoulders slouching and her head held down.

'One hundred dollar for an hour, one fifty for two.'

'How much extra is it for her to smile?' he added dryly. 'No thanks, not today.'

The Mamasan took her back to the other girls and scolded her on the way. 'You have to show some interest otherwise no-one will take you.'

'Got it in one,' thought Kristina.

As they approached their area, she saw the blonde girl in deep discussion with a short middle aged man, dressed in jeans and an open necked striped shirt. The Mamasan steered Kristina towards them.

'I'm not sure,' Kristina could hear the man say to the blonde girl, 'maybe yes, maybe no. I need to think.'

'He's waiting for a better price said the Mamasan to Kristina, 'but he'll go.'

'I'll give you a special Christmas offer,' said the Mamasan to the man.

'But it's not Christmas.'

'It is for you. Take two for same price' said the Mamasan pushing Kristina towards him.

Kristina felt a sudden pang of fear spread through her. The blonde girl's smile disappeared for a moment before returning but the smile was a tight pretence of the previous allure. The man looked from one girl to the other and pleasant thoughts passed through his head.

'OK, let's go. My name's John by the way' Without waiting for any further introductions he grabbed hold of each girl and led them out of the door, out of the hotel and into a waiting taxi.

Melda looked at the Mamasan with a look that said, 'Are you sure?' but she could see from her face the old woman was pleased with her bargain offer.

The taxi pulled up outside a large apartment block in an expensive part of town. John paid the taxi driver and gave him a large tip to keep his mouth shut. Without stopping, he led the two girls past the security guard who smiled as he looked the other way. By good fortune, the lift was waiting for them and they ascended to the third floor. The door to John's apartment was directly opposite and as he stooped to place his key in the door, he looked at both of them in turn and gave each a broad smile in anticipation of the impending fun. As they entered the flat, he closed the door, put one arm around each girl and squeezed.

'Let's get the business over first John,' said the blonde girl and held her hand out. John rummaged in his wallet and pulled out the one hundred dollars and placed it on the side.

'Take it when the business is over,' said John thinking it was a bargain.

The blonde girl quickly stuffed the money into her handbag and snapped it shut.

'It's OK, I'll take it now.'

Kristina excused herself to go to the bathroom.

'Don't be long,' John told her. 'I'm paying for this by the hour.'

As Kristina went to find the bathroom, the blonde girl started to strip off and John helped her to remove her final vestiges of modesty as her undies fell to the floor. She kissed John on the lips and teased his tongue with her own as her hands went down to his trousers, undid his belt, unbuttoned the waistband and carefully pulled the zip down. She knelt down, her hands moved into his under pants and took hold of his penis, massaged it to erection and brought it out of its hiding place and into the open. John closed his eyes in sheer bliss. The blonde girl wrapped her mouth around his erect member and moved it slowly in and out of her mouth, sucking, squeezing and tantalising him with the tip of her tongue.

'Where's the other girl?' rasped John.

'What?' said the blonde girl releasing her hold on his private regions and slowly looking up?

'Where's the other girl?' repeated John, 'I paid for two.'

The blonde girl looked around the room and saw a fully clothed Kristina sat on the sofa reading one of John's magazines. 'What do you think you're doing? Get yourself naked and over here. There's work to be done.'

'Mamasan only said 'take two' girls' said Kristina. 'She never said I would be doing anything.'

Eva sat in the kitchen waiting for the girls to come home. At around two am the doorbell rang and she rose to answer it.

'This fucking cow is never coming with me again,' swore the blonde girl as she strode in followed by a quiet Kristina.

Eva closed the door quickly so as not to wake the neighbours. 'Why, what's the problem?'

'What's the fucking problem? I'll tell you what the fucking problem is. She is! Tell the Mamasan never to send this cow with me again.'

'OK, said Eva, 'I'll see you don't lose any money. Leave it till tomorrow and Kristina and I will talk.' She unlocked the bedroom door and guided them in, gave a brisk, 'goodnight,' and then locked the door.

The Mamasan returned a little later with the few remaining girls and when they were safely locked in their room, Eva motioned for her to join her in the kitchen.

'It's not working is it?' the Mamasan said after Eva had recounted the blonde girl's story of the night's events.

'No, we need to call it quits,' Eva shook her head. 'Kristina's not cut out for working in the night clubs. I'll make some phone calls in the morning.'

The next morning Kristina was awoken by Eva shaking her shoulder.

'Follow me to the kitchen,' she whispered so as not to wake the others.

Kristina wiped the sleep from her eyes and followed Eva wearily, expecting to be shouted at. In the kitchen sat a middle aged woman dressed in a long drab shapeless brown dress which almost reached the floor. Her long black hair was unkempt and the lights reflected in her shiny olive skin.

'This is Madam Olga,' Eva announced. 'She's come to look at you.'

Kristina turned her head and looked at Madam Olga with distrust.

'Don't be shy. Take your pyjamas off.'

Kristina looked at Eva who replied with a curt 'do as you are told.'

Kristina pulled her pyjama top off over her head revealing her breasts.

'And the bottoms too,' said Eva, 'Madam Olga needs to see everything.'

Kristina slowly removed the pyjama bottoms and stood erect, naked except for a pair of black panties and stared at the far wall in an attempt to avoid their gaze.

'Now take those panties off,' said Madam Olga, 'and turn around slowly. I need to see how firm your arse is.'

Kristina did as she was told and turned slowly, as if she was on a turntable to allow Madam Olga see every aspect of her body. Madam Olga drew her tongue across her top lip in appreciation of the naked body before her.

Both women nodded in approval.

'How much did you say you wanted for her?'

'Twenty thousand dollars.'

'She's a pretty little thing, I'll give you that but I hear she's trouble?'

'Now whoever told you about Kristina?' asked Eva.

'These things have a habit of getting around. But I think I can knock her into shape. I'll give you sixteen thousand.'

'Eighteen and it's a deal,' said Eva and the two old ladies cackled as they shook hands. 'Go get your things. You're coming with me.'

Kristina looked at both women in turn unable to believe what she had just heard. Eva handed Kristina's passport over to Madam Olga and Kristina looked longingly at the little booklet responsible for all her woes. If only she could grab it back and run. But she knew there was no easy way out for her.

'Dmtry!' madam Olga called out. The door opened and in walked Dmtry.

'Hi Kristina,' he said, 'remember me? Shall we go or do you want to party with me and my friends again?'

Eva stood and walked to the door. 'Come with me and we'll get your things. Pick your night wear up off the floor.'

Kristina meekly followed her out keeping her eyes on Dmtry who just smiled back at her.

Eva unlocked the bedroom door and let Kristina in. 'Don't wake the others – they've been working most of the night.'

Kristina moved over to her mattress, found her suitcase and quietly packed her things.

'What's happening?' whispered Melda who had heard the door open and Kristina come in.

'Can you believe it? Eva's just sold me like a lump of meat to a woman called Madam Olga. Nobody said a word to me. I was sold for eighteen thousand dollars. It couldn't have taken more than two minutes.'

'Madam Olga runs a brothel,' said Melda, 'it means you'll not go outside anymore in case you run off. Look Kristina, promise me you'll start to play the game before things get worse.'

'How can they get any worse?' Kristina burst into tears.

'Oh they can get a lot worse. Madam Olga won't let you go until you've repaid the eighteen thousand dollars and some more. Now you're working inside, you'll get less money each time which means it'll take you longer to repay your debt.'

'It's not my debt,' hissed Kristina, 'I came here for a job as a dancer, nothing else.'

'All this is water under the bridge now. If you want to escape from this country and go home you'll have to repay the money and this means servicing men and making them enjoy it. If you don't do it with Madam Olga then it'll take forever.'

'If I don't do it with Madam Olga, where else can they send me? There can't be anything worse.'

Melda bit her tongue and refrained from telling her about the Chinese farm. 'Just promise me you'll start to play the game. Maybe they'll let you back here where you can pay the debt off faster.' She gave her a hug and Kristina turned and took one last look at the words written on the wall, 'I want to go home, Kristina.'

'Oh Mum, where are you!' She muttered to herself as she picked up her suitcase and left.

"I borrowed 2000 US Dollars to pay a travel agent in Bangladesh to arrange a visa for me to come to Almina to work as a tailor. When I arrived two men picked me up from the airport and took me to a flat where other women stayed and worked as prostitutes. I was confined and beaten because they wanted me to have sex with men. I persistently refused." She was held for four days whilst she was severely beaten as she would not give in to their demands. Once they realised they could not force her into the sex trade they put her up for sale for 1,100 Dollars. The men were caught in a sting operation when an undercover policeman posed as a buyer trying to buy the woman for prostitution.

Testament from Court records.

Chapter 20

'No, don't do it.' Tasha and Elena were talking on the phone and Elena was telling her of the plan. 'How can you be sure of finding her once you get there and worse still what will happen to Mikhail if you disappear too?'

'I have to go and at least try to find her,' said Elena. 'If they offer me a job you'll look after Mikhail whilst I'm away won't you; promise?'

'Of course I will but in return you must promise to keep in touch.'

'I have to get the job first don't I,' said Elena.

'Well let me know how you get on.'

Elena put the telephone down and looked again at the newspaper advertisement lying on the table by the phone.

She stared at it for some time,

'Do I, don't I?' she thought but the thinking was a waste of time because her fingers developed a mind of their own. A very determined mind of their own and she found herself dialling the number. Elena listened to the dial tone as if it were someone else doing the telephony.

Someone picked up the phone.

Elena was now on auto pilot, as if someone had taken over her body.

'I'm replying to your advertisement for dancers in the paper,' said a voice very much like Elena's; a voice coming from Elena's own mouth but one she had no control over.

'Oh, good, my name is Eva and I'm over here recruiting for vacancies in Almina. How can I help you?'

'I'm interested in working overseas,' said Elena, 'and your advertisement caught my eye.' Gradually, Elena's consciousness was now fighting for and winning the situation.

'What's your personal status,' asked Eva. 'Are you married? Divorced? Children?'

'I'm divorced,' Elena truthfully replied, 'With no children. My mother died just recently and so I'm at a loss. To be honest, if I died tomorrow no-one would miss me.'

Elena was pleased with this statement as she was sure it would help in what she now believed to be bogus auditions.

'I want a new start,' she continued, 'a new beginning, and to be honest, I need the money.'

'Thanks for being 'up front' with me,' said Eva, 'Why not come along for a chat and audition tomorrow afternoon at two.'

She gave Elena directions and the appointment was set. As she placed the handset carefully back into its cradle Elena thought,

'What on Earth am I doing?'

'Yes, I still have a good figure, but a professional dancer? It's so long since I did any dancing and at my age? Never mind, they can only say no.'

Elena picked up the phone once more.

'Hi Tasha, I rang the number and I've an audition in the city at two o'clock tomorrow. I won't be back by the time Mikhail gets home from school. Can he come round to your place until then?'

'Of course he can,' replied Tasha, 'but there's one condition.'

'What condition?' Asked Elena a little concerned Tasha was going to ruin her plan.

'That you tell me here and now all the names, telephone numbers and any details you have about these people. I've already lost a niece to them; I'll be blown if I have to lose a sister to them as well.'

'Not a problem.' Elena dictated all the names, phone numbers and details she had so far. Tasha wrote down the information and locked it in a drawer for safe keeping.

She went to bed filled with a cocktail of apprehension and euphoria. Euphoria she was at last doing something about her lost daughter and the apprehension, well that's obvious.

The next day Elena arrived in the city. Standing outside a cheap hotel she looked at the scrappy piece of paper and her own handwritten details. She looked at the doorway and checked she had the correct place.

Taking a deep breath she walked inside and in the empty foyer saw sign saying, 'Almina recruitment agency. Ballroom.' Elena followed the directions and found herself in a large empty space. At one end was a small platform meant to hold the band but on it stood a lonely CD player. The floor was empty but surrounded by tables and chairs stacked neatly around the edge. Eva, dressed in boots trousers and a bulky woollen sweater walked towards her.

'Welcome, my name's Eva'

'Elena. I'm here for the dancing job.'

'Don't mind me saying this,' said Eva eyeing Elena up and down, 'you do have a beautiful figure but you're a little older than I expected for a dancer.'

'Experience always beats enthusiasm,' said Elena defensively. 'Let me show you what I can do.'

'Have you brought your own music?' asked Eva.

'Yes,' said Elena, handing over a CD 'I'll dance to the third track. Where can I change?'

Eva pointed her in the right direction and placed the CD in the small player. Elena felt she needed to look young and so had bought a short top revealing her slender midriff and a pair of slinky black leggings which, if she was honest, made her bum look big.

Elena nodded at Eva who pressed the 'play' button. She started to move with the music and did fairly well. Had she had more time to prepare or even been a few years younger she felt she would have been good, or at least average. The truth is, the determination to find one's daughter doesn't a dancer make.

'I'm sorry, said Elena, 'I'll get it right with more practice. It's just the short notice between the advert and the audition.'

'Don't worry. Nerves affect us all. I've a few more people to see and then I'll be in touch.' Eva smiled at her, giving nothing away.

Elena left the city dejected since she had now blown her last chance of finding Kristina. On her way home she called in at Tasha's to collect Mikhail.

'I was crap,' she told her. 'There's no chance of my finding her now. I'm not going to be chosen, I'm sure.'

Mother and son walked home in silence. She knew her performance just wasn't good enough to impress anyone and she threw herself into bed and beat the pillows. 'Kristina, where are you?' she screamed, 'I've done everything I can do and don't know what to do next.' Eventually she went to sleep and was woken the next morning by the phone ringing.

146

'This is Eva.'

'Yes,' said Elena waiting to be told the worst.

'I'm really sorry,' said Eva, 'but I'm afraid you didn't get the job. You looked good and danced well but I, well we, actually, we felt you were a little old for the position we had in mind. All I can say is thank you for applying and good luck with your next application.'

'Oh God!' thought Elena, 'these people are for real. I thought they would take anyone desperate enough but it obviously isn't true. They actually are looking for talent.'

And then the dreaded thought came over Elena once again. How well did she really know her daughter? 'Is she capable of doing a runner and absconding? Is it really all my daughter's fault?'

That evening, Tasha visited Elena's house to hear how things had gone.

'Tasha, I tried,' Elena was distraught. 'What else can I do? I was crap. They said no. They must be legit otherwise they would've offered me a job.'

And this was how the next few days were passed. Elena sank into a deep depression as she tried to think of ways of finding her daughter and then becoming even more deeply depressed as she failed to come up with any other ideas. Three days later the phone rang. It was a man's voice.

'Hi Elena. How is Kristina doing?'

'Very well,' answered Elena realising who owned the voice, 'I'm sure she'll be sending money home soon. She just needs to get settled.'

'Good,' he said. 'Remember the interest is rising.'

Elena placed the handset carefully back onto the receiver and quickly did a personal audit. 'No daughter, debts to be paid, not good.'

No sooner than she had put the phone down than it rang again. It was Eva.

'Look, I'm sorry your application for the dancers job was unsuccessful but,' she paused for a moment. 'Don't feel insulted because if you're interested, we have a vacancy for a shop assistant in Almina. Someone has pulled out at the last minute and left us in a bit of a fix......'

"The investigation lasted four years resulting in the arrest of the Indian woman in Kerala. She has been charged with recruiting hundreds of women in India and forcing them to work as prostitutes in Almina. She used to target vulnerable women like widows, orphans, and those divorced and offer them good jobs but then forced them to work as prostitutes on arrival. The woman admitted her crimes saying that she used to charge clients between 27 and 54 Dollars to have sex with the girls. We believe she could have trafficked up to three hundred women. The investigation was a joint venture between Indian and Almina police forces and began when we were given a tip off when one of the victims escaped from a brothel seven days after she arrived."

Statement by Assistant Commissioner of Police.

Chapter 22

Kristina trudged into Eva's front room with her meagre belongings. Madam Olga smiled at her. 'Don't worry, we'll get on just fine.'

Dmtry's phone rang. He answered it with a short 'Ok.' He turned to Madam Olga. 'Taxi's outside. Time to go.'

Madam Olga took Kristina by the arm and the three of them made their way to the lift. They descended in silence 'like a condemned woman on her way to the gas chamber,' thought Kristina.

'Wait there,' Dmtry said as they stood in the entrance hall. 'I'll go out first and check for police.' He went through the double doors and looked carefully both ways before waving them outside. The driver opened the rear door of the taxi. Madam Olga and Kristina walked arm in arm onto the street; Kristina was blinded by the intense sunlight after spending so much time indoors and had to squint at the bright light.

She could just make out Dmtry sat in the rear of the taxi and saw him flinch as a pedestrian approached. He looked at Madam Olga with a concerned look on his face. Kristina took her chance and broke away from Madam Olga's grasp, running the ten metres to the pedestrian.

'Please, please help me!' She screamed. 'I'm being abducted by these people. Please help me.'

Dmtry and Madam Olga walked slowly but carefully towards the pair, not wanting to make a scene.

'You have to help me,' Kristina pleaded as she grasped his arm and looked into his expressionless eyes.'

The old Pakistani man looked at Kristina, then at Dmtry and once more at Madam Olga but just shrugged his shoulders. The true reality of her situation dawned on Kristina. She and the man did not share a common language. He didn't have a clue what she was saying. 'She's my daughter and we've arranged a marriage with a good man with excellent job prospects but she refuses to marry,' Madam Olga said to the pedestrian in a language and with reasons he understood. 'Children today have no gratitude for what we parents do for them.'

The pedestrian agreed whole heartedly and explained about his sister's child back home who'd tried to do the same. The family had beaten her into submission but now she was very happy and had a family of five. 'Three boys and two girls,' he added with pride.

They bade their farewells and Madam Olga led Kristina back to the car whilst Dmtry picked up her belongings and threw them into the car boot.

'Now that was a very silly thing to try,' said Dmtry. 'Firstly the police would have arrested you for having no visa and secondly, at Madam Olga's, every act of misbehaviour is punished.'

After a short silent drive through the suburbs, the taxi pulled up at a large villa surrounded by a high wall. There were no markings outside other than lipstick stains on the white plastic bell push surround where a lady had pressed her lips against it several times to make imprints.

'Subtle, but says everything,' thought Kristina. 'There's no mistaking that.'

Madam Olga used her key to open the huge metal gates for them to enter. As they slammed shut, it seemed to emphasize the beginning of Kristina's incarceration.

The double-storey, white villa was surrounded by plush lawns with sprinklers irrigating the grass. On the patio in front of the villa, three girls, dressed only in their flimsy house coats, sat on the steps leading to the garden attending to their manicure. They stopped briefly to say hello to Madam Olga whilst taking a sly glimpse at the new girl. It didn't do to show too much interest in new arrivals but they wanted to check out the competition.

The front door of the villa swung to one side.

'Afternoon Madam Olga,' said a young Asian man. He was tall, in his mid-twenties and dressed in jeans, shirt and sandals.

'Afternoon Hassan.' She turned to Kristina, 'Hassan's our cook and gofer. He'll attend to your every need. If you need food or anything from outside just ask Hassan and he'll 'gofer' it. You see, you don't have to leave the house for anything. Isn't that good?'

'Anything of a practical need,' said Dmtry punching Hassan on the shoulder playfully with his fist. 'He isn't a eunuch yet but he will be if he attends to anything other than a practical need.'

'I can't afford these girls on what Madam Olga pays me,' laughed Hassan. 'I'll go and make tea.'

'Dmtry,' said Madam Olga. 'Take Kristina through to the green room and explain to her what she did wrong outside the apartment building today.'

'Hi Miss Kristina,' said Hassan the next morning as he placed a tray by her bed. 'I've brought you tea and some toast.'

Kristina clutched the bedclothes and drew them over her naked body.

'No need to bother covering yourself here Miss. Naked ladies are a common sight; it's the ones with clothes on who take me by surprise.'

Kristina sat up and sipped the tea.

'Madam Olga is a good Madam,' he continued. 'Just treat her right, make her money and you'll get out of here in a year or two; then you can go on your own.'

Kristina's heart sank at the thought of two or three years in this place – and this was if she complied.

And if she didn't, how long then?

'When you're ready to settle in, just ring the bell by the bed and I'll take you to your room.' Kristina was left to consider her future.

George was in Almina for eight hours on a stopover He walked through immigration, collected his tourist visa and walked out of the airport into a whole new world.

'Now,' thought George, 'what can I find to do in eight hours?'

Most people would have taken the tourist sight-seeing bus. 'Almina in a day they advertised.' But not George. Buildings, views and touristy things just didn't attract him. No, George was happily married but away from home. No-one knew him and he had Carte Blanche to do whatever he wanted; provided he paid cash as his wife carefully checked all the credit card statements. An entry for 'Lotus Lily's massage parlour' on the statement wouldn't get past his business expenses account and certainly would arouse suspicion with the wife. Cash it had to be so he set off to find the nearest hole in the wall to get the 'needful.' He had searched the internet before leaving home in order to research the best of the 'nooky' places to visit in Almina. However, censorship had prevented any firm leads. Anyone foolish enough to openly advertise 'working ladies' in Almina was in for a short business life as the Almina police searched the web too and promptly arrested those crazy enough to give details of where they were to be found.

No, the old adages were always the best. 'If you want to know the 'whey hey', ask a taxi driver!' George hailed a taxi and climbed inside.

'Where to Sir?' asked the taxi driver.

'You tell me,' replied George, but I have fifty dollars for you here if you can find me a lady for an hour or two.'

'Ka-ching!' went the till in taxi driver's head. He pretended to think for a moment or two, knowing full well he was going to take George to Madam Olga's as he knew she would give him another fifty for bringing a customer to her whore house.

'I know a good place,' the taxi driver finally replied and set off in the direction of Madam Olga's; taking the long route just to bump up the taxi fare whilst he was at it.

Ka-ching!

On arrival, there were several cars and taxis at the front but this did not deter the driver. 'I'll come in with you, so you don't get cheated,' he said - knowing full well he had to go in with him otherwise they would treat George as a 'walk in' and not add the fifty dollar 'introduction fee' to his bill.

'How will I get a taxi back?' asked George looking at the deserted area and realising he didn't have roaming on his phone.

'Don't worry, I'll wait for you.'

'Ka-ching,' thought the taxi driver as he imagined the till ringing up even more money.

The driver rang the bell and Hassan opened the gate. 'Hello there,' said the taxi driver grabbing Hassan's hand and shaking it so vigorously it looked to George they had known each other all their lives.

'Welcome back,' replied Hassan, having no idea who the taxi driver was. Pretences had to be kept up, as here was a punter who didn't know the going rate.

Hassan escorted them into the house. The entrance hall was large with corridors going off at each side and George could see five or six doors leading off into rooms of unknown delights. There was a wide staircase which spiralled up to the promised land above – or at least George hoped.

'My friend wants a lady for a couple of hours,' the taxi man explained to Hassan.

'Anything in particular?' Hassan asked George. 'Black, white, yellow, skinny, fat? Madam Olga has them all.'

'I don't know really,' replied George. 'I'm not used to this sort of place.'

'Well we'll have to look after you then,' said Madam Olga appearing from nowhere. 'Hassan, ring the bell.'

Hassan moved to the side and pushed a switch on the wall. George heard nothing but gradually, one by one, the doors along the corridors opened and out walked some of the most beautiful girls he had ever seen. He moved his head from side to side as a bevy of beauties appeared out of the doorways and lined up along the corridors. He remembered to close his mouth as a string of sleek, long legged girls glided down the stairs to form a real stairway to heaven. George was truly overwhelmed. Never in his life had he been asked to choose which girl he wanted. When it came to women, he usually had to be grateful for the crumbs that fell from the tables of others and that hadn't been very often. He didn't even choose his wife as such – she chose him. It was all just too much for George and he couldn't make his mind up. He just looked from side to side, up and down the stairs, gawking at all the scantily clad ladies. He would have taken any of them and been happy. Spoiled for choice was an understatement at Madam Olga's!

'Where's Kristina?' whispered Madam Olga to Hassan. 'Go fetch her and put her on show.'

Hassan moved down the corridor as George continued to leer at the bare flesh before him.

'Come on Kristina, you know you have to come out and show yourself to the customers when the bell rings.' He led her to the door and stood her in line with the other girls.

Presented with nearly thirty gift wrapped female delights, George was panicking.

153

'Come on love,' said Madam Olga, 'which one do you want. Time is money.'

'How about the one on the stairs with the black hair?' chimed in the taxi driver wanting his money, hoping to move on and find more customers like George.

The girls showed off their legs and bodies in well-rehearsed stances smiling and even blowing kisses at him whenever he looked at them directly.

'You must decide quickly as we have other customers,' cajoled Madam Olga.

George spotted Kristina and looked her up and down.

'Not bad' thought George, wishing there had only been one lady and thus no choice to be made. His wife had made all the decisions in their family, so now he'd lost the knack. In any case this was one decision he couldn't ask his wife to make for him. George began to sweat as the onus of power took its toll.

He looked at Kristina once more. He studied her legs and moved his eyes up them and around the curve of her pert bum. He studied her breasts in detail. Moving his eyes up to her long aristocratic neck he started to feel excited. Something began to grow in his trousers.

'Maybe this is the one,' he was beginning to think to himself under the pressure of everyone watching and waiting for him to make up his mind.

'Yes take her,' the taxi man prompted.

'She's new, she's tight,' encouraged Madam Olga beginning to lose patience with George.

'Very nice girl is our Kristina,' encouraged Hassan.

George looked into Kristina's eyes and she looked directly back at his; a new experience. Normally women avoided eye contact and diverted their attention when George was near. He moved his attention down a little to her mouth and those beautiful full lips. Yes he could imagine placing his own on these and making sweet caressing kisses before using his tongue to part them wider and wider in order to gain an initial entry into the body that was to be his if only for an hour or so.

George thought he saw her lips open a little as he concentrated his full attention on her. He realised she was mouthing something to him but wasn't sure what it was. The movement of Kristina's lips silently repeated a phrase over and over again.

'Fuck Off. Fuck Off. Fuck Off. Fuck Off.'

Probably the only phrase with a universal meaning in any language.

'This one!' said George, realising what Kristina was telling him and grabbing the girl nearest him by the hand. 'I'll take this one,' he mumbled.

The girl gave a smug smile to the others as she led George to the bedroom and a couple of hours of bliss.

'He must be blind,' said the taxi driver to Madam Olga as he collected his money. 'She's the oldest and ugliest in the place.'

'Don't be nasty! When the lights are out all the girls look the same.'

The rest of the girls returned dejectedly to their rooms to await the next customer and the opportunity of working their way to freedom.

Apart from Kristina, who returned to her room with a broad smile on her face.

"My friend and I work as housemaids and were walking down the street in Almina when a car drew up and a man jumped out. They grabbed us and shoved us inside. Then they drove off. The whole thing took a matter of seconds. One of them tried to calm us down and told us they would find us better jobs in a hospital or in a shop but instead they took us to a house and locked us in a room with three other Asian women who told us they worked as prostitutes. One man returned to the room and tried to have sex with me but I refused and he beat me. A second man wanted the same but I grabbed a knife and told him to leave me alone. After they had left I borrowed a phone from one of the prostitutes and sent a text my sister who called the police." The two men lost their appeal against a ten year gaol sentence and were convicted of kidnap and unlawful imprisonment.

Testament from Court records.

Chapter 23

Nikki waved goodbye to Victor as she left the baggage collection area, passed through customs and outside to the greeters area where she stopped and lit up a cigarette. Taking deep drags, she replenished her nicotine levels. Looking around she saw Eva and the Mamasan leaning over the rail and holding a placard with her name on it. Nikki moved over to them.

'Are you Julie's friend 'Nikki'?'

Nikki nodded in acknowledgement.

'Follow us.'

The black BMW drew up and they all climbed in, Eva in the front with Nikki and the Mamasan in the back.

'This is Na'im our driver,' said Eva. 'He's been in Almina for five years – a long time.'

'Welcome to Almina, Ms Nikki,' said Na'im, 'I wish you a pleasant stay.'

'Thank you Na'im,' replied Nikki thinking he hadn't put much enthusiasm into his greeting.

The Mamasans mobile rang and she answered it. Nikki could not work out what she was saying as she spoke in English – a subject she had never bothered with whilst at school. The Mamasan disconnected and then rang another number and seemed to give directions to someone as her free arm flailed about from left to right in unison with the verbal directions given.

Eva went through her tour guide routine pointing out the main buildings and sites as they passed.

'Here's one hundred dollars in local currency,' said Eva passing over the usual thick wad of low denomination notes to Nikki. 'This is a float and we'll take it from your first month's salary.' 'Thank you,' said Nikki stuffing it into her handbag without counting it whilst inking she had already earned much more than this with her airport scam.

'We need to sort out your residence visa first thing in the morning. I'll need your passport for the authorities – we don't want to be illegal do we? Would you mind lending it to me for a day so I can make your stay legal? You can have it back tomorrow evening.'

'Yes, I know about the visa,' replied Nikki, 'Julie told me all about the passport.'

'Oh,' said Eva a little embarrassed, 'I'd forgotten for the moment you knew the business.' Not to be deterred, Eva continued from the script. 'What we've also done for you is to arrange a local SIM card for your phone. It's a different system here so yours won't work. If you let me have yours I'll change it so you can ring your Mother later.'

'Oh, thanks.' Nikki sounded grateful, 'I don't have a Mum or any relatives alive but there are one or two friends I'd like to ring to let them know I arrived in one piece.

Feeling pleased, Eva changed the SIM card collected the passport.

'Julie warned me about the SIM card too,' thought Nikki to herself, 'and you're welcome to the one you've just dropped on the floor of the car as it's already been cancelled by the person Philippe scammed it from – mind you, only after he had used it to ring half the world.' Julie had also pre-warned Nikki not only to keep her international SIM card hidden in her bag but to bring several photocopies of her passport along with her; plus a few stolen originals. Whilst she couldn't leave the country without the original, she could arrange almost anything inside it with just a copy.

The Mamasans mobile rang yet again and she talked in the same business-like manner as she had before. This was followed by an immediate but similar call to a second person.

'If these are business calls, can I have the next one?' Nikki asked, 'I might as well get straight to work.'

The phone continued to ring and at one point, the Mamasan held the mobile to one side and looked at Eva, who shrugged as if to say OK and so she continued her conversation. Nikki couldn't make out what she was saying but heard the words 'new' and 'tight' but little else.

The Mamasan broke into her thoughts. 'We'll drop you off now and you can shower there. His name's John, or so he says and it's five hundred dollars for all night. Take the money first but leave as soon as he goes to sleep. Afterwards, call this number and the driver will pick you up. We'll take your things to your room. When you understand the procedures, you can move in with Julie. By the way, you hand over all the money afterwards.'

'Great,' said Nikki and thought, 'I'm going to change that.'

They drove to 'John's' apartment and Nikki went up to his flat by herself. She rang the doorbell and 'John' opened the door.

'John?' she asked confidently. He nodded in response, 'I'm going to give you the best night of sex you've ever had in your entire life.'

John stared at her blankly with no response at all. 'What's up with this guy?' she thought. 'Am I at the right flat?' The realisation suddenly dawned on her that she was not speaking his language. Nikki pushed him into the flat, closed the door and embarked on an age long process requiring no translation.

Eva and the Mamasan waited outside for a few minutes until they were sure there was no possibility of Nikki returning early. 'We may as well go back to the airport,' said Eva. 'A new woman called Elena's arriving soon. She thinks she's coming to work in a shop.'

The Mamasan laughed as the car sped off to collect their next piece of air freighted merchandise for the company.

Elena followed the path trod by millions each year, through passport control, baggage collection, customs and out to the greeters area. She almost stopped breathing as the hot humid air entered her lungs. It was like walking into a sauna.

She moved over to Eva and the Mamasan who were holding a placard with her name on it.

As they drove off and Eva initiated the inauguration ceremony.

'This is Na'im our driver,' said Eva, 'he's been in Almina for five years – a long time.'

'Welcome to Almina, Ms Elena,' said Na'im, 'I wish you a pleasant stay.'

'Thank you Na'im,' replied Elena starting to feel a little afraid, thinking he hadn't put much enthusiasm into his greeting. After the ritual of exchanging the money and local SIM card in return for her passport and international SIM card, they drove home. Eva showed Elena into the bedroom and showed her the mattresses on the floor.

'You have the choice of the one on the left or the right,' said Eva as she pointed to the empty places. 'The other girls will be back soon.

I'll leave you now and let you get some sleep. We'll talk in the morning.'

Eva left and Elena heard the key turn in the lock. A wave of fear ran through her body but she tried to ignore it as she flopped on one of the mattresses. She left her suitcase in the middle of the room and took her mobile out from her handbag before throwing the bag onto a mattress. She dialled back home to let Mikhail know she was alright but nothing. She tried again to make sure she had the right international code. Nothing. She realised why Kristina had not contacted her; she had been conned out of her only contact with home. How could she ring Mikhail now? Elena burst into tears and flung herself fully dressed onto the mattress and cried herself to sleep; just as so many had before her and even more afterwards.

She was lying on the bed on the right; had she chosen the bed on the left, she may have been consoled by the small piece of graffiti Kristina had left behind.

Elena's sleep was interrupted by the unlocking of the door and the exclamation; 'Shit!' as Nikki tripped over her suitcase.

'Which idiot left that there?' the newcomer screamed. Elena pretended to be asleep and eventually calm was restored as Nikki bedded herself down for the rest of the night on the other mattress.

'Morning girls,' Eva said as she entered the room and woke Elena and Nikki. Get yourselves ready and come to the kitchen for some breakfast.

'Does the woman not understand what I did last night,' complained Nikki as she climbed off her mattress. She looked at Elena. 'Who are you?'

'I'm Elena, I arrived yesterday.'

'Nice to meet you, How're you enjoying the creature comforts of sleeping on the floor with a bunch of whores.'

Elena said nothing but smiled, picked up her suitcase with a meek 'sorry,' retrieved her bathroom things and went to shower and dress.

In the kitchen, Eva and Mamasan discussed the new arrivals.

'Nikki is sent from heaven.' The Mamasan smiled as she remembered Nikki's enthusiasm of the night before. 'She'll make us a lot of money.'

'And for herself,' said Eva. 'If only they were all like her. What do you think of Elena?'

'Hard to tell. She thinks she's come to be a shop assistant but deep down they all know what's happening and what's expected of them.'

'Not all, but most. I've no problem with Nikki, but Elena? To be honest she reminds me of someone, I don't know who but the feelings I'm getting aren't good.'

Elena and Nikki entered the kitchen for breakfast.

Nikki began to eat. 'I worked up one hell of an appetite last night.'

'Speaking of last night,' the Mamasan looked straight at her. 'Do you have some money for us?'

As Nikki handed over the five hundred dollars, Elena looked at the money wide eyed.

'And the tip?' the Mamasan held out her hand.

'How do you mean?'

'Well John always gives a tip and you hand it over too. At the end of the month we'll settle up and you'll receive your share of the earnings then. Don't worry, we won't cheat you!'

Nikki fumbled in her jeans pocket and produced another fifty dollars. Elena looked at the money on the table with disbelief, back home this was a fortune.

'Thank you and always remember we know everything.' She wanted the girl to know right from the start that she could not get away with anything

'Yes,' said Nikki thinking she would have some small change ready to hand over in future.

'Now,' continued Eva, 'is there anything either of you needs to ask me?'

'What sort of shop will I be working in,' asked Elena, 'What will I be selling?'

'SHOP!' exploded Nikki. 'The only thing you'll be selling is your body dear.' She saw the astonished look on Elena's face. 'Christ, she doesn't know does she? Sorry, I didn't realise. I thought you knew!'

'Well she does now,' retorted Eva. 'Is it going to be a problem for you?'

'Well, no.' Elena was thinking quickly, trying to recompose herself as fast as she could. If she was to find Kristina she would have to do whatever was necessary. 'But I've never done this sort of thing before.'

'Well you have,' Nikki laughed out loud. 'You just haven't charged for it before. Look, let's be friends. If it's alright with Eva why don't we work together until you get used to the business.'

'A great idea.' Eva welcomed the fact she would not have to call in Dmtry and his boys and the less she had to deal with Ari the better.

'Thanks,' said Elena gratefully, 'I'd like to work with you and I certainly could do with a friend.' She badly wanted to contact Mikhail, who would be worried sick, as he had not only had his sister disappear into thin air but now his mother too.

'How can we learn English?' asked Nikki. 'If we're to make real money out here then we need to be able to speak English.'

'Good idea,' said Eva, 'I'll arrange lessons. It's safer too. We had one girl who was new and was stopped outside by a plain clothes policeman. He asked for her name; she thought he was a customer and replied 'three hundred dollars' and so he said 'well Miss three hundred dollars, you're arrested.' She did three months in prison before being deported and we never saw her again.

That afternoon as Na'im drove them for their first lesson, Nikki and Elena exchanged a few pleasantries about where they had come from but each gave little away about their own circumstances - partly because they were still not sure how far to trust each other but mainly because Na'im was listening and seemed to understand their language.

'Did you learn much English at school?' asked Nikki.

'None.' She shook her head, 'and if I had, it's so long ago I'd have forgotten it all – and you?'

'We had lessons but no-one ever took any notice of the teacher. It was all about *learn this language for the culture and the great literature* which inspired none of us. If she'd linked the lesson to how the English language would help us later in real life it would have been better. In fact, if she'd said *'learn to speak English and you'll earn double as a prostitute in later life'*, we'd all been agog and done the homework as well!'

Elena laughed and then remembered she too was now a 'working lady,' and she felt sick at the thought of how she would get through this.

After a short drive, they arrived at a block of flats in a decent area of town and Na'im pulled up outside.

'It's apartment two zero four,' he said, I'll wait outside so don't try anything stupid like running away.'

'Don't worry, replied Nikki, 'With a hunk like you waiting for us we'll be eager to get back'.

They called the lift and ascended to the second floor. A sign on the far wall told them which way to turn and so they walked down the carpeted hallway to the flat and rang the bell. A middle aged lady opened the door. She wore a knee length blue dress, a light brown open cardigan and pink carpet slippers.

'Eva sent us,' said Nikki, 'We want to learn to speak English.'

'I'm Miss Velda, come in and sit at the table,' she said in their own language. Closing the door she followed them through to a table in the centre of the room. The room was cluttered with ornaments, photograph frames and knick-knacks seeming to have come from the 'everything a dollar' store. Elena thought it was far too fussy as there were frills on everything from the lamp shades to the cushions and she wondered how Velda kept it all dust free.

'Let's start with some basic conversation,' said Velda, 'My name is Velda, what is your name?'

Both girls repeated the sentence as best they could. 'Now try, 'how long have you been in Almina?' Again both girls repeated the sentence. 'Good; now try 'the weather is very good today'.'

'Can we stop there?' Nikki interrupted. 'It's business English we want to learn not conversational English.'

'Well what sort of Business English?' asked Miss Velda.

'Business 'business' English,' said Nikki in her own language. 'We want to know about the money and how to negotiate in it. We want to know how to ask the guy if he is ready to go to bed and fuck; we want to know how to ask if he wants to repeat the action and then how to ask if he's finished and can we go home now. We're hardly likely to discuss the weather in our line of work.'

Elena could see Miss Velda was not used to her students asking directly what they wanted but never the less she spent the rest of the lesson teaching them the Business English of a prostitute's trade. They found Na'im waiting for them and they drove off towards Eva and their new home.

'Do you have any family?' asked Nikki in a way of making polite conversation on their way back.

'Yes. Two children - a boy and a girl. My son's staying with my sister.'

'And the girl?' asked Nikki.

'I'm not sure where she is,' replied Elena trying to stop the tears welling up in her eyes. 'I worry about her.'

Nikki could see Elena was having trouble with her emotions when talking about her daughter and thought it best to leave this line of conversation for now. 'Have you talked to your son since you got here?' quizzed Nikki; fairly sure of the answer, in view of what Julie had warned her regarding Eva and the SIM cards.

'Mikhail, No. Eva has made sure I can't talk to anyone by taking my international SIM card.'

'Na'im, stop the car,' shouted Nikki, 'Elena needs to pee and there's a hotel there. She'll only be a minute.'

'Can't it wait?' asked Na'im losing patience with them both.

Elena was looking at Nikki in amazement and was just about to announce she was fine and didn't need the loo when Nikki jabbed her sharply in the ribs with something small but solid. Elena looked down and saw the mobile phone Nikki was now pressing into her hand.

'No, I really need to go,' said Elena. 'You can come and hold my hand if you like. I'll only be a minute and Nikki will stay with you here as a hostage.'

'But don't be long,' said Na'im, 'and don't tell Eva I let you go or I, actually 'we,' will all be in trouble.'

The car pulled up and Elena scrambled out. with the mobile cupped in her hand and out of Na'im's line of vision. She barely took time to look both ways for oncoming traffic before rushing across the road and entering the hotel.

'She really was desperate,' remarked Na'im.

'Something like that,' answered Nikki. 'Does the radio work in this car?'

Na'im found a radio station playing modern music and Nikki sat back; glad she now did not need to make conversation.

Elena raced into the hotel and had to force herself to slow down so as not to make a scene. She looked around. The lobby was huge with high ceilings and a glass wall stretching across the front of the hotel giving panoramic views of a pool, blue sky, blue sea and a palm lined beach. She could not see any signs to the toilets but then realised it was only Na'im who thought she was going there. She saw an empty seat over in a quiet corner of the foyer and moved over to it. Trembling with excitement she keyed in the numbers and listened.

'Beep, beep, beep, beep,' and then silence. She tried again with the same result. Elena became nervous as time was running out and she would need to get back to the car before Na'im came looking for her. She recalled the last number dialled on the screen and checked it carefully. 'No, that's it,' she thought and then realised she had not dropped the zero on the local codes when adding the international dialling code. Taking even greater care as the stress was causing her hands to shake and it was hard to hit the right key. She pressed the call button. A series of pauses and clicks came before it rang once.

'Mum is that you?' Mikhail must have been sitting by the telephone waiting for her call.

'Yes love, it's me.' Elena saw people looking at her and realised she must be shouting.

'Where've you been? We've been worried sick not hearing from you.' Elena could hear him holding back the sobs.

'I'm fine, love,' Elena said, trying to control her voice and talk calmly. 'There was a problem with the telephones so I couldn't ring before but it's all sorted out now. Look I can't talk for long as this isn't my mobile and calls are expensive but I'm here and I'm well. I've also met a very kind girl and we are becoming great friends so don't worry about me.'

'Elena, you there?' Tasha came on the line.

'Yes it's me and I'm fine.'

'Well don't do it again,' said her sister. 'We haven't slept since you left. Is there any news of Kristina yet?'

'No not yet, but its early days. I'll let you know when I've sorted out my own mobile. The one I brought with me doesn't work over here. It must be a different system and explains why Kristina hasn't telephoned. Listen, I've got to go now, please put Mikhail back.' There was a pause then, 'now listen Mikhail I'm fine. Don't worry about me. I love you. Ring you soon.'

'Love you too mum.' Elena disconnected the line before she broke down completely. She started to weep but noticed people were looking at her so she set off to find the toilets to wash her eyes and try to take away some of the redness.

'Thanks. I needed that,' Elena said as she climbed back in the car.

'I was about to come and find you,' said Na'im. 'You must've been saving up.'

The car drove off and Elena slid the mobile back to Nikki who mouthed silently 'ok?' Elena squeezed her hand and mouthed an equally silent 'yes, and thank you!' Elena's spirits were rising as not only had she contacted home but she felt in Nikki she had a friend she could trust.

'Any problems?' asked Eva as the three of them returned to the apartment.

'No,' replied Na'im to the girl's relief, 'they were as good as gold.'

'And how did the English lessons go?'

'Great,' replied Nikki, 'we're looking forward to trying it out for real.'

'Then get some rest and you can both go out tonight.' Eva was enthusiastic. 'I think you'll make a lot of money for everyone.'

They agreed but Elena was not as confident as she sounded. They went through to the bedroom which Eva unlocked for them and let them in. 'Don't worry, once you've settled in, you can have your own place. In fact one of our girls Melda, has just left. You'll no doubt meet her tonight.'

Nikki realised once Eva trusted a girl not to cheat her with money or run away, then she would be given a little freedom – if only to make space for other new girls. After a few minutes in the bathroom they settled down for a siesta. Nikki saw the graffiti on the wall by her bed and read it to herself.

'I want to go home, Kristina' and thought, 'stupid cow.' Why would anyone want to leave this place when there was so much money to be made? She looked across at Elena to say something but saw she was fast asleep. However, Elena's brain was racing; fretting over how she was going to pull it off tonight; and yet she had to, if she was to be creditable and stay to find Kristina.

After an hour of fretful sleep, Eva unlocked the door and told them it was time for the evening shift. Elena looked at Nikki and then at the blonde girl at the end of the room who was sitting up and wiping the sleep from her eyes.

'Hi,' said the blonde girl showing little interest in the new arrivals.

'I'm Elena and this is Nikki. We've just arrived.' Elena said in return and turned to look at Nikki who was now fully awake. 'What should I wear tonight? I thought I was going to work in a shop so I didn't bring anything red.'

'Don't bother,' said Nikki. 'Where we're going everyone will know who we are and what we're doing. To be honest it always surprised me why red should be associated with prostitution anyway. I mean why red and not blue? If anything red should remind men of a woman's period and that's definitely not related to sex.'

The blonde girl laughed, 'true. It doesn't matter what you wear. Some wear red from head to toe but for me, being normal, 'the girl next door,' seems to work. Mind you the blonde hair helps. Just think about going out on a Saturday night and dress and make up accordingly.'

Elena continued looking through her suitcase for something to wear.

'There's an iron in the kitchen Eva will let you use; you do have condoms with you don't you?'

'No, I thought I was coming to work in a shop!'

The blonde girl opened a small cupboard by her mattress and threw a box of twelve over to her. Don't take them all out with you as if you're stopped by the police with all those in your bag they'll arrest you for prostitution.'

'You're joking,' said Nikki.

'Sex outside marriage is illegal, so in their minds any single girl who has a condom in her bag is deemed to be a prostitute and arrested. Since married women don't need condoms either, they'll be arrested too, as they must be having an affair. Welcome to the logic of Almina! They used to stop us and empty our handbags and if they did find a condom, you were arrested, imprisoned and deported.

'So what do you do?' Elena was becoming intrigued. 'Have unprotected sex?'

'No way! We used to hide the condoms in our bras – one in each cup. The police couldn't search there without a reason.'

'And is it still like this?' asked Nikki.

'No, they had to stop looking for condoms. There were too many complaints when tourists and Western women were arrested but you still have to be careful.'

'Serves the Western women right, laughed Nikki, 'trying to do us poor working girls out of a living by giving it for free.'

'I need to get ready,' said the blonde girl, 'by the way, if you're not on the pill already then see Eva about it. Just in case you get drunk one night and make a mistake. Sex, pregnancy out of wedlock is illegal and so is abortion. The Orthodox Church has two or three newly born babies left on its steps each week.'

'But how could anyone just leave a child and walk away?' asked Elena.

'If you have an abortion you go straight to prison. If you give birth whilst still unmarried, go straight to prison. You cannot have a baby and take it out of the country without a passport for the bastard. To get a passport you have to report the birth and hello! Off to prison. Usually Eva and Mamasan hide the girl away until she gives birth and then dispose of the brat.'

'But that's awful.' Elena was appalled.

'No, they're actually good. Some send the girl to back street abortionists but most of them end up dead through infection. After all, when something goes wrong in an illegal abortion you can hardly go to the local A & E department. See Eva tomorrow, Elena and ask for the pill.'

When they were ready the Mamasan arrived and they met up with the girls from the room opposite. Elena looked at them discretely and was disappointed Kristina wasn't amongst them. They climbed into two taxis, arrived at the Almina Towers Hotel and took up their positions by the far pillar. Mamasan went to claim her corner by the bar and bought her usual pint of beer with two straws; with everyone in place, they were all set for business. Shop open!

It was a Thursday night, the beginning of the Almina weekend and the bar was filling up early. The Mamasan put down her beer and placed a beer mat on her stool to reserve it. She walked across to Elena. 'Let me introduce you to one or two customers.' She looked at Nikki, 'I don't think you need any help; you know more about this than I do.'

She took Elena on her usual tour of the bar introducing her to each and all as 'This is Elena, she's new, she's tight.' Fortunately Miss Velda hadn't included this in her business 'business' English lessons otherwise the normally reserved Elena would have been mortified to be introduced in this way. Nikki watched as the Mamasan paraded her new acquisition around the drooling hoard and saw the look of apprehension on Elena's face. She brought her back and advised her to keep looking at the men and smiling but Nikki could see Elena was struggling to keep her composure.

'Tell you what Mamasan,' said Nikki. 'Elena and I are a team. Let me find a punter who wants a double act for tonight - even if it means giving a discount. Elena can get used to the business and I can hold her hand and show her some of the tips.'

A look of relief spread across Elena's face and she used her eyes to plead with the Mamasan as if to say 'Oh please, pretty please.'

The Mamasan looked at them both and said, 'Sounds like a good idea. But only for one night mind you. The other girls will complain if you start to undercharge them.'

The Mamasan returned to her eyrie in the corner and sipped her beer.

'Come with me,' said Nikki as she led Elena over to an elderly looking man in the corner. He had his back to them so they came up behind him. 'I'll go one side you go the other and lean baby lean.' Nikki placed one hand on one cheek of his bum and squeezed. He turned around abruptly and she took hold of his hand. Elena went on the other side and leaned against him.

'I'm Nikki, what's your name?'

'Harold,' he replied.

'How long in Almina?' asked Nikki, the phrases learned in the afternoon flowing freely. This being business 'business' English for do you live here or are you a tourist?

'Two years. How about you two ladies?'

'We've been here six months,' lied Nikki knowing 'new' could be interpreted as 'desperate and cheap' but also to stay six months in Almina is business 'business' English for 'we're not tourists and have passed an AIDS test'. Being in Almina for more than a month meant she had passed a medical for her residence visa and so she was 'clean.' Reassured, Harold started to show interest. Nikki kept hold of his hand but with her free hand moved it up and down his chest. Elena followed suit and Harold started to feel an excitement he hadn't known for years.

'Is your family here?' asked Nikki which is business 'business' English for 'is your wife at home.' Nikki moved closer and rubbed her breasts

169

up and down Harold's arm.

'No,' said Harold, 'my wife's away on leave,' which is business *'business'* English for 'my flat is empty.'

Nikki leaned harder against Harold and Elena did the same. 'So, Harold. Would you like some fun tonight?' which is business *'business'* in any language.

'My friend and I both like you and want to come home with you.'

'How much said Harold?'

'How much would you like to pay?' she teased him, hoping Harold didn't know the going rate and would offer too much.

'One hundred dollars each all night.'

Nikki was disappointed. He knew how much to pay. 'Ok, but if we're really good, you give us an extra hundred between us.'

'It's a deal,' said Harold pleased with himself over the negotiations and looking forward to a night full of promise, 'but I don't want to be seen leaving with you ladies in case anyone I know saw me. You two leave now and wait outside. I'll be there in five minutes.' Harold looked around furtively to see if anyone was watching.

'Don't be long.' Nikki flashed her eyes at him and blew him a kiss as they walked away. 'Now look Elena, I'll do the business; you just watch and learn. In the taxi lean against him and put your hand on his thigh. At his place we strip naked, undress him together and lie one each side. You just keep stroking him from chest to thigh and do anything else you feel. The odd kiss from you will help but not essential. I will do all the rest. Got it?'

'Yes, and thanks.' Elena felt apprehensive at the thought of what lay ahead but she just kept thinking of Kristina and knew she had to play the part. Harold joined them and the three clambered into a taxi and drove off to a new experience for Elena.

"I was working on a market stall in Eastern Europe when I was offered a chance of a lifetime – to work in Almina as a nanny. When I arrived my passport was taken from me by Madame Anoush and I was sent to work in a brothel. She told me I had to work in the sex industry to pay back the money spent on bringing me out to Almina. There were days when she would beat us and not feed us if we did not work. She would line us all up and beat us with her shoe. One day when we were out, I complained that after all the work I had done she hadn't paid me any money. On hearing this, she rushed me into a taxi, took me home and proceeded to hit me with an iron bar.

After more than three years, I finally worked off my 'debt' and got my passport back but I couldn't leave Almina because I could not afford the fine for overstaying my visa." Records show that, in order to go home, the girl booked herself into an alcohol free hotel, drank several beers and lined the bottles up on the window shelf were they could be seen from outside. She then rang the police who arrested her, jailed her for two months for drinking before deporting her. Madame Anoush was sentenced to 13 years in prison for trafficking.

Report from Court records.

Chapter 24

The taxi pulled up outside an apartment block. Harold paid the driver and handed over a big tip. 'Always best to keep the driver happy so he doesn't drive off and call the police for the reward,' he thought, not wanting to push his luck. He knew full well it was illegal in Almina for a man to be alone in a taxi or even a flat for that matter with any female who was not close family. Elena felt a wave of panic as she saw the security guard sitting next to the lift but he just smiled back as the three conspirators waited for the lift.

'Don't worry.' Harold saw the fear on Elena's face. 'He knows me well and I give him a bottle of whisky every month. Some residents bring their 'visitors' in through the underground parking in the hope of avoiding his all-seeing eyes but there are closed circuit television cameras everywhere. He not only sees what's going on but turns up at the apartment door and interrupts the action just to get his 'baksheesh.' Being open about visitors is always best – providing you don't forget the whisky.'

He opened the door and let them in. The Sun had already gone down for the night and they could see the lights on in the other apartment blocks across the way. Harold moved over and closed the long, dark red curtains before returning to the front door where he locked it and placed the safety chain securely in place. 'We don't want any prying eyes or visitors do we? Don't worry; I've left the key in the lock so you can escape if you feel the need.' The room was painted white and had brightly coloured rugs scattered on the marble tiled floor. Large abstract paintings hung on the walls making the beige sofa set seem insipid in contrast.

He opened his wallet and counted out the wages of sin placing the notes on the shelf by the door. Nikki moved over and counted the notes carefully before placing them in her handbag and snapping it closed. 'You're supposed to leave the money there until the end,' Harold complained.

'Don't worry,' replied Nikki, 'you're going to have the time of your life. Do you have any vodka?'

He scurried off to find the vodka whilst Nikki found the bathroom. Elena could hear the sound of running water before Nikki returned in her shirt and panties and placed the rest of her clothes carefully over the arm of a chair. 'Why don't you go too,' Nikki whispered to Elena, 'and by the way, I wasn't washing my face.'

Elena looked at Nikki's panties with envy. They were clearly chosen as part of the 'uniform' to go with the job. Expensive, white lace cut high at the sides. Elena went to the bathroom and looked at herself in the mirror. 'Not as good looking as Nikki' she thought, 'and older too, but not bad. Not bad at all.' She removed her shoes and skirt to reveal the plain white cotton panties underneath.

'I'll need to go more upmarket if I'm to continue in this line of business,' she thought. The trouble was it had been a long time since she'd been undressed with a man and as the empty years had progressed, complacency had set in resulting in the panties of her youth being replaced with the knickers dictated by economics. Elena shrugged her shoulders and in the realisation that nothing could be done for now, removed the offending underwear, washed and dried herself carefully before slipping the cotton panties back on again. Picking her clothes up and placing them over her arm she glanced in the mirror once more and realised she still had her bra on. 'This had better come off too,' she thought and slipped it off from under her blouse. Elena examined the bra closely and saw it now for what it was, a piece of ironwork too big, too clumsy and designed never to be seen in public. 'This needs to go too. I need something sexy, something desirable - something expensive!' She returned to the room and, trying to look like she knew what she was doing, strolled over and placed her own clothes on the arm of the chair opposite to Nikki's discarded ones.

Nikki was clinging to a fully dressed Harold. One arm around his neck and the other arm hung down; her hand placed firmly on his crotch and squeezing his testicles through the material of his trousers in a rhythmic motion. Meanwhile her tongue was exploring his mouth with a finer precision than a dentist; from incisors at the front to molar at the back.

'I thought you'd run off,' he said coming up for air and motioning to a side table supporting a tumbler half full of vodka.

'No, just giving you two the chance to become acquainted,' replied Elena picking up the tumbler of vodka and downing half of it in a single gulp to steady her nerves.

'Careful, you don't want to pass out,' said Harold who was thinking of his investment and trying to balance the promiscuities a half drunken prostitute might put his way, against the risk of her passing out altogether.

Elena moved over to the other two carrying her glass with her. She could already feel the effect of the vodka and was starting to enjoy herself. She came up behind Harold and leant against his back. With her head on his shoulder she moved her free arm around the front and pushed Nikki's hand out of the way. She lowered his trouser zip and placed her hand inside. 'Who's a big boy then,' whispered Elena and took another large gulp from the vodka, emptying the glass.

'Got anymore?' asked Elena.

'Sure,' replied Harold and untied himself from the female knot and went to fill the tumblers once more.

'When did you last have sex?' asked Nikki using their native language.

'About ten years ago.'

'I can tell,' said Nikki looking at the two hard erect nipples stretching the material of Elena's blouse. 'You're not supposed to enjoy this work; you're just supposed to do it.' Nikki was starting to worry about Elena. The plan was to satiate the punter within a reasonable time and move on to the next one. Elena, she could see, was starting to enjoy the experience and, if Nikki wasn't careful, would spend the night here.

'Bloody amateurs!' she thought.

Harold returned with the replenished tumblers of vodka and handed one each to both girls.

'Cheers,' said Nikki, touched glasses with both Harold and Elena and pretended to drink herself.

'I'll take my vodka later and at home,' she thought, 'not whilst I'm working.'

Harold downed the full glass and to her astonishment so did Elena.

'Shit, we need to get out of here.'

Elena removed Harold's trousers completely; undoing the top button and belt before pushing them to the ground and off his legs - along with underpants and socks all in one movement. Sex is like riding a bicycle, one never forgets – even when inebriated.

Harold's member, now released from its constraints, sprang forward and bounced up and down several times, before taking up its forward erect position. Clearly his 'I'll follow you out in five minutes' from the hotel routine had nothing to do with not being seen with two girls but to give him the chance to go to the toilet and 'pop' a little blue pill.

Elena pushed Nikki out of the way and knelt down in order to caress the monumental appendage with her tongue.

'My turn now,' said Nikki trying to push Elena out of the way. But too much vodka and too much celibacy got in the way of common sense and Elena was having nothing of it.

Harold removed Elena's blouse and panties seeming not to worry they were not of the expensive designer type. She pushed him onto the sofa and started to climb on top of him.

'Elena, not without a condom,' Nikki said in a firm but singing voice but she was not listening and was starting to take aim at Harold's appendage.

'Elena, not without a condom,' Nikki said in a firmer and non-singing voice.

But Elena was now in her own world and was intent on pleasuring her body on Harold regardless of the 'health and safety' aspects of her job.

'Bloody amateurs,' Nikki wasn't impressed. 'What do I do now?'

'Harold. Would you like to see a lesbian act?' asked Nikki in a moment of inspiration.

'OH! YES.' Harold liked the idea and pushed Elena to one side, sitting back to watch the show.

Elena, having been one millimetre from a dangerous encounter with Harold, climbed off his body. After too many years of abstinence, she felt both deflated and frustrated at the interruption of her chance of glorious sexual pleasure.

Nikki reached out and took Elena's hand. She pulled Elena up off the sofa. Both naked, she placed her arms around Elena and pulled her close so their bodies pressed against each other from head to toe.

Whilst Elena's arms hung down limp, not knowing what to do, Nikki ran her fingers softly up and down the side of Elena's trunk as Harold, lying back on the sofa, began to pleasure himself.

Nikki gave Elena a peck on the cheek, then on the lips and then started French kissing with Elena pushing her tongue into Elena's mouth in a display exciting Harold even further.

Elena began to respond to Nikki's advances.

'Bloody hell!' thought Nikki once more. 'This is not for real; it's only for show.'

Panic was starting to engulf Nikki. How to get Elena out of here without upsetting the customer?

Nikki moved her hand onto Elena's breast.

Elena moved her hand onto Nikki's breast and started to tweak the nipple between her thumb and forefinger. Nikki felt a shudder move through her body as the seed of sexual excitement was planted in her. Harold started to work harder on his penis. Elena started to groan.

'Groan, who does that? Nobody groans these days' thought Nikki as she realised this situation was getting totally out of hand.

Nikki moved her tongue from Elena's lips to her ear. Moving her tongue in and out and around the ear; Elena became ecstatic. Harold almost wet himself. Nikki whispered to Elena, 'You're pissed. We need to get out of here. We need to get him unspunked in the next ten minutes and then go home. Understand?'

Elena nodded as only a drunk can.

'What a sad bastard,' thought Nikki as she looked at Harold and knowing that the meaningless gesture occurring between the two women meant so much to the watching man.

Nikki pushed Harold back on the sofa and put one knee either side of him. She reached across and removed a condom from her bag (placed strategically within reach from the outset) and unrolled it on Harold. Within two or three movements Harold was, to use the professional term, unspunked. Job done, the effect of the vodka and the unspunking had left Harold asleep.

'Come on,' she said, 'time to go.'

Nikki helped Elena dress, placed an unopened bottle of vodka from Harold's bar in her bag before both of them crept out of Harold's apartment and hailed a taxi to take them home.

Returning back to Eva's they rang the doorbell and were invited in.

'How did it go?' asked Eva.

'Don't ask,' replied Nikki supporting a drunken Elena.

'I'm going to throw up. Where's the loo?' asked Elena.

Eva and Nikki helped her to the toilet and hung Elena over the toilet seat. She felt awful being watched by these two almost strangers.

'She did well,' stated Nikki. 'Let's get her to bed.'

They dragged Elena to their room and she veered over to Nikki's bed space and collapsed on it.

Eva looked at Nikki as if to say 'what to do?'

'Leave her,' said Nikki and went over to sleep on Elena's bed.

Elena, fully dressed and almost comatose, turned over and through her bleary eyes read on the wall, 'I want to go home, Kristina.' She reached out and traced the letters one by one with her index finger and read the words again. 'I want to go home, Kristina.' Then, she passed out completely.

"I paid 1000US Dollars for a visa to come to Almina from Bangladesh. On arrival, I was met at the airport by a man who put me in a flat and forced me to have sex with strangers. One day a customer, also from my home country, gave me his number and offered to help me. I escaped and went to live with him but he also tried to force me to have sex with other men. When I refused, he tied my arms and legs and kept me locked up." A Syrian heard the girl crying for help from the window of the flat and reported the matter to the police.

Report from Court proceedings.

Chapter 25

'How's the new girl getting on?' asked Dmtry as he and Madam Olga shared a bottle of vodka together one night. 'She's been here three weeks. Has anyone chosen her?'

'No Dmtry, not a single one. She comes out with the others, stands well, displays the goods, but no-one chooses her. It's beyond belief. Kristina is a good looking girl; we have ninety customers a night and thirty girls, so each one on average, should perform three tricks a night. You can't beat the odds and yet here we are, three weeks – nothing. No-one chooses her.'

'Do you think she's a lesbian?' asked Dmtry.

'Well, there are plenty here who are and she hasn't shown any interest in sex of any kind.' Madam Olga was puzzled. 'Besides, if she is I can still make money from her. She doesn't seem interested in anything.'

'Maybe we should do some market research,' suggested Dmtry.

'Market research? We aren't high street grocers Dmtry; we're a brothel for Gods sake!'

'What I meant is, let's try her out. Who's your best customer? One you can trust and will give feedback.'

'Well Wally visits twice a week. Has done for years.'

'So let's give him a freebie. We'll ask Wally to come and select Kristina no matter what. He can tell us what happens and we can return his money. We've a big investment in Kristina and we can't let it go without trying to do something. Put them in the blue room. There are cameras and a partition behind the bed so you can keep a close watch.'

Kristina sat on the edge of her bed in the room she shared with four other girls. The other girls chatted away about what they would do as soon as they had earned their passport. Kristina sat cross legged, filing the rough edges from a broken nail on her left index finger, whilst thinking of home and her mother. She did this all the time and rarely had any desire to chat with the other girls. They had tried to make friends with her but she always spurned their advances. The bell rang and the girls stood up and went to the corridor to show their wares. Kristina stayed where she was − carrying on as if the bell hadn't rung.

It was not long before Hassan entered the room to perform the usual ritual.

'Kristina, Madam Olga says you've to come out or she'll fetch you. Please; don't make any more trouble for yourself.'

She stood up and went into the corridor where the other girls stood tall to give them height, smiling whilst gyrating from side to side. Kristina slumped and frowned.

She was confident she would not be chosen as the guy was a regular and always went for long legged brunettes.'

Wally looked up and down the row of girls in each corridor, taking a sly glimpse at Kristina as he did so. He ran his eyes up the staircase admiring all the good points of each and every girl who lined the banister.

'Take me, I love you' the fake smiles said as they really meant, 'I have a child and mother back home to support.'

Wally's gaze passed them by and the smile on each girl's face disappeared as quickly as it had been switched on. His eyes returned to the girls down the corridor and eventually rested on Kristina

'Shit!' thought Kristina. 'He is going to choose me.' A feeling of sheer panic took over. She tried the technique that had saved her so far; mouthing the words that were silent to everyone else but ever so loud to the punter.

'Fuck Off. Fuck Off. Fuck Off. Fuck Off.'

This just seemed to make matters worse. He still kept looking straight at her. She looked at the floor in the hope ignoring him may make him go away.

'I'll take that one,' said Wally pointing to Kristina. Since Madam Olga was paying, Wally thought he would push his luck.

'Two hours please − with everything.'

'A good choice,' said Madam Olga. 'Kristina's very good in bed.'

The other girls smirked as they walked past her back into the comfort of their room.

'This should remove the cobwebs from your cunt,' whispered one girl as she passed Kristina. 'Wally just comes and comes.'

'Go to the bar and get yourself a drink,' said Madam Olga turning to Wally. 'Hassan will call you when Kristina's ready for you.'

Wally left with Hassan, leaving Kristina and Madam Olga in the corridor.

'I'm not doing it,' said Kristina. 'I'm just not doing it.'

'Now listen here. You are not only going to 'do it' but you're going to 'do it' well.' Madam Olga had run out of patience.

Dmtry appeared from the far end of the corridor and approached them.

'Now come on Kristina, let's not have any trouble. You should be pleased. The customer chose you out of all these beautiful girls. He could have had any one; but he chose you. Think of it as a compliment.'

Dmtry took Kristina by the arm and forced her down the corridor to the blue room. Madam Olga went into the next room. The closed circuit television was already working and she could see Dmtry push Kristina into the room.

'Take your clothes off,' he said. She was adamant. 'No, I've told you I won't do it.' She was wearing a short nightie, the only clothing allowed in the brothel. Madam Olga kept their other clothes locked away for 'safe keeping.'

Dmtry reached out and ripped it off leaving her stark naked.

'Now get on the bed and lie down.'

'I won't do it,' cried Kristina holding one arm across her breasts and the other over her crotch - trying to cover her modesty as best she could.

Madam Olga opened a small trap door in the partition between the blue room and her own room. It was just behind the headboard so anyone in the blue room could not see it.

Dmtry pushed Kristina onto the bed so that her head fell on the pillows.

'Ouch! That hurts,' she screamed as she felt her head bang against the head board and her hair being pulled out by the roots.

'Hello, Kristina.' Madam Olga had placed her hand through the trap door and taken the opportunity of grabbing a handful of her hair when she had fallen back on the bed.

'It's me. I'm going to keep hold of your hair for the next two hours. Every time you refuse to have sex or if you don't throw yourself into your work with enthusiasm, I'll pull so hard your hair will almost come out in my hand.'

Taking a tighter grip on Kristina's hair, Madam Olga spoke to Dmtry through the trap door.

'We're fine here Dmtry. You can go now. Please ask Hassan to bring in Kristina's new friend.'

'Hello.' Wally spoke as he walked gingerly into the room and saw Kristina lying naked on the bed.

'How are you? You look beautiful.'

There was a pause before Wally saw her head bang suddenly against the head board and she let out a quiet guttural noise as her face turned into a grimace.

'Fine thank you,' Kristina spoke coldly.

'Better,' whispered Madam Olga releasing the tension on Kristina's hair.

'I'll undress then,' said Wally - not sure what to do with this girl lying flat on the bed waiting for him.

He removed all his clothes and stood facing her. He was glad he had taken the extra sex pill before leaving home but the girl didn't seem interested. She just lay there, flat on her back, staring at the ceiling.

'Well at least have a look at the goods,' said Wally. 'I'm over here, not up there on the ceiling. Well not yet anyway.'

Kristina didn't move at all but then she made a sudden movement of her head and grimaced once more. Madam Olga allowed some slack in her hair and she was able to raise her head a little to look at Wally's pride and joy.

'Now that's more like,' said Wally. 'Why not come over here, kneel down and let's start with a blow job?'

'Fine by me,' replied Kristina thinking this was a way of escape from Madam Olga's grip on her hair and possibly the entire situation.

Madam Olga gave a sharper tug on her hair.

'Oh no you don't!' she whispered to Kristina. 'Tell him to come over here.'

'Why not come over here and lie beside me?'

'Ok, but it had better become more exciting - and quickly,' said a bored Wally. He was becoming more and more exasperated with this girl, who refused to move off the bed.

Wally climbed on the bed and started to play with Kristina's nipples squeezing them between thumb and forefinger and rolling them gently between the two.

'Get off my boobs. Ouch!' said Kristina as Madam Olga pulled hard on her hair once more.

Kristina realised she would have to take control of the situation if she were to get out of it and decided on a way forward.

'It's ok,' said Kristina. 'I've just had my period and they're a little sensitive.'

Thoughts and images of things men are not meant to think of passed through Wally's mind and the once erect penis started to droop. The biggest form of erectile dysfunction is the thought of a woman's period which even the little blue pills can have problems overcoming.

'Don't worry, just be gentle.'

Wally started to explore Kristina's nipples once more fooling himself that they were beginning to respond to his stimulation.

He moved his hand down to her crotch and placed his fingers between her legs.

'Get your hands of my fucking … Ouch!' Kristina's head snapped back against the head board once more, in response to Madam Olga's tug on her hair.

Wally was getting more and more confused with this girl. Why did she not move from the bed? Why did she keep acting as if she was in pain? Why did she keep changing her mind?

'It's ok,' she said. 'Carry on.'

It's alright to say keep going but blowing hot and cold water over Wally's sexual exploits, even 'all expenses paid sexual exploits' was starting to annoy him. He was beginning to wonder if he could 'do it' even if this girl ever gave him the chance.

He gingerly moved his hand down to her crotch again, remembered what she had recently told him and then decided against it. He was then struck by a moment of resolve.

'Stuff it,' he thought. 'The girl is getting paid for this.'

Wally reached over to the bedside table where Madam Olga always kept an ample supply of condoms and slipped one on. He rolled over

Kristina and forced himself between her legs.

'Get off me... Ouch!' she cried, as Madam Olga tugged on her hair once more.

'I'm only going to fuck you,' said Wally as if Kristina thought he was going to do something bad to her.

'You're not,' retorted Kristina.

'Ow, that hurt!' She screamed as her head banged against the head board once more. Madam Olga was losing patience now and pulling extra hard.

'What's going on here?' asked a puzzled Wally. 'I don't understand this.'

'No problem, it's just too soon. Why don't we have some foreplay first?'

Wally brightened. 'This is more like it,' he thought.

Why not come up here and give me a pearl necklace?

Madam Olga smiled.

'Good she's given in. Not before time mind you.'

Wally took the condom off and moved to Kristina's head which was still inexplicably fixed to the pillows. He knelt astride her shoulders and gave his penis a few strokes to regain the erection.

Kristina brought her hands up and stroked it herself - fondling his manhood and making Wally delirious.

'Now let's put big boy in my mouth and we'll take him to heaven.'

Wally started to enjoy himself at the thought and put his hands behind him to feel her breasts.

Kristina put his penis in her mouth and ran her tongue over it ever so gently.

Then she bit it hard; sinking her teeth into s flesh as far as they would go.

'Get off me you bitch!' Wally screamed as tears came to his eyes.

But Kristina just bit harder.

'For God's sake, stop! You'll bite the bloody thing off.'

Madam Olga was taken by surprise but soon saw what was happening from the television screen.

She pulled as hard as she could on Kristina's hair but to no avail. Kristina just bit harder.

Dmtry and Hassan, hearing the noise, ran in and tried to force open Kristina's jaws but couldn't get enough leverage to open them.

Wally was screaming so loudly the other girls ran into the room.

Dmtry looked around for something to force open Kristina's jaws.

Madam Olga pulled as hard as she could on Kristina's hair but still Kristina held on.

'Hassan you go around the other side,' shouted Dmtry taking control. 'You hold her nose tight shut so she has to breathe through her mouth,' he shouted to one of the girls. On the count of three Hassan, we take one hand on the top jaw and one on the bottom and prise her jaw open.'

'For Christ's sake get on with it,' sobbed Wally. 'She's going to bite the bloody thing off in a minute.'

Under the intense pressure of Hassan and Dmtry prising open her jaws, the girl holding her nose and Madam Olga tugging hard on her hair, Kristina relented and let go.

As Wally rolled naked on the floor nursing his injury with both hands, Dmtry punched Kristina hard in the face.

'Enough,' said Madam Olga as she entered the room all flustered. 'I've reached the end of my patience. You're nothing more than a stupid cow and stupid cows end up on the Chinese farm. I'm taking you to market tomorrow.'

"I was a hairdresser in Pakistan but I was lured to Almina by a job in a salon. On arrival I was taken to a villa where I was told I would work in prostitution but I refused. She beat me and brought men to have sex with me. The Madam would drag me around the brothel on a lead attached to my hair. She tied my hair to a long rope and as I lay on the bed, she sat outside the room behind a slightly open door and watched. A Pakistani man paid 27 Dollars to have sex with me. If I refused and yelled or did not please him she pulled the rope to hurt me. After one month I wrote notes asking for help on small pieces of paper and threw them out of the window. After three days the police visited the villa, arrested the traffickers and saved my life. "

Report from Court case

Chapter 26

Elena watched as Kristina walked down the street. Her daughter was smiling, her hair flung back as she strode confidently along the pavement. Elena shouted out 'Kristina, over here,' but she did not hear.

Elena shouted more loudly, 'Kristina, I'm here for you.'

The girl kept on walking towards her but on the other side of the street.

Elena crossed over. A car - which Elena had not seen in her haste to find Kristina, swerved to avoid her. The horn blew but she did not care. It was Kristina over there, her daughter, and she was not going to lose her again.

Elena was now standing on the opposite pavement and Kristina was walking straight towards her.

She shouted out again, yelling this time, 'My dear, I've come to take you home!'

Kristina continued to walk towards her, not recognising her mother, who was now standing still, with arms outstretched to welcome her.

She reached out to touch Kristina, tears of joy in her eyes but her daughter passed by - tantalisingly out of reach.

'Elena! Wake up!' Nikki shouted. She shook her by the shoulder.

Elena shouted out once more, 'Kristina it's me, your mother.'

'Wake up Elena! You'll have everyone coming in here unless you stop.'

She opened her eyes and saw the white ceiling. She could see the blurred outline of someone sitting over her. When she sat up, the entire world spun around, making her so dizzy she had to lie back down. This made her feel nauseous and she could feel she was about to be sick. She sat up again and the room did one more spin – as if especially for her and for her alone. Staggering to her feet, she made her way to the bathroom.

'Sorry,' said Elena as she returned to the bedroom avoiding Nikki's amused smile. She raised her head sheepishly and gave Nikki an embarrassed look of apology.

'Enough said?'

'Yes, enough said,' Elena replied. 'It was the first time. I was so nervous. I didn't eat anything and then I drank. Not a good combination.'

'No,' mused Nikki. Do you remember anything? Anything at all?'

'I remember going out to work at the bar, talking to someone and then going somewhere in a taxi but nothing else.'

'Well it's probably for the best. Some things are best forgotten.'

'True,' said Elena. 'But I can't help feeling there was something I should remember. Something very important.'

'Well, at least he paid us and this is the important thing. Mamasan is pleased with you. I didn't tell her about the rest.'

'Thanks Nikki.' She replied as she continued trying to remember what the very important thing was.

'I can't face breakfast,' said Elena 'I can't. I just can't.'

'Oh yes you can' Nikki told her. 'We've more work to do, to build our reputation as the top earners in this place. Have a shower and let's go to work.'

Elena stood quickly and realised it was a mistake, 'you go down first, and I'll follow.'

'By the way,' asked Nikki. 'Who's Kristina?'

'Kristina?' replied Elena trying not to let the alarm show in her voice. 'What do you mean?'

'Well you were shouting out to someone called Kristina as you came around.'

'I don't know any Kristina,' said Elena, quickly gathering her thoughts. 'It must've been the vodka.'

'Yes,' it must have been the vodka.' Nikki did not believe a word Elena had said. She knew Elena was hiding something regarding this 'Kristina' and she was determined to find out what it was.

Later, at the Almina Towers Hotel, Nikki looked across the bar and blew a kiss to a man on the other side but he turned away and avoided her advances.

'Waste of time today,' she said to Elena. 'Not many in and those who are here have only come to look. Let's wander around and survey the field.'

'Hi there,' Nikki spoke in her sweetest voice to a young European man. 'You thinking of taking a lady today?' asked Nikki in her most persuasive tone.

'You show me a lady and I'll take her,' he replied.

'We're all ladies,' retorted Nikki, 'you just need more beer to realise it.'

'You know,' she pontificated, 'everybody thinks it's exciting being a whore but it's not. Most of the time we spend standing around, bored to death, trying to find a customer. When we do eventually find one, we try our best to do the job as quickly as possible in order to return here and stand around, bored to death again, waiting for the next customer. For every thirty minutes I spend screwing, I spend two or three hours standing around waiting. And you know what? The screwing is more boring than the waiting.'

'Are we not feeling happy today?' asked Elena.

'No we're bloody well not. In real life I wouldn't give time of day to these morons if they asked me out for a date but I do it for the money. What's the old saying, 'Wham Bam thank you Ma'am? Well in my book it's 'wham, bam thank you ma'am; 'ka-ching;' and the money is in our hand. Or better still, ka-ching, wham bam thank you ma'am.'

'I take it your friend is not very happy?'

'Pardon,' asked Elena as she turned to the man standing next to her.

'Sorry, I was eavesdropping and heard your friend just now.'

'Oh, don't worry about her. She's just bored when things are quiet.'

The man next to her was in his mid-fifties, well dressed and wholly respectable.

'I'm James,' he introduced himself. 'What's your name?'

'Elena,' she replied thinking he was the only male in the universe not called John.

'Nice to meet you Elena,' said James, taking her hand in his.

'Don't get carried away,' interrupted Nikki, 'holding hands in public is OK if you are both men but a man and a woman holding hands in public is asking for trouble - even if they're married.'

'You're not a happy pixie at all today are you?' remarked James. 'You're like a legless dog.'

'Are you calling me a dog?' asked Nikki pretending to take offence.

'No,' certainly not. 'I was thinking more like 'me-no-paws'.'

'You'll be called 'me-no-dick if you aren't careful.'

'Wouldn't be good for business though would it?'

'Fancy a three some?' said Nikki. 'My friend is dynamite in a threesome, especially after a couple of bottles of vodka.'

'Is this true?' asked James.

Elena went a little red and ignored the question.

'No, I was thinking of just me and Elena actually. But there's no chance as my wife's at home.'

'Why not do a three some with her then?' asked Nikki.

'I don't think she'd appreciate it somehow.'

'You could go back to Elena's place?' Nikki continued.

Elena turned in shock; as she clearly could not take James back to the Mamasans with all the other girls watching.

'Is it possible?' asked James.

'No, but there are places to go,' spoke Nikki confidently.

'How much?' enquired James.

Nikki gave Elena a nudge and she spluttered out 'One hundred dollars for one hour?'

'Sounds good,' replied James. 'I'll go and settle my bill. Stay here pretty lady.'

James went off to the bar.

Elena looked at Nikki, 'and just where am I supposed to take him?' she asked.

'Ring this number and book a bed for an hour. She'll give you directions on how to find the place and confirm if they have a bed free.' Nikki took Elena's phone and put a number in the memory.

'It's behind Almina Park hotel,' she told her friend. 'Ask for directions on the way.'

When James returned, they left and started to look for a taxi but there were none to be found.

'Private taxi sir?' asked a man pointing to his private car.

'Yes,' said James wanting to keep a low profile and not wanting hassle with a legal taxi driver since he had consumed alcohol and was about to enter a car with a woman who was not a close relation. An illegal taxi driver would not report him as he would bring the law down upon himself.

'Where too?' Asked the taxi driver as they sped off.

'Behind Almina Park hotel,' she managed to mutter. 'I'll find out exactly in a moment.' Elena started to ring the number.

'Shirley's? I know Shirley's,' said the taxi driver.

On their way, James and Elena exchanged shy glances and touched hands once or twice – by accident of course.

'Hi Shirley? Do you have a bed for an hour?' enquired Elena over her mobile.

'I'm a bit busy at present but I'm sure I can find you a place.'

'Pass the phone to your driver and I'll give him directions.'

Elena tried to pass the phone over.

'No, it's Ok. I know Shirley's,' he said.

'But what's your flat number?' asked a panicking Elena.

'Flat 103,' was the abrupt reply terminated by the phone going dead.

The taxi pulled up outside a modern, 20 storey apartment block. The Almina Park hotel was directly in front of them - but nowhere near a park. James asked the driver.

'How much?'

'As you feel,' he replied.

James handed over ten dollars. Far too much for the short journey but James based it on 'half for the half fare, the rest for 'shush' money'.

As they went inside, Elena was trying to show an air of confidence, as if she had done this many times before but the cracks were showing.

Entering the lift they were joined by a fat man who stood behind them. They ascended in silence. As they left the lift Elena thought she heard a voice from behind say 'have fun,' but they ignored it and went to find Shirley's.

'This way,' said Elena taking charge. She remembered Nikki telling her. 'You're the boss. This is what they're paying you for.'

A young Philippina girl opened the door.

'Hi. Shirley?' asked Elena timidly.

'Come in,' said Shirley giving a broad smile and acting as she and Elena were lifelong friends.

They walked into the apartment. It had a kitchen off to the left with a breakfast bar separating it from the open lounge and hallway.

'Sit down,' said Shirley motioning to some bar stools around the breakfast bar. 'It won't be long. We're busy at present. Beer?'

'Yes please,' replied James.

'No thanks,' said Elena feeling sick at the thought of more alcohol.

Shirley opened the can of beer and placed it before James.

'Three dollars for the beer and fifteen dollars for the bed.' James handed over a twenty dollar note.

'What's your role here?' asked James thinking he wouldn't mind an hour with Shirley.

'I'm just the doorkeeper here,' she replied quickly seeing the look on Elena's face.

A couple came out from the behind the curtain at the far end of the lounge. They came towards James and Elena. The man gave James a shy nod of the head.

'Don't leave together. Man leaves first,' Shirley reminded them. The man left followed by the girl a few minutes later. Shirley went behind the curtain and busied herself with the bed.

'OK. Clock starts now,' she said emerging from behind the curtain. Elena took James's hand and led him behind the curtain. There was a double bed, mattress, sheet and nothing else. A gaudy blue curtain with bright red flowers covered a small window and stopped the bright Sun floodlighting their afternoon tryst. They went to opposite sides of the bed. James sat on the bed and started to unbutton his shirt as he looked across at Elena who was in the process of removing her blouse and bra.

'Haven't you forgotten something?' asked James.

'Forgotten something?' Elena looked at her bag on the side then back at James. 'How do you mean?'

'Money? 'Don't you want your money?' He took his wallet out of his trouser pocket and handed over a one hundred dollar bill.

'Oh, thanks. I always hate this part; asking for the money,' Elena was embarrassed, not wanting to let on she had never, ever asked before. She placed the money in her bag and returned to undressing.

'Nice!' said James as he eyed her body. He stood up, undid his belt and removed his trousers. Elena was now lying naked on the bed, her head propped up on one arm as she watched James remove the last vestiges of dignity.

He lay down beside her and put his arm around her. Their bodies moved together to give intimate contact from head to toe. Elena could feel his erection growing. She kissed him full on the lips and used her tongue to full effect. James was hard and big by now and responded by using his own tongue to push Elena's forcefully back into her own space. Anyone who says prostitutes don't kiss either hasn't been with one or hasn't paid enough. Elena, mindful of the time limit, felt under the pillow for the condom she had placed there earlier. She reached down and unrolled it over James erection. She lay back down on the bed and opened her legs; took hold of James by the waist and guided him so he was now over her and ready to enter. She smiled at James; he smiled back and pushed his penis deep inside her.

Elena felt a tingle of pleasure rush through her entire body.

James removed his penis completely, looked directly into Elena's eyes and prepared to enter her once more.

'Ah! Ah! Ah!' He shouted.

'Shush,' whispered Elena. 'They'll hear you.'

Outside in the kitchen, Shirley heard the noises of bliss and thought, 'good girl, you can come again. Why wait the hour if you can be back on the game after thirty minutes.'

Shirley's phone rang. 'Yes, no problem. Come now I have one bed just finishing.'

'Ah!' James repeated and came down hard on Elena – missing the mark and stabbing her in belly with his penis.

'Ow! That hurt,' shouted Elena forgetting her own words of caution. 'You are squashing me' she whispered. 'James, Get off me you are hurting.'

But he did not move. He was lying on top of her and she was pinned to the bed peering from behind James's right ear at the ceiling. She tried to push him off but he was too heavy.

'James,' she whispered. 'Are you OK?'

There was no reply. Elena suddenly realised what was really meant by the phrase 'dead weight.'

Since she couldn't push him off, Elena put her arms around and rocked gently from side to side. Each time she rocked further and further until she managed to slide out from underneath his body. She sat up and looked at James who had gone a deathly white colour.

'Oh no! What do I do now,' she thought.

'James, are you OK?' she whispered in a vain hope of getting a response but none came. James was dead.

Elena knelt over him and taking both hands tried to resuscitate him in the way she had once seen in a movie. Unlike the movie, James did not respond.

But what to do now?

Elena listened for noises from the other side of the curtain. She could hear Shirley talking to someone but it was normal conversation and it was clear no-one knew of the drama developing behind the curtain.

She climbed off the bed and opened her bag. Taking out her mobile phone, she pressed the keypad ferociously. It was ringing.

'Please Nikki, don't be working. Answer the phone. Answer the phone. I need you.'

'Mmmmmm,' came a voice from the other end of the phone in English. 'That's nice.'

'Nikki, is that you?'

Elena tried to keep the panic from her voice and speak quietly as she could hear Shirley talking to new customers, who were clearly waiting for their turn in this bed.

'Just keep going lover boy.' Nikki's voice came over the phone again.

'They won't be long,' Shirley's voice wafted through the curtain, 'only a few minutes left.'

'Nikki, is that you?' hissed Elena. 'Don't mess about, this is urgent.'

'Oh! Push harder big boy.'

'Nikki?'

'Course it's me' answered Nikki in Elena's own language, so the punter couldn't tell what was being said.

'What are doing?' asked Elena.

'Working,' answered Nikki.

'Just keep going that's how I like it,' said Nikki once more in English.

Elena heard an indistinct man's voice on the phone.

'No, I'm not talking to a friend. This is one of those numbers were you get to listen to dirty talk during sex. It really turns me on. By the way, you'll need to pay extra for this service.'

'So, what's up?' asked Nikki in the language only she and Elena could understand.

'Should you be on the phone when you are working?' asked Elena forgetting about her own predicament for a fleeting moment.

'No, it's OK I'm working *hands free* at this part of the task. So go on, what is so important you had to ring me in the middle of my work?'

'My punter is dead. He's just died on top of me.'

What? Are you joking?'

'No! He really is dead.'

Nikki pushed her customer to one side and sat up quickly.

'What's going on?' the man asked of her.

'Your time's up.'

'OK. I will pay extra. Just let me finish.'

'No problem,' she replied. 'In a minute, just let me listen to this next bit. It's getting really dirty and interesting.'

'Can I listen if it's so good?' asked the man.

'No, it's not in English,' replied Nikki.

'Where are you?' asked Nikki to Elena.

'I'm at Shirley's. James is dead on the bed. We're still behind the curtain and there are more people waiting for us to leave so they can come in. What do I do?' Pleaded Elena.

Are you both dressed?' asked Nikki.

'No, we are both stark naked.'

'Well get yourself dressed get out of there at once.'

'But what about James?' asked Elena.

'Leave him there,' replied Nikki coldly. 'Under no circumstances get caught there with a naked, dead man or you'll be thrown into prison for the rest of your life. Once you're well away from the place, ring the Mamasan and ask her to tell Ari to sort it out but as for you, get far away and fast - and make sure you don't leave anything behind.'

'OK, I will.'

Elena dressed quickly. She found her bag, took out a hair brush and tidied herself up. 'No mirror,' she thought to herself. 'Well they would expect her to be a bit dishevelled, knowing the purpose of her visit. Elena was just checking under the bed to make sure she hadn't left anything when her phone rang. It was Nikki.

'Did you have sex with him?'

'Sorry?'

'Did you fuck this James guy?'

'Yes of course I did,' replied Elena. 'Why else would I be here?'

'You must be one exciting lady,' replied Nikki. 'Where's the condom?'

'What do you mean, where's the condom?'

'Well it'll have your DNA on it and will be easy to trace you if something goes wrong. You need to take it with you. Where is it?'

Elena looked over at James. He was on his back, staring blankly at the ceiling and going whiter by the minute, which made the red condom look like a burning torch.

Elena sighed. 'He's still got it on.'

'Well remove it and take it with you, packet and all.' Nikki hung up.

Elena moved slowly towards James.

'Five more minutes,' Shirley's voice came through the curtains. 'There are people waiting.'

'No problem,' replied Elena moving towards him. James still had an erection and the condom was still firmly in place. Elena wondered how long an erection lasted after death or was it rigour mortis already setting in.

Keeping her head as far away as possible and trying not to look, she stretched out her arms and gingerly took hold of the condom, delicately unrolling it. She placed it in a tissue and put it, along with the wrapper in her bag.

She went to the curtain, turned around and took one last look at the body.

'Sorry James,' she whispered. 'You didn't deserve this; you were a nice guy.'

'Men leave first,' Shirley said.

Shirley stood behind the bar. Opposite her, sitting on two bar stools, was a young Chinese girl holding hands with a fat old man, who had clearly had too much to drink. He looked lustfully at the young girl now his turn had come.

'He's still got another five minutes left,' explained Elena. 'He said he was not feeling well and wanted a few minutes to compose himself.'

Shirley gave Elena a sneer as if to say don't do it again.

'You must be one hell of a girl,' the fat man slurred but was stopped short by a poke in the ribs from the Chinese girl.

'You better believe it,' said Elena as she calmly opened the front door and left – immediately making a run for the lift and freedom. Her phone rang as she clambered into a taxi which, luckily was passing by the front of the building.

'Are you out of there? Asked Nikki.

'Yes,' replied Elena. 'Just.'

'I'll meet you back at the Mamasans.'

She shuddered; she never thought she would be thankful to return to that place.

'Here comes the black widow spider,' said the blonde girl as Elena entered the room to a round of applause.

'Yeh, the Russian rabbit,' said Nikki.

'Do you mind?' said Elena pretending to be hurt. 'I might screw like a rabbit but I'm not Russian. What's happened about James?'

'Don't worry about him, Ari will sort him out.' Said the blonde girl.

'Nikki came over and gave Elena a hug. 'You had me worried for a minute there. I thought I'd lost you.'

'What about Shirley and the 'rent a room' if the police catch her,' Asked Elena turning to Nikki and then to blonde girl.

'Don't worry about her,' said the blonde girl. 'She's been pushing her luck for too long. The writing's been on the wall for years now.'

'What did you say?' asked Elena.

'I said, she's been pushing her luck for too long. That's all. I mean in the same apartment building for years now. Same telephone number; she's asking for trouble.'

'No, no,' afterwards.'

'I just said *the writing was on the wall*. What's wrong with that?'

'Nothing.' Elena walked across the room. She flung the toys from the back of Nikki's bed as memories of a drunken night flooded back to her. There on the wall she saw the words. 'I want to go home. Kristina.'

'Can we swap beds Nikki?'

'Why? What's wrong with yours?' asked Nikki somewhat puzzled.

'Nothing,' replied Elena. 'I just want to sleep over here. I think after today I've earned it. Don't you?'

'Ok, if you must. I'm so busy these days, I hardly sleep there anyway.'

Elena quickly moved their things over and lay down on her new bed. She turned to face the wall and gently stroked the writing with her fingers. She could recognise the childish handwriting anywhere.

'I want to go home. Kristina.'

"I was widowed nine years ago and I was desperate for money to support my children so I came to Almina looking for a job. I did not find anything so I left my contact details with friends and returned to India. A man rang me and offered me a job as a maid on 220 US Dollars per month which I accepted and returned to Almina. On arrival I was taken to a flat and locked up. The men used force to make me have sex with up to seven different men a day. I became severely ill but luckily I still had my phone and local number from my previous visit so I rang the police." Almina anti-human trafficking police stated the woman was locked inside the flat and had guided them to the place by phone whilst looking out of the window. When they arrived one man broke out through the kitchen window and tried to escape but was caught on the roof of the building.

Testament from Court records.

Chapter 27

Innis sat on the grass under the shade of a tree. The weather was warm but he still wore a black leather jacket over his blue jeans and white T-shirt. Two boys, big and mean watched him from their viewpoint - a bench on the opposite side of the field. A third boy was leaning against a tree to Innis's right. He too was watching, waiting. Every now and then the lone boy would glance towards the other two boys on the bench and nod his head in Innis's direction, shrugging his shoulders as if to say 'Well?' The bigger of the two boys sitting on the bench would shake his head and say a silent 'no,' and all three kept watching. A girl, scruffy looking and in her teens came up to Innis and sat beside him. They exchanged a few sentences and then the girl passed Innis some money. He looked around for anyone in authority, saw none, opened his leather jacket and quickly took a small sachet from his inside pocket and passed it to the girl. Sliding it through the neck of her dress, she tucked the package into her bra, after which, she stood and left.

Innis pulled his feet towards him, wrapped his arms around his folded legs and rested his head on his knees. Thinking.

Two boys aged twelve or thirteen came and sat either side of him. He looked up and glanced at the surroundings. There was a short conversation. Money changed hands before Innis reached into his jacket inside pocket and transferred two small sachets to the boy on his left. They quickly stood up and moved away. The boy leaning against the tree looked across at the two on the bench again and mouthed 'now?' The bigger of the two boys again shook his head to say 'no.' They watched as a constant stream of young people came and sat at Innis's side and, with little variation, acted out exactly the same scene. The tide of visitors eventually subsided and Innis stood up and brushed the stray bits of grass from his trousers. The boy leaning against the tree looked across at the two on the bench and the bigger of the two boys nodded his head and all three began to walk towards Innis.

He saw them approaching and looked from one to another, realising what was coming; he turned and began to run but a fourth youth, the biggest of them all, who had been in hiding behind him all the time, caught and held him until the others arrived.

'I just rang the hospital,' said Dorgan. The red colour of his large round face displaying his losing battle against high blood pressure. He spoke to no-one in particular but placed his mobile down carefully on the large desk in front of him. The other two men sat in leather and chromium chairs at either end of the desk. They were in a modern office three floors up and the large windows overlooked the gloomy sprawl of old grey concrete houses. The two thin, casually dressed men looked towards him and waited for more details. 'Innis will be out of action for at least two months. The bastards waited until he'd sold out of merchandise, took all the money and then beat him near to death. Broken ribs, arm and probably internal bleeding. Do we have anyone else at the school who could take over until Innis is back at work?'

'No,' the middle aged lackey lounging in a chair to the right of the desk remarked. 'We don't have anyone there who can take over.'

'The High School is a good earner,' said Dorgan. 'It's not just the money from the drugs we sell to kids today, which is good business in its own right, but once we get them hooked at school they're customers for the rest of their lives. We need to find someone to replace Innis and quickly.'

'Any ideas or suggestions?' asked Dorgan looking from one to the other.

'What about the Elena woman who borrowed money to send her daughter someplace. What was it called? Almina?' asked the grey haired flunkey on the left.

'What about her?' asked Dorgan. 'Is she overdue on repayment?'

'Yes, a little late,' continued the man on the left. 'But it's not that. From the time she borrowed the money to send her daughter away, no-one's seen the daughter and now no-one's seen hide or hair of the mother. She never answers her phone when we ring and the rumour in the village is she's run away and disappeared.'

'Well how does this help us in our situation with Innis?' asked Dorgan.

'She has a son called Mikhail, she left him with her sister. He's at the same High School Innis went to.'

'Is he an addict?' asked Dorgan.

'No he's clean and really into sport.'

'And what are you suggesting may I ask?' Dorgan already knew what the 'suggestion' was going to be.

'Force feed him a few doses and get him hooked. He'll deal for us then if only to get a fix.'

'Get me the sister's phone number.' Dorgan realised this was an excellent opportunity.

'Ready and waiting,' said the man on the left. He smiled as he passed a slip of paper with a phone number written it over to Dorgan. 'Her name's Tasha.'

He looked at the number and picked up his mobile.

The phone rang in Tasha's hallway.

Tasha picked up the phone on the second ring.

'Your sister Elena borrowed some money from me a while ago and I was wondering when I would get it back?' Dorgan used the smoothest unemotional tone he could muster.

Tasha froze as she realised who it was. 'Sorry, what did you say?'

'I think you heard me perfectly well the first time,' said Dorgan. 'Now where is your sister and when will I get my money?'

'There was a problem with Kristina and her job and Elena has gone to sort it out. Don't worry. She'll be back very soon.'

'Well I hope so. For both your sake and hers.' He rang off.

Tasha placed the phone back onto its cradle slowly.

'Oh Elena! Where are you? Why don't you ring?'

Tasha spent the rest of the evening worrying about Elena and the phone call. Apart from the first call over a week ago she'd heard nothing. Her thoughts were interrupted when Mikhail came home.

'Hi Auntie Nikki, I'm home,' he shouted as he came in through the front door.

'No news is good news,' she thought. She must not let him know anything was wrong. 'How was choir practice?' she asked as she went to lock and bolt the front door.

Mikhail looked at her as she did this and wondered why she was increasing security.

'Is everything alright?'

'Yes everything's just fine. It's just there have been one or two burglaries in the area of late and so I want to be sure we're not next.'

Tasha spent a fretful night either wide awake or dreaming Elena and Kristina had met every kind of harm possible.

The next morning she made breakfast and sent Mikhail off to school before returning to bed to try to catch a little more sleep.

As Mikhail walked to school, two boys came up from behind and walked each side of him.

'Mind if we join you,' one said. 'We've a proposition for you.'

Back home, Tasha was half asleep, having visions of Elena being beaten by two large strong men and heard the telephone ringing in the background. At first she thought it was part of her nightmare but then realised it was her own telephone ringing downstairs. 'Oh no!' she thought. 'Dorgan is after his money again. I won't answer it. But what if it's Elena?' Tasha ran down the stairs and picked up the telephone.

'Hi Tasha,' said a familiar voice. 'It's me, Elena. She was here. Kristina was here.'

'You mean you've found her?' Tasha asked excitedly.

'No, not yet,' replied Elena. But I'm on the right track. She was staying at the same place where I'm staying but has moved on. She's still alive, I know she is. How's Mikhail?'

'Oh he's OK. Don't fret about him. Everything is just fine here so don't worry about us. Just find Kristina quickly and come home.' Tasha felt guilty about not telling her sister about the telephone call from Dorgan. They'd always told each other everything but she felt Elena had enough to worry about as it was. 'Do you have a phone number I can contact you on?'

'No not yet. This mobile belongs to a friend. I hope to get a number fixed up soon.'

'But I thought you had roaming on your old phone. Why doesn't it work?'

'It's, it's a different system out here,' she stuttered. 'The card doesn't work.' Now it was Elena's turn to keep things from her sister. She didn't want to tell Tasha her phone, and probably Kristina's too, had been taken from them on arrival.

'I have to go now. Give my love to Mikhail and you too.' Elena felt the tears starting to well in her eyes.

'Look after yourself and be safe,' replied Tasha. 'Bye.' She slowly replaced the receiver.

'Bye,' whispered Elena to a dead line and stared at the mobile as she slowly moved it away from her – fighting the desire to call back and say some more, to hear her sister's voice again and tell her how awful everything was in Almina and how much she hated it.

Elena slipped the mobile into her handbag and went over to the sink where she washed her hands and dried her eyes. Looking into the mirror she saw they were red from shedding a few tears so she moistened a tissue and dabbed them away, gave her make up a quick renewal and returned to the bar at the Almina Towers Hotel.

The Mamasan watched from her eyrie in the corner of the room at the end of the bar and tapped her watch to indicate to Elena she had been away too long.

Elena nodded an apology and joined Nikki in their allocated spot.

'Thanks,' she said returning the mobile quickly to Nikki. 'I needed that.'

'Everything Ok back home?'

'Yes, everything's fine.'

'Nice to have someone to call. I don't have anybody to care for me.'

'Maybe it makes it easier,' said Elena automatically, her mind clearly elsewhere.

'One day, you and I are going to have a talk about this Kristina,' thought Nikki. 'Come on, don't get depressed. What you need is a good punter with a lot of money. Let's try those two over there.'

Nikki led Elena across the bar to two middle aged men deeply engaged in a serious conversation.

'Hi, guys, you taking a lady home tonight?'

'Maybe,' said the taller of the two making a deliberate show of looking Nikki up and down.

'Why not take a good look at my arse whilst you are at it,' said Nikki turning around and sticking her bum out so he could have a better look.

'I'm a tit man myself,' said the other man.

'It's why you two get on so well,' thought Nikki not wanting to say it in case it harmed business.

'Maybe later,' said the 'tit man' whilst really meaning, 'we're only here to look and not to spend.'

'Ok, later.' Nikki led Elena away. 'We may as well call it a day as it's almost the end of the afternoon session and the depressed look on your face would put a sex maniac off. What was said in the phone call to make you so sad?'

'Nothing, I'm just a bit home sick that's all.'

'I've spent my entire life being sick of home,' said Nikki. 'In my experience, 'Home is where the grief is.' Come on; let's go back to the flat. Mamasan will not be pleased but we'll work much harder tonight.'

It was clear the other girls had fared better than they had as they had the room to themselves when they returned. Elena stretched out on her new bed with her back to the room and stared at the writing on the wall.

'I want to go home, Kristina.'

She ran her fingertips slowly across the words as if she were a blind person reading them in braille.

She felt a thud on the bed beside her as Nikki flung herself down. 'Now tell your auntie Nikki all about this Kristina and who she is. I'm not leaving until you've told me everything because not only is this Kristina making my new best friend miserable but more importantly, it's bad for trade and losing me money! Remember what they say? 'A problem shared is a problem broadcast around the world!' No, sorry. I shouldn't have joked. Come on Elena, tell me. You can trust me and maybe I can help. I do want to help. Honest.' Nikki put her arm around Elena and lowered her head so Elena could see her face.

She looked Nikki straight in the eyes and decided in an instant she could be trusted. Flinging her arms around her, she blurted out the whole story amidst a flood of tears and a flurry of tissues.

Elena had just finished recounting the whole saga to Nikki when they heard the Mamasan coming towards their room.

'Quick, sit up and dry those tears. No-one must know about this.'

Elena sat up and made herself as presentable as possible. The door opened and the Mamasan entered the room. She looked at them both sitting on the one bed, arms around each other.

'I'd never have thought of the man mad Nikki as 'one of them,'' she remarked.

'I have to take sex where I can find it,' replied Nikki giving Elena a big kiss on the lips.

'Stop taking the piss! What's up with her? Why is she crying? She's not pregnant is she?'

'No, just homesick,' said Elena sadly.

'Well I've good news for you Nikki,' continued the Mamasan. 'We've new recruits arriving tomorrow so we need the space. Nikki, you've made such an impression on Eva she's decided we can move you out into a flat with one or two other girls and you can work from outside.'

'But what about Elena?' asked Nikki.

'She's not ready yet. Elena stays here for a while longer until Eva feels she can trust her.'

Elena felt her heart sink as she realised she was about to lose her only friend and confidant in Almina; maybe forever.

'Well I'm not going without Elena. If Elena stays, I stay. Let someone else leave instead of me.' Elena looked at Nikki in astonishment and gratitude.

'If Eva says you go, you go. End of story.'

'I must be Eva's best earner in this place. If I'm unhappy, the money will stop coming in and you'll have to bring me back here. What'll you do then? Please Mamasan. Let's not fight over this. Let me take Elena with me. I'll look after her. Then you have two places for your 'recruits.' Nikki stressed the word 'recruits' knowing full well these girls thought they were coming to Almina for respectable jobs. The Mamasan looked from one to the other and saw the terrified look on Elena's face. 'Let me talk to Eva and see what we can do.' 'Oh! Thanks,' the girls said together and both sprung up together and gave the Mamasan a hug. 'I only said I'd try. I never promised anything.'

'It's all we ask,' replied Elena.

'Well I can't do anything until you let go of me can I? Look, the other girls are returning from work – where you two should have been.'

'We'll work extra hard tonight if you let us stay together,' said Nikki.

'Well take some rest then,' said the Mamasan, breaking free and leaving the room.

'Don't worry,' Nikki whispered, 'I'll help you find your daughter Kristina if it kills me. It's time I did one good deed in my life.'

'What's up with you two?' said the blonde girl entering the room. 'Make way for the worker. At least I earned money and played 'hunter gatherer' today.'

'Cunter gatherer more like,' replied Nikki. 'Come on Elena, we need rest if we're to make lots of money tonight to impress Eva.'

They both lay on their beds; Nikki feeling the joy of 'do-gooder' for the first time in her life and Elena imaging what would happen if Eva said 'no.'

Helped by the weekend trade, Nikki managed three one shot punters plus an all-nighter to Elena's one-hour hit plus a thirty minute blow job with a client who drove around in his car whilst Elena undid his trousers and satiated his need. The Mamasan was well pleased with them both.

Nikki returned home the next morning and rang the doorbell. She heard the key enter the deadlock and turn as the door opened.

'Come in Nikki,' the Mamasan whispered. 'Eva wants to talk to you in the kitchen. The rest of the house is asleep.'

Eva smiled, 'I wanted to talk to you alone without Elena. Are you sure you want to do this? I mean take her with you?'

'Yes, I am, Eva,' replied Nikki firmly.

'You do realise what we're offering you? Freedom of sorts. The chance to have some sort of life. Of course we'll keep a firm watch on you but it must be a better life than here. Are you prepared to give everything up for Elena?'

'Elena will be fine. Let her come with me and I'll look after her. We'll make you more money than you've ever seen.'

'I'm not sure Elena is ready. I don't trust her. I think there is something going on but I don't know what it is. Sometimes she is here in body but her mind is elsewhere and it's affecting business. Look at how long she spent in the toilet this afternoon. The Mamasan said it was near half an hour. How much business did she lose?'

'Sorry, but I'm not leaving without her. I know better than to threaten you but I want her to come with me. I'll look after her and I'll guarantee she'll be fine.'

'Guarantee is a strong word in the company we keep. Are you certain you're personally prepared to 'guarantee' Elena?'

'Yes, I'll look after her.'

'Alright. You can move out together but Ponytail Ari will keep a close eye on you both and if there's something I should know about, then please tell me now. Nikki, I like you, so let me ask you one more time; if there is something I should know about then please, please tell me now. You know what Ari is like.'

'There's nothing. Elena is just a little homesick. I'll look after her.'

'I hope you know what you're doing,' said Eva. 'I wouldn't do it if I were in your place. Ari will hold you responsible for everything.'

'Go and sleep. We need to find somewhere for you and Elena to stay this afternoon.'

Nikki went to bed and thought 'I hope I know what I'm doing too. This daughter of Elena sounds like trouble.'

When Nikki opened her eyes after a few hours of hard earned sleep, all she could see was the hazy outline of Elena's face looking down at her. As the drowsiness faded away she realised Elena was sat on her bed gazing at her with a beaming smile.

'Eva has told me. I can come with you. Thanks for saving my life.'

'Come on you two,' said the Mamasan poking her head around the door.' Come down to the kitchen. We need to talk about where you're going to live.'

They showered and dressed, excited at the prospect of moving out.

'We need to find you something quick, as our new recruits are arriving later.' Eva poured out two cups of coffee.

'Well there's a newspaper here,' said Elena excitedly and reaching over to the nearby coffee table, picked it up and opened it.

'*Naked man found in sea,*' she read on the front page. Staring back at her was a head and shoulders picture of James. He looked respectable and prosperous in his tie and suit. Elena remembered him as she had last seen him; naked and dead in a flea bitten whore house on the wrong side of town. '*James Broadman was found early yesterday washed up at the side of the sea by two fishermen,*' the newspaper story continued. '*James, a British national, had lived in Almina for fifteen years with his wife and three children. Police sources revealed a brain aneurysm was suspected as the likely cause of death due to high blood pressure but it was not known how he came to be in the water completely naked.'*

Elena quickly put the paper back on the coffee table - face down to stop James smiling at her.

'Oh James!' she thought to herself. 'I'm really sorry. You didn't deserve to end like this. Why couldn't that bloody Ari have had more respect and have found a better way; a decent way to move you?'

'There's no time,' said Eva smiling quietly to herself as she too had seen the article about Elena's unfortunate lover in the paper. 'We do have several places and we're going to move you into a two bedroom apartment and we're moving your friend Julie in with you too. You'll make a happy threesome.'

'Which of us is going to share?' asked Elena, not sure if Nikki would choose her long-time friend Julie over her.

'You'll all share the one bedroom,' said Mamasan giving a look of surprise at Elena's naivety. This leaves the other one free to take punters back to. Three girls, two rooms.'

'Oh, sorry.' Elena was embarrassed.

Eva looked over at the Mamasan and gave her a look which said, 'Are you sure Elena is ready for this?'

'Yes. Now go and pack,' she directed the girls. 'You're leaving in half an hour.'

'What are you two so excited about?' the blonde girl asked as they went back to their room.

'We're leaving,' Elena explained. 'Eva is moving us out of here and into a flat so others can move in here.'

'You're moving out! You!' The blonde girl was now fully awake. And staring at Elena.

'I can understand Nikki but... You? I've been here two months, worked harder than you, and I'm still here.'

'Wasn't there a problem of keeping tips back from Eva a few weeks ago?' asked Nikki. 'And didn't Eva find out, give you a good beating with her shoe and threaten you with Ari if you did it again? I think that may have something to do with it.'

'Perhaps,' she said sulkily.

Nikki and Elena started to pack their meagre possessions.

'If you've been here two months,' asked Nikki casually, did you ever meet this Kristina who desecrated Eva's wall over there?'

Elena bit her lip, stopped what she was doing and tensed her entire body waiting for the response - determined not to miss a single piece of her answer.

'Oh, her? Right stupid cow,' the blonde girl replied. Elena felt an unstoppable urge to defend Kristina but Nikki gave her a severe look making her think better of it. 'The cow refused completely to work. They tried everything. Friendly persuasion, force. Even had three guys break her in but she still wouldn't play game.' Elena remembered just how stubborn Kristina had been as a child.

'I want to be a dancer,' the blonde girl mimicked in a mocking tone. 'That's all she would ever say. 'I want to be a dancer.'

'Was she here long?' asked Nikki.

'No, week or so,' the blonde girl continued. 'Maybe two weeks max. That's a long time for one of Eva's investments not to pay dividends.'

Elena was dying to ask some questions herself but she was too busy trying not to cry.'

The blonde girl leant over and started looking for something in her bag.

Nikki looked across at Elena and placed a vertical finger across her lips and motioned 'Shhhh.'

'Finally, they sold her,' said the blonde girl looking up.

'What!? Said Elena in far too loud a voice for someone supposedly with a casual interest in the girl. 'I mean, what do you mean, 'sold her'?'

'They sold her,' said the blonde girl. 'These people can sell us like meat at the local market. They trade us, barter us, and sell us from one to the other. As long as they have our passports, we're a commodity to be traded like any other commodity. What's the price of sugar today? It's gone up owing to shortages. What's the price of an Eastern European lady today? Oh, I can sell you one of those cheap as they are flooding the market. They sell you and hand over your passport to the new owner, like you hand over the log book when you buy or sell a car.'

'Do you not want to go home?' asked Elena.

'Of course I want to go home! But how can I?' The blonde girl shouted back.

'Shhhh,' warned Nikki. 'They'll hear you downstairs.'

'Sorry,' the blonde girl whispered. 'But how can I? I was so excited when I got the job. Working in a shop they said. A posh shop selling high end fashion. My husband had left me and never gave us any money. I have a mother and baby at home and we struggled so much to make ends meet. This was the answer to our prayers; money for Mum, a good school for my son and a respectable job for me. I was even so stupid to think I might find a new husband. A lovely man with a good job paying lots of money. Someone from Europe or the States. I dreamt it all. There was I; beautiful house, a western husband, a green card for me and my son. Did I dream? What respectable man is going to marry a whore? Who'll take the risk of taking his ex-whore wife to a company party, only to find half the men there have already had her for a hundred dollars or less?'

'Is there no way of leaving?' asked Elena suddenly finding some empathy for her.

'I read about a working girl, who was locked in a room like ours and wanted to escape so much she somehow managed to find some bottles of beer. She sat on the balcony and after she drank them she lined the bottles up along the rail for all to see. Someone reported her to the police and they came and arrested her for prostitution. She served one year in prison followed by deportation. She was happy and thought the year in prison was well worth it.'

'Well was it?' asked Elena.

'Total waste of time!' the blonde girl said without any trace of emotion. When she finally arrived home the bastards had got to her family and beaten the shit out of her mother. Her mother was so brain damaged she didn't even know who her own daughter was when she reached home.'

Elena felt herself beginning to panic as she realised the seriousness of the situation she and Kristina were in.

'So what do you plan to do?' asked Elena.

Shut up and put up – with any and every man who'll have me until I have worked my way out of this mess. In the end, they wear you down and you give in. What's the saying? 'Abandon hope all ye that enter here?' Well they should put the sign over the arrivals gate at Almina airport for all the single girls from Eastern Europe, Africa and China to read as we enter.'

'Are you two ready?' Mamasan shouted from downstairs. 'The car's here.'

'Coming,' shouted Nikki.

'So what happened to her?' asked Elena.

'What happened to the girl I once was? I'll tell you. She died. All the life was squeezed out of me by this place. All there is left of the girl I once was, is this empty shell you see before you.'

Nikki picked up her bags and turned towards the door.

'No, not you,' asked Elena hiding the rising urgency in her voice. 'The girl, Kristina. When they sold her, who did they sell her to?'

'Come on you two, the car won't wait forever.' Eva shouted from downstairs once more.

'Poor cow. They sold her to a brothel.'

'Which brothel?' asked Nikki.

'Madam Olga's brothel. I haven't been there but it's on the outskirts of town. I haven't heard any news of her but I expect the worst.'

'Come on you two or do I have to come upstairs and drag you down here.' Eva's shouted impatiently.

Elena picked up her bag and moved towards the door. She turned to look back at the blonde girl who shrugged her shoulders in a sign of defeat.

Don't mind me,' the blonde girl said. 'I'm just depressed at the thought of you two leaving and me staying here. Go on. Good luck to you both. One day I'll be there with you on the outside.'

Elena put her bags down on the floor and rushed over to the blonde girl, bent over, hugged her and gave her a kiss on the cheek.

'Yes, and when you do, come and stay with us. It's an order.'

She picked up her bags and both she and Nikki went down the stairs.

'I thought I'd seen her before,' 'thought the blonde girl. 'She's the same nose as that Kristina girl. I wonder if Eva has realised it too.'

"I arrived at Almina airport for a job as a hotel receptionist but was met by a stranger who said he had paid 4000 US Dollars to bring me here. He said he needed my passport and identity documents to make copies and I handed them over. I was taken to a flat where there were several frightened Moroccan women and another man who said he had paid 4100 Dollars for me and that I had to work as a prostitute until I had paid it off. I cried, I screamed but they beat me for ten days. I tried to run away but they caught me and the beatings worsened. I was given a handler whose job it was to provide me with birth control pills and make sure I did not escape. A driver would drop me off at the home of a client who would inspect me and if he didn't like me he would send me back and ask for something else. The going rate for each visit was 410 Dollars which the handler kept to pay off my debt. He even forced his own wife of five months pregnant to sleep with clients for money. Eventually, one of the handlers got drunk and left the key in the door which allowed us to escape." In all, 14 women escaped from the flat and sent to government shelters for trafficked women.

Proceedings of Court case.

Chapter 28

Tasha heard the key turn in the front door lock and shouted out to Mikhail.

'Quick, your Mum's on the phone.'

He ran down the hallway and almost snatched the telephone from her hands.'

'Mum, where are you?'

'Oh, Mikhail it is so good to hear your voice. How's everything? How are things at school?' She could feel the tears welling up in her eyes as she heard her son's voice.

'Fine Mum, just fine. Have you found Kristina yet?'

'No, not yet but I'm on the right track.'

Tasha looked at Mikhail's animated face as he spoke to his Mum. 'How did we get into all this?' she thought sadly. 'It was only a few months before we were all one big happy family. Broke maybe, but happy none the less.' She watched the boy as he talked to his Mother. Her eyes ran up and down his body. 'He's growing too. He'll soon need a new coat.' Tasha studied him a little longer thinking somehow something was different. 'It's the shoes,' she almost said out loud. 'Mikhail was wearing new trainers. Expensive new trainers. Where did he get the money for those,' she wondered. She hadn't bought them and he did not have any money. Where on earth were they from? As soon as he hung up the telephone, she asked him.

'Where did you get those?' she asked.

'Get what?' He could not look her in the eye.

'The trainers. They're new aren't they?'

'Oh these? One of the boys in the choir had them. His Mother bought them on the Internet but they didn't fit so he gave them to me.'

'Did he not want any money for them?' Tasha asked, hoping the answer would be no.

'No, he said I could have them; it would've cost too much to send them back. I'm going to my room to do some homework.' Mikhail ran up the stairs leaving Tasha with a very uneasy feeling in her stomach.

Elena handed the mobile back to Nikki. 'Thanks. I must sort one of these out for myself one day.' This was one of the advantages of the three girls living in their own flat. There was no-one to watch them or listen in to their conversations. It hadn't taken long for the three girls to move in and unpack. The flat was sparsely furnished but had all the basics, including real beds and built in wardrobes. Anyone would have thought they had won the lottery on seeing their reaction to this discovery. There were some travel posters on the wall to places none of them had ever heard of but otherwise the walls were bare.

'Time to clean ourselves up and go earn some cash. I'll take first turn in the bathroom, then Elena then you Julie,' declared Nikki.

After she had finished her shower and Elena was safely out of the way taking her turn in the bathroom, Nikki explained to Julie about Kristina, and Elena's plight to find her.

'All we know is, she was sold to some brothel run by a Madam Olga.' Nikki was wearing a pale blue towelling bath robe and sat at the dressing table and adjusted her hair with a set of heated curling tongs.

Julie lay on the bed scanning a fashion magazine. She was dressed in a Chinese style black dressing gown adorned with a red dragon which contrasted with her pale white skin and brittle blonde hair. Too much time spent out of the sun and inside smoky bars had taken its toll on both her hair and her complexion. The black roots of her hair had started to show. 'Oh, Madam Olga's,' she replied 'I've never met her but I heard she's a bad old cow.'

'Do you know anyone there or even where the place is?' Nikki continued to work on her hair. She'd decided to be curly tonight and the heated tongs were working their magic. 'Psst' they went as Nikki pushed the button at the end to release a burst of steam to set the curl.

'No, I've never been there but I think there's a girl at the place I hang out at who's just bought her passport back and is working freelance. I could ask her if you like.'

Nikki nodded and smiled at her.

'It's not like you to help someone for free. Have you gone soft?'

'Maybe I'm just getting old but I feel sorry for Elena. She obviously loves her daughter very much.'

'Psst,' as Nikki pressed the button on the end of the curling tongs and released another burst of steam.

'What's this place like where you work? Is it better than the Almina Towers Hotel?'

'The Palace hotel? It is more upmarket, so you can earn more money each time. Every place has its own price and woe betide any girl who undercuts the others. The Almina Towers Hotel is bottom end – if you excuse the pun, so you can't charge a lot. At the Palace we have to pay the management seven hundred dollars a month plus another thirty a night to go in but the minimum price punters pay to take a girl is double, sometimes triple, everywhere else.'

'Psst,' as the curling tongs released another burst of steam. 'We may have to go ...' Nikki stopped mid-sentence as the doorbell rang.

'I'll go.' Julie moved to the door. 'Who's there?' she shouted.

'Cut out the party jokes and open the fuckin' door,' came the voice from outside. It was a voice Julie feared and recognised only too well and opened the door without delay.

'Where are the two new girls?' Ari marched into the bedroom without being asked, strutting in as if he owned the place and all within, which to all intents and purposes, he did. He was wearing an open necked white shirt with dark trousers. He wore no jacket in deference to the afternoon heat. 'Ah, here's one of them. Which one are you?'

'I'm Nikki,' she said, placing the curling tongs slowly back on the dresser and turning to look at Ari.

'And how are we today?' asked Pony Tail Ari as he walked up to Nikki,

'All the better for seeing you my sweet Ari,' she replied. 'Have you come for a fuck, because if you have you're out of luck; the house boy has just gone out.'

He gripped her upper arm in one hand and squeezed hard. Twisting it around, he lifted Nikki up from her chair and moved her body so he was now looking her in the eyes. 'Don't be bloody sarcastic,' said Ari.

215

'You're hurting me,' she winced. 'You'll give me a bruise which will frighten the customers away and this will upset Eva.'

He threw her down in one vicious move. Nikki rubbed her arm to ease the pain.

Ari saw the curling tongs. He leaned over her and picked them up. Holding them above his head and examining the long blades. He pressed the steam release button, fascinated by the sound as the steam came out of tiny holes all down the length of the central cylinder. Ari smiled like a child who had found a new toy.

'Oh! Sorry.' Elena emerged from the bathroom fresh from her shower and wrapped in a towel.

'No need to apologise lady.' Ari carefully placed the curling tongs back on the dressing table; setting them down as if they were some rare and priceless object. He walked over to Elena.

'Eva has put you three in my care so I came to say hello.'

Ari stopped in front of Elena. 'Eva said I had to take special care of you.'

He reached out and started to pull the towel away from Elena. She was about to say 'stop' but saw Julie shaking her head in warning and against her better nature, she let Ari disrobe her. He let the towel fall to the floor. As she stood naked in front of him, Ari slowly, very slowly looked her up and down with his cold piggy eyes and examined every inch of her body in a show of total power.

'So this is the deal. You keep all of your earnings, including tips, until the end of the week. I'll come around and collect the money and I'll decide how much of your earnings you can keep. Don't spend a penny until I've taken Eva's share and if you dare to short change me, you will regret it. Is that understood?'

They all nodded in unison.

'Good, then get to work ladies. Don't worry, I'll let myself out.'

'Maybe Julie's right,' mused Nikki as she cast a bored eye around the bar in the Almina Towers Hotel.

'How do you mean?' asked Elena.

'Like she said,' continued Nikki. 'Maybe we should go more upmarket so we can earn more money every time.'

'But it's a lot of money to put up. What if we don't get any customers? How do we pay the fees?'

'Well, you know what they say, 'If you don't 'put up' you won't get

216

'put up!"

'What about the Chinese girl over there?' continued Elena nodding towards a heavily tattooed, big breasted girl in the opposite corner of the room. 'They say she's the top earner in this place and makes over ten thousand dollars a month.'

'Yes, but she'll go with 'anything in a condom'. We have our standards to maintain.' Nikki spoke, using an impressive imitation of a pompous present day politician.

'Judging by some of the men I've seen you go with,' laughed Elena. 'Your standards are pretty low.'

'Meow!' laughed Nikki. 'Do you see the Iranian guy over there?' She nodded towards a fat, well-dressed man directly across from them.

The man nodded at the two girls, realising they were talking about him. He smiled, sure they must be saying something good. 'Well I've known three girls who have been with him at different times and they all said the same thing. Apparently he always goes back to their place or some cheap 'rent-a-bed,' strips naked, and then puts on three condoms. I mean, how's this supposed to make a girl feel? Three condoms!'

'Well, maybe he has a wife and is scared about taking back some dread disease,' suggested Elena.

'Scared shitless maybe,' continued Nikki. 'However, the worst is yet to come. As soon as the girl has taken her working clothes off and is ready for the business (by the way, we must be the only profession in the World that actually has to take our working clothes off in order to go to work) he produces a pair of latex rubber gloves from nowhere - the sort doctors wear, dons them and then starts feeling the woman's boobs. It ends up more like a trip to the gynaecologists than doing a trick. I've heard of playing Doctors and Nurses but that's ridiculous!'

'Bugger off,' said Elena practising some of the new vocabulary Nikki had taught her. 'He never does!' Elena thought she had better be more careful about what she learned from Nikki, in case she started repeating things when she was finally safely back home.

'Absolutely true! Now, I wouldn't let my standards fall so low.'

Their conversation was interrupted when Nikki's mobile rang.

''Toys are us.' Would you like a plaything delivered to your home tonight,' she asked?

'One day you will have a shock and find it's the police,' muttered Elena finding her friend's antics amusing.

'It's OK,' Nikki grinned. 'It's Julie.'

'Has she found anything out about Kristina?' Elena suddenly began to take an interest.

'If you'll let me listen, I'll find out won't I? Hi Julie, Yes, yes. Did she? Good on her then. But you don't know where she is now? OK. Thanks. Bye.'

'What did she say?' asked Elena eager to know if there was any news.

'Well, apparently, Julie met a girl who left the brothel just after Kristina arrived. It seems they tried to make Kristina work but it just wasn't happening. When they tried to force her, she almost bit some idiot's dick off! Good girl. I mean, how stupid are men? Putting their one and only crown jewel between some stranger's teeth which are designed to rip a 'T' bone steak to shreds in five minutes - and they're actually hoping for a good time! Afterwards, they sold Kristina to some Chinese guys who run a cheap brothel for labourers.'

'Does she know where Kristina is now?' Elena was frantic. She had to find her.

'No, it was a cheap brothel. None of our girls work in those sorts of places so she's no idea.'

'But how will we find her now?' Elena was desperate. 'I'll have to go and search for her.'

'Elena.' Nikki spoke softly. 'You, I mean 'we,' we can't.'

'But why not,' asked Elena sharply.

'Because, my dear, we are women and women don't go into a Chinese brothel. Not without being press ganged into working for the next two years at the first place we visit. No, we need to think this one through.'

At this point the door to the bar swung open and around twenty men swarmed in. They were all dressed as Elvis 'lookalikes.'

'Shit!' said Nikki. 'This is all we need. A bloody stag party and everyone dressed as Elvis Presley. Don't they know he's dead? We might as well go home now, as all they'll do is chat everyone up, waste our time, bugger off to the next nooky bar and then go back to their wives.'

Elena, turned her back towards the Elvis look-alikes. 'Hopefully they'll ignore me.' The group all wore black pompadour Elvis wigs and large black sunglasses, white suits with high collars and red capes draped around their shoulders. Three of them had inflatable plastic guitars.

'I think it's too late,' Nikki grimaced as she watched an 'Elvis' walking towards them. The other Elvis boys watched, whilst the three with the inflatable guitars manipulated their instruments in front of them so the necks rose and then fell in a very suggestive way.

'Does this mean, 'Elvis has risen' and is on his way to 'heaven'?' asked Elena.

'If what you mean by 'heaven' is my delightful body,' Nikki smiled. 'Then he's in for a shock – and looking at the age of this Elvis, if he's truly 'risen' then he's been on the little blue pills. Oh shit! He really is coming over to talk to us.'

'Now remember you have standards Nikki,' joked Elena.

'Excuse me ladies, 'Are You Lonesome Tonight',' asked Elvis?'

'No, I'm with my 'Little Sister',' replied Nikki.

''Tell Me Why'?'

'She's a 'Hard Headed Woman'.'

'But 'I Want You, I Need You, I Love You',' continued Elvis.

'Then 'Treat Me Nice', replied Nikki – keeping in the same theme of Elvis' song titles.

'But 'you're 'The Devil in Disguise',' said Elvis.

'Yes but I do have 'One Broken Heart For Sale,' added Nikki; beginning to think adding an 'Elvis' to her list of customers might help her CV.

'Why don't we become 'Kissin' Cousins',' asked Elvis.

'Well then, you'll have to 'Kiss Me Quick' otherwise, if you take too long, you'll have to re-mortgage Graceland,' replied Nikki.

'Do you have any 'Love Letters' from France,' asked Elvis?'

'Of course,' replied Nikki. ''I love Rubberneckin' and certainly don't want to 'Do the Clam', or worse still, catch a 'Burning Love'.'

'So what are you two doing in 'Heartbreak Hotel'' said Elvis moving his hips as he aped a poor 'Elvis the Pelvis' motion.

'Don't Ask Me Why!' said Nikki finding it hard to keep a straight face and almost being the first to break into a giggle. Nikki found herself actually beginning to like this Elvis.

From across the bar the other Elvis' were waving to the man and motioning they were about to leave.

"I'm Leavin' said Elvis. It's time to go our, 'Separate Ways'.'

'Well, 'I Need Your Love Tonight'' said Nikki. "I Beg Of You'. 'Anyway You Want Me' or, if you like, just go 'Way Down' way 'Way Down'.'

The rest of the party across the room were becoming more demonstrative in their desire to move on. The three with the inflatable guitars were standing leaning back, each with his pelvis thrust forward. The necks of the guitars were strategically placed between their legs becoming erect and subsiding at fever pitch.

'It's 'Now or Never',' said Nikki pursing her lips.

"Love me Tender," Pleaded Elvis. "Wear My Ring Around Your Neck!"

'Piss off,' said Nikki as she tried to feign a look of disgust but ended up laughing. 'I'm not having a dead Elvis wanking on me.'

'Come on' the other Elvis' shouted across the bar. 'We're moving on.'

'Don't you recognise me,' asked Elvis?

'Of course I fucking recognise you,' said Nikki. 'You're Elvis Presley!'

'No, no,' said Elvis starting to walk away and join his friends. 'I'm Victor. We met at the airport. You sold me a ticket to queue jump.' He lifted his dark, Elvis sunglasses to reveal his face.

'Victor!' shouted Nikki in delight whilst grabbing his arm and pulling him back. 'Elena, quick. Grab hold of Elvis and give him a big kiss.'

Elena wasn't sure just what was going on in Nikki's mind - but she knew enough by now to know there would be a reason for all this - and a modus operandi.

Both girls grabbed Victor from either side. They turned him to face the other Elvis lookalikes and in unison, gave him a big kiss on each cheek. The boys across the room gave a cheer and so Nikki responded to the audience by moving her hand down to Victor's crotch and, in plain view of all, squeezed his crotch. The Elvis' cheered even louder. Nikki moved her mouth to Victors ear, thrust her tongue into it in movements giving the Elvis spectators glee and whispered, "Viva Las Vegas', you're my 'Good Luck Charm'. I'll take you to the 'Promised Land' and include my 'Hound Dog' over here for free anytime you like. I need a favour. I still have your card. I'll ring you tomorrow. It's been 'Such a Night'!'

Victor walked across the bar to join his look-alikes and continue the pub crawl. He looked back from one girl to the other in wonderment, blew them both a kiss and left.

"The 19 year old girl was from my village back in India and a colleague told me of her situation. I decided to try to help her and visited her as a client but there was no way I could get her out of that hell by myself. I returned to the apartment with two friends, again posing as clients and we managed to escape with the girl and set out for the Indian consulate. Within ten minutes the agents had tracked us down and beat us and took the girl away. I then went to the Indian consulate and gave them the phone numbers of the agents and they ordered the agent to hand the girl over or face the consequences."

Report from Court proceedings

Chapter 29

Victor walked into the room and nodded at the man in charge who was standing just inside the door. He was a fat Chinese man in his mid-fifties dressed in shirt, loose calf length cotton trousers and sandals. The top of his head was completely clean shaven. Victor handed over twenty dollars and the man held out his arm to display a long polished bench running against the wall. Perched on which were nine cheaply dressed labourers, all squashed together at the top of the bench, leaving the bottom end empty. He motioned to Victor to sit down, which he did beside the ninth man but quickly inched away as the smell of dried sweat hit his nostrils. Their visit here was probably the reward for a hard day's toil in the hot sun but Victor wished they had bathed before coming to such a place.

'Number ten,' thought Victor.

Above his head, the blades of a ceiling fan whirled around, making little effect other than mixing the putrid aromas from the unwashed bodies into one foul smell that stung Victor's nostrils. A window air conditioning unit mounted in the wall at the far end of the room hummed away, as it struggled to compete against the heat given from the bodies in the room. Every now and then, it would send a waft of cool fresh air as a blessing to Victor, but not often enough. On the opposite wall were a series of white curtains hanging from a crudely crafted rail, precariously placed one metre below the ceiling and looking as though they would fall down at any instant. From behind the curtain in front of him came the gentle swaying noises of a bed, rocking to and fro; almost drowned by the more feverish sounds emanating from behind the curtain at the far end of the room - 'knock, knock, knock' as headboard crashed against the wall.

'Christ,' thought Victor, 'How can anyone do it in a place like this?' But 'did it' they did as he was now well aware.

It had been over four weeks since he had agreed to help Elena and Nikki find Kristina. He had lost count of the number of places like this he had visited and was now wishing he had said 'no.' What if someone who knew him saw him? What would they think, or worse still, say?

'Guess where I saw Victor Musgrove last night!' he imagined. 'In a 'twenty dollar' a shot brothel. He must be desperate or broke.'

However, he knew this was never going to be a problem. No-one in his circle would ever venture near places like this; his secret was safe. But what if the police raided the joint and arrested him? This was always a possibility. He shuddered at the thought of appearing in Court; to be charged for paying for sex in the lowest place of the low. The thought of his photograph plastered across the front page of the Almina Times was his worst nightmare. He could just see the headline.

'Local business man Victor Musgrove arrested in sex joint.'

His thoughts were disturbed by the curtain on the far right swinging open and a man walking out with a smile on his face and a spring in his step. Through the open curtain Victor just caught a glimpse of the back of a naked Chinese girl squatting over a plastic bowl, douching herself, before the curtain quickly closed again.

'You.' The fat man in charge pointed at the man sitting at the top end of the bench. This was all it needed. The man stood up, straightened his trousers, walked over to the empty cubicle and entered – closing the curtains behind him. They rest of the men slid their backsides up a place along the bench, not even bothering to stand up, so the top end of the bench was now fully occupied once again.

'Number nine,' thought Victor.

He needed no instruction on this type of queuing as it was standard practice in Almina and proved to be a most effective and civilised way of queuing. It happened at all the government departments and saved any arguments and pushing in. One merely sat at the far end of the bench, moved up a place, as people before you were served and eventually one ended up face to face with the person you had come to see. There was a knock on the door and all the men on the bench turned to see who it was. The fat man in charge opened the door and motioned to an older looking Pakistani man to enter. He handed over the money and came to sit next to Victor. Victor examined the newcomer's orange, henna dyed beard and managed a small smile in greeting whilst trying not to inhale the unwashed fumes flowing from his body.

It dawned on Victor the Chinese girl in cubicle three could not be Kristina and he would be wasting his time venturing in there. The curtain from cubicle one opened and a man walked out briskly giving a guileful wink on his way out to those sitting on the bench. Victor saw nothing of the girl inside. The fat man in charge pointed to the man at the top of the bench and said 'you.'

He stood up straightened his trousers - which was pointless as they were soon to come off and lie on the floor anyway, and walked into cubicle one. They all slid up towards the top of the bench.

'Number eight,' thought Victor, as he slid up the bench.

Everyone was silent except for two Indian men who were presently numbers four and five – three ahead of Victor. They clearly knew each other and chatted away in whispered tones in a language Victor could not understand.

The curtain to the middle cubicle opened gently and an African man with dark curly hair emerged. He looked at the floor in a mild embarrassment as he made his way to the exit.

'You,' said the fat man in charge to the man sitting at the top of the bench. He stood up, straightened his trousers in respect for the lady he was about to meet and entered the cubicle. The men on the bench all slid up a place.

'Number seven,' thought Victor. He looked at his watch, calculating on average it was taking eight minutes per session.

He hadn't wanted to do this but the two girls had been so desperate. The look on Elena's face as she had pleaded with him to help her find her daughter was one he just could not say no to. Besides, he was beginning to like Elena. He could see her face as he went to sleep. Did it matter she was a whore? Probably he thought. Think of the shame if people found out. What would his employees think if they found out his 'lady' was a hooker.

The curtain to cubicle one opened.

'That was quick.' Victor looked at his watch. It had taken less than six minutes from trousers on to trousers on!

'You,' said the fat man in charge and the next man stood, straightened his trousers and went into cubicle one. Try as he may,

Victor could not get a good look at the girl inside.

They all slid their backsides along the bench.

'Number six,' thought Victor as the door opened yet again and another hopeful punter joined the line.

The two Indian friends were now numbers two and three and it was clear from their conversation they were becoming increasingly excited at the prospect of sexual intercourse – with a real woman.

Victor had never even thought of having sex in these places. He treated it as a job to help to find Elena's daughter. In normal life, it was bad enough in the gent's toilet trying to have a piss with a queue behind you. No matter how desperate you are to relieve oneself it was impossible as soon as a line of men formed behind you waiting for the same urinal. Whistling, thinking of flowing water helped for naught. In these situations, Victor usually pretended to have finished, shake himself, wash his hands and walk out in order to come back later. So making love, sorry having sex when a line of men are waiting for you to finish? No, he just couldn't! He would talk to the girl, thank her and as soon as he had established she was not Kristina, he would leave a generous tip and leave.

'What nationalities of girls do you have here?' asked Victor of the fat man in charge.

'Sorry?' said the fat man in charge.

'I mean,' said Victor, 'what are the nationalities of the girls behind the curtains?'

'What does it matter?' he replied. 'Is there any difference?'

'I prefer Eastern European to Chinese as they have bigger tits,' said Victor.

Our Chinese girls have big tits,' said the fat man in charge. 'We pay to have them enlarged.'

'I don't like to play with implanted tennis balls,' said Victor. 'Do you have any Eastern Europeans?' Victor thought if they were all Chinese he might as well go home now.

'The girl in cubicle one is Eastern European,' said the fat man in charge. 'The other two, Chinese.'

'Can I have her?' asked Victor.

'No, you get what comes in your turn,' the surly man replied. 'Chinese better. She too quick. Too many men.'

The curtains to cubicle one separated as a man squeezed through the parting like a grown baby emerging from his mother's vagina.

'You,' said the fat man in charge once more and the next man in line stood up, straightened his trousers and entered cubicle one. Again, Victor could not see the girl inside. They all slid up a place.

'Number five,' thought Victor. The girl in cubicle one was certainly playing havoc with his averages. The other two were averaging ten minutes per client but she was now below six.

Victor wasn't supposed to be here at this place tonight. Elena and Nikki had been finding the places they wanted checked out, but when the taxi arrived at their suggested port of call, it had been shut down by the Almina police the day before. 'Lucky escape' thought Victor and trembled. Too close a call. It was the taxi driver who had suggested this place. It was a little off the beaten track and so, as he had said, 'safe'.

The two Indian friends were now one and two and had moved into silent mode as the expectation rose.

The door opened and another man entered. They all looked around to inspect the new entrant. He handed over the money and the fat man in charge motioned him to join the end of the queue on the bench.

Victor needed to think quickly as he needed to see the Eastern European girl; otherwise the whole night was a waste of time.

'I need to go to the loo?' He told the fat man in charge.

'Can't you wait till after?'

'Not and come at the same time,' replied Victor. 'If I miss my turn I miss it. It's my problem'

'OK,' said the fat man in charge and Victor went outside into the corridor. When he returned, he slipped a one hundred dollar note into the fat man's hand and said, 'Eastern European girl?'

'OK,' the fat man in charge showed no emotion as he slipped the money into his pocket. Victor returned to his seat, still 'number five'.

The curtains to cubicle two opened and a tall Asian man came out. Victor had stopped timing by now and just wanted to tick this place off his list.

'You,' said the fat man in charge to the first Indian man. He stood up, straightened his trousers and slid behind the curtain to cubicle two.

Victor looked up and prayed to the ceiling fan in the sky, 'God, please don't let me straighten my trousers when I stand up.'

They all slid along the bench.

'Number four,' thought Victor.

The curtain to cubicle one slid open. A grey haired man trooped out muttering he hadn't had the time he had paid for – but nobody listened.

'You,' said the fat man in charge. The second Indian man stood up, straightened his trousers and went inside cubicle one.

'Shit,' thought Victor. 'That's the one I wanted.'

They all slid along the bench and the door opened and someone else came in and joined the end of the queue.

'Number three,' thought Victor.

He looked at the fat man in charge as much to say 'are we on?' but the fat man looked away.

'My hundred dollar tip has gone down the drain,' thought Victor.

'Your times up,' the fat man in charge shouted to the Indian man still in cubicle two.

'But I haven't finished,' came the breathless voice from behind the curtain.

'Doesn't matter, times up he replied.

Slapping noises of flesh against flesh came from behind the curtain in cubicle two as he frantically tried to finish.

The curtain to cubicle one opened and the second Indian man came out. He waited near the door for his friend.

'You,' said the fat man in charge and the man at the front of the queue stood, straightened his trousers and entered cubicle one.

'You, your time's up,' angrily shouted the fat man again at the curtains of cubicle two. 'Come out now.'

The slapping noises of flesh against flesh reached a crescendo but still he couldn't come.

'I haven't finished,' came the voice from behind the curtain. 'I haven't finished!'

Victor heard the girl shout something in Chinese to the fat man who pressed a bell push on the wall. Within minutes, two large Chinese men brandishing baseball bats ran into the room and threw open the curtain to cubicle two revealing the Indian man pumping the Chinese girl for all he was worth.

They dragged him off and started to beat him with the baseball bats. Blood flew everywhere as the bats opened wound upon wound. The Chinese girl stood in the corner of the cubicle trying to keep out of the way. She tried to hide her modesty with her hands as there were no bed sheets in this place and she was 'on view' to the rest of the spectators. The second Indian man went to help his friend but was bludgeoned back by the flailing bats. The first Indian man, now unconscious, was dragged naked from the cubicle followed by his blood-soaked friend limping afterwards.

The room went quiet. People looked from one to the other in complete disbelief.

'You,' said the fat man in charge to the first in line.

'Cubicle two.'

He stood, straightened his trousers and went into cubicle two. He left within seconds no longer having the appetite for sex with someone whose lover had just been beaten to near extinction. A black widow spider had nothing on this. Victor was now first in line.

'No, please no,' thought Victor. Not cubicle two.

'You,' said the fat man in charge pointing to the man in second place behind Victor. 'Cubicle two.'

'But...' sputtered the man in second place not wanting to find the same fate as the last lover.

'You!' said the fat man in charge. 'In there now.'

The man in second place stood up, straightened his trousers and went inside.

The curtain to cubicle one opened and the man who had clearly been waiting behind the curtain for the fuss to die down, crept sheepishly out of the room.

'You,' said the fat man in charge pointing at Victor. Victor rose, bent to straighten his trousers but thought better of it and walked into cubicle one.

Closing the curtains behind him, he looked at the girl, lying naked on the bed. She was completely white and so thin the bones protruded from her skin. Her hair colour matched the description of Kristina and yet..? It was hard to compare this girl to the healthy, happy specimen in the photo Elena had given him. He raised her arm and saw the multitude of injection sites. She just lay there staring at the ceiling.

'Get on with it,' she said in a sudden outburst. 'Time's money.'

'I like to talk a little first said Victor. 'Otherwise I can't do it.'

'Not my problem,' said the girl on the bed. 'You've five minutes. That's your lot.'

'Where are you from?' asked Victor.

'Anywhere you like that gets this over with,' she responded flatly. What's your name?' asked Victor.

'Whatever turns you on,' said the girl, totally disinterested in answering his questions.

'Don't you want better than this?' asked Victor sitting on the side of the bed.

'What are you? A bloody social worker?'

'No I am looking for a girl,' said Victor.

'Well you are in the right place,' she said.

'No, a special girl. A girl called Kristina who needs to go home.'

'I want to go home,' said the girl on the bed.

'Now get on with it and help me.'

'How will it help?'

'I need eighteen thousand dollars to get my passport back. You pay twenty dollars for sex with me. I get fifty percent less my lodging and other things I need to take to help me to forget. This leaves me fifty cents per fuck. Thirty fucks a day, gives fifteen dollars a day; that's three full years and I'm free to go home. So get on with it, fuck me and then get the fuck out of here.'

Victor was not sure this was the girl he was looking for but sure as hell it was someone in the same situation. He took the photo Irena had given him out of his pocket and held it by her face. There was a likeness but not enough to be sure.

He took a chance and said 'Your brother Mikhail thinks you are a crap dancer.'

'Mikhail always said that,' she replied. 'But he always loved me.' And then she laughed a quiet knowing laugh.

'What about your mother Elena?' he asked. 'Do you remember her?'

'Times up,' said a voice from outside.

The girl on the bed sobbed quietly into the pillow.

Victor stood up, took out his mobile phone and, making sure the flash was off, took a picture of the face of the girl on the bed.

'Don't worry,' he said, 'I'll be back. Your mother's looking for you.'

230

'That's a few nearer,' he said as he left one hundred dollars on the side and turned to leave.

She started to sob and he heard her whisper, 'I want to go home.'

Victor gently pulled the curtains aside, strode out into the room and said to the men on the bench, loud enough for the fat man on the door to hear;

'Best fuck I have ever had.'

"I went to a flat in Almina with some friends and a Chinese man was waiting behind the door. I sat waiting in line while my mates went off to have sex. We heard my friend quarrelling with a girl behind one of the curtains and a pimp went to my friend and asked him to hurry up. I heard the prostitute talking to the pimp in Chinese. My friend told him he had not finished, at which point the pimp pulled him out and asked him to leave. We argued with him and he made a phone call. Ten minutes later, nine Vietnamese men rushed in waving swords and knives. They attacked me first and tried to stab me but I managed to escape. I was bleeding and fell unconscious but my friends carried me to the hospital. My friend, who took too long to finish was stabbed to death." The nine Vietnamese ran off but were later caught by police and Courts sentenced them to 10 years in gaol.

Proceedings of Court case.

Chapter 30

Tasha sat across from Dorgan. The big desk separated them. Dorgan leaned back in his chair and put his hands across his great stomach, interlinking his fingers as he did so. He looked across at Tasha but said nothing.

'Nice body,' he thought.

Sitting to one side, some distance away was one of Dorgan's henchmen, Bruno. The one who had suggested they 'hire' Mikhail. He looked from Durgan to Tasha but his gaze finally rested on Tasha's tits. 'Very nice,' he thought. 'I wonder if she's up for it.'

'So,' said Dorgan, finally breaking the silence. 'You wanted to see me?'

'Yes,' replied Tasha. 'I thought it best to come and explain things.'

'Explain? Do you mean there's a problem?' said Dorgan sitting up straight for effect.

'No, no,' stuttered Tasha. 'Only you keep ringing me about Elena and the money she owes, so I thought it best if I come to see you in person and explain.'

'That's OK then,' said Dorgan leaning back relaxing in his chair once more. 'We don't like problems do we Bruno?'

Bruno was suddenly interrupted in his mental undressing of Tasha. 'No Boss, not if it concerns money.'

'Good,' continued Dorgan. 'So if there's no problem, why're you here? Did you bring an instalment on Elena's loan?'

'Err, no.' said Tasha quietly. I just wanted to explain.'

'Then explain.'

'It's just you keep ringing me about the money and I don't have any. I know she borrowed it so she could send her daughter to Almina for the good job she'd been offered but when Kristina didn't phone or get in touch then Elena went as well; to try to find her.'

'And has she found her,' enquired Dorgan?

'Well no, not really.'

'But there's no problem you said,' asked Dorgan?

'Oh no, there's no problem. In fact Elena has a job over there whilst she looks for Kristina.' Tasha was fighting hard not to show how nervous she was becoming but the muscles in her nipples started to contract – something that always happened when she became nervous. This caused them to stand up and become hard and Tasha was embarrassed as she could feel them pushing against her bra and blouse.

Dorgan watched in fascination as the two pimples tried to push through her blouse.

'It's just it will be a little while before we can pay you and I was hoping if I explained, you might stop ringing me every day for the money.' Tasha knew well what was happening with her body and started to blush.

'How long do you need,' asked Dorgan? 'One month?'

'Oh, I'm sure I'll have something by then. Thank you. Thank you!' Tasha stood up from her chair and started to make for the door.

'You do know how much she owes,' asked Durgan as she had made half good her escape.

'Tasha stopped and turned to face Durgan. 'Err, no I never asked and Elena never mentioned it.

'Well, including interest, its five thousand dollars up to now and rising at two hundred dollars a week. So in a month's time it will be five thousand eight hundred dollars. There's no problem is there?'

Tasha thought her heart had stopped. So much money! 'How could Elena possibly pay back so much?'

'No, there's no problem,' said Tasha and almost ran out of the room.

'You were a bit mean Boss, telling her how much it was. I thought she was going to wet herself.' Bruno stood up and walked over to the table. 'And you see those tits and how they stood up?'

'Yes, I saw. How is this Mikhail getting on with selling the merchandise?'

'He's doing Ok Boss. Not as good as Innis, but he's learning.'

'And is he using our products too?'

'He took a lot of persuading, but yes, definitely Boss.'

'Good!'

Tasha didn't stop until she reached home. She fumbled in her bag to find the front door keys but her haste made her confused and so at first she thought she had lost them. Finally, finding the keys in the deepest corner of her bag, she turned the key in the lock, entered the house and closed the door firmly. She leaned back with her body pressed tightly against the door as if to give added security. Only when she was in the safety of her own home did she feel she could relax. Dealing with Dorgan had made her feel dirty and she felt she needed a long hot soak in the bath.

But it had not been as bad as she feared. She had expected a difficult meeting with threats and demands but there were none. It was Dorgan himself who had proposed the extension to the loan. Tasha had expected to have at least had to beg him for more time. In the end it had been easy - too easy. A sudden feeling of unease passed over Tasha. Dorgan had a reputation for being difficult and yet he had been as nice as nice could be. It suddenly didn't feel right. She saw Mikhail's jacket on the chair by the telephone. It would be a long time before he could have a new one if what Dorgan had said was correct and Elena actually did owe him nearly six thousand dollars. She felt herself going weak at the knees as the thought of all that the money came back into her head. It was a fortune! How could Elena possibly back pay so much? What made her borrow it in the first place? She looked again at Mikhail's jacket. It didn't quite look right.

'Mikhail. I'm home,' she shouted.'

'I'm in my room working,' came Mikhail's voice from upstairs.

Tasha moved towards Mikhail's jacket to examine it more closely but was interrupted by the phone ringing. 'I thought Dorgan had agreed to stop ringing me,' she thought, as she picked up the receiver.

'Hi Tasha, it's me Elena. How are things?'

'Thank God you've rung. I went to see Dorgan today and he has agreed to give you a month's extension but we must have something by then.'

'Don't worry, it'll be Ok. I should be getting paid tonight so I'll send it to you soon,' said Elena.

'Well that's a relief,' said Tasha meaning exactly what she had said. The thought 'maybe Mikhail will get his new jacket sooner rather than later,' passed through her head.

'Yes, I've been working hard, so I should get a bonus tonight.' Elena went a little red in the face when she said this. 'If only Tasha knew what she meant by working extra hard!' It didn't help that Nikki was making knowing faces at her as she talked about her 'job'.

Tasha picked Mikhail's jacket up as she talked to Elena. She examined the collar to see just how threadbare it was. But it wasn't - It looked like new. In fact, it didn't look like Mikhail's jacket at all.

'Is that Mum?' asked Mikhail, suddenly appearing next to Tasha and taking the phone from her.

As he talked excitedly to his Mother, telling her how much he missed her and loved her and what he had been doing at school, Tasha examined the jacket in more detail. The label was from an expensive shop – one they had never been able to afford to buy from. Mikhail watched his aunt as she went over every detail of the jacket and suddenly his conversation became distracted; as if he was now more interested in what his aunt was doing rather than talking to his Mum.

'I need to talk to Mikhail after he has finished on the phone,' thought Tasha.

'Bye Mum. Love you!'

'Bye darling. Love you too.' Elena pressed the 'end call' button and, with tears in her eyes, handed the mobile back to Nikki. She missed him so much but there was nothing she could do.

'Everything all right,' asked Nikki?

'It will be if Pony Tail Ari leaves us with some of our takings tonight,' replied Elena.

'Correct! Tonight is Thursday when the day of reckoning is upon us and we receive the wages of sin! The doorbell rang. Oh shit. That will be him now.' Nikki went to answer it and Ari strutted in.

'How are Eva's little chickens?' asked Ari. 'Hopefully they've been laying golden eggs this week. How much have we earned?' Elena and Nikki laid out their money in separate piles on the table. 'Where's the book?' Elena produced the book Eva had told her to keep with the accounts of every customer and how much they had paid. He counted out Elena's money, one thousand two hundred dollars.

'Ok. This checks out. Not bad for the first week,' commented Ari as he passed her five hundred dollars. Elena looked in amazement as so much money had been taken from her. Ari saw the look and said 'We've the rent to pay and then there's Eva's commission.'

He turned to Nikki and counted out her money; two thousand three hundred. 'Where's the book?' Nikki produced the book and Ari flicked through it. 'It's not complete. There are some days with no entries.' Ari flung his left hand out and hit Nikki across the cheek with the back of his hand. She fell back onto the bed. 'Don't worry it won't leave a mark.'

'I didn't have time. I was working so hard but all the money is there. Honest.'

'Doesn't matter how hard you work. Eva wants the book filled in so you fill it in.'

Nikki rose from the bed rubbing her cheek to take away the pain.

Ari counted out some money and handed it to Nikki.

'What's this?' she asked. 'My share should be more than this.'

'Fill the book in and you get your share. Mistakes cost money.' He opened his long black coat and sunk a hand into the pocket. The pocket was deep – like those in the coats worn by poachers in olden days to hide the prizes of their nocturnal pursuits and so he had to reach far down into the lining. He took out a huge roll of one hundred dollar bills from the inside pocket; there must have been forty or even fifty thousand Dollars there. He added the money from Nikki and Elena, wrapping it around the outside and making the roll even larger. Snapping the elastic band back around the outside – just for effect, he returned it to his pocket. Elena and Nikki drooled at the sight of so much money - which was the effect Ari had intended.

'Where's Julie,' he asked?

'She's out on a job,' replied Nikki quickly.

'Well this is the second time this month she's missed collections. You tell her if she misses it again there'll be trouble.'

'But if she's working, she's working,' Nikki argued.

Ari grabbed hold of Nikki's hair and pulled her head sharply back. He turned her head so she was looking straight at him. 'You tell her to take care. If she misses another collection, I'll make sure she never works again. Is that clear?' He gave a sudden jerk as he let go which threw her onto the floor. Ari moved to the door in silence, staring back from one girl to the other. He opened the door and left; closing it quietly behind him.

'That guy frightens me,' said Elena.

'Me too,' said Nikki and shivered as she spoke.

'Just where is Julie? She knew Ari was coming tonight.'

'I don't know,' answered Nikki as she clambered to her feet. 'But what I do know is one day I am going to kill that bastard.'

"I admit I brought several hundred girls to Almina from Armenia," testified the accused. *"But I helped them by teaching them English. I warned them not to drink and lose their heads and not to fall in love and ruin themselves. I will bear my punishment for doing these good deeds."*

One witness testified;

"We were forced to work in prostitution. We were beaten with an iron bar for the smallest offences and we lived in constant fear of an enforcer known as 'Pony Tail Ali."

Almina authorities had tried to stop the 'huge problem' caused by this madam by refusing to give visas to Armenian girls under the age of thirty, but the accused simply sent them to Russia first and arranged false passports. As the judge sentenced her to 13 years in gaol, she hurled abuse at him.

Proceedings of Court case.

Chapter 31

'Toys are us,' said Nikki as she answered her mobile.

'I've found her!'

'What!'

'I said I've found her!'

'It's noisy in here just wait 'till I go outside.' She hurried out of the bar and into the foyer. This was not unusual in the Almina Towers Hotel as most girls did this when a client made a 'telephone reservation'. In fact some girls did this to pretend they had a customer. It was often embarrassing when they had been standing around all night and not scoring when other girls had been with two or three clients. Pretend you had a phone client, rush outside and then either go home or move on to another bar was par for the course.

'You mean you know where Kristina is,' Nikki made her way to the foyer.

'More than that. I know where she is and I have spoken to her. It's Kristina alright.'

'How is she? You didn't, you know, you didn't.....'

'No I definitely did not fuck her thank you very much. She was in a bad way. I hardly recognised her she looked so ill. In fact I wasn't sure it was her until she recognised Elena's and Mikhail's names. I have photos as well.'

'Victor, you're fantastic and I forgive you the Elvis outfit! Just wait till I tell Elena.'

'There's something else I need to tell you but I don't think Elena should know,' continued Victor.

'What can't we tell her?'

'She was high, Nikki. I mean out of it. They're feeding her with so many drugs she's just not with it. I found her body but that's all there was.'

240

'We need to talk privately Victor. Just the three of us. Can we do this?'

'Well yes, but how do we arrange it,' he asked?

'Well if you use your bloody imagination, it won't be difficult will it. *You man; we working girls,*' come and pick us up and we'll take you for a threesome back at our place.'

'Oh, I hadn't thought of that,' Victor sounded a little embarrassed. 'I'll come now.'

'And Victor, dress normally this time. The girls haven't stopped ribbing me about last time with Elvis.'

'Well, actually I do have a cowboy outfit. Will that do?'

'No Victor! Come now before someone else plucks us two flowers.'

She ended the call and went back inside; Elena was in deep conversation with a man in his twenties.

'You're too young for her,' said Nikki. 'You should be ashamed of yourself; she's old enough to be your mother.' The young man started to move away.

'Maybe later,' Elena called after him. 'What was all that about?'

'Victor has found Kristina and he's coming over now to spill the beans.'

'You mean he knows where she is?'

'He says he not only knows where she is but he's talked to her and has her photo.'

'He didn't, he didn't...'

'Of course he didn't fuck her. How could you even think of such a thing from such a nice person as Victor,' said Nikki righteously. 'He's on his way here now and when he comes we're going with him as though it's a threesome. We're taking him back to our place and using the office.'

'What office? We don't have an office,' said a puzzled Elena.

'In our line of work the spare bedroom is our office – where we entertain the clients.'

Victor came into the bar. He looked around trying to find the girls but it took time for his eyes to become used to the dimness. They waved frantically at him, blowing kisses until he saw them and moved over. Elena and Nikki met him halfway, linked arms with him and led him to the door.

'That was quick,' said a girl near the door. 'What do they have that

241

we haven't?'

'Home James!' said Nikki to the taxi driver. Elena cringed on hearing the name James, remembering her experience with her own 'James.' She was sure Nikki did it on purpose to embarrass her.

'How is she?' All three sat on the edge of the bed in the 'office' and Elena was eager to know Kristina was well.

Victor related his story to the women who listened to his every word.

'And that's about it said Victor as he finished his story. "If it wasn't for the police having raided the brothel you sent me to and the taxi driver suggesting this one, I might never have found her.'

'Well, we now know where she is but the question is, how do we get her out?' Elena knew it would be difficult.

Victor reiterated her thoughts, 'It won't be easy.'

'Can I see her picture?' asked Elena.

Victor looked at Nikki quizzically?

'She's very tired,' she said. 'Her photo doesn't do her justice; and cameras in mobiles aren't so good. They always make you look worse than you really are.'

'Victor, just show me. I want to see her.'

He opened his mobile and showed Elena her daughter's picture. Elena said nothing but reached for a tissue to wipe away the tears.

Finally Elena turned to Victor and looked him straight in the eye. 'Thank you Victor. I....., I mean we, couldn't have done it without you. I don't know how to even begin to thank you.'

'Well, actually,' said Nikki. 'It's already arranged. I promised Victor a threesome if he did this for us. So come on Elena, let's start the instalments.'

Nikki pushed Victor back on the bed and started to unbutton his shirt.

'You don't really have to do this you know,' said Victor.

'A promise is a promise,' said Nikki. 'Get your kit off Elena, we have work to do.'

Nikki knelt over Victor, one leg either side. She looked straight into his cool blue eyes and maintained the eye contact. Starting at the top she undid her blouse button by button until the two front sides fell apart revealing her breasts cocooned in a plain white cotton bra – the only piece of decoration being a small pink bow at the centre of the cleavage. Nikki shed the blouse, placed her hands behind her back and removed the bra. She held a breast in each hand, squeezed them from the sides so they pushed forward.

'What do you think?' asked Nikki.

'Nice, very nice.' Victor studied the small nipples and the surrounding areola; pink and slightly oval. He reached up and ran a finger over the five or six little lumps around the nipple.

Nikki let her breasts fall and unbuttoned Victor's shirt. She ran her fingers through the hair on his chest - dark black hair. Not too much but enough. She moved her body inch by inch down his legs to reveal his waist, undid his belt, unbuttoned his trousers, dismounted and stood by the bed. She took hold of the bottom of each trouser leg and pulled, removing the trousers and socks in one well practised go. She gently manoeuvred Victor so he was now lying on his side facing her. Nikki knelt at the side of the bed and gently massaged his penis. It grew a little but remained soft. Nikki bent over and used her tongue at first to tease the tip, then followed on with her whole mouth – using long slow strokes in an attempt to excite him.

'You don't have to do this,' said an embarrassed Victor. 'It's my age. I don't always get a hard on these days.'

'Just lie back and relax,' said Nikki taking a moment's break from the task at hand in order to answer. 'We'll do all the work.' She continued to massage his limp penis with one hand whilst the other started to caress his testicles.

Elena, now naked too went around the other side of the bed and lay next to Victor so their bodies touched from head to toe. She lay on her side and Victor could feel a nipple move along his back. Nikki felt Victor start to stiffen.

'Here we go,' said Nikki. 'I told you it would work.'

Victor turned his head so he could see Elena. She smiled at him. Nikki felt his penis stiffen further. He saw Elena's dark red nipples surrounded by their areola. They were at least twice the size of Nikki's and had twenty to thirty little lumps on each. He reached out and touched one. Immediately Elena's nervous system sent messages and the muscles contracted causing the nipples to harden and stand whilst the areola puckered up causing the little lumps to become even more prominent.

Victor's brain responded by sending signals to his penis. Nerve cells in the two long cigar shaped regions running along the inside of his penis produced nitric oxide. The nitric oxide molecule sent signals to nearby cells which produced an enzyme leading to the muscles in his artery walls relaxing. The arteries in the spongy cigar shaped regions got bigger and allowed blood to flow in at a far greater rate. The veins taking blood from his penis became squashed and restricted the flow of blood out. Elena kissed him on the lips and used her tongue to force his mouth open. Victor, with blood pouring into his penis at a far greater rate than it could leave, felt it inflate like a balloon and become hard. Very hard.

Elena moved her hands down to his member and pushed Nikki's away so she was now merely a bystander. She watched for a minute or so and thought, 'I'm not needed here,' and crept slowly out of the room to go to the kitchen to think.

Elena's brain was working overtime and sending out signals to her whole body and she was now sexually aroused like nothing before. Her labia minor, the two flaps of skin at either side of the vagina opening became swollen and puffy allowing salt water to flow through the vagina walls. Victor moved his hand to Elena's vagina and quickly found the magic button; the clitoris - the only organ in either sex having no known purpose other than providing pleasure. As Victor tantalised the eight thousand or so nerve endings concentrated in this one place, Elena's clitoral hood, the protective hood of skin over the clitoris pulled back whilst her clitoris hardened and expanded. Glands at Elena's vagina entrance were now providing extra lubrication. Victor rolled her onto her back and climbed on top of her. He thrust his penis inside Elena and moved it in a way going back time immemorial. As to whether there is a G spot or not didn't matter, Victor would find it if it were there.

The thrusting movements produced friction which caused the labia minor to gently massage Elena's clitoris whilst Victor's penis worked its magic inside. Elena moved her hand downwards and used her finger to help the clit on its way to the ultimate goal.

As they both moved towards orgasm, the regions of their brains behind the left eye started to shut down taking away their ability to reason and control their bodies in the fast approaching orgasms. In Elena's brain the regions controlling both the 'flight or fight' and 'fear and anxiety' responses were shut down. Elena was now feeling safe and relaxed and ready to enjoy the orgasm. Better still, the region in her brain associated with pain switched on so she could fully benefit from the connection between pain and pleasure.

Both Elena and Victor were ready for orgasm and orgasm they did.

They both lay contented in the calm after the storm. Lying on the bed with their head and shoulders propped up by the pillows. Victor had his arm around Elena and she snuggled her head against his chest. Their brains releasing the hormone oxytocin - the same hormone released in childbirth creating the mother/child bond and now responsible for the emotional bond between Elena and Victor.

They felt contented, bonded; happy in a way.

Nikki popped her head around the door.

'Since its gone quiet now, I'll come in.'

She had two mugs of coffee with her which she placed on the tables at either side of the bed.

'Sorry,' said Victor sheepishly. 'I didn't mean to ignore you. It just; well it just happened.'

'Don't worry about it. It gave me time to think. I know how to get Kristina back.'

'How?' replied Elena not wanting to remove her head from Victor's chest.

'Easy; we buy her!'

'How can we buy her?' Eva will kill us, or at least Pony Tail Ari would if she thought we were going into competition with her.'

'Not us, Victor buys her. We move up market to the Palace Hotel, work our butts off in a manner of speaking and Victor goes along and buys her; passport and all.'

'I'm not sure we could ask Victor to do that,' said Elena hoping he would disagree with her.'

'After what I've just seen, he'll be putty in your hands – well perhaps that's the wrong phrase. Victor? What do you think?'

'It's possible, but it depends on how much you two can earn. I don't mind helping with money, either.' The only part of the plan he was not happy about was the thought of Elena working her butt off with other men.

'We'll talk later. I'll leave you two, so you can have your seconds.' Nikki moved towards the door, opened it but paused and turned back to face them.

'By the way, if you hadn't noticed, it wasn't sex going on between you two. There was chemistry there - a lot of chemistry there. It's also known by the name of 'love'. Bye!'

She left the room and closed the door. Victor and Elena looked at each other and smiled. He lowered his head and kissed her on the forehead.

'No,' he thought. 'You can't marry a prostitute. You just can't.'

"The leader and five gang members locked me up in a brothel where one man raped me five times. They compelled me to have sex with numerous male clients. After suffering lock up for one year I pleaded with one of the customers to lend me his phone. I rang my brother who contacted the police." The Police set up a trap whereby they offered to buy the 17 year old Bangladeshi girl for 700 US Dollars. The gang accepted and were arrested as soon as the money was handed over. The leader was sentenced to life imprisonment whilst the other gang members were given five years each. Almina Court prosecutors told reporters that they always ask for the maximum sentence in cases of human trafficking in order to stop the trade.

Proceedings of Court case.

Chapter 32

Tasha slammed the front door shut and threw her keys on the table in the hall. 'That was the worst moment in my life. I felt so ashamed.'

Mikhail said nothing but held his head down. 'To be called in by your headmaster to be told you'd been missing school is bad enough but hearing you told your French teacher to 'go screw herself,' is just the end. You used to be so good.' Tasha softened her voice to try to reason with him. 'What's happened Mikhail? Don't you think your Mum has enough trouble with Kristina going missing, without you adding to her problems?'

Mikhail remained quiet.

'And these new clothes you keep coming home with. Where are they coming from? I haven't given you any money for them. I couldn't afford them in any case. Where are they coming from?'

'I told you, from a friend at school,' he replied.

'Don't lie to me as well. You haven't been to school as I've just found out. Just go to your room and get out of my sight.'

Mikhail trudged up the stairs.

'And you're grounded for the next week,' she shouted after him.

He stopped for a moment. 'Grounded. But how could he work for Dorgan if he was grounded?' He went into his room and closed the door behind him, knowing he would have to wait until his Aunt had gone to work and then disobey her. He needed to work in order to get his fixes.

Downstairs the telephone rang.

'Yes,' Tasha answered sharply.

'It's me, Elena. Are you OK?'

'No not really, it's been a bad day.'

'I just rang to say I've sent five hundred dollars. There'll be more soon.'

'Thank God,' said Tasha. 'Have you any more news about Kristina?

'No, we're working on it but it'll take time, is there a problem?' Elena sensed something was wrong.

'Yes, there is. I didn't want to tell you but its Mikhail. He's been missing school; he's coming home with new, expensive clothes and he won't tell me where they're coming from and, and........'

'And what?' Elena was worried. Mikhail was usually so good.

'I don't know what but there's something. It might be my imagination but there's something odd going on. It's the way people look at me and him in the street and then Dorgan....' Tasha paused for a moment. 'Dorgan's being too nice. You need to come back here as soon as you can. We've lost Kristina and now we're losing Mikhail as well.'

'I can't come now I'm so close to Kristina. Try and sort it out for me will you? Please?'

'I'll do what I can,' Tasha promised. 'But try to get back soon.'

Elena pressed the 'end call' button on the mobile and passed it back to Nikki.

'Problems back home,' asked Nikki.

'Yes, now my son is going off the rails. I have one foot at home and one foot in Almina and I'm being pulled both ways at once. We need to move Kristina out of there as soon as we can. Let's hope Victor is successful tonight.'

Victor was sitting on the bench. The stench of unwashed bodies attacked him from either side. He had already given the fat Chinese man in charge one hundred dollars to make sure he saw the 'white girl' and was waiting his turn. Slapping noises and groans came from behind the curtains. Victor thought of Elena. Did she do this too? Sex for hire? But still, he could not get her out of his mind. He thought about her all the time. Elena was the only reason he was here; doing this. However, there could be no future. Marry a prostitute? Never!

Finally the curtain at the far end opened and a man walked out. 'Total waste of time,' he muttered under his breath as he walked past him.

'You,' the fat man at the door said as he pointed at Victor. He rose and went inside closing the curtain carefully as he entered. He sat by the side of the bed.

'Kristina,' he whispered. 'Kristina, your Mum has sent me.'

'Get on with it, you're wasting my time,' said Kristina drowsily.

'No, I want to talk to you,' he whispered. 'Your Mum has sent me.'

'Talk, fuck, who cares? You've six minutes.'

Kristina lay flat out and naked. She said nothing but just stared blankly at the ceiling. There was nothing but a bag of skin and bone on the bed.

'Your mother asked me to tell you she loves you and she's come for you. See, she's sent you this.' Victor removed a silver chain with a small silver bear hanging from it. It had been a present to Elena from her own mother and she had worn it all her life. He held the chain above her head so the bear hung a few centimetres above her eyes. Kristina stared at the bear and smiled. Suddenly she sat upright and snatched the necklace. 'Mum,' she shouted.

'Shh!!' whispered Victor. 'Keep quiet. It's our secret.'

'Your time's up,' came a voice from outside.

'OK,' he shouted and turned to the girl. 'It's our secret. Don't tell anyone. Your Mum's here in Almina and she's come to take you home,' He whispered into Kristina's ear.

'Home, yes. I want to go home.'

Victor took one last look and reluctantly parted the curtains and left, cringing at the sight of the next customer who stood and moved towards Kristina's cubicle.

'Can I see the owner?' asked Victor.

'If you're going to make a complaint about that one I wouldn't bother. You'll only end up with a broken skull.'

'No,' he said rather too quickly. 'I want to make him a business proposition.'

'About what?'

'The girl,' replied Victor nodding towards the end cubicle. 'I like her. I want to buy her.'

'Wait here,' said the fat man. 'I'll see what he says. Your next,' he said to the man at the top of the bench. 'Go in when the next one comes out.' He left but returned in a few minutes. 'The boss will see you. He's through the door over there. Just walk in.'

Victor walked across the passage, tapped gently on the door opposite and walked in. The room contained two Chinese men. A bald round faced man sat at a desk whilst the other, thin and wrinkled, rested comfortably in an arm chair, to one side. Both wore traditional Chinese smocks which hung over Western trousers.

'So, you want to buy my Kristina,' said the man at the desk.

'Yes,' replied Victor. 'I like her and want her for myself. Private if you know what I mean.'

'How do I know this is not a police sting operation?'

'Do I look like an Almina policeman? In any case, if I was the police I've enough on you now to close you down. No I just want the girl for myself. Safer this way.'

'And how much are you offering?'

'Five thousand Dollars,' Nikki had told him to say this. They would want more; especially as Victor was Western. Five thousand, she reasoned was enough to get them interested since they would have bought her cheap.

'She's a good earner is my Kristina,' lied the man. 'She's very popular with the punters. I'm not sure I want to let her go.'

'Any girl will do in a place like this,' Victor reasoned with him. No-one knows who they're getting until they are in there. You could easily replace her with another girl for a thousand and keep the profit.'

'I need to speak to the owner, said the Chinese man. 'Come back tomorrow and I'll see.'

Victor rose and held out his hand in offer of a handshake. The Chinese man ignored it; leaning back in his chair and placing his hands, fingers intertwined, on his fat belly.

'See you tomorrow,' Victor muttered clumsily, as he turned and left the room.

The Chinese man immediately leant forward, picked up the phone and keyed in the numbers.

'Hello, Eva? I've just had a strange request. A Westerner has just come in and offered to buy your Kristina from me.'

'She's not 'my Kristina,'' corrected Eva. 'I sold her. Did this Western man give a name and in any case, how does he know her?'

'He's called Victor and he's fucked her twice now. Asked for her specially, - both times.'

'Did he know her?'

'I don't know,' continued the Chinese man. 'First time he just asked for an Eastern European. Second time he asked for the same one again.'

'So are you going to sell her to him?'

'Why not? She's useless so I might as well get some money back somehow.'

Eva put the phone down. She was with the blonde girl; sitting in the kitchen drinking tea. 'Strange, someone has just offered to buy Kristina from the Chinese brothel.'

'Well he's not interested in sex, if he's after Kristina.'

'No,' said Eva, 'but what we can't understand is how he knows her and why he wants to buy her. His name's Victor but no-one seems to know who he is. He's certainly not in the business or we'd know him. There's something very odd about Kristina and all this. I always felt she'd be trouble.'

The blonde girl picked up her tea cup in both hands and raised it to her lips but stopped before the cup touched them. She didn't drink but looked over the top of the cup at Eva. 'What I always found odd about her was how much alike she and Elena are.'

'It's probably they just come from the same region,' said Eva.

'Yes it's probably just that,' said the blonde girl; still holding the cup to her lips, not touching a drop of the tea but knowing she had planted a seed of doubt in Eva's mind.

"We came to Almina to work as cleaners but we were forced to entertain 23 to 25 men a day. What if I have contacted some disease? I have three children back home and I have not been paid at all. Since I came here I have only managed to call home once when one of the agent's guards took pity on me and gave me his mobile phone. I phoned home only to find my father had died. I desperately wanted to go home and asked for my passport back but he denied us. When we refused to entertain any more men, they locked us in a flat. They brought us food for the first couple of days but then that stopped and we were left alone. We found a screwdriver and managed to unscrew the door lock and escape. A kind man found us at a roundabout and took us to the Indian Association who helped us."

Proceedings of Court case.

Chapter 33

'What about him over there?' asked Nikki, motioning to a middle aged man across the room.

'Oh, him,' shrugged Julie. 'We call him Mr Stingy. He pays but he expects it all inclusive – room and taxi home included. He's ok if you can't find anyone else.'

'And the one at the end of the bar?'

'No chance,' continued Julie. 'We call him 'Mr Chinese waste bucket.'

'How do you come to give him that name?' Nikki looked puzzled.

'Well, you know the waste bins they have in offices? Well, he only takes Chinese rubbish.'

'So how do you and Elena like the Palace hotel?' Asked Julie. They both looked around and smiled. Much better! It had the appearance of a high class night spot with crystal lights on the ceiling, red and gold interior and a live band. The girls were dressed to kill in designer outfits and all the men had dressed to impress.

'It's better,' said Nikki. 'Like you said, a big investment but when you score, you score big.'

'Now the guy over there looks nice,'

'Now you're really wasting your time. He's 'bumstruck;' boys only I'm afraid.'

A West Indian man walked towards them and motioned for Julie to go with him.

'That's what I like,' said Julie. 'Customer satisfaction brings in repeat business. Bye.' She walked over to the man and they left together.

'Toys are us,' said Nikki as she answered her mobile. 'Hi Victor. How did you get on?' Nikki listened intently nodding her head from time to time.

'Well?' asked Elena when she had finished.

'Seven thousand dollars is the last price and we have until the end of the month or they'll pass her on to someplace else.'

'That's a lot of money!' Elena was shocked. 'Especially when Pony Tail Ari is taking so much.'

'Do what I do.' Julie spoke quietly. 'Don't hand it all over. As long as he gets enough, he's happy. They never really know how much you earn.'

'I'm not sure he's so stupid,' Nikki interrupted. 'He looked pretty upset when you weren't there the last time he visited. Come on Elena, we'd better get to work.' Nikki and Elena started to work the room using the five phrases ample for their trade; 'Hi, What's your name? Where are you from? How long in Almina? Where do you live? Are you taking a lady tonight?'

It was a good night and both girls had more than cleared their costs and made money. Tired from a long, hard working and sleepless night, they slept in until mid-afternoon.

'Wakey, wakey!' said Nikki shaking Elena by the shoulder. 'Time to wake up and get ready to donate money to the 'Pony Tail charity'. Elena sat up slowly and stretched her arms.

'Is it that time already?' She rubbed the sleep from her eyes and looked around the room. 'Where's Julie?' she asked.

'Don't know,' Nikki looked worried. 'She didn't come home this morning.'

'But Pony Tail Ari is due soon and remember what he said last time?'

'I know, and with what she was saying about keeping money back it worries me. I think she's being stupid.'

Both girls showered and dressed and had only just finished tidying their hair when the doorbell rang. They looked at each other as if to say, 'what now.'

'Don't worry,' Nikki moved to the door and opened it. 'Pony Tail Ari, what a pleasure to see you.'

He looked at Nikki's sweet smile and grunted. He barged in, in his usual ungracious manner and walked over to the hall table.

'Money? Books?' He said abruptly. The girls made two piles of money on the table, opened the account books for audit and then stood back out of his reach. Ari counted each in turn, muttered 'better,' and handed them their share. The girls sensed he was in a bad mood but said nothing.

'Where's the other cow? Julie?' he snapped.

'She's working,' Nikki spoke quickly.

'I thought I told you to tell her to be here. Did you tell her or not?' Ari looked straight at Nikki with his half closed piggy eyes.

'Yes, I told her,' said Nikki feeling the fear from his stare. 'She must be working.'

'Do you want another slap?' He demanded.

'No. Please. I told her.'

Ari dug deep into the inside pocket of his long coat and pulled out the customary wad of one hundred dollar bills. He added the notes from the girls, replaced the elastic band and pushed it deep back into his coat.

'I'll find her,' he muttered as he walked slowly to the door, letting himself out and closing it silently behind him.

'We'll never get the seven thousand by the end of the month at this rate,' said Elena as she counted her money. 'Maybe Julie was right and we should keep some money back.'

'No, Julie's wrong; very wrong. We hand it all over. We've got to try harder. In any case, Victor said he'd help. Come on, let's go; we won't earn anything here.'

After another repetitive night's work followed by a long lie-in, Elena woke to the sound of voices.

'What are you playing at?' whispered Nikki trying not to wake Elena. Keeping money back and avoiding Ari will land you in deep shit.'

'I'll be fine,' said Julie quietly. 'They'll never find out exactly how much I earn. I avoided Ari as I had to send money home to cover my mother's medical bills. I'll earn some more and he can have that.'

'But he needs it all. Don't you see?'

'And he can have it all - the next time.'

'What are you two arguing about?' asked Elena drowsily.

'Oh, nothing,' replied Nikki. 'Come on lazy bones all three of us have to go and earn some money. I'll take the shower first.'

'Psst' went Nikki's hair tongs as she rolled strands of hair around the short stubby cylinder of the tongs and pressed the button to release the steam.

'Hopefully there'll be some fresh customers in the bar tonight,' said Julie as she lazed on the bed reading a magazine and waiting her turn in the shower.

'Hopefully an aircraft carrier load of US sailors desperate for love,' answered Nikki. 'We all need the money.'

'True, but why are you two so desperate to earn money so quickly?' It's not as if you've been here forever. And what is so special about the end of the month.'

'Psst' went the steam curling tongs as Nikki set another curl giving her time to think whether she should confide in her long-time friend. Julie knew about Elena's daughter but not that they had found her and were in the process of buying her back. 'Elena's son is ill and needs medical attention,' deciding caution to be the best policy.

'Next,' said Elena emerging from the bathroom.

'About time too,' Julie threw the magazine on the floor and stood up. 'I could have done two blow jobs in the time you spent in there.'

'Two blown jobs more like,' answered Nikki as her mobile started to ring. 'Toys are us, ..., yes, both of us, ..., yes outside of the hotel at seven thirty. Bye.'

Nikki put the mobile down and turned to Elena. 'Great start to the night. A punter we met last night wants us both for four hours before his ship leaves. This means we've time for a couple more before the bar closes. We'll have to get a move on though.'

'Psst' went the curling tongs as Nikki set the last curl.

'Are you girls going out already,' Julie emerged from the bathroom dressed in a bath towel and shrouded in a cloud of steam. Looking from one girl to the next she saw they were dressed to kill.

'Yep, we got a hot date with the navy straight out. He wants a threesome,' Elena spoke proudly.

'Good for you,' said Julie. 'I hear you need it. I hope your son gets better soon.'

'What?' asked Elena.

'You know, your son going into hospital,' Nikki butted in quickly. 'The money will help with the cost.'

'Oh, yes, my son,' said Elena slowly catching on. 'The money will come in very handy. Are you ready Nikki?'

'Sure am, Seven thirty time to be dirty!'

'May I borrow your curling tongs Nikki?' asked Julie as the girls made their way to the door.

'Yes, no problem. Just make sure you unplug them before you leave so as not to burn the house down. Bye.'

'Thanks, if I go curly some of the locals might forget they've been

257

with me twenty times already and buy again. Bye.'

'Psst' went the steam tongs as Julie started on the first curl. She heard the key turn in the lock and the door open.

'What's up, forgotten your condoms?' asked Julie as she turned to look at the door. She froze as soon as she saw it was not the girls who had returned but Pony Tail Ari.

He stared at Julie for a moment then turned his back to her and gently closed and locked the door.

'No, my little chicken,' he said gently. 'They've gone on a wild goose chase so we can have a little talk in private.'

Julie placed the tongs on the dressing table. 'If it's about the money, I can explain. My Mum's been ill and I had to send it home as an emergency. You can keep everything for the next few weeks in order to pay you back.'

'But Madam has been checking on you,' Ari walked slowly towards her. 'Eva thinks you've been keeping money back and stealing from her.'

He was now standing over Julie who was sat on the stool looking up at him.

'No, I wouldn't, honest.' Fear started to spread throughout her body.

Ari grabbed hold of her hair and pulled her head back so he could look straight down into her eyes. 'Eva wants me to make an example of you to keep the others in line. I like Eva,' said Ari in his most threatening voice.

With his free hand he ripped the towel from around her and forced her naked body onto the floor. Letting go of his grip on her hair and still fully dressed, he moved between her legs forcing them apart with his knees.

'If you are going to rape me, go ahead, it happens two or three times a night,' Julie instantly regretted her words.

Ari looked down at her and smiled. 'No, I promised you would never work again.' He placed his left hand over her mouth and pressed hard so she could now only breathe through her nose.

'Mustn't disturb the neighbours he said. With his right hand he felt for the dressing table and picked up the curling tongs. The electricity cord stretched taught so he gave it a fierce tug and ripped the plug from the wall socket. He moved the hot cylinder slowly before her eyes. Still smiling he gradually stroked it down her body, between her breasts burning them as he did so. He traced a line down her stomach, rested it on her naval as he moved them slowly down further and further until it rested upon that most special place between her legs.

Then pushed fiercely.

'Pssssssssst.'

'What a waste of fucking time,' said Nikki as she pulled her keys out of the open door and walked in. First the two punters never pitched up and then in the excitement I left my membership card for the Palace bar at home.'

Nikki walked into the apartment followed by Elena. 'Wait here, I won't be a minute, it's in the bedroom.'

Elena waited in the hallway whilst Nikki went to collect her card.

'Strange,' said Nikki from the bedroom.

'What is?'

'Julie's bed's made. She never makes her bed. All her clothes have gone too. In fact it's as if she were never here.'

Elena joined Nikki in the bedroom and looked around. All trace of Julie had gone. 'She's taken your curling tongs too,' said Elena looking at the empty box lying on the dressing table.

Nikki took out her mobile and called up a number from the memory. 'Victor? We need to meet and soon. Can we come to your place tomorrow morning? It's not safe here anymore.'

Indian police are investigating claims that a prostitution gang were exporting women to Almina. Thirty six women were arrested in New Delhi as they were about to board a plane for Almina – allegedly to work on stage shows. One of the gang members arrested is allegedly involved with a hotel chain with properties in Almina and is thought to be the assistant to the chains CEO. Police would like to interview an airport official for allegedly taking bribes to allow women to leave India without being questioned. He is believed to be on the run.

Police statement

Chapter 34

'There you go,' Victor placed three mugs of steaming coffee down on the table. The room was quite elegant, with plush sofas surrounding an expensive glass coffee table.

The girls had taken places on separate sofas and both smiled at Victor.

'Thanks,' said Nikki moving to one side to make way for him.

'Move up,' Victor nudged Elena and sat next to her.

Nikki noticed the move but didn't take offence. 'Ow! That's hot,' she said having picked up the cup and taken a sip. She put the mug down, picked up a tissue from the open box on the table and wiped her mouth.

'Hot? Just like you two ladies.' Victor turned to Elena and smiled at her.

'Why do you have such a big apartment when there's only one of you?' continued Nikki.

'I like the space and sometimes I get lucky.'

'You'd have to get lucky with the whole convent choir to fill this place,' grinned Nikki as she cast an eye around the spacious lounge.

'To be honest, I have two kids and they come and visit me from time to time.'

'How old are they? Boys or girls?' asked Elena joining in the conversation for the first time.

'One of each. My son Justin, is fourteen years old and my daughter Rebecca, is twenty one next birthday. That's them over there,' said Victor pointing to a photograph by the television.

'So where are they now?' Elena asked, trying not to be put off by Nikki who was nodding her head towards Victor and mouthing 'get in there kid.'

'We separated long ago and the divorce came through last year. The kids are with my ex but they come and visit at least once a year.'

'I've a son about the same age,' said Elena wistfully. 'He's at home with my sister.'

Victor placed his hand on Elena's forearm and squeezed gently. 'You must miss him.'

'More than you can imagine but I need to sort Kristina out. I have to sort Kristina out.'

Victor turned to Nikki, 'so, why the sudden rush?'

'It's getting dangerous. A friend of ours, Julie, disappeared within a matter of hours. We think Pony Tail Ari is behind it and if so, well, things have taken a sudden turn for the worse.'

'Pony Tail Ari.' Who's he?'

'Victor, don't ask. You don't even want to know,' Nikki shook her head. 'We need to get Kristina out of there before they sell her to someone else; if that happens we would have to start over.'

'OK,' Victor looked from one girl to the other. 'What's the plan?'

Nikki looked across at her best friend and stared at her intently but Elena kept quiet.

'Well we need to buy her back,' continued Nikki still looking at Elena and pleading silently for her to speak but Elena said nothing.

'Well we've already decided that,' said Victor a little perplexed.

Elena still said nothing.

'But we need to buy her back quickly,' Nikki was still looking straight at Elena and motioning with her hands for her to say something.

Elena said nothing but started to turn red as tears began to well in her eyes.

'Elena it's your daughter,' said Nikki. 'For God's sake, tell him.'

Victor turned to Elena, 'Tell me what?'

Elena started to sob, took a deep breath and blurted out, 'We need to buy Kristina back as soon as possible before we lose her but we haven't enough money so we want to borrow some from you and we can't take her to our place as Pony Tail Ari will be there and we don't know who they'll put in Julies' place at our apartment so we want her to stay here with you and we'll pay you back everything as soon as we can and I know I don't have the right to ask but there is nowhere else I can turn.'

Elena held her head low. She was mortified. He put his hand under her chin and raised her head so she was looking at him in the eye. 'Please,' she begged resting her head on Victor's chest and sobbed her heart out.

'Great performance,' thought Nikki. Exactly on target as Nikki had told her earlier. 'If you ask him he will; if I ask him he won't. However, in Elena's case it wasn't a performance at all. She was pleading for her daughter and the stakes were high - very high indeed.

'How much do you need?' asked Victor to Nikki, knowing she was the brains behind all this.

'We need another three thousand dollars.'

'Shit,' thought Victor, 'I thought getting rid of my ex was expensive but these two are taking the record as the most expensive in my life.'

'And if I bring Kristina back here, what about this Pony Tail Ari? I don't want to end up in the sea on dark night.'

'Don't worry,' said Nikki. 'He'll never link you with us.'

Victor wasn't too sure but he looked down at Elena. The desperation she was feeling was obvious and his heart went out to her.

'I know I am going to regret this. I'll do it.'

'Give me whatever money you have. I always keep enough Dollars for an air ticket out of here in case things turn nasty in Almina. You never know.' As Nikki placed a pile of one hundred dollar bills on the coffee table, Victor took out a scrap of paper from his pocket, picked up his mobile and called the number scribbled on it.

'Mr Charlie? I'm ringing about the girl Kristina. I've the money. May I collect her tonight?' Victor paused whilst he listened to the voice at the other end of the phone. Nikki and Elena sat up on the edge of the sofas leaning forward so they could catch every word. 'Yes, eleven tonight. I'll be there. You'll have all her papers too? Good.'

Charlie put the phone down and turned to his associate. Our friend is coming to collect Kristina tonight. Have all her things ready.'

'Shall I go and remove her from the shop now?'

'No, she might as well keep working until he comes to collect her. He might not pitch up. Just tell her to pack and in the meantime we'll make as much money from her as we can.'

Charlie picked up the phone and rapidly keyed in some familiar numbers.

'Eva? Our friend Mr Victor has just rung. He's bringing the money and collecting your Kristina tonight.'

'I told you Charlie, she's not my Kristina. I sold her on to Madam

Olga and she sold her on to you; body and soul.'

'But Eva,' joked Charlie. 'I got the body but I'm still awaiting the soul.'

'Nobody pays for the soul in your business Charlie; they only want the body.'

'True, but I thought you'd be interested. It's strange a Westerner buying a commodity from us. I've never known it before.'

'Do me a favour Charlie and send someone to follow this man. Find out where he's taking her. It may be useful to us in the future.'

'I've already arranged it,' said Charlie. 'I'll inform you of your Kristina's future whereabouts. On another matter, do you have any more girls you want to pass on? I'm one short now and a white girl adds a bit of class to the establishment.'

'There's another batch arriving tomorrow but I want to see if they'll work upmarket first. I'll let you know.'

Eva replaced the handset on its cradle.

'Problems?' asked the blonde girl who was sitting in the kitchen, concentrating on filing her nails, whilst talking with Eva. They were at the table drinking endless tea. The blonde girl had her feet on an empty chair next to her and was wearing a red silky housecoat with nothing underneath. The housecoat hung down to reveal her long slender legs.

'I don't know,' replied Eva. 'That was Chinese Charlie telling me someone called Victor has found the money and is collecting our Kristina tonight.'

'He should have tried 'Buy one get one free' with Chinese Charlie. He has enough of them.' The blonde girl continued attending to her nails taking especial care with the nail on her little finger whilst she waited for Eva's response.

'It's strange. No-one's heard of this Victor before, and why Kristina? She's the worst working girl I've ever had.'

'Maybe he's into necrophilia,' said the blonde girl wanting to keep the conversation going and find out more. 'With Kristina, it must be the nearest thing to screwing a lifeless body - and you don't have to keep finding a replacement.'

'I thought about what you said.'

'Said about what?'

'What you said about Kristina and Elena looking alike. I checked

Elena's passport against a copy of Kristina's.' Eva paused.

'And?' asked the blonde girl putting her nail file down and giving Eva her full attention.

'You may well ask. They're both from the same country, the same region and they both have the same surname. But..'

'But what? Come on Madam, but what?'

'It's a very common surname. Half the people in the country have the same name. It may just be because they come from the same region they've similar looks.'

The blonde girl picked up her nail file and resumed her manicure.

'Still strange though. On top of all this a guy called Victor wants to buy your Kristina.'

'I wish people would stop calling her 'my Kristina.' I sold her. She's not my problem anymore. Sold as seen, no refunds.'

The blonde girl concentrated on her nails. 'It was you who brought her here and there's no such thing as 'sold as seen' in this business. If there's a problem, Chinese Charlie will blame you won't he?'

'But I don't understand why this guy wants to buy her outright.'

The blonde girl looked up from manicuring her nails, 'maybe you need someone to keep an eye on Elena. Someone you can trust. Someone who can report back to you and tell you what she's up to. Isn't there a free place in their apartment?'

"I arrived from Bangladesh for a good job but was forced to work in the sex industry as soon as I had landed. At first I was sent to work in a massage parlour for two months but since I could only speak my own native language they told me I could not continue there but must work as a prostitute. I refused but they beat me until I agreed and was given a salary of 370 Dollars a month. After twenty days I couldn't take any more so I pleaded with them to send me home. They refused and beat me. They locked me in a room for three days and raped me twice." The Almina human trafficking hotline received a call stating where she was being held and police freed her and arrested the traffickers.

Proceedings of Court case.

Chapter 35

'Tasha, I told you I can't come home,' Elena sobbed into the mobile. She looked around the '*office*' in the apartment; in the daytime it was a cold friendless place. A double bed as a workplace. Two cabinets, one at each side of the bed with nothing else but a box of tissues on the top and a supply of condoms inside. No real pictures on the walls - none meaning anything personal to Elena anyway and here was Tasha was pleading with her to go home. She remembered her own bedroom with photographs of her family and life, soft toys, lace and frills everywhere. 'For one thing I don't have my passport and secondly I'm hoping to save Kristina in the next day or two.'

'But not only is Mikhail selling drugs he's using them too.' Elena cringed as she heard what her sister had to say. The one thing she always dreaded was her children using drugs. Just about the worst thing any mother could discover. 'He's also been thrown out of school; not that it matters much as he stopped going anyway. It's bloody Dorgan. He wants your money and your family too. Why you ever borrowed money from him, I'll never know.'

'Tasha, I was desperate. I still am. Please try and sort it out for me. I can't come home until I've saved Kristina. I can only do one thing at a time. I'll sort Mikhail out then. In the meantime, please do what you can for me.'

'I'll try. Love you.'

'Love you too,' said Elena as she put the phone down. She went back to the bedroom and Nikki.

'Remember me,' asked the blonde girl, as Elena walked in.

'Oh, yes.' Elena was taken by surprise. 'What're you doing here?'

'I'm your new roommate.'

'This is Anastasia and she is taking Julie's place,' Nikki told Elena. She turned to the blonde girl. 'Is it OK if we shorten your name and call you 'Nasty'?'

267

'Why not, everyone else does.'

Elena handed the mobile back to Nikki. 'What's up with your phone? Not working?' Nasty asked.

'No the battery's flat; I need to charge it,' Elena did not want to tell her Nikki had international dialling.

'So where are we going to tonight? I'm free at last so I want to enjoy my first night.'

'We've been going to the Palace. Julie put us on to it,' Elena explained. 'Trouble is you have to clear it with the hotel first, so you won't get in just yet.'

'But just for you, we'll try the Almina Towers Hotel tonight,' interjected Nikki thinking it may be a good idea to keep an eye on their new visitor for a while.'

'Is your phone ringing Elena?' Nasty asked with a smirk. 'Your battery must have recharged all by itself.'

'Shit! This is going to be difficult,' thought Nikki as Elena answered her mobile.

'Oh, hi,' Elena just managed to stop herself from using Victor's name out loud. 'Later tonight? Yes I'm sure I can fit you in later. Just give me a ring when you're ready.'

'Did you really say 'I'm sure I can fit you in'?' asked Nasty. 'Just how big is this guy?'

Elena ignored her, as she had more important matters on her mind and continued her telephone conversation. 'I'm going to work now. Thank you. Thank you.'

'Well Elena, I wonder how Victor got your phone number?' thought Nikki. 'I certainly never gave it to him. She knew the 'spark' between them was leading to something special.

Victor replaced his mobile in his pocket. He felt the thick envelope in the inside pocket of his jacket, making sure the money was still there. Putting the car into drive, he left the underground parking at his home to go and collect Kristina. He had wanted to take someone with him for protection but after going through a mental list of his friends and colleagues, he decided there was no-one he could trust and no-one he wanted to get involved. He drove through the evening traffic; always a busy time in Almina with people making their way home from work or just driving around in their huge, shiny four wheel drives trying to relieve the boredom. It was after ten and it had long gone dark.

Victor clambered out of the car and removed his jacket, transferring the money to his trouser pocket. He remembered from a gangster film he had seen long ago that jackets were usually worn to conceal a gun and he didn't want any trouble. He left the car unlocked, took a deep breath, and plucked up the courage to push open the front gate. The door to the villa opened as he walked up the path towards the door.

'You here for lady?' asked the fat Chinese man, peering through the half open door and not recognising Victor in the dark.

'I have an appointment with Mr Charlie,' replied Victor.

'Ah, Mr Victor. Come in. Mr Charlie expecting you.'

'Why did I use my real name?' thought Victor. On second thoughts he decided it was best as if they discovered he had been lying to them, the whole deal could have gone very wrong. He glanced into the working area of the brothel as he passed. There was a queue of seven men in the 'shop' waiting patiently for their turn.

'Mr Victor,' Chinese Charlie rose to his feet and offered Victor his hand in a rare friendly gesture since money was to be had. 'How are you?'

'Good,' lied Victor, 'very good.'

'Sit down,' continued Chinese Charlie, 'and fetch Mr Victor some tea.'

'No, I'm fine,' Victor wanted to do the deal and get out of there; but it was too late; one of Chinese Charlie's underlings was already pouring him tea from a flask on a table at the side of the room.

'Thanks,' said Victor as the clear glass cup containing the hot tea was placed in front of him. He could see the single large sugar lump lying at the bottom. Unstirred and undissolved as was customary out here. He took a sip of the sweet liquid, being careful not to drink it all as the tea would keep coming as often as the cup was emptied.

'I have the money,' said Victor. 'Is the girl ready?'

'May I see the money?'

'What about the girl?'

'Don't worry Mr Victor. No-one's going to cheat you. I'm happy with the deal and in this business, with us all being visitors, we must all remain friends with no falling out.'

Victor took the envelope from his trouser pocket and placed it carefully on the desk in front of Chinese Charlie who picked it up and counted the money carefully and without embarrassment.

'Good it's all there.'

'And the girl?' asked Victor.

'She's packing her things. Have some more tea.' Chinese Charlie nodded at the underling who left the room.

'The white girl.' The underling said to the fat Chinese doorkeeper in the brothel. Where is she?'

'She's in the end cubicle with a customer.'

The underling went to the last cubicle. The line of waiting customers went very quiet as he passed, as anything out of the ordinary usually meant trouble.

The underling threw back the curtain and revealed a naked Indian man pumping away at Kristina. She was totally emotionless, staring at the ceiling. Her left arm outstretched so it overhung the side of the bed, her fingers held tight in a fist.

'Get off her!' the underling snapped. The Indian guy stopped pumping and looked back in surprise. 'Get off her, she's wanted elsewhere.'

'But I haven't fin..,' he stuttered but knew better than to argue.

He stood up by the bed, his erection slowly disappearing. The underling grabbed Kristina by the arm, pulled her off the bed and walked her naked into the open room. The doorman stood at the entrance to the cubicle along with a young Chinese girl who was now standing by his side. She was naked apart from a towel wrapped around her. As the underling walked Kristina out of the room, the doorman pushed the Chinese girl onto the bed and removed the towel from around her.

'You can have five extra minutes,' he said to the Indian guy. 'Enjoy.' He left closing the curtain behind him.

Victor turned as the door opened and a naked Kristina was escorted in. In the full lighting of the room, he was horrified by what he saw. She was drained of all colour and her bones were protruding through her skin as if they were trying to get out. She reminded him of some pictures he had seen of young girls who were dying from anorexia.

The underling took a carrier bag from one corner and threw it at Kristina.

'Get dressed.' Like an automaton, she took some jeans, a blouse and some slippers from the bag and started to put them on. It was not easy for her as she would not unclench her left hand.

'Must have given up on underwear long ago,' thought Victor who was making a deliberate effort not to watch her dress.

'Here's her passport,' said Chinese Charlie handing over the document. Victor took it and opened it. Whilst one would never recognise Kristina as the healthy specimen in the passport photograph, it was clearly hers. He checked the visa and saw it had expired long ago.

'Visa expired,' said Victor. 'It could be a problem.'

'Only if you let her out of your bedroom,' replied a smiling Chinese Charlie.

'I've included a few supplies which will keep her happy for the next two or three days. These are free of charge. She'll need her medicine. When you want more, just ring this number and ask for a coconut pizza and we'll deliver.' Chinese Charlie handed over a business card which read, 'Almina Bizarre. Home delivery pizza.'

'I don't think I'll need any thank you,' Victor said trying to return the card.

'You will. Kristina has a strong need for her medicine. She takes much.' Chinese Charlie rose indicating their business was closed. 'If you need any more girls I'll be pleased to do business with you again. Help Mr Victor to his car with his purchase.' The underling pushed the carrier bag into Kristina's hands and led her forcibly by the arm.

'Don't hurt her,' pleaded Victor.

'Don't worry, Kristina feels no pain,' retorted the underling snappily.

He put Kristina in to the passenger seat and threw her carrier bag onto the back seat. Victor was shocked. Her entire belongings fit into one carrier bag.

He drove away and as he turned the corner at the end of the street a motor cycle came from the back of the villa carrying a Chinese rider wearing shorts, a red shirt but no helmet. On the back of the motorcycle was a large box bearing the inscription 'Almina Bizarre. Home delivery pizzas.'

Elena's mobile rang. Even though she had been holding it in her hand all night, she fumbled to open it and almost cancelled the call in doing so.

She was so nervous she could barely say hello but Victor was calm and controlled and straight to the point.

'I've got her, Elena. She's in my home and we're alone. Why not come over and say hello.'

'Yes, I'll come now. All night did you say?' She closed the mobile and looked directly at Nikki. 'I've an all-night customer. Someone I've been with before. I've got to go now.'

'Good luck,' Nikki shouted as Elena walked away.

Anastasia, took out her own mobile and sent a text.

'Elena, all night customer; eleven pm' and sent it to Eva.

'How is she?' asked Elena, as Victor opened the door to let her in.

'She's fine. Tired but safe. She's asleep in the spare bedroom through here.'

Kristina was lying on the bed. She had lost so much weight she hardly made a dent in the mattress.

'She is as they gave her to me,' said Victor not sure if 'gave' was the right word to use. I can't get her to release her left hand; it's all clenched up.'

Elena rushed over to the bed and pulled Christina to her breast.

'Don't worry; mama's here,' she whispered gently. Kristina said nothing but started to sob quietly. Elena ran her hand down her daughter's left arm and tried to open her clenched fist.

'No, don't steal it. It's mine.' She said as she pulled her arm away.

'Looking at how many possessions she has in the carrier bag, it looks like just about everything she had has been taken.' Victor was standing at the bottom of the bed.

'Don't worry darling. I won't steal anything from you. I'm your mother. You'll hurt yourself, if you don't let go.'

Kristina released her grip and let Elena open her hand. There inside was the little bear necklace Elena had given to Victor to pass on to her.

'She must have had it there all the time,' Victor said but neither of them were listening to him; they were both sobbing their hearts out.

Realising he was not needed Victor left the apartment and hailed a taxi.

'Where to Sir?'

Victor wasn't sure. He just needed to get away for a while. 'I need a drink,' he thought. 'Almina Towers Hotel please,' he heard himself say.

In the bar he could see Nikki across the room, talking to another girl.

'Hi Nikki, I needed a drink after all this.'

'After what?' asked Anastasia sharply. If something was going on she wanted to know about it.

'John, you're back.' Nikki replied, rather too quickly for casual conversation. 'John, I'd like you to meet Nasty. Nasty's our new flat mate.'

'She doesn't look flat to me,' quipped Victor putting on an air of jollity he certainly didn't feel.

'John's just come back from partying with two girls,' continued Nikki. 'No wonder you need a drink. Is everything OK?'

'Yes, I left the two girls very happy. Very happy indeed. Look, you two are working and I just want a quiet drink and recover my strength. If you don't mind I'll go over to the bar and not frighten away your customers.

Victor moved over to the bar, ordered a drink and spent the next thirty minutes trying to drink his beer, using both hands to hold the glass, in a failed attempt to stop them shaking and spilling the liquid onto the floor.

Nikki watched him from afar. She felt Anastasia watching her with interest and so broke off her vigil with a start. 'I'm going to work the room. Coming?'

'No, I'll stay here and let them come to me – said the spider to the fly.'

'The only flies you'll get near are on a pair of trousers,' Nikki retorted.

'Are you taking a lady tonight?'

'How long in Almina?'

'Where you from?'

She resorted to the well-worn phrases used by all the girls to start a conversation but her heart wasn't really in it. She kept thinking of

Elena and Kristina and found her eyes wandering over to Victor propping up the bar. She kept working the room but found herself gravitating towards him.

'Do you play cards? Well, play them right and you could come home with me,' she spoke to one customer before she found herself next to Victor. Putting her arm through his she whispered, 'Come on. I don't know about you but I need to go back and see how they both are. Drink up and let's go.'

Victor took one last gulp from his drink, left the last few inches in the glass and he and Nikki walked out together, not noticing Nasty pick up her phone.

'Nikki's just left with a guy called John.' she reported.

'Thanks,' said Eva. 'You're a good girl.'

The Almina Supreme Court rejected the final appeal of three Bangladeshi men against the death penalty for the murder of a Bangladeshi man known for helping prostitutes escape from their captors. Evidence showed that the men were furious when he intervened as they were taking a prostitute back to their premises. They went to the victim's home, attacked him and tied his legs and feet together. He was beaten with a pipe before being strangled.

Proceedings of Court case.

Chapter 36

'Shit!' thought Victor as he and Nikki stood in the lift in his apartment block. Standing opposite him was his neighbour, a lady in her mid-fifties with whom Victor often exchanged pleasantries whenever they met. Tonight she said nothing but smiled knowingly as she avoided his eyes.

'It will take some time to live this one down,' he thought, looking at the length of Nikki's skirt.

The lift came to rest and the doors slid open.

'After you,' said Victor to his neighbour, hoping he could let her go ahead and casually pretend Nikki was not with him. In the bar she was camouflaged amongst the other girls but in the cold light of reality, there was no mistaking her for the hooker she was.

'No, after you,' said the lady with a knowing smile.

Victor and Nikki walked down the corridor saying nothing and keeping a respectable distance between them. The lady walked behind. As bad luck would have it they came to Victor's apartment first and they stopped as Victor unlocked the door.

'Have a good night,' said the lady as she walked on to her own apartment.

As Victor and Nikki went inside, they saw a light coming from the kitchen. 'Is everything alright' he asked, as he saw Elena sitting at the table sipping coffee.

'Oh, yes. Kristina's finally sleeping. I can't thank you enough.' Elena was very tearful and emotional.

'Well our problems are only just starting, said Nikki. 'Do you have Kristina's passport?'

'Yes it's here,' handing it over.

Nikki looked at it, flipping the pages over quickly. 'The bastards never finished the residence visa. They just reported her as an absconder to save money. This means she's overstayed. At best it's a

276

fine; at worst it's prison.'

'What are you two talking about?' asked Elena. 'We've her passport. Isn't it enough?'

'Will you tell her or shall I?' asked Nikki looking at Victor. 'It's not easy to get out of Almina. There are thousands of normally law abiding citizens who are locked up here, for simply bouncing a cheque, let alone staying here illegally.'

'But couldn't we just pay the fine?' Elena was still unaware of the problems they may have to face.

'In theory, the answer is yes,' said Victor. 'Since I 'bought' Kristina and I have her passport, we could just pay the fine. It will be a big fine mind you.'

'How much?' asked Elena knowing the answer would be depressing.

'One hundred dollars per day,' said Nikki. 'So we're looking at a lot of money.' Elena went pale - even more money and she was already in debt both to Victor and at home.

'Add to that, since Kristina has been force fed drugs, which take months to get out of your system, if they do a blood test then she could be in prison for years to come,' added Victor.

'So what can we do?' Elena was worried now.

Victor looked over at Nikki and sighed. 'The problem is not only Kristina, it's you as well.'

'How do you mean?'

'Kristina I can sort out through my company. I employ her, pay the fines and as long as she can stand up as she goes through the airport, no-one will bother her. All this country is interested in is money. If they get their money they'll never stop anyone from leaving.'

'I'll pay you back everything Victor, you know I will. You've been amazing and I'll never forget what you've done. Why am I the problem?'

'What Victor is trying to say is we have just swapped one problem for another. Yes, we can get Kristina out but what about you?'

'I can go with her, take her home. What's the problem?'

'The problem my dear is you have no passport. Eva has it. How do we get you out of Almina?'

'Well, I could just …' Elena was perplexed. She had not thought this through at all. It was going to be difficult.

'No you couldn't,' interrupted Nikki. 'Not until you've paid Eva back and it could take years.'

'And then what about the loan sharks back home?' asked Victor. 'How will you pay them back without Almina salaries?'

'I can't,' said Elena finally. 'You two have obviously thought this one through. As long as I get my daughter Kristina out of this hell hole I'll stay here forever. So what do we do? I've no choice.'

'There is a way, but it's risky and I need to look into it.' Victor did not like to see her upset.

'What way?' asked Elena. 'We'll try anything.'

'I'll need to ask around,' he continued, 'but I've heard of people doing 'a runner' from Almina when their debts are so large they can't repay them.'

Why would anyone 'do a runner' over their debts?' Elena was incredulous.

'Because in Almina, any loan is secured by an undated security cheque. When a person can't repay these loans, the lender writes in the current date and presents it for payment. Since it's a criminal offence in Almina to 'bounce a cheque,' the person goes to prison until the loan is repaid. When in prison, they earn no money so they are stuck there, added to which they can't pay their other bills and so other lenders go after them as well. Hence people do runners to avoid debts. Nikki tapped Elena on the shoulder. 'We need to get back.'

'Yes, Kristina will be fine here with me. Come whenever you like,' continued Victor. 'However, you two must continue as normal for the time being otherwise people will become suspicious.'

The girls walked out of the front door and Victor knew he did not mean what he had just said. He did not want Elena to carry on as 'normal' at all. He wanted her to stay in his home with him.

But you could never marry a prostitute.........could you?

"I was working in my sponsor's kitchen when this man burst in, gagged and blindfolded me and then pushed me into a waiting car. He drove me to a flat where he said I had to work as a prostitute." The police rescued the pregnant housemaid when they raided the flat following a tip off.
                    Proceedings of Court case.

Chapter 37

As they walked into the foyer of the Almina Towers hotel for a 'business lunch,' a man came out of the bar to their left. He was dressed in a suit with a flower pinned to the lapel and he was clearly drunk. He gave them both a broad grin and moved off in the direction of the toilets, stumbling up the few stairs as he went. The security guard at the door couldn't prevent himself from smiling and as Nikki looked around, she saw the same amusement on the faces of all the hotel staff.

'What's going on?' she asked the security guard as she handed over the entry fees in return for the two 'free drink' vouchers. Since they were now working semi-independently, they had to pay their own way.

'We've a wedding reception,' he told her proudly, as if this sort of thing happened every day in what was generally accepted to be a 'hookers' bar.

As their pupils reacted to the gloom of their surroundings, they could see the dance floor emerge on their left; not that anyone ever danced on it mind. The only 'dancing' done was a mental tap dance, as girl and client negotiated a price but today it had been cleared and one long table had been set. There were pristine white table cloths, metal cutlery and in the middle, a huge floral centre piece. Standing or seated around the table were a dozen or so people who were all dressed in their 'Sunday best' and wearing corsages. The regular working girls were standing back, keeping at a respectable distance, watching in awe. Not just at the spectacle of the couple having their wedding party in such a place as this but at the realisation the hotel actually had such refinements as metal tableware.

Nikki looked around the room and spotted two men visiting for the first time. Walking over to them, she stood close. Elena followed. 'Hi, could you help us out please?' She said with a smile to the taller of the two, on the basis he would have to look down at her and would be able to see down her cleavage. 'We had to pay to come in and they gave us these tokens for free drinks. We don't want a drink, so we wondered if you two kind gentlemen would give us the money and then use them to buy your next drinks.'

The man took his eyes off Nikki's breasts and examined the tickets in her hand. She held one of the vouchers between finger and thumb and turned it towards him so he could see the name of the hotel, the date and the writing 'one free drink.'

'Sure. All the same to me,' he smiled as he and Nikki exchanged cash for tokens.'

'Thanks. Catch you later.' The two girls blew them a kiss and walked away to lose themselves in the crowd.

'What are they doing celebrating here?' Nikki asked a Chinese working girl she knew vaguely.

'They married this morning and are celebrating their reception here. I never thought this sort of thing would happen to one of us.'

Elena looked at the group and scanned each face in turn. In her home country she would have found it odd that all the men were old and Western whilst the girls were all young and either Eastern European or Chinese but here in Almina, it did not surprise her at all. She had become used to seeing and doing things that would have shocked her in her home country only a few months ago. However, in this 'other' world, it was the norm and the everyday life was certainly different. For a second she imagined she was the bride and Victor the groom and they were celebrating with her children, Kristina and Mikhail. Mikhail would have given her away and Kristina would have been her bridesmaid but no, men like Victor never married whores.

'Those drink tokens are no good?'

'Sorry,' she said as her day dreaming was suddenly interrupted.

'Those drink tokens you sold us are no good. They can only be used for soft drinks and not alcohol. What do we want with lemonade in a place like this?'

'What's the problem?' asked Nikki, sliding her hand through the man's arm and leaning against him. She had seen the problem only too well and had returned to help Elena.

'Those tokens are no good. They can only be used to buy soft drinks.

It says so at the bottom.'

'That's why I held my thumb over the bottom of the token you prick!' thought Nikki.

'They must have changed the rules. It's never happened before,' Nikki smiled sweetly. 'Tell you what, take us both home with you and we'll deduct the money from the price. A deal?

'Bloody cheating cow,' he muttered as he walked away.

Nikki was about to give her reply with a hand gesture but was interrupted by her mobile ringing.

'Toys are us?' she answered. It was Victor.

'I have the name and contact details from my friend regarding the shipment. Do you understand?' Victor was taking great care with his choice of words. In Almina all telephone conversations often were listened to by the police; similarly with emails. Any key word triggered an automatic alarm at the police electronic listening station. Anyone under suspicion would have a full time 'tap' on his/her phone. Victor had chosen to contact Nikki rather than Elena as he knew she was much more guarded and would not let anything slip in the conversation.

'Yes I'm with you. When will you get the loading documents?'

'Today, I'm just leaving now.'

'And the cargo? Is it OK?'

'It's fragile but safe. Is it possible for Elena come around and look after the cargo whilst I go out and organise the final details of the shipment?'

'You don't need to ask. In any case, her long face is driving my customers away so I'll be glad to be shut of her. I'll ask her.'

'I know this is a lot to ask,' Nikki turned to Elena, 'but Victor wondered if you could help him out and go look after Kristina for him whilst he's out.'

'Try to keep me away,' Elena was elated. She wanted to be with her daughter more than anything.

She pretended to talk on her mobile to make it look like she had a customer and made her way to the exit and the ever waiting taxis.

On arrival at Victor's apartment block she pressed his apartment number into the electronic security key pad by the door and was reassured when she heard his voice on the intercom. As the door 'buzzed' it opened and she walked in. Across the road a Chinese man was sitting astride a motor bike, watching her whilst speaking into his mobile. On the back of the motor bike was a carrier box with 'Almina Bizarre pizzas' emblazoned on it.

'How is she?' Elena asked as she entered Victor's apartment.

'She's fine,' he answered. 'She's sitting up in bed now, still shaking but not so badly.'

Elena went into Kristina's bedroom and rushed over to the bed. Sitting next to her, she put her arm around her and gave her a hug.

'What Kristina really needs,' said Victor, 'is some 'home food.' If I'm honest, I think it's what Mum needs too; to cook for Kristina. Here's the phone number of the corner shop. They'll deliver what you need and I've an account there. Why not ring them up and order what you want?

Before he left the apartment, Victor switched off his phone and removed the battery. He remembered from the New York nine-eleven disaster police had been able to trace the bodies in the rubble by their mobile phones; and he didn't want anyone tracing him where he was going.

Elena rang the grocery and ordered vegetables and the other essential ingredients for her daughter's favourite food. Within a few minutes the ingredients arrived and she set to work in the kitchen.

Whilst she cooked, Elena and Kristina talked of home, of Mikhail, Tasha and a life seeming so long in the past. Had she been to Victor's before, she would have known the grocer's shop was run by a Pakistani who had never employed a Chinese delivery man such as the one who had come to her door.

'Hello Eva, this is Chinese Charlie. How are you?'

'Fine Charlie, at least until you rang. What's up?'

'Well do you remember your Kristina and the westerner Victor?'

'I already said Charlie, she's not my Kristina, I sold her to you 'sold as seen.''

'If you bring trouble to me, I bring trouble to you. There's no such thing in our business as sold as seen.'

'So what's the problem?' Madam Eva did not need trouble from Charlie.

'Well, my man has been outside Victor's apartment block for the last few days non-stop, and he's just seen your Elena enter the building. Now is she your Elena or not?'

'Oh yes, she's my Elena and this is getting interesting.'

'So what do you plan to do about it?'

'As I see it Charlie, this Victor bought Kristina fair and square so we cannot complain but if he's thinking of helping Elena to escape, then I'll have to act. I've invested too much money in her already and she's far too valuable an asset to just let her go. No Charlie, if this man tries to take Elena then we'll have to kill him.'

'I thought you might say that. I'll stop my men from watching her now. This is for you to sort out.'

Eva placed her mobile down slowly and began to think. She picked up the telephone and dialled.

'Is that you Ari? We've a problem.'

"I was promised a job as a secretary but when I came from the Philippines to Almina I was forced to work in the sex industry. They advertised me by giving out business cards with my phone number on. I paid money for them to bring me here but they took my passport, held me in a flat where one man raped me. He said customers would ring me for sex. They distributed cards offering massage services but I was made to work as a prostitute for a month. I texted a friend's husband asking him to save me and sent him my address. He reported to the police who rescued me."

Testament from Court records.

Chapter 38

Wonderful!' said Victor as he mopped up the last of the soup with a piece of bread. 'You can certainly cook.'

'And thank you too. I really enjoyed cooking for Kristina. She's sleeping now, which is the best thing for her.'

'I'll drink to that,' and Victor held up his glass of wine and clinked glasses with Elena. As they did so, their eyes met and held each other for a moment before an embarrassing silence forced Victor to look away.

'How did you get on?' asked Elena.

'OK. Nikki's coming soon; so let's wait until she's here and then I don't have to repeat it. Apparently she's with two local men who are paying her a fortune - as only Nikki can. Victor stood up and started to clear the plates.'

The domestic scene of Elena washing and Victor drying was played out as they chatted, enjoying the closeness of doing something together. They had just finished drying the last of the cutlery when Nikki arrived.

She looked around the kitchen. 'Wow! Is this something from fifties television? Daughter asleep in bed, Mummy and Daddy washing up after the evening meal, it's enough to make you throw up.' Looking at their faces, she realised they did not find her comments amusing.

'Sorry. So how did you get on Victor?'

'Good. My company's 'Mr Fixit' has sorted out Kristina's visa and fines and so she's booked on a flight home the day after tomorrow. She'll have to change flights halfway, so I'm going with her until there. I'll make sure she boards the flight for the last leg before coming back. There won't be any problems once she's left this place. Elena, you need to arrange for Tasha and Mikhail to meet her at the airport.'

'That's great but are you sure about accompanying her out of here?

It's a big thing to ask of you.' Elena was ecstatic but worried they were asking too much of Victor.

'It's no problem. I think it is better if I'm with her when she leaves Almina in case there are any problems. She's on my visa now so I'm her sponsor and I can sort things out if need be.

'As for you Elena we've a problem. With no passport it will be hard for you to leave without working your way out of here. By that I mean paying Eva back. The trouble is, having worked so hard to earn the money to get Kristina out of here they'll not let you go cheaply. You're too valuable to them. Think of yourself as a salesperson; the more you sell, the higher your next month's target.' He cringed at the thought of Elena selling her body.

'I don't mind,' said a righteous Elena. 'As long Kristina is safe; it's all I want.'

'Well there's a way but it's dangerous,' he continued. 'I talked to some people today who can arrange things. '

'Do you mean escape by boat?' asked Nikki.

'No it's too dangerous. The customs people search the boats all the time. I mean crossing the desert and then over the mountains to Kajan. It's the neighbouring country and from you can get help from the embassy as you're not a criminal in Kajan. You can even catch a boat home.'

'Sounds risky.' Nikki was thinking Elena was too naïve to accomplish this journey.

'It is,' continued Victor but what's the other option? Having sex with strange men for the next five years to earn her passage home?'

Nikki realised Victor found this option unacceptable; perhaps more so than Elena.

'So,' she continued, 'If, as you say Kristina goes to her homeland, and Elena makes it across the desert, what then?'

'How do you mean?' said Victor trying to avoid the question. He knew what she was thinking.

'Well, do you and Elena go your separate ways never to see each other again?'

Victor tried not to look at Elena, who he knew was staring at him; waiting for his response.

'One step at a time Nikki. We're taking huge risks here.'

'It's OK Victor,' said Elena moving over to him and putting her arm around his waist. 'I can't thank you enough for what you've done for Kristina and myself already. I ask for nothing else.' He smiled at her as he began to speak again.

'Come round here at four tomorrow afternoon. They wouldn't give me any details of the trip, as there are others leaving with you and they don't want anyone talking and landing us all in prison. However, they said to pack a small rucksack with enough clothes for four or five days. You must wear jeans or trousers and a burqa that covers your body from head to toe. Put the rest in a suitcase and Kristina will take it for you; she has very little of her own and it'll look more realistic if she has more clothes. I'll take you to the people who'll make good your escape and then Kristina and I will go to the airport.

'A burqa? Elena was confused. 'You mean the robes people wear that cover everything? I don't have one of those.'

'Then buy one today. It's imperative you get one Elena. This is a very dangerous thing you're doing. We mustn't make any problems.'

At this point Kristina walked into the room. She was wearing a T shirt and pair of knickers and wiped the sleep from her eyes as she walked. 'Did I overhear you talking about going home?'

'Yes dear, tomorrow.' Elena spoke as she walked over to her daughter and gave her a hug. 'Now go back to sleep; you'll need all your strength for the journey.'

'Are we going together?' Kristina asked Elena.

'No, it's not possible,' Victor told her. 'I'm taking you half way and your Auntie Tasha and Mikhail will meet you at the other end. Your Mum has to go a different route and unfortunately we cannot go with her.'

'Wait there,' said Kristina, as she untangled herself from her mother's arms. She went back into the bedroom and returned with the little bear on a chain her Mother had asked Victor to give to her in the Chinese brothel.

'Take this for good luck,' she said and placed it in her Mother's hand.

'No you keep it,' said Elena. 'It's yours now, I gave it to you.'

'Well, keep it with you and when you come home, you can give it back to me.' Kristina closed her mother's fingers around the bear and then let go.

'It's time we moved out of here.' Nikki could not cope with all the emotions and feelings. 'Kristina needs to rest, Elena needs to pack and I want to catch a last customer before the bars close. One of us has to earn some money.'

Nikki moved to the door. Elena took a step forward but then stopped and turned to look at him. 'How about one last night of lust Victor? It's free.'

Victor was fighting with his feelings. He wanted to tell Elena how much he loved her, how much he cared. He wanted to tell her he would protect her and keep her from harm but the words wouldn't come. Instead he looked at her, staring into her expectant eyes but all he could manage to say was, 'no, it's a long day tomorrow. Its better we finish it like this.'

As Elena followed Nikki out of the door, she turned and took one last look at him mouthing, 'Bye,' and gently closing the door before starting to sob.

Victor stood for a while watching the door, hoping against hope it would open once more and Elena would walk back in. That she would run to him and hold him tight. The door remained silently closed.

As soon as he realised Elena was not coming back, he went to the kitchen to finish off the bottle of wine.

After all, you can't marry a prostitute; can you?

"They paid my parents a large sum of money and said they were bringing me to Almina for a good job. I was only fifteen years old but they forced me to sleep with men. They humiliated me and beat me until I capitulated." The Almina police received a tip off and met the girl as she returned from an assignment. They persuaded the girl to help and an undercover agent approached her captors and asked to take the girl for three days. The gang leader accepted and was arrested as soon as the money was handed over. Searches revealed the victim's passports, money transfer receipts and a ledger recording transactions of the money made from prostitution.

Proceedings of Court case.

Chapter 39

At the appointed hour Victor's doorbell rang and Nikki and Elena entered the apartment. The building security guard recognised them and let them into the building without question. Kristina was already dressed in jeans and a black top; she leapt up from the sofa as soon as she saw her Mother and ran across and hugged her tightly.

Elena was happy to see Kristina looking so much better.

'Glad to see you're on time.' Victor came in from the kitchen with a mug of coffee. 'We'll need to set off soon. We're meeting Elena's transport in a lay-by on the main route out of here, so we'd better say our goodbyes here. There's no need for me to say goodbye to Nikki of course,' he laughed, 'as we'll see each other in the bars from time to time.'

Nikki nodded, feeling sad Elena was going and nothing would ever be quite the same again. Victor moved over to Elena and put his arms around her waist. He held her to him becoming aroused immediately. 'I'll never forget you Elena. Kristina has my postal address and you remember my phone number. The people who're taking you said you mustn't have any identification or addresses on you in case things go wrong; which they won't,' he added quickly.

He gave her a kiss on the lips and he moved away. Elena sprang back at him and holding him tightly, gave him a long passionate kiss.

'I can't thank you enough Victor, and you too Nikki. Without you both I'd never have managed this.'

'Forget it.' Nikki was embarrassed by emotion; she didn't want to lose control of herself. 'Now, let's get going or we'll still be here tomorrow.'

They took the elevator down to the underground parking. Victor and Elena exchanged smiles but no-one said anything. They put the bags in his car, got in and drove out into the fading sunlight. Elena watched carefully as they drove past the well-known landmarks;

taking one last look in the knowledge she could never return and see them again. She looked longingly at Victor, knowing she would never see him again either. The thought tugged at her heart. In a different place, at a different time, who knows? 'Why doesn't he say something,' she thought. 'I know he loves me.'

Victor said nothing; he was lost in his own thoughts and his own turmoil whilst trying to concentrate on his driving.

Eventually the buildings dwindled away and they were out in the open country.

'There they are,' said Victor pointing to a 4x4 parked in a lay-by ahead.

Elena's heart started to race as this was goodbye and the last time she would ever see him. He pulled in behind the waiting car and got out.

He pointed to Elena. 'Her name is.'

The driver stopped him abruptly. 'No, no names. No talking for the next four days. It's safer this way.'

Kristina held her mother tightly.

'I'll see you in a few days. Thanks Mum. I love you.' She returned to Victor's car. Nikki hugged Elena, squeezing her until she could hardly breathe.

'I'll miss you even though I'll make a hell of a lot more money from now on. Look after yourself and keep in touch.' She let go and Elena looked across at Victor.

As they walked towards each other he held out his hand and took Elena's in his. He looked into her eyes but a huge lump in his throat prevented him from saying anything. Words deserted him.

'I don't know what to say,' he stammered.

'Not bloody difficult,' thought Nikki, who was listening in. 'Why not try 'you are the love of my life, will you marry me?' What's so bloody difficult about that?'

Victor held Elena close to him and she placed her head on his chest.

'Thanks again for everything Victor. Thanks for giving me my daughter back. I'm so going to miss you.'

'You'd better go,' He spoke softly. 'Farewells are best kept short.'

'Does it have to be farewell?' asked Elena, knowing the answer already.

Victor swallowed. 'Don't make this any more difficult than it already is. Goodbye and good luck. Let me know when you both reach home safely.'

'But what about the money I owe you? I'll try and send you some every month, as soon as I find a job.'

'Forget the money. I don't want it back. I'm glad I could help and it was worth it just to have met you. I'll never forget ...' His voice tailed off; he was overcome with emotion as he led Elena to the waiting car and helped her into the back seat, squeezing her hand and blowing her a kiss. Tears were running down Elena's face. She felt so lonely and desolate.

There were two English men in the car escaping with her. She would at least have company on her miserable journey.

As he walked back to the car, Nikki caught him up. 'What the hell are you doing?' She asked.

'What?' he said sharply 'I'm going back to the car.'

'How stupid can you be? You love her, she loves you and yet you are still prepared to let her go. Go back and ask her to marry you whilst you still have the chance.'

'I can't do it, Nikki. I can't marry a prostitute! How many men has she been with every month; every week; every day? Every time we made love I would be wondering if it was for real or whether she was just acting for the paying customer. I can't marry a whore.'

'I'm the whore,' continued Nikki. 'I'm the one you can't marry. It's why it never worked between you and me but Elena only did this for her daughter. She'd never have done it if she hadn't been desperate to save her.'

Victor stared at the vehicle in front of them and saw the water vapour from the exhaust glistening in the moonlight as the engine started.

'There's still time. Run. Tell her how you feel. You can't end it like this. You know you've strong feelings for her. Don't deny them.'

He continued to watch the four by four. Elena was looking at him through the rear window. As the car drove off she waved, seeing nothing as the tears filled her eyes.

He managed a weak movement of his hand in reply and watched in silence as the car disappeared into the distance. Finally he started the engine of his car.

'Victor,' said Nikki. 'Without a doubt, you are the biggest prick I've ever met!'

"The men dragged us off the street and into their car and drove us to Almina where they sold us to colleagues for the sum of 680 Dollars to work in prostitution. We contacted a friend and he called the police who rescued us." The police raided the building where they were being held and discovered 23 women held there.

Proceedings of Court case.

Chapter 40

'Stop the car,' Elena screeched.

'What?' said the driver. 'We can't. We're on our way. We can't turn back now.

'I have to go back to Almina. I've left something at the apartment I must have.'

'Can't you get someone to post it? Asked the driver. 'We've got to keep going.'

'No, either we go back or I'm not going.'

'So what's so important we have to risk everything to go back for?' asked one of the Brits sitting next to her.

'I can't explain,' continued Elena, 'but it is simply something I have to have and I've left it behind.'

She realised that when she had packed, she had left the little bear necklace she had promised Kristina she would take for 'good luck' on the dressing table at the apartment. 'I'm not going to let my daughter down again she thought.'

'Look the journey will take four days, another thirty minutes to go back won't make any difference will it? Take me back and I'll pay you extra. Please.'

The driver, placated by the thought of extra money, turned the car around and made his way back to Almina, following Elena's directions.

'I'll only be two minutes,' she said as the car pulled up outside her apartment block.

'Hurry up,' growled the Brit next to her. He was feeling decidedly unsafe.

Elena rushed into the building, stabbed the lift button for her floor and spent an anxious moment waiting for it to arrive. She had to wait whilst a family took an interminable time struggling to prise a pram out of the lift before she could enter.

'Come on, come on' she thought as the floors slowly ticked past.

Eventually, she arrived at her floor and went to the apartment. Taking her keys out, she tried the handle but it was unlocked.

'Nikki must be here,' she thought. 'She'll be angry with me for coming back.'

'Hi Nikki, it's me,' she called out but there was no answer. She raced to the dressing table to find the bear but it was nowhere to be seen.

'But I know I left it there,' she said to herself.

Slowly the front door closed and Elena turned as she heard the latch click into place. Standing behind it was Pony tail Ari. He held the chain in his fingers so the bear hung freely down. In his other hand was an iron bar; fifty centimetres long and three centimetres thick. He tap, tap, and tapped on the little bear with the iron bar as he moved towards her.

'Have we forgotten something?' he said smirking as he moved towards her.

'No..., no. I am just off to work and I need some more condoms.'

'Not good enough. Eva knows all about your beloved shit of a daughter and you. Eva knows her little chickens are about to flee the nest but you little chicken, are going nowhere. You are well and truly plucked!'

Ari threw the bear onto the bed and Elena watched where it fell. He grabbed her by the throat and pushed her against the wall. He was so close all she could see was his round face and piggy eyes staring at her. He stroked the iron bar across the top of her head.   'Now should I start here with a little tap, tap, tap?' He gently tapped her forehead with the bar enjoying the fact his teasing was frightening her half to death.

He moved the bar down between her legs and stroked it in and out.

'Or should I start here and push, push, push? It doesn't matter where I start really because my little iron bar is going to explore every part of your body before we finish.'

Ari's face was so close she could taste his breath. Elena, now totally frightened out of her life felt a warm wet feeling in her jeans as her bladder uncontrollably emptied its entire contents.

'Now that's the effect I have on women,' said Ari as he permitted himself a rare smile.

She stared at his ugly face, hating his cold stare as he relished the thought of what damage he was going to inflict upon her.

The smile disappeared and she stared in disbelief as his eyes rolled upwards towards the ceiling. He fell to the floor with a bang. As his face slid out of view, she saw Nikki standing there with a knife in her hand. Its five inch stiletto blade covered in Ari's blood. He was dead; he would never torture or maim anyone ever again.

Nikki looked at her. 'I never told you about my little pal did I? A good friend of mine called Philippe gave it to me a long time ago and told me to take it with me wherever I went; to look after me in case there was any trouble and he wasn't there to protect me.'

'But how did you get here,' asked a shocked Elena.

'I was across the street and saw you come home so I followed you up here. I don't know why, I just felt there was something wrong so I came in here quietly.'

'Well thank God you did,' said Elena.

'Elena, you stink! Go get a shower and there's a pair of my jeans you can have in the bathroom. I can hear the sound of a car horn from outside. I think you friends are getting tired of waiting.'

Elena went into the bathroom and whilst she was out of the way Nikki took the opportunity of going through Ari's pockets. She counted out some dollar bills from the huge roll and put the rest in her own pocket. The gun she placed in her handbag.

When Elena returned Nikki asked her, 'How much money do you owe back home?'

'Don't remind me,' said Elena. 'I have it all to face when I get back.'

'Will this lot clear it?'

Elena looked at the stack of dollar bills. 'Well yes.' she said warily. 'It's more than enough.'

'Take it. A present from Pony tail Ari.'

Elena looked at Ari lying in a pool of blood on the floor.

'But what about him?'

'Don't worry about him just get the hell out of here.' Nikki pushed the money into Elena's hands gave her a peck on the cheek and walked her to the door. 'Leave this life to me and the professionals - and this time, don't forget the bear!'

"There were seven of us recruited by this man to come from Bangladesh to Almina to work as maids. As soon as we arrived he took our passports, locked us in an apartment and forced us to work as prostitutes. In order to take our revenge we invited him to the apartment with an offer of a massage by all seven of us. Part way through, we strangled him with a cord."
Report from Murder trial.

Chapter 41

Elena and her fellow travellers continued in their planned exit. The journey out into the desert seemed endless and they were both relieved and afraid when they eventually came to a stop.

They were surrounded by sand dunes and the quarter Moon just gave enough light to see the undulating mounds going on forever. There was nothing but sand; miles and miles of sand.

'This is where I stop,' said the driver. Get out here and take your belongings with you.

Looking at Elena he said pointedly. 'And don't forget anything this time.'

Elena and the two men clambered out; the car drove away leaving them alone and stranded in the middle of the desert.

'What happens now?' asked one of the men looking around hopelessly.

'I don't know.' Elena was bewildered as she looked around and saw nothing but emptiness in every direction. The millions of stars dotted like jewels in the black night sky above her made her feel lost and small. Her heart beat fast as she wondered if Victor had been cheated. Had he paid the money for us to be left here to die? No, he would never fall for it. Victor would look after her; she knew this with all her heart.

'What's that?' One of the men could hear something in the distance.

'What's what?' asked Elena. She heard nothing.

'That?' he said. 'Can you hear it?'

Elena listened intently and yes, she could hear the noise of motor bikes approaching; powerful motor bikes. As the noise grew louder and louder they managed to see dust trails approaching in the moonlight. Eventually the bikes arrived and swung to a halt in front of them. She prayed it was not the police.

'Get on,' ordered the driver of the first bike. She did so hoping it was safe.

There were three bikes and each one of the travellers climbed on to the pillion seats and was whisked away in a flurry of sand and noise.

The next two days were spent travelling by night and sleeping by day to avoid the border patrols. There was little cover so they had to manage as best they could. On the third day they reached the mountains. Hard, rock mountains with no soil or greenery anywhere. The passes were difficult. They rode along paths little more than one metre wide and when by chance she had happened to look down, all she saw was a vertical fall of two thousand metres or more. She kept her eyes straight ahead, concentrating on the driver's back. As they rode on she gained a great respect for the driving skills of her helpers. There was one time she panicked thinking they had been seen when a border patrol helicopter flew over with its search lights blazing. They had all spent a worried thirty minutes pressed hard against the mountain wall as the beams of light probed every nook and cranny. As luck would have it, it missed them.

Any attempt at talking was frowned upon and stopped immediately.

'Better no-one knows anything about each other, in case we get caught,' she was told.

As they came down from the mountains in the night-time on the final leg of their journey, the riders saw headlights in the distance. It was clearly a cause for consternation among their guides as it was too soon to meet the next link in their escape chain. As they rode down the track, the lights grew bigger and brighter. The riders discussed changing their route but there was no other way. They had to keep going towards the oncoming vehicle. The road was rough but still the car headlights came towards them and then it seemed to slow down and wait for their approach.

'Shit, we've been caught,' muttered one of the men.

Elena's heart fell at the thought of being returned to Almina.

The bikes pulled up in front of the car lights. The driver of the car got out and held his hands above his head, to show he was not a danger. As soon as she saw him she knew.

'Victor!' yelled Elena as she clambered off the bike and ran towards him.

'What are you doing here?'

'Kristina's back home with your family and I realised I can't live without you; but only if you give up the night job!' He smiled.

'What about your friends and your business associates when they see you with me? Can you live with that?'

'If we go somewhere else, it won't be a problem. This place is finished anyway. The money's gone and it's time to get out. We'll go on the boat together and I'll see you home. Once we've tidied up your life we'll all go to Europe, You, me, Kristina and Mikhail.'

'Are you sure?'

'I've never been surer in my life. In fact, the boat trip can be our honeymoon cruise.'

"We had no visas so we paid the agent 420 Dollars each to cross the mountain range that separates Almina from its neighbour. We often had to hide in a mountain ridge to prevent circling police helicopters from spotting us; they are always on the look out for illegal people crossing. We had to tread carefully as one wrong foot meant plunging to our deaths. We had five bottles of water and some bread but that soon went. We walked the whole day sleeping at night. Along the way we came across skeletons. After eight days we came across a small village where a pick up van was waiting for us."

Statement of illegal immigrant.

Chapter 42

Epilogue.

'Ari's dead' Nikki announced.

'I know,' said Eva, 'and Elena's run off with her daughter.'

'I heard that too, Eva.'

'She took off with all the money.'

'What a bastard she was,' said Nikki with feeling.

'You need to get out of here Nikki ASAP because Ari was murdered in your apartment and there'll be questions.'

'I know Eva, but I haven't got my passport.'

'I can sell it back to you cheap.'

'I'm grateful Eva, but if I'm to protect you, I need to get out of here tonight before the police start to ask questions and I don't have the money.'

Eva went to the safe on the wall and keyed in the combination.

'Here you are, Nikki, your passport. Take it. Now get out of Almina before the police find Ari's body.'

'But I need my airfare, Eva. Where will I get that from?'

She looked at Nikki's angelic face, thought for a second and without further ado, she handed over three thousand dollars from the safe.

'Thank you Eva. What will you do now you no longer have an enforcer?'

'Keep our heads down until the Boss sends someone else. We'll be OK. It'll just take time. But you need to disappear in order to protect us all. What will you do Nikki? Where will you go?'

Nikki put her hand in her jacket pocket and felt the roll of hundred dollar bills, liberated from Ari's pockets. There was over one hundred thousand dollars in cash. She picked up her suitcase and tottered towards the door on her high heels. As she turned to say goodbye, she replied.

'I don't know. I haven't thought as yet. Maybe you'll read about me in the future. Who knows?'

E.M. is a member of the Honduran group 'Mothers of Progresso' whose sole aim is to find their daughters who have fallen into the hands of human traffickers. "We have had to turn into private detectives to try to find our children, because if we don't, no-one else will."

Many of the missing girls end up in Chiapas, Mexico where the consul is said to have received hundreds of phone calls from women claiming to have been sold into brothels.

Each year some of the members of the Mothers of Progresso travel to Chiapas to try to find their lost daughters. They go from nightclub to nightclub, brothel to brothel clasping photographs of their daughters in the hope of finding some information. There have been sightings but most of the time the leads fizzle out as the sex workers are too frightened to talk. However, these mothers have been successful in finding three of the missing girls.

E.M. said, "We're not scared of anything or anyone. We won't give up until we find out what has happened to every one of our children."

Source: The Times. Friday June 8th 2012.
Channel 4. "Honduras: The Lost Girls."

THE END

Authors note:

Nikki

I felt that there was no way a respectable mother such as Elena could travel half way across the world, take on the trafficking gangs single handed and win – hence Nikki. It needed someone who was basically as bad as they were and someone who knew the ropes. All the cons she and Phillippe pulled are ones taken from real life (except one) and have happened to someone, somewhere. Thankfully not the same person! So which one wasn't? The one at the airport with the ticket machine. I was stuck in this situation and thought, 'now what would Nikki have done?'

Kristina

The inspiration for the book and Kristina came from a lady I met in a bar. It was a nameless bar in a nameless city that could have been anywhere in this world we live in. I was early and my friends were late and I saw her, Victoria, sitting by herself and crying into her beer (it was tequila actually). We got to talking and she told me she was celebrating. She told me how she had been promised a well-paid job in a high end dress shop. She told me how excited she and her family had been at the prospect of real money; money that would put an end to an existence of living from hand to mouth, day after day. She told me of her young son who she had left with 'babushka' since her husband disappeared as soon as he was born; how she had dreamed of a university education for her child with the money she was to make.

Then she told me of her arrival and how she was met at the airport, escorted to a flat where she was locked in like a prisoner along with several other girls. She told me how she was beaten and gang raped

until she lost the will to fight back and gave in to their demands –
prostitution. She told me how it all works, of the beefy Mamasans or
'managers' who would oversee large groups of women, escort them
to a bar and arrange hour long liaisons with a man – any man
regardless of age, nationality or personal hygiene; all that mattered
was that he had the money. She told me of the enforcer who would
beat an errant girl with an iron bar before raping her; of the cigarette
burns and other means of teaching a bad girl a lesson.

Why was she celebrating you may ask? Well after being forced to
work in a brothel for the last two years, that morning her boss had
come in and handed her passport back. He said she had repaid the
debt she owed to the traffickers for bringing her over and that she
was free to go. That is when I met her in the bar. When she was
celebrating.

Whilst this book, its people and the locations are all fictional, the
story lines are all true and based on anecdotes related to myself by
Victoria and others like her or from the proceedings of actual court
cases where traffickers have been found and prosecuted.

Kristina's story is Victoria's story – but in Victoria's case no-one
came to save her. She spent two years locked up in a brothel with no
escape. Whilst you tuck yourself up in your cosy bed tonight, just
spare a thought for the thousands of girls like Victoria; forced into
prostitution through no fault of their own and for no other reason
than they wanted a better job and a better life for themselves and
their family.

R J Flo

Acknowledgments

There are many people to whom I am indebted in the writing of this book.

Brenda, who read through the early drafts and recommended several changes and Hilke and Romy who found too many typos in the first proof. Any errors still there are mine.

In particular I would like to thank Tom for his encouragement and advice and for his recommendation to 'put the girl in jeopardy from page 1!' The cover blurbs owe a lot to his input and are better for it. The liquid lunches every Friday kept us both writing as, after the initial greeting we would each ask the question of the other: 'how many words have you written this week?' One had to have a good answer!

If you would like to help stop human trafficking sign up at
www.50forfreedom.org/

Made in the USA
Las Vegas, NV
25 August 2023

76612801R00175